2

# The Wild Card

# *The Wild Card*

## TERESA CRANE

LITTLE, BROWN AND COMPANY

A *Little, Brown* Book

First published in Great Britain in 2000
by Little, Brown and Company

Copyright © Teresa Crane 2000

The moral right of the author has been asserted.

A CIP catalogue record for this book
is available from the British Library.

HARDBACK ISBN 0 316 84819 0

Typeset in Palatino by
Palimpsest Book Production Limited,
Polmont, Stirlingshire
Printed and bound in Great Britain by
Creative Print and Design Wales

Little, Brown and Company (UK)
Brettenham House
Lancaster Place
London WC2E 7EN

For Chris, With Love

# *Prologue*

## London, October 1944

The spacious room was eerily shadowed and, after the swift, running footsteps had receded and the street door below had clicked shut, suddenly very quiet. The clear, metronomic ticking of the clock on the mantelpiece served more to emphasise the silence than to break it.

Beyond the closed windows a wet and windy darkness was settling upon the drab streets of a weary, war-torn London.

The ashes of yesterday's fire crumbled in the grate and the air was cold.

There was no movement; nor would there be ever again from the still figure that lay slumped across the desk, one hand still stretched out towards the telephone. Blood dripped upon the polished wood of the floor.

Mellowly the clock struck the hour; but in the still silence of the room there was no ear to hear it.

Death was in the air. Indeed, for long-suffering Londoners a particularly fearsome and silent death had quite literally been in the air for months now. In Europe and in the East the tide was turning and running fast the Allies' way; but Hitler was by no means finished; still he clung to the conviction that if London could be destroyed, or its people roused to revolt, all would not be lost. His first so-called 'retaliation weapon' – the V1 – had been a pilotless plane full of high explosive, launched from Northern Europe and aimed at the British capital. Since the success of the D-Day landings most of these launch sites had been overrun and destroyed; not so the rocket-launching sites of the V2s, further east. These unnerving weapons came without sound or warning and killed and destroyed without discrimination.

The room darkened. The clock ticked on.

The explosion, when it came, fractured the deathly quiet, ripping the heart from the building and shattering the gas main beneath the pavement of the street outside. In a matter of seconds the destruction was complete: an elegant terrace of handsome houses that had stood for the best part of a hundred years was a smoking heap of dusty rubble and splintered timbers. There was a moment of shocked stillness, broken only by the dangerous hiss of gas and the trickling tumble of broken masonry. Then there came the roar of flames, and someone began to scream.

Amazingly, there were survivors. But others had not been so lucky. Eight shattered bodies were eventually recovered from the shambles of the wrecked buildings. Seven had been killed by the blast. Not surprisingly under the circumstances, there was little left to indicate that the eighth had not.

# PART ONE

# Chapter One

## Summer 1929

Mary McCarthy shaded her eyes against the dazzling reflection of sun upon sea and automatically – almost unthinkingly – counted heads. The children were scattered, singly and in groups, across 'their' piece of the beach; three Cloughs, four Barkers and, sitting apart, his back against a sea-smoothed boulder, elbows resting upon his knees, long-lashed eyes brooding upon the glittering horizon, her own Liam. At fourteen the boy was too thin for his height, and his hands too big for his narrow, bony wrists. His shock of curly hair was black as coal; as was the scowl on his face.

Mary sighed.

One of the older girls, carrying a spade and a bucket of sandy pebbles, stopped for a moment, watching a small boy as he prodded at a motionless crab with the handle of his spade. 'Oh, for heaven's sake, Ned! Come and help with the castle and leave the poor thing be. It's as dead as a doornail.'

'No, it isn't.' The boy Ned, small, slight, his fair hair sun-bleached almost to silver, poked at the creature again. 'I think it's pretending.'

Distracted from his reverie, Liam turned his head, dark brows lifting. 'If it is, 'tis good enough to be on the stage at the Coliseum.' The words were dry, the voice soft with a trace of the lilt of Ireland.

Unexpectedly Ned flashed him a quick, bright smile and giggled.

His sister Christine pursed her lips. 'Come on. Come and help with the castle.' There was nothing cajoling about the words; this was an order.

'Don't want to.' The narrow, elfin face was dangerously mutinous.

Christine ignored him. 'Get some water in the buckets, Liam. I want to make a keep with towers and the sand's too dry.'

Liam looked at her levelly and without moving for a long moment. Then, without a word, he stood, picked up a couple of buckets and padded on bare, sandy feet down to the sea. The watching woman let out a breath that she had not realised she was holding. The boy was in a very difficult position, no-one knew that better than she; given his temperament, it was surprising he did not flare up more often at the high-handed young miss who as often as not treated him like a servant.

'Come *on*, Ned! Come and help!' Christine reached out to take the child's arm, and began forcibly to haul him to where a dark chubby girl a couple of years her junior was heaping and patting sand into a huge, flat-topped pile.

The boy's face went puce. His sunhat fell off as he dragged away from her. 'Don't want to!' he shrieked, this time at the top of his voice.

'Don't be such a bully, Chris.' Another lad, of about the same age as Liam, lifted his head from the book he had been reading. The mild, amused friendliness of his tone was somehow more chastening than sharpness would have been.

Christine flushed deeply. Her colouring was the same as Ned's – unlike Emma, the middle Clough child who was labouring so earnestly upon the castle, they both took after their small, blonde mother. 'I'm not a bully!'

'Yes, you are!' Ned was gleeful. He wriggled from her grip, capered on the sand. 'Alex just said so! Bully, bully, bully! I shall tell Mother!' He glanced towards the house that stood above them atop the sharp rocky incline – dignified in the children's minds as The Cliff – that dropped directly down to the beach.

'Now, now.' Mary carefully closed her waxed-paper and bamboo sunshade and climbed, not without effort, out of the deckchair. 'Come along, my dears. T'would be a shame to spoil the day. Let's have some lemonade, why don't we? Ned, put your sunhat back on, there's a good child.' Her accent was much stronger than her son's; she all but sang the words. She raised her voice. 'Josie? Tom? Lottie? Lemonade for you here.'

Josie and Tom – the two youngest Barkers – had been hunkered down, heads together as always, peering into a small rock pool. These two were often taken to be twins; a mistake easily made. They were square-built, spry children with vivid colouring – bright-cheeked, red-lipped, hair and eyes the shining brown of new-picked chestnuts. At this moment they were, as so often, so totally absorbed in each other that they did not hear Mary's call.

'Josie? Tom!'

Liam, coming back from the sea, water slopping from the buckets, made a detour. 'Will you come on, you two? Lemonade up.'

They scrambled to their feet. Despite Josie's eighteen-month advantage over her brother, they were of exactly the same height. Their faces were an odd, triangular shape, broad at the brow, narrow at the cheekbones and with sharply pointed chins. The hands they reached to each other were identical: competent, square-palmed with short, strong fingers. Hand in hand, they raced across the beach towards the others.

Charlotte Barker, the last of the party, who had been

paddling in the shallows on her own, sauntered up to Liam, bare white legs gleaming in the sunshine. Beneath the wide brim of her sunhat her pale eyes glinted and her smile was mischievous as, neatly and unselfconsciously, she untucked her skirt from her knicker legs and shook out the creases. 'Playing navvies?' she asked, not unkindly.

'Somethin' like that.' He smiled down at her. In common with most people he found it easy to smile at Lottie Barker. There was no trace of malice in Lottie – nor, it must be said, much trace of thought for the world about her. She took things as they were, looked to her own concerns and left it at that. With her startling mop of flaming hair, pale freckled skin and light eyes she looked almost transparent in the brilliance of the day. In build she was fragile as a fairy and – to her chagrin – looked younger than her thirteen years. Liam had already discovered how deceptive that particular impression could be.

When they joined the others, Christine and Ned, over their lemonade, were still bickering.

'I don't *want* to build a castle,' Ned was whining in his most irritating voice. 'Castles are *boring*.'

'Ours won't be,' his sister said, briskly. 'We're going to have turrets, and passages and a moat and a draw-bridge.'

'I don't *want*—'

'What do you want, Neddie?' It was Alex again, patience and reason personified, shouldering manfully his role as the eldest and most responsible of the group. Christine threw him a look of irritated exasperation.

'I want—' the child brightened, 'I want to build a Zeppelin!' he announced.

Christine let out a scornful and unladylike shout of laughter. 'Oh, don't be so daft! You can't build a *Zeppelin* out of *sand*!'

The wide, soft mouth trembled. The easy tears began to well. A wave of bright colour rose in the child's face.

There was not a member of the group who did not

know what would happen if Ned decided it was time for a tantrum.

Mary made a hasty move towards him, but before she could reach the child Liam had dropped casually to his knee beside Ned, turning him away from the grins of the others, a thoughtful look on his dark face. 'Sure – you know, a Zep would be a wee bit difficult. But I tell you what—' Ned watched him, waiting. When purposefully deployed, the long vowels and soft consonants of south-west Ireland could be very persuasive.

Ned gulped, hiccoughed a little and screwed up his face, giving due warning of what could be to come. 'What?' he asked, defensively cautious.

'We could try building a *Bluebird*. Would that be to your liking?'

Ned's attention had been caught. 'Like the motorcar, you mean,' he flapped his small hands, 'that's the fastest one in the world?'

'That's the one. What d'you think?' Liam smiled one of his rare smiles, made a fist and pretended to graze the boy's jaw with it. 'Captain Malcolm Campbell Clough, is it?'

'Could we do it?'

'You can do anything if you try,' Liam said, straightfaced, climbing to his feet and throwing a slightly caustic glance towards his mother. 'Or so I'm reliably told. Come on. Bring your spade. Let's see what we can do.'

'It's getting a wee bit late, don't you think? Shouldn't the children come up off the beach before the wind chills down?' Siobhan Clough was standing at the open window, looking down upon the activity on the beach. The shadows were lengthening. 'The boy really shouldn't get cold. Should I send down to Mary to bring them up?'

Pamela Barker, sitting with her feet up on the couch and placidly knitting, did not even look up. 'The boy will be fine, dear. You really mustn't cosset him so. Mary will bring them up when she's ready. The air will do them good.' She glanced up and smiled at her companion, her hands still moving, assured and busy. 'That is what we brought them here for, remember?' she added, gently. 'Sea air, and exercise. They're getting both. So just stop worrying and come and sit down. It's your holiday too.' She was a tall woman, lean rather than slim, her dark straight hair, cut in the popular bob, as severe as a man's, the plainness of her strong features tempered by dark, intelligent eyes and a smile of quite remarkable sweetness. Her voice was attractive; low and well-modulated. In all the years they had known each other, and even with four lively children to keep in check, Siobhan could not remember hearing Pamela ever raising it to anyone.

Which was more, she thought ruefully, than anyone could say about herself.

She crossed the room, picked up a magazine from the table and settled into a chair, kicking her shoes off and curling her legs under her.

Pamela watched her with affection as she leafed through the pages. It never failed to amaze her that Siobhan, after fourteen years of marriage to the overpowering George Clough, three extremely difficult births, four miscarriages and the constant worry of a sickly son, still quite artlessly contrived to look the pretty, vulnerable child that she, Pamela, had first met all those years ago. By tragic chance – her parents had been visiting American relatives – Siobhan had been orphaned at the age of ten by the San Francisco earthquake of 1906 and within weeks had been bundled off to an English boarding school by a disinterested guardian who did not know what else to do with her. Pamela it had been who had rescued the child from almost suicidal misery and despair. Envied for her pretty face and cloud of fair, curly hair, bullied for her Irish background, her timidity, her nightmares and her lack of sporting prowess, grieving for her doting parents, Siobhan had been an isolated and desperately unhappy child with neither the stoicism to accept what was happening nor the strength to fight it.

Pamela, though only a few months her senior in age and, like Siobhan herself, an only child, had taken her under her wing, protecting and caring for her like an older sister. And so it had remained into their adult lives. They were, if anything she supposed, closer than most sisters. The only near-rift between them had come when Pamela, in the year that the world was rushing towards war, had met a young solicitor, David Barker, fallen in love in a most uncharacteristically impulsive manner and – even more uncharacteristically – had promptly, and with no second thoughts, married him. It had perhaps not been surprising that within the year Siobhan had met and married a man twelve years older than herself, a man of some property and means, a man of strong views and stronger temper; a self-centred, self-made man whose wartime business dealings went on to make him a great deal of money.

Pamela did not like George Clough, though she did her sensible best not to show it – at least not too often. The feeling, she knew, was mutual; and she cared not a jot.

Siobhan tossed the magazine aside, jumped to her feet restlessly and wandered on stockinged feet to the window again, throwing it open and leaning out, elbows on the sill, to watch the children on the beach below. Like Pamela's, her hair was fashionably short – though unlike Pamela's it was unfashionably curly and no amount of painstaking effort could straighten it. It feathered about her head and face like a cap of gold, gleaming in the sunshine. She was wearing a short, pleated skirt and a loose short-sleeved blouse pulled down to her hips; though, like her curly hair, her neat, curvaceous figure refused to conform to the uncompromisingly boyish vogue of the day.

'I wish—' she said, and stopped.

'What?' Pamela laid aside her knitting and joined her at the window. 'What do you wish?'

'I wish—' Suddenly and impulsively she turned, her grey-blue eyes wide, 'I wish we could go to Ahakista. It seems such a very long time since we were last there.'

'It was. Ned, Josie and Tom were tots. It must be five or six years.' Pamela looked at her curiously. 'I thought it was your idea to come to the south coast again this year rather than go to Ireland?'

Siobhan shrugged evasively.

'Wasn't it?'

'George thought it best. He said the children are more settled here. We've taken this house so often for the summer they think of it as home.'

'As you think of Ahakista.' The words were gentle.

'No.' The denial was fractionally too forceful. 'No, of course I don't.'

'But, Siobhan, it *is* your home. Or it was, for the first ten years of your life. It's very important to you. And to the children. It's in their blood as well as yours.'

'George—' Siobhan stopped, turned back to the window, shrugged again. 'You can't blame him,' she said after a moment. 'It's much easier for him to get to see us here than in Ireland.'

Then why doesn't he come more often? The question was such an obvious one that Pamela, though it was on the tip of her tongue, could not bring herself to ask it. Her own husband joined them each Friday night, to leave again to return to London on Monday morning. George Clough had honoured them with his presence just once in the past month. Pressing business kept him away. Pamela had her own opinion of what that business might be, as she had her own opinion of George's reluctance to allow his family to spend any time in the house on the hillside above the little fishing village of Ahakista, on Dunmanus Bay, in which three generations of his children's forebears had been born. The fact was that when faced with – and attracted to – the young, lovely, malleably eager-to-please Siobhan O'Sullivan he had inexplicably failed to take into account the fact that any child of the union would have as much Irish blood in its veins as English; an odd oversight that he rectified by ignoring it, and expecting everyone else, including the children themselves, to do the same. One of his many obnoxious and entirely predictable habits was completely to disregard his wife's sensibilities in his frequent declarations that the Irish were, in general, a race of savages and nothing but trouble.

Pamela glanced back down at the beach to where the dark lanky Liam and the small fair Ned were industriously excavating a large hole. It was impossible to spend any amount of time with the Clough household and not to sense the undercurrents that swirled around young Liam. To his credit the boy did his best to stay out of George's way, and when that was not possible kept a still tongue and a quiet eye under all but the worst of provocations. For all his difficult and sometimes surly nature, Pamela felt sorry for Liam; life was never going to be easy for a fatherless child. The situation had always intrigued Pamela; the advent of Mary McCarthy and her child had been the one time in her life that Siobhan had ever actually stood up to George. Not even Pamela knew the whole story, though Siobhan told her most things. All she knew was that Mary was a distant cousin who, some ten years before, had turned up out of the blue with the four-year-old Liam trailing at her skirts. There was talk of a father dead in the war, of debts, a lost home and destitution. Siobhan, with two small and energetic children to care for, a hopeless way with servants and in the middle of a difficult pregnancy, had welcomed her with open arms; and Mary had been unstinting in her devotion to her ever since. Providentially it had happened that George had at the time been away on an extended business trip to America. By the time he came back Mary was a fixture, a combination housekeeper, nursemaid and companion. George, swayed no doubt by the fact that a dysfunctional and chaotic household had been reduced to comfortable order in a matter of weeks, condescended to accept the situation. He had not then, nor had he since, accepted Liam. The boy was here on sufferance, unwanted baggage that came with his mother.

As if she had picked the thought from Pamela's head, Siobhan leaned across the sill, pointing. 'What on earth are Liam and Ned up to?'

Pamela smiled. 'Lord knows. Displacing half the beach by the look of it. No doubt we'll find out later. Shall I ring for some tea?'

The beach party returned an hour or so later, scrambling up the short steep path to the house, erupting into the big kitchen, depositing buckets, spades, paddling shoes, balls and diabolos in an untidy heap and, squabbling amiably, clattering on up the stairs to the drawing room where Siobhan and Pamela waited, leaving Mary and Mrs Turner the cook to look at each other with affectionately shaken heads and eyes cast to heaven.

'Liam – bring the bucket with the shells up, will you?' Christine called over her shoulder.

Liam grunted.

'Mama! Mama! I built a *Bluebird* out of sand. It had a real seat I could sit on. And we made a steering wheel out of a spade and a bit of wire!' Ned ran to lean against the arm of his mother's chair, his head tilted to look at her. 'I wanted to build a Zeppelin, but we decided it would be too hard. Liam helped me quite a lot,' he added as a charitable afterthought.

Siobhan put an arm about him, drawing him to her as she glanced around at the bright faces of the other children. 'Did you have a good day?'

'Lovely!' Emma held out the bucket Liam had brought upstairs. 'Look what we found. We brought one of every different kind of shell we could find to show you.'

'It was my idea,' Christine said, quickly and sharply.

Siobhan smiled at both of them; it never failed to amaze her how different from each other these two daughters of hers were; Christine slender, quick and as fair as Siobhan herself, Emma solemn, brown-haired, brown-eyed and plump, a thoughtful child, generous-natured and self-effacing, not exactly words that could be used to describe her older sibling. Siobhan spread out the magazine on her lap. 'Tip them on here. Let's see how many we know.'

'That's a mussel!'

'And the pointy one's a limpet.'

'There's a whelk and a winkle and the square one's a razor shell.' The children poked the shells about with grubby fingers. Sand spattered on to the polished wooden floor, and the salt smell of the sea was in the air.

Alex had walked to where his mother sat and bent to kiss her cheek. She smiled warmly up at him. Although she would deny it to the death to anyone but herself, this, her first-born, was her favourite child. Not that that meant anything in terms of indulgence; on the contrary, perhaps because of it she was occasionally aware of being harder on him than on the others. The two younger ones had been a conspiracy since they could talk, and Lottie – Pamela's eyes followed Lottie as she danced to the window and stood, swaying a little, looking dreamily out to sea – Lord only knew where Lottie had come from, with that startling hair and those pale green eyes. A fairy child, her father called her. A changeling, self-possessed and self-absorbed; and, her mother suspected, beneath the fragile, pretty surface with a will of iron. It was very rare for Lottie not to get her own way, yet it was always difficult to discover exactly how she had achieved it. Not with tantrums, nor with argument. It simply happened. Pamela watched as Liam joined her daughter at the window, saw his slow smile as she turned to speak to him. It was typical of Lottie that she could make even Liam smile. But Alex – tall, quiet, clever Alex – he was Pamela's pride and joy.

'There's someone at the door,' Christine said, and lifted her voice above the hubbub. 'Come in.'

It was the little maid, Agnes, with a letter held awkwardly on a small silver tray. She bobbed a quick curtsey, not meeting anyone's eyes, uncomfortable colour rising in her cheeks as she found herself the focus of so many eyes.

'Letter for you, Ma'am. Just come by Special Delivery,' she whispered to Siobhan.

Siobhan smiled at her reassuringly and held out a hand. The child was so excruciatingly shy it was an embarrassment to behold. She all but threw the envelope into Siobhan's lap and scuttled out of the room.

'What a very strange girl she is,' Christine observed, truly puzzled.

Emma shook her head. 'She can't help it, she's just shy. She finds us all a bit overwhelming, that's all.'

'I sometimes find you so myself,' Pamela said, drily but with a smile.

Siobhan had opened the letter and scanned it rapidly. Everyone waited, watching her expectantly. She lifted her head, refolded the missive, smiling very brightly. 'How lovely,' she said, looking from one to the other of her older children. 'Your Papa is coming to visit. Tomorrow. For three or four days. Isn't that splendid?'

Beside her Ned had frozen, and visibly paled. Quietly, her eyes still on her daughters, her hand found his.

At the window the Irish boy's most thunderous scowl was back in place.

'As long as it doesn't mean we can't have our picnic,' Christine said, with the practical self-interest of a confident child. 'Mrs Turner's promised to make egg mayonnaise sandwiches. They're my favourite. Mother, may I ring the bell for tea? I'm *starving!*'

'No need.' Liam was already at the door. 'I'm off down anyway,' he said, his newly-gruff voice cracking a little. 'I'll tell Mrs Turner.'

Ned sidled closer to his mother. 'I had rather a lot of lunch,' he said in a small, apologetic voice. 'If you don't mind, I don't think I'm going to want any tea.'

# Chapter *Two*

Ned sat on the upholstered stool of his mother's dressing table, shoulders hunched, small hands tucked beneath his thighs, legs swinging as he surveyed his reflection glumly in the mirror. The English summer had once more run true to form; the sunshine of yesterday was gone; beyond the rainwashed window the skies were grey and the dark waters of the Channel surged in fierce, white-topped breakers up the beach.

The room was very quiet.

The small face that looked back at him was pale beneath its heavy thatch of silky fair hair, and the huge eyes were shadowed. He had not slept well last night.

Footsteps sounded in the hallway outside and his swinging legs stilled as he tensed, listening. Half an hour before he had watched from the window as his father had arrived; big and brisk and handsomely dressed, paying off the taxi and running up the wide steps that led to the front door with the impatient vigour of a man half his age. Most of the other youngsters had gone off for a walk along the rainswept beach; Ned hoped devoutly, but with little real faith, that no-one in the house knew that he had not gone with them.

The footsteps passed. He relaxed a little. After a moment

he leaned forward and, gently and quietly, eased open the drawer of the dressing table. His mother was not a tidy person; the drawer was a jumble of combs, brushes and hair grips, small boxes of powder and rouge, bottles of nail varnish and perfume, several lipstick cases. The child poked around the clutter with an inquisitive but careful finger, inspecting bottles and jars and boxes, occasionally picking one up, opening it to sniff at the contents, then replacing it in exactly the position in which he had found it. After a while he pushed the drawer quietly shut, slipped from the stool and went to the small chest of drawers that stood beside his mother's bed. These, too, he went through, methodically, one by one. Stockings and underwear that smelled, sweetly, of his mother's special scent. He touched them softly and smiled. A small bundle of letters that he left undisturbed; he had read them before. A little notebook that he leafed through, though he already knew it contained nothing more exciting than his mother's haphazard attempts to organise her life; addresses, hair appointments, birthdays, reminders—

He lifted his head sharply. Footsteps were coming up the stairs. He slid the drawer shut, flew back to the dressing table. When Pamela opened the door he was once again sitting hunched upon the stool, short legs swinging, eyes wide and expressionless upon his own reflection.

'Ah, there you are.' She smiled over his shoulder into the mirror. 'Your father's asking for you. He's in the drawing room with your Mama—' The child had stiffened. Pamela put a not unsympathetic hand lightly on his shoulder. 'Come along, dear. You know he doesn't like to be kept waiting.'

'So, young Edward – how far can you swim now?' George Clough was a tall, well-made, handsome man with a quietly controlled, clipped voice that somehow made itself heard more effectively than any shout. He stood with his back to the large, empty fireplace, his hands behind his back, rocking a little on his heels. Rain streamed down the window.

Ned stood dumb.

'Well?' The word was crisply impatient.

'George, the weather hasn't been—'

Siobhan's husband bent a dark, quelling look upon her. 'I'm talking to the boy, my dear.' There was nothing of warmth in the endearment. He looked back at his son. 'Edward?'

'I d-d-d—' Ned blanched, took a huge breath and controlled his stuttering tongue, though not before he had seen the thunder building in his father's face. 'I don't like swimming, Father. Mama said—' he trailed off, looked imploringly at his mother.

'The boy's young yet, George,' Siobhan said softly, 'and not as strong as he might be since the fever. The tides here—'

'The tides here are no stronger than the tides anywhere else. And it is his very weakliness that must be tackled by activity strenuous enough to strengthen him. I left instructions last time I was here that the child should be taught to swim, and that he should go into the water at least once a day. Are you telling me that those instructions have not been carried out?'

There was a short, oppressive silence.

'I see,' George said, quietly ominous.

Siobhan tried again. 'I could find no suitable instructor, George. And the weather has been very changeable. Look for yourself how bad it is today,' and she gestured towards the drenched morning beyond the window.

Her husband lifted a dismissive hand. 'It's as well I came, I can see. As usual I suppose I'll have to make the necessary arrangements myself. Didn't it strike you that young McCarthy might as well at least do something to try to earn his keep? As I remember it, the little beggar swims like a fish.'

'Liam?' Siobhan shrugged, helplessly. 'No, I'm sorry, it didn't occur to me.'

'What does?' George, dismissively, turned back to Ned. 'So, young man. If you haven't been learning to swim, what have you been doing?'

Poor Ned's mind, predictably, went as blank as a newly-cleaned blackboard. 'I—'

His father waited, caustically patient.

'I've p-played on the beach, and – had picnics, and – we went to B-Brighton and rode on—' he struggled for a moment, then got the word out whole, 'donkeys.' Ned glanced at his mother again, hoping for a prompt. It was a mistake. Her pale, pretty face was so full of helpless sympathy that it brought on the sudden – and under the circumstances absolutely unthinkable – welling of tears. He cleared his throat, and clenched his face fiercely. 'Um – we've played games, and Mama is reading us *The Children of the New Forest*. It's a topping story. I don't know how it ends yet because she hasn't f-finished.' He caught himself, biting his lip, hesitating, casting about desperately. 'Chris and Emma keep building huge castles with towers and moats and things, and L-Liam and I built Captain Campbell's *Bluebird* out of sand. Liam said that we c-couldn't build a Zeppelin—' He trailed off, looking down at the floor to avoid his father's eyes. The rug had a strange, asymmetrical pattern that made his eyes feel funny. He closed them for a moment.

'We're going to have to do something about this child's stammer,' his father said, matter-of-factly, over Ned's head to his mother.

Siobhan said nothing. *The only time he stammers is when he speaks to you.* What was the point of saying it? 'Will I ring for tea?' she asked, softly and pleasantly. 'It won't be long before the other scraps are back and we won't have time to draw breath.'

Liam, summoned, climbed the stairs reluctantly and pushed

open the door of the drawing room. George Clough, seated at a small writing desk in the window, swung in his chair to face him. 'Ah. McCarthy. Did no-one ever teach you to knock, boy?'

'I'm sorry.'

George stood up, took his stance in front of the fireplace. 'I beg your pardon?' he said, pleasantly.

'I said – I'm sorry—'

'Sir. I'm sorry – Sir.'

There was a long and tense moment of silence. Liam swallowed. Then, 'I'm sorry, *Sir,*' he said, very clearly, his eyes steady and defiant upon the man's face.

George's lips tightened. He clasped his hands behind his back. 'I've a job for you.'

Liam said nothing.

'I want you to teach my son to swim. He is to go into the water at least once a day. Without fail. Is that clear?'

'Yes,' there was a noticeable pause, 'Sir,' said Liam.

George turned back towards the window. 'That will be all. But, McCarthy—'

Liam, who was already at the door, stopped and turned, waiting.

'You should learn,' the man said, very quietly, 'that insolence – especially dumb insolence – will bring you nothing but trouble.' He turned to face the boy, a dark silhouette against the grey light behind him. 'You understand?'

'Yes. Sir.' Liam said, his voice completely expressionless, and closed the door very quietly behind him.

'What's made *you* so grumpy?' Cheerfully and with no invitation Lottie threw herself down beside Liam on the battered sofa at the far end of the big kitchen. On the other side of the room Mary and Mrs Turner were busy preparing a lunch that was, on George's instructions, to be taken formally in the dining room.

'Nothing.' Liam's scowl deepened.

The bright, pretty face beneath its halo of marigold-red hair lit to laughter. 'Well, goodness me! Perish the thought of coming across you when you weren't quite feeling yourself, then! You've a face as black as an undertaker's hat!'

This time Liam, albeit reluctantly, smiled back. He shrugged. 'Mr Clough,' he said, simply.

Lottie sobered. 'Ah,' she said, the single syllable conveying instant understanding. Since George Clough had arrived that morning few people had escaped the odd uncomfortable moment.

'I'm to teach Ned to swim.'

'Ned doesn't want to swim. He hates the water.'

'I know.'

She pulled her legs up to sit cross-legged on the sofa, her fingers clasped about her narrow ankles, her light summer skirt slipping apparently artlessly about her pale thighs. Liam averted his eyes. 'Oh, well,' she said, lightly, watching him steadily, a gleam that might have been amusement in her eyes. 'Best it should be you rather than some stranger. Ned trusts you.'

'I'm not a bloody servant!' The words were very low and very violent. Across the kitchen Mary McCarthy lifted her head, her attention caught by the fierceness of her son's tone, though – fortunately – she did not catch exactly what he had said.

Lottie's eyes widened at the forbidden word.

'I'm sorry,' Liam muttered, the apology half-hearted. He was picking viciously at a fingernail, his face grim. 'Yes, *Sir*. No, *Sir*. Three bags full, *Sir*!' He was talking as much to himself as to her. 'Who the hell does he think he is?'

'The master of the house,' Lottie said, practically though not unsympathetically. 'Which is exactly what he is.' She laughed, suddenly and infectiously. 'Why he even informed *Mother* this morning that it was high time little Tom was sent away to school.'

Liam's blue eyes widened. 'And what did she say to that?'

'She said—' Lottie giggled, then put on her mother's most caustic tone, '"Thank you, for your advice, George. I'll bear it in mind."'

Liam grinned, and for a moment the dark, well-boned face lit to a startling charm. 'I like your mother.'

She nodded. 'So do I.' With a swift movement she slid from the sofa and held out her hand. 'Come on. We'd better get ready for lunch.'

He shook his head, still smiling, the black mood lifting as quickly as it had descended. 'There's at least one advantage to being a skivvy,' he said, drily. 'I'm not invited.'

The girl pulled a laughing face. 'Be grateful for small mercies,' she said.

'I am. Believe me, I am.' The tone was heartfelt.

With rain still driving against the windows, lunch was taken, for the most part, in a rather strained silence. George Clough took his food seriously, and he detested idle chit-chat at the table. The Barker children darted sidelong looks at each other, daring each other to laugh; Pamela watched with faintly raised brows and a glint in her eye that could as easily have been encouragement as warning. Emma applied herself stolidly to her plate, whilst Ned, sitting beside his mother, eyes downcast, pecked pallidly at his food in a way that quite clearly irritated his father. Only Christine seemed unintimidated by her father's presence.

'Papa,' she said, unexpectedly, as Mary cleared the plates and brought a large trifle to the table, 'may I come back to London with you for a couple of days? It's Martha's birthday on Monday and I thought—'

'No.' The word was brusque and brooked no argument. Pamela flicked a look at Siobhan, who kept her own eyes downcast, fixed upon the creamy trifle that Mary had placed before her.

'But—'

'No,' George said again. 'It would be most inappropriate.'

'But, Papa, Martha's my very best friend, and—'

'Christine, did you hear me? I said no. I meant no.' George's voice had dropped, and bright spots of colour had appeared on his handsome cheekbones.

'Christine,' Siobhan said, quickly.

But Christine was not her father's daughter for nothing. Her face, too, had flushed with the blood of temper. 'That isn't fair! Spencer's at home, isn't she? She could look after me. I wouldn't be any trouble.'

George's face was thunderous now. Siobhan looked nervously from one to the other. 'Christine, be quiet, there's a good girl.'

'But, Mama, it *isn't* fair! I want—'

George slapped the table with the flat of his hand, making Ned jump almost from his skin. 'It seems to me, young lady, that you get altogether too much of what you want. Leave the table.'

Christine's chin came up as she glared back at him challengingly.

'*Leave the table!*'

There was a moment's utter silence. Then, slowly and quietly, the girl pushed back her chair and stood, never taking her eyes from her father's. Stubbornly she took a breath and opened her mouth.

Siobhan, quite audibly, caught her breath.

George's index finger came up sharply. 'One more word,' he said, ominously quietly, 'and I'll take a strap to you. Do as you're told. Now.'

She stood for a moment longer, the focus of all their eyes, staring at him; then, head high and back straight as a ramrod, she turned and marched to the door.

As it snapped shut behind her, small Tom let out a breathy, nervous giggle. Under the table, Josie kicked him. Emma and Ned were avoiding each other's eyes.

'I say, Aunt Siobhan,' it was Alex who braved the awkward silence, 'that trifle looks awfully good. Could I have some, please?'

The spell broken, the other children fidgeted in their chairs, Ned picked up his spoon and promptly dropped it, flinching a little as he glanced at his father, expecting a reprimand. But George had not noticed. He was staring at the door, which had closed with a sharp and defiant click behind Christine, with an expression that boded ill for his elder daughter.

Liam was in the kitchen with his mother when Christine, with neither a look nor a word for either of them, burst through one door and out of the other into the rain.

'Christine?' Mary ran to the open back door. 'Christine! What in God's name are you about, child? You'll catch your death! Christine!'

Christine, running down the path that led to The Cliff, took no notice.

'Liam, will you go after her! Here—' Mary reached to a peg near the door and lifted down two jackets. 'Take these.'

Liam, bemused, threw on one of the waterproofs, then set off, running, after the flying figure that had just disappeared down on to The Cliff pathway. By the time he reached the top Christine was on the beach. She stood below him, panting, staring out to sea. The rain had turned into a drenching drizzle, sweeping in a wet and shifting curtain from the south, directly into her face.

Liam scrambled down the slippery path. 'Christine!' His voice was almost drowned by the monotonous crashing of the surf. '*Christine!*'

Only then was she aware of him. She glanced quickly and angrily over her shoulder, then turned away again. 'Go away!' She began to walk, very fast, along the beach.

He ran to catch up with her. 'Don't be so daft! Ma's right, you'll catch your death! Here – at least put this on.' He held out the jacket.

She increased her pace. 'I said – *go away!*'

He caught her arm. She swung to face him. He stood,

awkwardly, still holding her, the jacket hanging loose to the wet sand. 'Are you – are you crying?'

'No.'

There was a moment's silence, broken only by the thunder of the waves.

He proffered the jacket again. 'Put it on,' he said, gruffly. 'Or I'll get it in the neck from me ma. And yours too, probably.'

She snatched it from him, struggled into it. He did not offer to help. When she started to walk again, more slowly this time, he kept pace with her in silence.

'Liam, I asked you to go away. Will you do that, please?' She hesitated. 'Thank you for the jacket.' The thanks were dismissive.

'Thank Ma, not me,' he said, shortly. Then, 'What's wrong?'

'Nothing.' Realising the clear idiocy of that, she shrugged. 'I quarrelled with Papa at the table. He sent me away like—' She swallowed and he saw her clench her face against fresh, furious tears. 'Like a naughty child! It was – it was *humiliating*.' She hissed the word; he barely heard it over the sound of the sea. 'He threatened—' She stopped.

'What?'

'Nothing.'

They walked on for a moment in silence. Both of them, bareheaded, were drenched. Christine's fair hair was plastered to her face and neck. Liam shook himself and water flew from his black curls as if from a dog's shaggy pelt. 'What did you quarrel about?'

For a moment he thought she would refuse to tell him, but the urge to justify herself proved irresistible, as he had suspected it might.

'All I wanted to do was to go back to London with him for a couple of days. It's my best friend's birthday on Monday. I haven't seen her for *ages*. He's all alone in that great big house. Although Mary and Cook have come with us, Spencer's there – she's only a maid, I know, but for goodness' sake, how much work is there for her to do with only Papa in the house, and him out at work all day? She could have looked after me! He wouldn't even know I was there. Then all he'd have had to do was put me on the train and Mama could have met me, here at the station.' She had worked out the plan during the night, had been so absolutely certain that it could be accomplished that even now she could not accept its brusque dismissal. She had envisaged the others' envy at her grown-up adventure; the thought of their sympathy – worse, perhaps even their relish of her discomfiture – was insupportable.

'Your father – didn't like the idea?'

'No.'

'I suppose – fathers can be like that,' he ventured.

'How would you know?' The self-centredly irritated retort was totally unthinking.

He stopped.

She walked on.

'Enjoy your walk,' he said to her retreating back, cursing the crack in his unreliable voice. And by the time she had turned, surprised, he was striding away from her, shoulders hunched, hands in pockets, back through the drifting rain towards the house.

'May I ask you something, George?'

The uncomfortable lunch was over. The children had scattered to various parts of the house, notably the kitchen with the left-over trifle. George, Siobhan and Pamela were taking coffee in the drawing room. Pamela, standing at the long window looking out into the rain, turned, looking enquiringly at the man who stood in his accustomed place, brandy glass in hand, in front of the fireplace.

'Of course.'

Pamela hesitated for a moment. Siobhan looked worried. 'Was the child's idea such a terrible one? She's right – Spencer would be perfectly capable of looking after her. We've been here for nearly five weeks. She's missing her friend. Would it have been so difficult to take her back with you for a couple of days?'

'Pamela,' Siobhan said, softly, her voice distressed.

George quelled her protest with a glance. 'It wouldn't have been difficult. It would have been impossible.'

'Why?'

'Because Spencer isn't at the house. No-one is at the house. I gave Spencer leave of absence for the summer – she has an aged mother, if you remember – and moved into my club.' He waited for a moment. 'Hardly the place for a thirteen-year-old girl,' he added, drily.

Siobhan's eyes, blue as forget-me-nots, had widened. She said nothing.

'You – didn't tell us that,' Pamela said, quietly.

'There seemed no reason.' The words were blandly polite. The line of his mouth was not. 'An empty house – be it in Holland Park, Brighton or the highlands of Scotland – is hardly the most congenial place to find oneself. I decided to take myself off to more amenable surroundings. That's all. Did I require your permission?'

'Of course not, George.' The words were quiet but far from submissive, and the tone did not bespeak belief.

Siobhan glanced at her friend and then away again.

'Well,' George, sardonically, half-bowed to Pamela, 'if you wouldn't mind, Pamela, I'd like a word with my wife. About our children.' Both pronouns were emphasised, very slightly.

Pamela knew defeat when she saw it. She smiled. 'Of course.'

George barely waited for her to leave the room. 'On my way back to London,' he said, brusquely, 'I intend to stop off and speak to Miss Warner of St Catherine's. She wrote some time ago to say that there was a place for Christine, if we so wished. I shall call on her and make arrangements for this September.'

'Boarding school? Oh but, George!'

'The child is a little minx and needs discipline. St Catherine's has an excellent reputation. The Dorsey girls go there. Charles is extremely pleased with the establishment. Whilst I'm there I shall make arrangements for Emma for next year. As for Edward, it's a pity that Belfairs doesn't take pupils under eleven.'

Siobhan was on her feet, her hand at her throat. '*Ned?* George – the boy's only nine years old! And he's very frail. The doctor says the fever has affected his heart.'

'Doctors?' George made a dismissive sound. 'You know my opinion of doctors. Anyway, as you know, I wish him to go to my old school and that unfortunately isn't possible until he's eleven. He needs toughening up, Siobhan. You baby him too much. You spoil him. And another thing, my dear—'

'Yes?'

'I do wish you wouldn't encourage that – priest – to come to the house quite so much. I don't believe him to be a good influence.'

Siobhan's head came up at that. 'Father O'Donnell doesn't come to the house as a priest, as you well know,' she said, very quietly. 'When I married you I agreed to give up my religion, and I did so. Do you doubt me?'

'No, of course not, but—'

'Father O'Donnell comes to see Ned purely as a singing teacher.'

'I know the boy has a pretty voice, but—'

'Pretty? Is that what you think? He has a glorious voice. It's the one thing that he does better than anyone else.'

'Exactly!' her husband snapped. 'And what good, pray, is that going to do him in life? You're making a namby-pamby of the child, and I intend to stop it. It's a hard world out there, and he's going to have to take his place in it. As his mother, you should realise that. I wish you would help rather than hinder me in this. Now – it seems the rain has stopped at last. I think I shall take a turn along the beach. Would you care to accompany me?'

Siobhan had sat down again, neatly and prettily, her long

lashes veiling her eyes. 'No, George, I think not. I haven't
finished my coffee. Perhaps a little later?'

She was still sitting so, very still, very straight-backed,
when the door opened. 'Shall I send down for fresh coffee?'
Pamela asked, gently.

Siobhan shook her head, and very carefully set her half-
empty cup on the table. 'No, thank you.'

Pamela's dark eyes were sympathetic. 'Tough?'

Siobhan lifted her chin. 'Christine is to be sent away to
boarding school, Emma is to follow next year, Ned is a
namby-pamby, and Father O'Donnell is to stop coming
to the house,' she said, calmly. 'If Belfairs took babies, as
some of those awful places do, Ned would be going away
too. The doctor who says that Ned has a weak heart is a fool.
That about covers it, I think.' The words, despite their quiet,
were savagely bitter. She turned her head to look directly,
almost challengingly, up at her friend. 'Pamela? May I ask
you something?'

'Of course.'

'Do you believe that George is staying at his club?'

The silence was answer enough.

'No,' Siobhan said, very composedly, 'neither do I.' She
stood up, walked to the fireplace, stood for a moment
watching her reflection in the mirror that hung above it.
Then, slowly, she turned, and Pamela, who had known her
for a very long time, noted with some satisfaction the stubborn set of the soft mouth. There were times when George
Clough underestimated his wife. 'Next year,' Siobhan said,
'I intend to take the children to Ahakista for the summer.
Would you and your family care to join us?'

Pamela smiled. 'We would. We would indeed.'

# Chapter Three

## Ireland, 1930

Lottie Barker rubbed the misty condensation of her breath from the dormer window and peered out. The rain that had prompted this infantile game had almost stopped. A sudden shaft of sunlight struck the wide, calm waters of Dunmanus Bay, and a rainbow curved, perfectly symmetrical, above the hills on the opposite shore, its colours vibrantly clear against the still-dark storm clouds. Downstairs she could hear the voices of the younger children as they clattered around the house looking for her.

'Found you! Found you!' That was Ned. Lottie heard Emma's laughter as she was pulled from the huge airing cupboard on the landing. They'd be up in the attics any time now. She supposed, in the spirit of the game, however silly, that she really ought to make more of an effort and find somewhere proper to hide.

She was about to turn away from the window when she stopped, as a movement caught her eye. To her right, a little further up the mountainside from Hill House, stood a small and ancient stone circle. Only two or three of the stones, which stood perhaps shoulder-height to a man, were

still upright; the others had long since tilted and fallen
in a bracken- and bramble-covered jumble. It stood above
the little fishing village of Ahakista, silent and mysterious
testimony to the presence of man on these shores at a time
before history had begun. In the couple of weeks that
they had been at Hill House with the Cloughs, Lottie had
never seen anyone visit it. The younger children sometimes
played there, and they had all picnicked there a couple of
times, but she had never seen anyone from the village come
to the place. Now, however, a man stood leaning against
one of the stones. He was very tall and broad-shouldered.
He wore a long, navy blue raincoat and a matching, wide-
brimmed hat that, at least from the angle from which Lottie
was watching, completely hid his face. He was rolling a
cigarette, very deftly, his eyes not on what he was doing
but upon the picturesque scene below him. Lottie leaned
to the window, curious, trying to get a better look. This
was no farmer – no countryman at all from the look of him
and the cut of his clothes; in fact he had the unmistakable,
if indefinable, air of the town about him. As she watched,
his hands stilled for a moment and he leaned forward a
little, watching attentively. Lottie followed the direction of
his gaze.

A tall, rangy figure had emerged, head ducked to avoid
the low doorway, from a little whitewashed cottage on the
shore below. The cottage stood alone, situated on its own
tiny rocky peninsula that jutted into the bay. Liam, flat cap
in hand and a broken shotgun hooked casually across his
shoulder, stood for a moment head tilted to look up at the
sky; then, obviously deciding that the rain had stopped for
good, he slapped the worn cap on to his unruly hair, tucked
the gun under his arm and set off up the track that wound
up the hillside, past the house and the stone circle out on
to the open mountainside above. Lottie, her own attention
caught, watched him with a small, speculative smile on her
lips. In her opinion – and she counted herself as something
of an expert on the attractiveness or otherwise of the young

human male – Liam McCarthy, even at his most surly, had always been a good-looking boy. Lately, however, he had undoubtedly become something more.

Liam and his mother had come to Ireland a few weeks before the two families, to prepare Hill House for its influx of guests. When the Cloughs and the Barkers had arrived – tired and quarrelsome after the long journey – it had been to find the old house polished and sparkling, fires lit welcomingly against the chill of a fresh sea wind, pantry stocked, staff hired from the village, beds fresh and inviting. It had also been to find a brown-faced, shock-haired Liam whose young strength had split the huge pile of logs that were neatly stacked against the east wall of the house, whose newly and swiftly acquired skills with the rod and the shotgun had put food on the table, and who was so clearly at home here in the land of his birth that the almost permanent defensive scowl was all but gone. With all the bedrooms in Hill House taken, he and Mary lived in the one-up, one-down cottage by the sea that had been the first habitation on the land. Mary spent her days at the house, whilst Liam, for the most part ignoring the other youngsters, spent his roaming the mountainside with the old gun he had found in the cottage or rowing out into the bay to fish. Ned saw most of him, tagging along whenever he was allowed, or running down the steep track to the cottage whenever he saw the tell-tale column of smoke rise from its chimney. The new, rather unnervingly easier-going Liam tolerated the boy's presence with something close to an offhand affection; the new, rather unnervingly easier-going Liam, thought Lottie as she watched him swing confidently up the path towards the house, would turn a few heads if he ever bothered to learn how.

The sound of the hunt was coming closer.

'She's in the attic.' Josie's voice, firm and clear.

'In the attic,' Tom agreed, stoutly.

'Which end?' That was Ned.

'Ip, skip, sky blue,' Emma chanted, 'Who's it? Not you! East end.'

Lottie grinned as she heard them clatter up the wrong stairs. She'd slip down to the kitchen and be sitting with her feet up and a lemonade in her hand before they found out their mistake.

As she turned to the door she noticed that the man who had been standing in the stone circle had gone.

Liam, level with the house now, looked up and caught sight of her. He lifted a casual hand in greeting. She waved back, and saw the glint of his smile.

She stood, thoughtful, for too long. 'Got you!' said Ned, with huge satisfaction from the doorway. 'Come on – it's Josie's turn to hide her eyes.'

Lottie shook her head. 'The rain's stopped. I think I'll go for a walk.'

Liam was whistling through his teeth as he walked, splashing through the small rivulets of rainwater, shining in sunlight, that trickled down the stony path. The sun was already warm. He took off his jacket and slung it over his shoulder. Hill House stood to his right, a grand house in the context of rural Cork, built some eighty years before by Siobhan Clough's grandfather, who had made his fortune through foresighted investment in the then newfangled railways of England and had retired here to his beloved west coast of Ireland, with a new young wife and their small son, Siobhan's father, John. There were some in the village who still remembered John O'Sullivan; an other-worldly man with a passion for butterflies and no head for business. He had met and married Siobhan's mother late in life – a pretty woman, everyone conceded, but of no great fortune and with a brother who lived in San Francisco, which was, tragically, to prove the death of them both. Liam, glancing now at the house, caught, in the fresh, glittering rays of sun after rain, a movement, a glimpse of a pretty, smiling face in one of the high attic windows that pierced the long roof.

In the clear light the sheen of Lottie Barker's marigold hair was unmistakable. He lifted a hand and grinned, hefted the comfortable weight of the gun tucked under his arm and strode on. After the morning's downpour, there'd be rabbits on the hillside soon.

The weathered stones of the circle were still wet from the rain. Carefully propping the shotgun beside him and tossing down his jacket, he leaned with his back against the tallest stone, as he always did when he passed this way, and studied the glorious view. He never tired of it – the brackened mountainside, the huge sweep of the bay, the distant blue hills across the water, which rolled on down to the most south-westerly point of Ireland. One day – when he had made his fortune – he would come back and live here.

He smiled a little at the thought, then put a hand to his pocket and pulled out a battered tin. Opening it, he extracted a stub of half-smoked cigarette, which he lit, tilting his head back to draw on it deeply. Then, as he glanced down to slip the tin back into his pocket, he saw to his surprise that he was not the only smoker who had stood here recently. He bent to pick up the cigarette at his feet; it was a roll-up, and it was barely damp. Puzzled, he looked around. In the far distance, walking fast, a tall man strode up the path that led across the hills to the Bantry Bay side of the peninsula. As the boy watched, he disappeared behind a rocky outcrop and was gone.

Liam shrugged, reached for his tin again and carefully deposited the cigarette in it. Whoever the stranger was, his tobacco was as good as anyone else's.

'Well, well! You're a one, aren't you? Does your mother know you smoke?'

Startled, he turned. Lottie had crept up behind him and was sitting on a fallen stone, swinging her sandalled feet, head tilted mischievously. The sun lit her hair to a fiery halo about her pointed, freckled face. She was wearing a pretty pale green dress, short-sleeved, short-skirted and much the same colour as her eyes, her legs were bare and she had a very large smudge of dirt on one cheek.

Liam smiled and shrugged.

'I shall tell,' she said, virtuously, grinning like an imp.

'Ah, come on – you wouldn't be gettin' me into trouble, now, would you?' Artfully he broadened his accent, his eyes gleaming with laughter.

She giggled. 'You don't need me to get you into trouble, Liam McCarthy. You're capable enough of doing that yourself, I'm sure.'

He pinched out the cigarette and stowed the last of it back in the tin. Lottie jumped up and came to join him, gazing out across the bay. 'It's very beautiful, isn't it?' she said quietly after a moment.

'Yes. It is. I was just thinkin'—' He stopped.

'What?' She cocked her head to look up at him. 'What were you thinking?'

He shook his head. 'Ah, 'tis silly. I was just thinkin' that I'd like to live here one day.' He glanced down at her, his mouth crooked into a self-deprecating smile. 'After I've made me fortune, you understand.'

Her huge eyes widened further in delighted surprise. 'How are you going to do that?'

He leaned back against the stone, folding his arms and narrowing his eyes as he looked out across the hills. When he spoke his voice was thoughtful, speaking as much to himself as to her. 'Well, to be truthful, at the moment I can't say I've any idea. But I'm goin' to do it. Mr Fletcher says the same as me ma – that you can do anything if you really try – if you really want to.'

'Who's Mr Fletcher?' The words were abstracted. Lottie had picked a bracken leaf and was carefully stripping it with long, thin fingers.

He smiled a little. The girl had the attention span of a butterfly. 'A teacher,' he said. 'And a good friend, too. A friend who's shown me that education's the thing. Education's the key to gettin' to *be* someone—'

'A teacher? How on earth can you be friends with a *teacher?'* Lottie was aghast. 'Lord – after I leave school – which'll be just as soon as I possibly can – I never want to see or speak to another teacher again!'

'This one's different. He thinks I could really make something of meself. He's found out about a scholarship—' Liam stopped. Lottie had reduced her piece of bracken to a skeleton and, humming quietly to herself, was making patterns on the rock with the sunshine. He shook his head, faintly exasperated. 'Lottie, will you tell me how you managed to get that great lump of dirt on your face?'

She looked up, surprised. 'Have I?' She rubbed vaguely at her left cheek. 'It must have been when I was up in the attic. Ned had us all playing hide-and-seek—'

'Wrong cheek. Here.' Liam turned her to face the sun, pulled a grubby handkerchief from his pocket. 'Stand still a minute.' He licked the handkerchief. Lottie screwed her face up, but stood obediently still as he scrubbed at the dirty mark.

'And what do you two think you're playing at?' Christine Clough, in knee-length shorts and open-necked shirt, stood, hands in pockets, surveying them coolly.

Liam turned away.

'Don't be daft. We're not playing at anything.' Lottie rubbed the palm of her hand over her cheek. 'I'd got a smudge of dirt on my face, that's all. Where've you been?'

'Oh – around.'

Liam had walked back to where the shotgun was propped against the stone. Christine followed him. She watched as he picked it up, snapped it shut, tucked it into his shoulder and sighted along the barrel. 'Can you really shoot that thing?'

'Yes.'

'Who taught you?'

'Tim O'Mahony, from the village. I help him out on his boat sometimes.'

'Did it take long?'

'What?'

'Learning to shoot.' She was impatient.

'Oh – well, no. Tim says some people are just natural shots.'

'And you're one of them?' Her voice was faintly mocking.

His chin came up. 'Yes,' he said, simply.

She held out her hand. 'May I see it?'

For a moment, all too obviously, he was tempted to refuse, though to be truthful even he would have been hard put to explain why. He saw the tightening of her lips. Shrugged.

She took the gun from him. 'Is it loaded?'

'Of course it isn't.' The tone was withering.

She broke the gun, snapped it shut again as she had just seen him do, hefted it in her hands. 'It isn't as heavy as I thought it'd be.'

'It's a twelve-bore.' He watched in silence as she curled a finger about the trigger, lifted the gun awkwardly and sighted along it. Then, unexpectedly, she held it out to him, abruptly.

'Shoot something.'

'What?'

'I said shoot something.' She was impatient.

'What sort of something?'

'Oh – anything. There – that.' She pointed.

At a distance of perhaps twenty-five yards a large stone rested upon a boulder.

'And what's the poor thing done to offend you?' Liam asked, drily.

'Don't be silly. Just shoot it.'

'Why?'

'Because I want you to.'

'Stamp your little foot, why don't you?' The words were very quiet. Lottie glanced at him, startled.

Warm colour flooded Christine's suntanned face. For a moment he thought she would flare, but then she rammed her hands back into her pockets and lifted her chin. 'I only want to see you shoot something,' she said in a perilously reasonable tone.

'Cartridges cost money.' He broke the gun and slung it across his shoulder again.

'Oh, for goodness' sake – I'll pay for some.'

He raised his black eyebrows.

'I will. I mean it.' She smiled a small smile. 'You're afraid you won't hit it,' she said. 'Aren't you?'

He stood for a moment longer, then slipped a hand in his pocket for a cartridge.

Christine watched closely as he loaded the gun. 'I thought you were supposed to put two in?'

'I'll only be needin' the one.' He brought the gun up, clicked the hammer back. The sound of the shot made Lottie jump and put her hands to her ears. The stone at which Liam had aimed flew into the air and landed in the bracken. 'There. Satisfied?' he asked Christine.

'Can I try?'

He stared at her. 'What?'

'I said, can I try? It doesn't look too hard.'

His mouth twitched a little caustically at that. 'Have you ever shot a gun before?'

'No, but—'

'Well, there you are, then.'

'But neither had you until a few weeks ago!'

'That's different.'

'Why? Why's it different? Because you're a boy and I'm a girl? I think not! You just said some people are natural shots. How do you know I'm not?' she asked, heatedly.

It was, he knew, a reasonable question. He dodged giving the reasonable answer. As so often, this small, arrogant girl had put him thoroughly out of sorts. 'And what do you suppose your mother would say if she knew I was letting you fool around with a gun?'

Her eyes narrowed dangerously. She planted her hands on her hips. 'There you go again. Why would I be fooling around? Is that what you do? Fool around?'

'Of course not.'

'Well then! Show me how. Let me try.'

'You might try saying "please", Christine,' Lottie said, mildly acid, then shook her head, grinning, as Christine scowled at her. 'P'raps not.'

Christine turned back to Liam. 'All right,' she said after a moment, more in defiance than defeat. 'Please,' she emphasised the word flatly, 'will you let me try?'

Lottie's laughter tinkled. 'You might as well give in, Liam. You know Chris. She's not going to give up until you do.'

'I'll pay for some cartridges,' Christine said. 'I promise. As many as you like, not just how many I shoot,' she added, craftily.

For a lad as hard up as Liam was, this was temptation beyond resisting. He shrugged. Why not? The worst that could happen was that she'd land on her arse in the bracken. He almost smiled at the thought. 'All right. On one condition.'

'What's that?'

'That you do *exactly* as you're told. This thing's not a toy. You've got to take care how you handle it.'

She nodded and took the gun he handed her, examining it in fascination.

'You're right-handed, yes?'

She nodded.

'So – left foot forward, like this. Bend your knee a bit – no, you're too far forward. Balance your weight – that's the way. Practise it a couple of times. Stand up, then forward; up, then forward.'

Christine opened her mouth, glanced at his face, shut it again and practised the movement a perfunctory couple of times. Lottie, cross-legged on a fallen stone, watched in undisguised amusement.

'Give me the gun a minute.'

Christine handed him the gun. He swung it easily up into his shoulder, his elbow high. 'When you mount the gun it's got to fit into your shoulder. And you must hold it firmly, or you'll lose it when you fire – here, you try.'

She took the thing eagerly, swung it awkwardly up to her shoulder.

'Jesus, Mary and Joseph, girl! Pull the trigger holding the thing like that and you'll smash your shoulder to smithereens. Look – like this.' He reached out and took her elbow, lifting it, slipping his hand into the hollow of her shoulder that the movement created. 'There – feel it? – get the stock settled there.' Seeing that she still looked puzzled, he took her narrow hand and laid it in the hollow of his own shoulder, lifting his elbow so that she could feel the movement of bone and muscle. ''Tis like a cradle for a babe, d'you see?'

There was a small silence. Her hand was warm and firm through the tough material of his shirt. She snatched it away. 'Yes,' she said, shortly, 'I see.'

For some reason he felt the blood rising in his face. 'You try it again, then,' he said, gruffly. She practised a couple of times. 'That's the way, you're getting it. Mount the gun, head over, so.' He reached to tilt her head; her hair was springy, thick and sun-warm beneath his hand. 'Aim at that bunch of bracken growing in the rock there.'

'I haven't got any cartridges in the gun yet.'

'Did I say to shoot the thing? I did not. I said to aim at it.' He was suddenly aware that his hand was still resting on her hair and – oddly confusing – that the feel of the silken, curly tousle of it was far from unpleasant. He stepped back, his hand dropping to his side. 'Right you are; now try both together. Left foot forward, knee bent, mount the gun, balance it, aim at the rock – that's the way. Try again.' He walked around in front of her, watching her movements. 'Balance,' he said again. 'Balance the gun and balance yourself. Hold it.' She had the gun in her shoulder. 'Comfortable?'

She hefted the gun a little. 'Yes.'

'Sure?'

'Yes.' There was an edge of impatience in the word.

Liam took a quick step forward and with no warning thumped the heel of his hand hard on the end of the gun-barrels, pushing her completely off balance. Had it not been for the stone behind her she would certainly have fallen. As it was, with a shriek, she stumbled back against the stone, the gun flying from her upflung hands. Neatly, Liam caught it.

'You *beast*! What on earth did you do that for?' She was outraged. For a moment Liam thought she would fly at him. He held up a hand placatingly. Lottie was doubled up with laughter.

'It's what would have happened if you'd pulled the trigger holdin' the gun like that. An' with another bullet in the barrel most like. I told you – it's not a toy.'

She surveyed him suspiciously for a very long moment. 'All right,' she said at last, evenly, 'let's try again.'

Lottie had long since got bored and wandered off by the time Liam was ready to let Christine try a shot. He stood behind her and sighted along the barrels, held rock-steady in the small hands. 'That's the girl. Perhaps a little higher.' She adjusted her aim. He had already slipped a single cartridge into one of the chambers. 'Hammer,' he said. The hammer clicked, clear and steady. 'Now. Squeeze. Don't snatch.' He moved closer to her, ready to steady her if necessary. The sun gleamed on the fine, fair hairs on her bare arms. Unlike Lottie, Christine's skin had turned to honey in the sun and wind. She laid her smooth cheek against the stock.

The shot rattled, echoing, along the mountainside. She rocked back a little. He caught her shoulders, steadying her. 'I hit it,' she said, very quietly, and turned. Her eyes were shining. 'I did hit it, didn't I?'

'You surely did.'

'I told you I would.'

'You did, so.' His tone was dry.

'I'd like to try again.'

'I was sure you would.' The tone had not changed.

Christine ignored – or perhaps did not notice – it. She held out the gun. 'Would you load it for me, please?'

He smiled pleasantly, handed her two cartridges. 'Load it yourself.'

Ten minutes later, having proved that her first success was no fluke, she gave him back the gun. 'It's not like shooting at something that's moving, though, is it?'

He shook his head. 'No.'

'Would you teach me that, too?'

He hesitated.

'I'll double the number of cartridges,' she bargained, slyly.

He shrugged. 'Done.'

'I hear Christine's been having shooting lessons?' Pamela poured two cups of tea and handed one to Siobhan. Her voice was mildly amused. 'I must admit that I find the idea of Christine let loose with a shotgun rather a daunting one.'

Siobhan laughed a little. 'That was my first thought. But I've had a word with young Liam, and he assures me there's no danger. I trust the lad. He'll be careful. Though I must admit—' She stopped.

Pamela looked at her enquiringly.

'Well, I did wonder whether it's quite – proper – for the two of them to be seeing so much of each other.'

'Proper?' It took a moment for the inference of that to sink in. When it did, Pamela shook her head with a small snort of laughter. 'Oh, don't be silly, Siobhan. If I know those two, they spend the best part of their time together quarrelling. Anyway, the others are always about. Young Ned follows Liam around like a puppy.'

'You don't think we're letting them all run a little too wild? They've been roaming the countryside like a gang of young gypsies.'

Pamela leaned forward and patted her friend's hand.

'Don't be silly, Siobhan. Just look at them. They're all having a wonderful time. Isn't that what we wanted? In a month or so they'll be back home; back to school, back to order, back to rules and regulations. Let them have their heads. They're a sensible bunch on the whole. I'm sure we can trust them.'

Obviously still uncertain, Siobhan nevertheless nodded. 'I suppose you're right. I just wonder if George—' She stopped.

'George isn't here,' Pamela said, briskly. 'And George isn't coming. And what George doesn't know can't hurt him, can it? Which reminds me,' she added, 'I've booked Sean Flynn's taxi from Durrus to pick David and Alex up from Bantry on Saturday. They'll be on the three o'clock train, hopefully. I thought I might go along to meet them – would you like to come? We could go early and do some shopping in Bantry if you'd like?'

Siobhan shook her head, smiling. 'No, no. It's your day. I'll wait here. You'll have a lot to talk about. I'll stay here with the children. I might even look in on one of young Liam's shooting lessons.' She smiled, affectionately. 'I have to admit it would be quite a novel experience to see my daughter taking orders instead of giving them.'

'Liam McCarthy, how *dare* you speak to me like that?'

'I only said—'

'It's not what you said, it's the way that you said it! Who the devil do you think you are?'

Inevitably Liam's temper rose to match the girl's. 'I'm the one who's in charge here, that's who I am! And if I tell you you're doing something wrong, then you're doing something wrong! Will you tell me why you must argue with everything I say?'

'I don't!'

'You do!'

'I *don't!*' Christine was scarlet with fury and mortification.

Liam slung the gun on to his shoulder and, turning away from her, set off up the mountain path with long, angry strides.

Beside herself with temper she watched him go. 'I hate you!' she yelled at his departing back.

Liam turned. ''Tis mutual, Miss Clough,' he said, grimly. 'Believe me, 'tis mutual!'

# Chapter Four

'I wish *I* had a bedroom up a ladder,' Ned said, pulling off his shoes and socks and wriggling his pale toes. 'It must be really fun!'

Liam, sitting on a rock beside him, grinned and tossed a pebble into the water. Behind them stood the little white-washed cottage; before them spread Dunmanus Bay, sparkling in the sunlight. Further along the shore Josie and Tom were busily filling a galvanised bucket with mussels, the sound of their constant chatter mingling with the easy lap of the waves. Not for the first time Liam wondered what on earth the two of them found to talk about all the time.

Ned got to his feet and stuck a toe in the water, laughed at the chill of it, and then waded in up to his knees.

'Don't be gettin' your shorts wet, or your ma won't be happy.'

Ned bent over, peering down into the crystal-clear water, fascinated by the light that rippled over the stones and shells and waving seaweed. Birds – curlews and gulls – wheeled and called overhead. A heron perched like a hunchbacked old man on a rock not far from them. Ned stood up, splashing the water. Disturbed, the bird lifted gracefully into the air, great wings beating. They both watched it. 'I wish we could stay here for ever,' Ned said, suddenly.

Liam leaned forward and ruffled his hair. 'We've still a couple more weeks.'

A flock of gulls were fiercely mobbing the heron, driving the bird away. 'Why are they doing that?' Ned asked.

'Protecting their territory. He's a stranger. They see him as a threat. They want him away.'

The younger boy kicked a spray of water into the air, sparkling and glistening. 'That doesn't seem fair.'

Liam grinned. 'Life isn't,' he said, lightly. 'Didn't you know that?'

Ned shrugged and changed the subject. 'Lottie's in trouble,' he said, offhandedly

'Oh?'

'She went walking on the mountain with that Sean O'Donovan from the village.'

Liam raised dark eyebrows. 'Did she indeed?'

His companion turned to look at him. 'What does "no better than she should be" mean?' Both the words and his blue eyes were altogether too ingenuous.

'I think you know very well what it means. Why d'you ask?'

''Cos that's what Chris said about Lottie.' A flashing, elfin grin lit the narrow face with mischief.

'Ned? Ned – have you seen Emma around?' Christine's voice, calling from behind them.

'Talk of the devil,' Liam said, very quietly.

Ned lifted his head. 'No,' he called back, 'not since lunchtime, anyway. She was going off with a book last time I saw her.'

Christine joined them. 'Where was she going, did she say?' She ignored Liam. Liam, returning the compliment, leaned forward, his elbows on his knees, and very deliberately turned his head to look in the opposite direction.

'Nope. No idea.'

'Oh, bother! She's always disappearing with a book! Mama wanted her for something.'

Liam's interest had been caught by a figure who was

standing a little way along the road that ran along the edge of the bay. He was a big man, dressed in tweed jacket and trousers and with a wide-brimmed hat pushed to the back of his head. He was leaning against a rocky outcrop, fingers busy with a roll-up cigarette, his eyes scanning the far hills on the other side of the bay. Yet Liam had the instinctive feeling that, until he had turned, the stranger had been watching them.

'She might have gone up to the circle,' Ned offered helpfully. 'She likes it up there.'

Christine turned, still grumbling. 'Wretched girl! I s'pose I'd better go and look.'

The stranger was lighting his cigarette, head bent, hand cupped about the flame against the sea breeze. For a second his eyes met Liam's. Liam frowned; there was something quite hauntingly familiar about the man, but he could not for the life of him put a finger on what it was.

Ned had hauled a skein of bladderwrack from the sea and was busily popping its slimy pods. 'Alex has promised to take me on an expedition to the Sheep's Head, to see the lighthouse. Mama has said I can go. Do you want to come? I'm sure Alex won't mind. He's arranging a pony and trap to take us along the peninsula until we come to the bit where you have to walk. We're going to take a picnic lunch and everything. It'll be fun.'

The stranger had turned and was strolling away, his back to them. Liam watched him for a moment, still frowning a little. 'Yes, sure. Why not?' He turned back to the child. 'Ned, have you seen that man around here before?'

'What man?'

Liam indicated the retreating figure.

Ned shook his head. 'Don't think so. Why?'

Liam shrugged, not sure himself why he had asked. 'Just wondered,' he said.

He saw the stranger again a couple of days later.

He was coming off the mountain, the gun over his

shoulder and a brace of rabbits dangling from his belt, when he heard footsteps behind him.

'Good day to you.' A quiet voice, strongly accented. 'I see you've had some luck with the gun.'

Taken entirely by surprise, Liam turned. How the man had managed to get so close behind him without being heard he could not imagine.

The stranger held up a quick apologetic hand, the fingers heavily stained with nicotine. 'Sure, I'm sorry, lad. It wasn't me intention to startle you.' He was a strikingly handsome man, tall and broad-shouldered, his bright eyes as blue as the skies, the hair that curled from beneath the rakishly-worn hat thick and black as Liam's own. His mouth was straight and firm; his smile attractively lopsided. Again something stirred elusively in Liam's memory, and was lost.

'It's all right,' he said.

'You've a good supper there.' The man nodded his head towards the rabbits.

'Yes. Ma cooks a good rabbit.'

Again the smile. 'Lucky lad. You're local?'

Liam shook his head. 'We're here staying with the people at Hill House. Ma works for them.'

'Ah.' The sound was non-committal.

Liam eyed him curiously. 'Yourself?' he ventured.

The blue eyes had been thoughtful. At Liam's question the man stopped and held out his hand, 'I'm Dermot. Dermot – Sheehan.' Had Liam imagined that slight hesitation? 'I've been over in Bantry on business. Thought I might see a bit of the countryside while I was hereabouts. I'm stayin' yonder.' He jerked his head to indicate some unspecified spot on the other side of the mountain.

Liam took the hand. It was warm and very strong. 'Liam McCarthy. How do you do?' he said, politely.

The smile lit the man's face almost to laughter. 'Grand. I do just grand. An' it's pleased I am to meet you, Liam McCarthy. Perhaps we'll see something of each other in the next few days? I'm round and about most of the time.' They had reached the stone circle. He stopped, dipped into his pocket and brought out a tobacco pouch, a pack of papers neatly folded into it. 'I'll not come further today,' he said, equably. 'The further down I go, the further 'tis to come back up.' He put his hand to his inside pocket and brought out a battered flask. 'I've got good company.'

Liam grinned.

The man extended the flask towards him. 'Join me?'

Liam shook his head. 'Best not.' He slapped at the rabbits at his belt. 'I've these to skin, and the knife is sharp.'

'Sensible lad.' Dermot Sheehan hitched himself on to one of the fallen stones, turned to survey the staggeringly beautiful view of the bay. 'Sharp knives and strong liquor – it's a troublesome combination, an' isn't that the truth?'

Liam lifted a hand. 'I'll be seeing you, then.' He turned and walked away, stones slipping from the tramp of his heavy boots on the path.

'Indeed you will,' the man who called himself Dermot Sheehan said, very quietly.

Liam did not hear him.

He was outside the cottage, skinning the rabbits, when a small figure came hurtling down the path towards him. Ned's thin, fair-skinned face was scarlet and tear-streaked; he could barely take a breath to speak. 'Liam! *Liam!* You've – g-got to – c-come.'

Liam wiped his hands on a rag, caught the child by the shoulders. 'Steady, Ned, steady! What is it?'

'Chris – th-they've got her – they're – being *horrible* to her – I'm afraid they'll – h-hurt her – I ran away.' The tears were running again, the words only barely intelligible.

Liam shook him, and not gently. 'Ned! Calm down! Who's got Christine? And where?'

'D-down in the wood – where the s-stream is – n-near the little waterfall.'

Liam, towing the child behind him, was already on his way. 'Who?'

'S-some boys from the village. Emma's gone off again and w-we were looking for her – where are you going?'

Liam had crossed the road and had flung a leg across a low dry-stone wall. 'This way. It's quicker.' He leaned towards the slender child and with little ceremony and no effort picked him up by the scruff of his neck and swung him over the wall. 'Watch your ankles. It's rocky. Just follow on.' He let go of the sobbing child and began to run.

Christine stood, flushed, dishevelled and defiant, her back, ramrod straight, set against a tree, watching warily as her tormentors circled her.

'So, yer snooty little English bitch.' The leader of the group was a big lad, a young man Christine had seen before, down by the little harbour, helping when the boats brought in the fish. 'Will yer be tellin' me what's yer favourite colours?'

'I don't know what you're talking about.'

'Would it be black an' tan, d'yer think?' He addressed his appreciative audience rather than the girl. 'Suit her, wouldn't it? Go with the yeller hair, wouldn't it?'

Christine stood silent.

There were about half a dozen of them; at least a couple looked uneasy at the sport, but obviously lacked the courage to stop it.

The lad advanced on her, thrust his face into hers. 'Me father died in Dublin, fightin' for Ireland. In 1916. Three months before I was born. Fightin' the fockin' English.' He saw her flinch a little, and repeated, 'The fockin' *fockin'* English.' His voice was very quiet.

'Sure, and can't you always trust the English for a bit of bad timing?' The conversational voice came from behind him. Liam stepped into the clearing. 'Six months earlier and, beGod, the world would have been saved some grief, Jonty O'Mahony. Christine—' He held out a hand, his eyes steady on the lad who had turned, and stilled, on seeing him. 'Party's over, Jonty.' Liam's voice was acid with disgust. 'Fancy your chances up against a pint-sized girl, do you?'

Christine, slowly and with her eyes flicking from one to the other of the group, was sidling towards him. He almost grinned at the sudden, unpromising look she threw him.

'Makes you feel good, does it?' he added, gently.

'Fock you, McCarthy! Call yerself an Irishman?' Jonty O'Mahony spat over his shoulder. 'You? You're an arse-lickin' traitor. Go back to England an' take the little English bitch and all her kin with you.'

Christine had reached his side. 'Oh, I will.' Liam was peaceable. 'When I'm good and ready.' His eyes flicked around the circle. 'Well, well. All your little half-brothers are here, I see.' He raised his brows in the most insulting way possible. 'Your mother's a true patriot, Jonty. All true sons of Ireland. What does it matter who fathered them?'

The other youngster launched himself at Liam like a bull. Christine let out an involuntary yelp and jumped backwards. Ned, who had just caught up with it all, flew to her.

The two were well matched. Blood flew. No-one interfered. The scrap was brief and brutal, but it was a fair fight, and one to savour. With honours relatively even, they drew back.

'You're a bastard, McCarthy,' Jonty said through bloody and broken lips.

'That's very possibly true.' Liam's face was less marked than his opponent's, but a purple bruise was swelling on his cheekbone, and blood ran from his lower lip. 'And beGod you're a shite yourself.' His voice was amicable.

'Jonty.' One of the younger boys shifted from foot to foot. 'Think we should be goin'. Ma'll be lookin' for us.'

'Home to Mammy, Jonty,' Liam jeered, grinning.

'Fock off.' Jonty turned and traipsed off into the wood, followed by his henchmen.

'Irish savages!' Christine said, coldly furious. 'Father's right. I don't know why we don't hang the lot of them!'

Liam – bruised and unthanked – turned, eyeing her with sudden and graceless dislike. The swelling on his cheekbone was darkening by the moment. And it hurt. 'D'you not think it's time for you to accept that you're half-Irish yourself, Missy?' he asked, bluntly. 'Perhaps you should sometimes remember that?'

Ned looked worriedly from one to the other, and, predictably, took the safest option. His voice lifted in a tearful wail. 'I want to go home.'

Liam, more battered and bruised than he had cared to admit to his mother when he had explained the cause of his colourful cheekbone and split lip, did not sleep well that night. The evening had stilled, and fog had rolled in from the dead calm water, clammy and thick, billowing against the tiny dormer window of his loft-bedroom.

He was awakened from a restless sleep by the sound of voices; whispers that were loud in the all-enveloping silence that had folded around the cottage on the shore.

'You'll stay away from him! If it's the last thing I do, Dermot McCarthy, I'll make sure you stay away from him! He believes you're dead. Everyone does. Leave it so!' His mother's voice was low and passionate. 'Who the hell d'you think you are to come walking in here like this? Fifteen years, Dermot! *Fifteen years!* Never a word. Never a penny. Never an enquiry if we were dead or alive. You abandoned him and you abandoned me. You left us in debt and homeless. God alone knows what would have become of us both if it hadn't been for Siobhan Clough! And for what? For what did you leave your wife and son? For the gun and the bullet. For the company of thugs! Well, you made your choice and by God I'll make sure you stick by it! Leave Liam alone! He knows nothing about you. I don't want him knowing anything about you. He's a decent lad.'

'He is that. From what I can see you've made a wonderful job of the boy.'

There was a sudden silence. 'How would you know that?' Mary asked, very quietly.

The man did not reply.

Liam slipped out of bed, winced, pulled on a pair of trousers.

'*I asked – how would you know?*' His mother had not raised her voice, but there was a precariously sharp edge to it. She waited for a moment. Then, 'You've spoken to him. Haven't you?' she said, flatly. 'How *dare* you? What *right* do you have to come near him?'

'Mary, I'm the lad's father.'

'No.' The word was bitter. 'You fathered him, yes. But do you know anything – *anything* – about him? What's his favourite food? Is he good at football? Can he swim? What does he like to read? What does he want for his birthday? When *is* his birthday, Dermot?' The words were scathing. 'Can you even answer me that?'

The silence was heavy.

'You? His father? What have you ever done to deserve to be called so? Go away, Dermot. Go back to your patriotic friends and your dangerous politics. Go away and leave us alone.'

'Ma?' Liam, easily practised, shinned down the wooden ladder into the big sitting room below. His mother's bed was neatly made up, the sheets folded back ready for use, in the alcove beside the big old iron range. A brass oil lamp flickered on the scrubbed table, casting shadows. The fire in the great open fireplace had died to a glimmer. Fog blanked the window that faced the sea. 'What's going on?'

The two adults, arrested where they stood, stared at him. His mother was in her dressing gown, her long hair loose and freshly brushed; the man he now knew as his father stood with his back to the door, bare-headed, his hat in his hand, beads of moisture from the fog glistening in his black curls. And now, clear as day, Liam could see it; the set of the head, the blue of the eyes, the very cast of the face was his own. This was the haunting familiarity that had puzzled him so; quite literally a mirror image. 'What's going on?' he repeated, and for the first time in a long while his voice cracked a little. He cleared his throat.

In the silence that followed, a charred log shifted and collapsed in the fireplace, sending up a little puff of white ash.

On bare feet Liam walked forward and leaned his hands on the table, looking across it, intently, into the man's face. 'You're my father?'

He heard his mother catch her breath to speak, but for the moment did not look at her.

'I am,' the stranger said quietly, then added, a hint of amusement in the attractive, musical voice, 'Lord, boy, you've been in the wars from the look of it?'

Liam ignored both the comment and the amusement. 'Why are you here?'

'It was as I said on the mountain – I was in Bantry on – business.' He shrugged disarmingly as he hesitated over the word. 'You well know how gossip flies around here. I heard the Cloughs were at Hill House for the summer—' He stopped.

Liam's narrowed eyes were savage, and very steady on his. 'Go on,' he said, evenly.

'Sure what's to go on? I thought I'd come over to Ahakista and—' Again, easily, he let his voice tail off, and again he shrugged.

'And – look us up, like?' Liam was relentless. 'See if I was worth claiming?'

Dermot McCarthy was too wily to answer that one.

Liam walked around the table to stand in front of him. 'Tell me,' he said, perilously softly, 'why did the fact that the Cloughs were at Hill House mean anything to you at all?'

Mary McCarthy, who had been watching her son, turned her eyes, with his, to the man by the door.

'I knew your mother was distantly related to Mrs Clough,' Dermot said, carefully.

Liam let the awkward silence lengthen before saying, 'Go

on.' His face was bleak. His tongue teased at his split and swollen lip.

Dermot McCarthy's expression was wry. 'Sure – you're a chip off the old block, lad,' he said, quietly, and then, eyeing the damaged face and bruised ribs, 'in more ways than one.'

'If you knew,' Liam said, relentlessly, refusing to be diverted, 'that Ma worked for the Cloughs, then you didn't have to wait till we came to Ireland to find us. Did you?'

Unable to sustain the fierceness of the boy's gaze, Dermot's eyes dropped. He tossed his hat on to the table and reached into his pocket for his tobacco pouch.

Mother and son stood in silence as he rolled his cigarette. Mary's face was watchful.

The lighter flared, illuminating the planes and angles of the handsome face. Liam swallowed, the line of his mouth tightening painfully. 'Well?' he insisted.

The curly head lifted. 'No,' Dermot McCarthy admitted, simply.

'You could have found us at any time.'

'Yes.'

'But you didn't.'

The man did not reply.

Liam turned and walked to his mother, put his arm about her shoulders. He was already almost a head taller than she. 'We don't need you,' he said, quietly. 'Ma's right. Go away and leave us alone.'

Dermot studied the fierce young face for a moment. 'You really mean that?'

'Yes.'

'I see.' He stood in silence for a moment before reaching for his hat and settling it firmly upon his head. 'I'm sorry, lad. I'm truly sorry.' The note of regret in his voice was persuasive. Liam's arm tightened about his mother's shoulders.

Dermot McCarthy looked from one to the other, then, shrugging a little, turned and opened the door. Fog drifted

eerily into the room. Liam and Mary stood watching him,
limned in the soft light of the lamp that stood on the table
behind them. He opened his mouth as if to speak, then
shook his head and walked out into the darkness, closing
the door very quietly behind him.

Mary McCarthy turned and for the briefest of moments
rested her forehead on her son's shoulder. Then, collectedly,
she walked to the stove and put a large black kettle on
the hob. Liam sat down, very suddenly, put his elbows on
the table and, closing his eyes, ran his fingers through his
already wild hair. When he lifted his head his mother had
seated herself opposite him. 'You've seen him before?' she
asked, gently.

Liam nodded. 'He's been hanging about for a while. I
only spoke to him once.'

'Do you want to—' Mary paused, 'ask me anything?'

'I don't know. Yes, I suppose so. But I don't know—'

There was a moment's quiet. Then Mary asked, 'May I
ask you something?'

Liam lifted his head, watching her, and waited.

'Did you mean what you said to him?'

He hesitated only for a moment. 'Yes.'

'You're sure?'

'Yes.'

'Then will you promise me something? Will you promise
me not to talk to him again? I can't make him go away. I
can't make him leave us alone. I'll answer any questions
you might want to ask, and I'll answer them honestly. Just
don't speak to him again. Don't have anything to do with
him. He's a wicked man.'

Liam let his face drop back into his cupped hands for a
moment.

'Please, Liam!' His mother's voice was quietly urgent. 'I
know what the man can do! Sure, no-one knows better!' Her
voice for a moment was bitter. 'He may be a rogue but he's
a charmer, I don't deny that. You've seen it for yourself.
He'd beguile the devil himself, given half a chance. But

he's worthless and, worse, he's dangerous. He'll do you nothing but harm. Please. Give me your word you'll not speak to him again.'

Still he said nothing.

She got up and went back to the stove, where the kettle lid was rattling as the water boiled. Liam lifted his head and watched as she went through the comfortingly familiar ritual of tea-making. She brought the steaming cups to the table, set the sugar bowl in front of the boy, then went to a cupboard and produced a jug. Liam's eyes widened a little as she brought it to the table and he caught a strong whiff of its contents. His mother looked at him whimsically, and for the first time she smiled, faintly. 'Sure, 'tis for emergencies, is it not? And if this isn't an emergency I'd like to be told what it is.' She poured a little of the poteen into both cups and pushed the sugar towards him. 'Help yourself.'

'Thanks.' Liam spooned two generous helpings and stirred his tea, his eyes thoughtful.

'Your father's a maverick, Liam. And trouble follows him around like a dog follows its master. Please, if you meant what you said, then promise me you'll not speak to him again. If you didn't—' She stopped, blinked quickly, ducked her head and reached for her own tea.

He reached across the table for her hand. 'Ma, don't upset yourself. Please.'

'I'm not upset.' She sniffed loudly, squeezed his hand.

'You're always telling me not to tell fibs,' he reminded her gently.

She smiled a faint and slightly watery smile. 'That's true.'

'I won't speak to him again,' Liam said, quietly. 'There's no reason to. I promise I won't. On my life I promise.'

This time his mother couldn't prevent the overspilling of tears. She lifted the cup unsteadily to her lips.

Equally unsteadily, Liam laughed. 'Ma, will you tell me what you've got against that tea? You've diluted it once, and now you're doing it again!'

She set the cup down. 'Oh, get on with you. Before we
do anything else I should put some more iodine on those
bruises. I only hope young Christine's grateful for what you
did for her.'

Liam pulled a face, and flinched. 'Pigs might fly, I suppose,' he said, 'but in my experience not too often.'

Dermot McCarthy watched Liam as, gun on shoulder, he
tramped slowly up the path that led from the cottage past
Hill House and the stone circle to the rocky hillside above.
Even from this distance the lad looked tired; the usual swing
was gone from his step, the bruises on his face stood out
lividly, and there were dark rings about his eyes. He was
walking stiffly and had obviously not seen the man who
stood above him. Dermot drew back behind the tallest of the
standing stones, his eyes still upon the tall, rangy figure of
his son. Almost without thinking about it he found himself
rolling a cigarette. There must have been some talking done
in that cottage last night after he'd left, he reckoned, wryly.
But then, why not? The boy deserved to know the truth;
and there wasn't much that Mary could have told Liam
that he, Dermot, could in honesty have denied or even
defended, if he had stayed. He wasn't sure himself what
impulse had taken him down to the cottage last night. Any
more than he had understood why he had spoken to the lad
the other day. To be truthful – and Dermot, whatever his
deviously devised code of practice with others, was always
truthful with himself – he had been astonished at his own
reaction upon meeting the lad. His motive for coming to
Ahakista had been pure – almost idle – curiosity, nothing
more. On hearing in Bantry that Siobhan and her family
were at Hill House, he had wondered if Mary and their
son might be with them. With a few days on his hands
whilst waiting for unfinished business to be completed –
and in the long-ago-acquired knowledge that if idle time
needed to be whiled away it was always better to while it
away in a spot that was as far as possible from the nearest

army post or police station – he had decided on the spur of the moment to come and see. It had never been his intention to make himself known to either of them, let alone to make any claims on the boy. He shook his head. Mary had had every justification last night; he had no rights in Liam. What good would either of them be to the other? The lad himself, to his credit, had told him to go. Best leave it at that.

And yet—

The fog still hung over the bay and obscured the higher slopes of the mountainside. The gorse and bracken dripped water, the stones were wet. Dermot heard Liam's boots skitter on a slippery rock, then splash through a patch of peaty bog. The lad took after him in one way at least; he didn't go round things, but straight through them. The thought brought a grin.

He waited until Liam was almost upon him before stepping into his path.

Liam stopped. He did not look surprised. There was a long moment of silence.

'I'd give you top o' the mornin' but,' Dermot gestured ruefully, 'it doesn't exactly seem appropriate.'

Liam said nothing. Neither did he smile. The bruise on his cheekbone was a picturesque shade of greenish purple. His eye had begun to close.

Dermot reached for his tobacco pouch and offered it with a questioning lift of the eyebrows.

Liam shook his head. He was studying his father with steady, unreadable eyes.

Dermot shrugged and tucked the pouch back into his pocket. 'Guess you know a lot more about me than you did this time yesterday?'

Still no reply. And still the eyes so like his own did not waver.

'Sure – you won't catch somethin' just by speakin' to me, you know.'

Liam shook his head and turned away, walking into the circle and standing with his back to his father looking out across the fog-bound waters. 'I promised I wouldn't.' The young back was very straight and still.

'An' you keep your promises,' Dermot said quietly at last.

'Yes.'

'No-one can say better than that, lad. It's glad I am to hear it. Strikes me you're a boy to be proud of.' Dermot's roll-up had gone out. Liam heard the click of the lighter as he relit it. 'Everything she's told you's true, boy,' he said, softly, after a moment. 'I abandoned her, and you. An' you not three months old. Likely I'd do it again. It's not in me to have me slippers by the fire and the stew on the stove. But as I say, you're a lad to be proud of, and though it's none of my doing, that I am. I thought – just one thing – before I go—'

Liam had not moved. His head was back and his jaw tight. Dermot could not see his face.

'It happens that me business takes me to London some-times. I stay in a friend's flat, round White City way – very convenient for an Irishman, that.' Liam could hear the smile in the words. 'Sure, I've been goin' to the dogs one way or another for years.' He waited, hoping for some sign of unbending. None came. 'I've written down the address. Just in case, like. You never know.' His voice had taken on a peculiar and, to Liam, horrifying note of uncertainty. 'Would you take it? Anyone there will always know where I am. If you should need me, that is.'

Liam turned.

His father extended a torn scrap of paper.

Wordless, and after only a moment's hesitation, Liam took it and stuffed it in his pocket.

Dermot stepped back with a bright flick of a smile. 'Well, then. I'll be on me way.' He took a couple of steps backwards, his brilliant eyes still on the young, marked face, suddenly intense, as if memorising it. Then he turned and, very quickly, head down, his long raincoat flapping about his legs, strode along the steep path, up and away, into the hanging, clinging fog.

He did not look back.

So he did not see the tears that were coursing almost unnoticed down his son's face as he watched Dermot walk away.

# Chapter *Five*

'May I come in?' Christine's voice, by no means as crisply sure of itself as it usually was, came from the open door of the cottage.

Liam, who had been sitting with his back to the door, chin resting on his fists, studying a book that lay open on the table in front of him, jumped to his feet and turned.

The girl took a sharp breath, and deep colour rose in her cheeks as she saw his face.

'If you want.' Liam was wary.

She walked into the room, stood before him, hands clasped before her as if about to give a recitation. 'I came—' she said. And stopped.

'Yes?' He made no effort to disguise his surprise.

She tried again. 'I came—'

Liam waited, baffled.

'I came to apologise.' The words came out in a rush. 'I'm sorry. I was horrible to you the other day, when you'd – when you'd been so brave. I'm sorry,' she said again.

Completely taken aback, he stared at her.

She pulled an uncomfortable face. 'Well – say *something.*'

'I—' Liam shrugged and spread his hands.

'It isn't so astonishing, is it?' Christine, recovering herself, was mildly indignant. 'You got hurt because of me, and I didn't even thank you. So – thank you.' The last two words were briskly spoken.

Liam grinned, genuinely amused. 'That's all right.'

Christine, never one for beating about bushes herself, took him at his word. 'Good.' She looked around her. 'What a nice cosy room this is. I've never been in here before.' She pointed to the ladder. 'What's up there?'

'My bedroom.'

'Up a ladder? What fun!' She was wandering about the room, touching things, examining things, openly inquisitive.

Liam watched her with exasperatedly amused eyes. 'Would you care for a glass of lemonade?'

'Yes, please.' Christine had stopped at the table and was flicking through the book Liam had been reading. 'Shakespeare?' she said.

The unthinking astonishment in her voice brought a hint of a smile. 'Shakespeare,' Liam agreed, drily.

'I didn't know—' She suddenly realised how tactless she was being, and for the second time in as many minutes blushed rosily.

'A teacher at school's coaching me. There's a scholarship—' Liam stopped, lifting a shoulder. 'You'll not be wanting to hear about that.'

'Oh, but of course I do.' She hitched herself on to the table and sat with her legs swinging. 'Tell me.'

Liam handed her a glass of lemonade. 'My free schooling ended last year. Ma's struggled to pay, but she can't. Mr Fletcher – he's a teacher – persuaded them to let me stay on, at least until Christmas. Now he's found a scholarship I can go in for.'

Christine was frowning at him over the rim of her glass. 'Why do you want to stay at school?'

'Because if I want even half the things that you take for granted, I'm going to have to work for them,' Liam said, bluntly. 'And I won't get them by labouring in the docks or clocking on to a factory floor.'

Christine cocked her head, interestedly. 'I see. What do you want to do?'

'I'm not sure. But I know sure as eggs what I don't want to do.' Liam turned from her to gaze across the bay. 'I don't want to scrape a hand-to-mouth living for the rest of my life. I don't want to live in a slum and die of tuberculosis. I don't want to touch my cap to men who are no better than I am. I don't want to save pennies in a pot so that I can maybe enjoy a pint on a Saturday night.'

'This Mr Fletcher seems to have put some ambitious ideas into your head?'

Liam turned, unsmiling. 'He didn't put them in there. He just encouraged them when he found them.'

She drained her glass and jumped to the floor. 'Well, good luck to you, I say.' She walked to him to hand him the glass, stood very close looking up into his face, and then to his surprise lifted a very gentle finger to the savage bruise on his cheekbone. 'I really am sorry about that,' she said, softly. 'And you really were brave. I'm sorry I was so horrid afterwards. It was just – well, shock I suppose. I had been very frightened.'

'You didn't look very frightened. You looked as if you were about to take him on yourself.' Her finger was soft and cool on his face.

She grinned, a quick, elfish grin very like her brother's. 'Who would you have bet on?'

'He wouldn't have stood a chance.'

Laughing she swung away from him, and then paused at the door, a slight, dark shape against the sunlight, her hair lit to gold. 'Oh, by the way – did I hear Ned say that you were going with him and Alex to the lighthouse?'

'I thought I would, yes.'

'I'm coming too. It'll be fun. It's on Thursday. See you then.' And she was gone.

Liam walked back to the table. She had not, of course,

bothered to keep his place in the book. He flicked through until he found it, and sat down, his finger holding the heavy book open. But it was a long time before he started to read.

When the pony and the ancient little wooden cart that Alex had managed to hire wound its way down from the big house to the coast road on Thursday morning, Liam, a small knapsack slung across his shoulder, was waiting by the roadside. Alex was driving, with Christine beside him.

'Good mornin' to you.' Liam swung himself up and over the side to settle himself in the back beside Ned.

'We're going to see America!' Ned said, excitedly, then chanted, sing-song, 'We're going to see America, we're going to see America!'

Liam raised surprised brows. 'Are we indeed? Sure, perhaps I should have brought more than a sandwich, then?'

Christine turned, laughing. She was wearing a white shirt and knee-length khaki shorts, long socks and walking boots, and had a bright red jumper slung around her shoulders, a matching ribbon keeping her hair from her face. 'Mama says that's what they say here when they go up west – to the end of the peninsula. There's nothing between there and America – so the standard question after you've been there is "Did you see America, then?"' She made a fair fist of her mother's accent.

Alex clucked to the shaggy pony and the small cart started off. Ned leaned forward, peering at Liam. 'Does it still hurt?' he asked.

'What?'

'Your face.'

'Oh, that. No. Not much, anyway.

'It's still a terrible colour.'

'Thanks.'

'Does it hurt to smile?' Ned was fascinated. Liam felt like an exhibit at a touring show.

'A wee bit.'

'You were *very* brave.'

Liam shook his head. 'Jonty O'Mahony's no great shakes.'

On the rough bench that was the driving seat Christine and Alex were laughing easily together. 'I love it,' Christine was saying, 'I really do. I didn't expect to, but it's absolutely super. Not stuffy or anything. I've got a really good friend called Agatha. Our housemistress said last term that we weren't so much friends as a conspiracy. We have some great times.'

Alex cast her an amused look, but Liam missed what he said. Ned, bouncing on the seat beside him, was still intent on making him a hero. 'But Jonty is older than you, isn't he?'

'A bit, I suppose.'

'*And* there were a lot of them.'

'Ned—'

The huge, flower-blue eyes were still fixed on his face. 'I think you were *great*,' Ned said.

'Well now, it's grand of you to say so, and thank you. But will you look out there,' Liam pointed out across the still waters of the bay, 'd'you see what that is?'

Ned turned. 'Where?'

Liam put his arm about Ned's shoulder and, bending his own head to the boy's soft fair one, pointed again, sighting along his finger. 'There. See it?'

'A seal! Christine, look! There's a seal!'

'And there's another.' Liam pointed.

Alex and Christine were laughing again.

'*Christine!*' The tone of Ned's voice was the equivalent of a stamped foot. 'Look at the seals!'

'I see them.' His sister glanced across the water, then turned back to Alex. 'So crotchety old Miss Myers was standing there saying—' she put on an exaggeratedly refined tone, '"Miss Charling tells me that a ball has been found in the quadrangle. Will the girl who has mislaid it please report to Miss Charling to collect it?" And someone put up her hand and said, "Please, Miss, what colour is it?" "Red, I believe," she said. So,' Christine grinned mischievously, 'so I put up my hand. "Yes, Christine?"' Again the slightly cruel mockery. '"Please, Miss," I said. "What shape is it?"'

Alex's grin matched her own. 'Idiot! What did she say?' Christine shrugged, airily. 'She gave me a hundred lines.' Her voice this time lifted to a ladylike drawl. '*I must not be facetious. I must not be facetious. I must not be facetious—*'

'And,' Alex grinned, 'have you stopped being facetious?'

She cast him a withering glance. 'Course I haven't!' She threw back her head and let out a shout of laughter.

Liam, obscurely and inexplicably put out, leaned back and contemplated the countryside.

It was worth contemplating; the rough road ran along the coast, with the sparkling water of the bay always on the left, the lift of craggy hillsides on the right. Tiny white-washed farmsteads dotted the hills, and sheep cropped the sparse turf. An ancient watchtower, ruined by time, looked sightlessly across the water. They plodded through the little village of Kilcrohane, with its picturesque bridge and square-built, rather dour church and then, the scenery becoming ever wilder and ever more mountainous, on towards the far point of the little peninsula. The rocky track began to climb, winding steeply up. The views were breathtaking.

At about midday they reached the point where it was necessary to get out and walk. They piled out of the cart. Alex unharnessed the pony and tethered her where she could graze. They were high on a clifftop; almost vertiginously high. Far beneath them was a tiny bay, a couple of primitive shepherds' cottages crouched into the cliffsides as if huddled against the elements. A buffeting wind gusted, and clouds had started to scud across the sky. The water, here where the bay met the vast reaches of the Atlantic Ocean, was choppy and fierce below them.

Alex hefted a haversack out of the cart. 'What say we have

something to eat now, then walk out to the lighthouse, then come back and finish the picnic before we go home? That way we won't have to carry a lot.'

'Good idea. I'm starving!' said Ned.

They perched on rocks and, staring seawards, munched sandwiches in a companionable silence. The wind was rising. 'Come on.' Christine, impatient as always, jumped to her feet. 'Let's get going. It looks as if the weather's changing.'

They walked, scrambled and sometimes half-climbed across the high, rocky terrain, skirting bogs – or sometimes, perforce, squelching through them – fording streams, pausing in delighted astonishment at the little tarn that glimmered, brown and still, high up on the plateau. A combination of exertion and the ever more wildly gusting wind made breathing difficult and speech all but impossible. Ned was hauled up rocks, handed across streams, helped up the steeper slopes. Within a few yards of starting out he had slipped his small, childishly pliable hand into Liam's, and from there on relinquished his grip only when it was absolutely impossible to retain it. It took them the best part of an hour to reach the far western point.

The cliffs were towering; the vastness of the ocean that confronted them was awe-inspiring. In the spray-hazed distance was nothing. Nothing, until America.

Ned's hand was cold in Liam's. Tired though he was, he jumped up and down and shouted against the wind. 'Can you see America? Can you?'

Liam grinned and shook his head.

Alex swung the small knapsack he carried from his shoulder and pulled out a very large bar of chocolate, brandishing it like a trophy. He pointed. Nearby a huge rock loomed against the increasingly cloudy sky, offering at least some shelter. In its lee the sudden quiet was astounding. Christine rubbed her ears ruefully. 'I wish I'd brought a hat.'

With a small, strong pocket knife Alex was breaking

up the chocolate, handing around big, irregular chunks. They chewed on it in silence for a moment, grinning with enjoyment when they caught each other's eyes.

'Ten minutes or so,' Alex said, eyeing the sky, 'and then I think we should be starting back.'

'Yes, Sir,' Christine said, saluting solemnly. She was sitting cross-legged, and had a smear of chocolate on her chin.

Alex opened his mouth, but before he could speak she put a laughingly placating hand on his arm. 'I'm sorry. Only joking. Someone's got to take charge of the ship, we all know that.' She raised a subversive eyebrow. 'Anyone here made of sugar?' There was a small silence. She patted Alex's arm comfortingly. 'Then none of us will melt if it rains, will we?'

Liam, leaning back comfortably on the rock, had reached into his pocket for his cigarette tin. Flipping it with his thumb he opened it.

Ned watched, fascinated. Christine's eyes were interested. Alex looked uncomfortable.

Liam, suddenly very still, ignored them all.

How could he have forgotten?

In the tin there were two whole cigarettes, a half-smoked one – and an almost-complete roll-up. The one he had found at the stone circle. He picked it out of the tin, carefully.

The wind buffeted about the rock, whistling through crack and crevice.

He sat for a moment, his face totally impassive, looking at the thing. Then, very slowly, one-handed, he broke it up and let the tobacco scatter into the wind.

Ned blinked. 'Why did you do that?'

Liam shrugged and said nothing.

'Liam? I said why—'

'Ned.' Christine's eyes were on Liam's face, and her voice was sharp. 'Mind your manners. What business is it of yours?'

'But—'

His sister quelled him with a glance, though her own expression was faintly puzzled as she looked at Liam.

Liam took the half-smoked cigarette from the tin and lit it. Then he stood up, leaning on his crossed arms on the rock, his back to the others, looking with narrowed, savage eyes out to sea. The wind nearly lifted the cap from his head.

There was a long and strangely awkward pause in the conversation. Then, 'It doesn't seem possible we've only a few days left before we go home,' he heard Christine say.

Alex replied, but the words were drowned by the sound of the wind.

Home?

Liam dropped the cigarette, ground it with his heel and turned. 'Best we get going, I think. Young Ned's getting cold.' Unsmiling, he bent to lift the child to his feet, before setting off, wordlessly, down the path.

'Liam – wait for me.' Ned's voice was plaintive.

The wind was behind them on the trek back, which made the going a little easier. Once back at the cart they were hungry again, but at Alex's suggestion decided to eat as they travelled.

'It's my turn to sit up the front,' Ned announced.

Christine shrugged. 'If you want. It's not very comfortable.' She clambered on to a wheel and swung her leg over the side of the cart, jumping down to sit beside the silent Liam, and then reaching for the knapsack that held the sandwiches and lemonade that Mary had packed for them. 'Here, everyone,' she handed round the sandwiches. 'There's cake for later.'

Alex had finished harnessing the pony and had swung up beside Ned. As the cart began to move, Christine took a swig from the lemonade bottle and grinned at Liam. 'Why do things always taste better outdoors?'

He shrugged. 'I suppose because you get hungrier outdoors.' He knew he was being brusque, but the dark mood that had come upon him so suddenly refused to lift. He did not want to make conversation.

Christine, to her credit, tried again. 'I reckon the others missed a smashing day. Don't you?'

Liam nodded, his eyes on a gull that swooped and battled with the wind above them, a faint scowl drawing his brows together.

'Emma and Lottie could have come, though Aunt Pamela said that since we already had Ned to look after, Tom would have been too much of a responsibility, and Josie wouldn't come without him, of course. Emma had her nose in a book, as usual, and Lottie—' She let the words trail off, then sat watching him for a moment, jolting with the movement of the cart. When he said nothing she leaned forward suddenly and passed her hand in front of his unsmiling face, in the manner of a hypnotist. 'Hello? Anyone there?'

He turned his head and attempted, not very successfully, the faintest of smiles, but still did not speak.

Christine shrugged her shoulders and turned to face the front, pulling away from him a little. 'Suit yourself,' she muttered under her breath, with more than a touch of her usual quick-tempered acerbity, and quite loudly enough for him to hear.

They travelled on in a silence broken only by the gusting wind and the cries of the sea birds, a silence that, in the way of such things, got more difficult the longer it lasted.

It was a considerable time later that Liam realised that the girl beside him was shivering. She had hunched her shoulders and shoved her hands up the sleeves of her jumper, and her face had whitened with cold under the pale gold of her tan.

Wordlessly he slipped out of his jacket and handed it to her.

She looked at him in surprise, her hands still tucked up her sleeves.

He jerked the jacket towards her. 'Take it.'

She studied his face for a moment. Shook her head. 'Why should you get cold just because I was daft enough not to bring a jacket?'

Liam nodded at the rucksack at his feet. 'I've a pullover in there. I'll not get cold.'

She pulled her hands from her sleeves and took the jacket. 'Thank you.'

'Here.' He leaned forward and held it for her as she struggled into it, then settled it on her shoulders and tucked it around her legs. The jacket, warm from Liam's body heat, completely swamped her. She snuggled down into it, closing her eyes for a moment as the blissful warmth enveloped her. 'Thank you,' she said again; and, lulled by the warmth and the movement of the cart, within five minutes was sound asleep.

She woke as Alex drew the pony to a stop outside the cottage on the shore. Liam vaulted over the side of the cart, reached in for the rucksack, lifted a quick hand in farewell and turned away.

It took a moment or two for her fully to wake, and then: 'Wait!' she called, starting to struggle out of the coat. 'Liam, wait! You've forgotten your jacket.'

He did not turn, but called over his shoulder as he went, his voice tossed by the wind, 'Keep it. You can give it me back tomorrow.' He swung on down the path that led to the cottage, pushed the door open, ducked his head and disappeared.

Christine, torn between relief at not being exposed to the elements for the last few minutes of the journey and irritation at what she saw as Liam's uncalled-for and ill-mannered brusqueness, watched him go with exasperated eyes. 'Honestly, that *boy*!' she exclaimed, furiously, and then subsided; lost, for once, for words – a very rare state of affairs, as she would have been the first to admit.

The next day, under Pamela's discreetly organising eye, they started to pack, in preparation for the return to London.

With both Christine and Emma away at school, the Clough household that autumn was as quiet and peaceful as it had ever been. Unlike the unpretentious Barker home situated a couple of streets away, the Clough house was very big, four storeys and an attic high, part of an imposing terrace built in the previous century in a quiet crescent in Holland Park. The ground floor was taken up by an impressive reception hall, an equally grand dining room, a breakfast room and a large, half-basement kitchen. On the first floor was a formal drawing room and a smaller, prettier sitting room that overlooked the large garden, and which Siobhan had taken as her own. George's masculine study, all leather and mahogany, was also on this floor, while the family bedrooms and the two smart new bathrooms were spread over the next two. The attics were a warren of rooms that were given over to the permanent staff, of which there were three – Mary McCarthy, Mrs Turner the cook and Peggy Spencer, the live-in maid. Maud, who helped Mrs Turner in the kitchen, lived out.

Liam, who had the smallest broom-cupboard of a room to himself, spent every spare minute he could manage crouched over the tiny gas fire studying; he was to sit the scholarship after Christmas and it was the most important thing in his young life that he should pass. The books Mr Fletcher had lent him were piled on the postage stamp of a floor, on the narrow windowsill and on the shelf he used as an improvised desk. Isolated above the activities of the household, he worked his way doggedly through the mock-examination papers Mr Fletcher had set him, getting up at five each morning in order to carry out the chores that were required of him, so that every moment of the evening and into the night could be devoted to his studies.

'You'll be straining your eyes if you don't look out,' Mary scolded him fondly, steering her way through the clutter and shifting a pile of papers in order to set a steaming cup of cocoa beside her son.

Liam, not taking the eyes in question from his book, shook his head and smiled. It was three weeks before Christmas, and from Siobhan's sitting room below came the sound of a piano, and Ned's pure and quite staggeringly beautiful voice rose as he practised a carol. Mary turned her head to listen. 'Sure, an' isn't that like the voice of a little angel?'

'It is.' Liam nodded a little wryly. 'The shame is that the little angel only seems to know one song. He's been singing "Once in Royal David's City" ever since I got in. 'Tis becoming just a little tedious. As a matter of fact, I'm thinking of wringing his little angel neck.' He lifted his head to look at his mother. 'I assume the master of the house isn't home?'

'You assume right,' Mary said, collectedly. 'Now – no midnight oil tonight, young man. Nine o'clock and it's into bed with you, you hear?'

Liam grinned. 'Yes, Ma.'

Just over a week before Christmas the girls came home, and the house became considerably more lively. The Barker children were in and out, parties were planned, secrets whispered, festive preparations made as the excitements of the season began to build. Liam, in his eyrie, saw little of any of them. With everyone, including his mother, preoccupied with the coming festival he ignored them all, kept his head down and went on working. All he asked, for now, was to be left alone.

It was not to be.

The storm broke totally unexpectedly, three days before Christmas. There was to be a dinner party that evening and – reluctantly – Liam had allowed himself to be co-opted into the kitchen by his mother to help Mrs Turner and Maud. He was at the sink peeling a huge pile of potatoes when an unusually subdued Christine slipped into the room and stood, hesitantly, by the door.

All eyes turned to her, surprised and questioning.

'Liam—' She cleared her throat. 'Liam – I'm sorry, I truly am. Papa wants to see you.'

Liam, frowning but as yet unworried, put down his knife and picked up a towel to wipe his hands. 'What for?'

'It's my fault. It's all my fault.' Suddenly and alarmingly he realised she was very close to tears.

'What is?' he asked, warily.

'I told him—' She stopped. 'I didn't mean to – Emma mentioned that we hadn't seen much of you since we came home. So I told her – about the scholarship and everything. Papa was there—' She bit her lip.

Liam stared at her, a sudden, unsettling chill in the pit of his stomach. He clenched his hands. 'So?'

'He – was furious. He sent me to get you. He wants to see you. Now. In his study.'

Silence fell. Maud, a scruffy, thin-faced girl, threw a scared glance at Liam. George Clough terrified her at the best of times.

Very slowly Liam put the towel down on the draining board and, face set, walked to the door.

Christine, after a swift and embarrassed glance at the other two, followed him up the stairs into the hall, where a tall, beautifully decorated Christmas tree stood, the fragile glass decorations glittering in the light. 'Liam – I am so sorry.'

He ignored her. He took the graceful sweep of staircase that led to the upper floor two at a time.

He entered the room without knocking to find George Clough, as he had expected, standing with his back to the fire, his hands clasped behind his back, his face like thunder. 'You wanted me?'

'Your manners, McCarthy, are those of a guttersnipe. Do you never knock before you enter a room?'

Liam said nothing. His instinct had already told him that whatever the man intended, there was little he was going to be able to do to deflect it.

'My daughter informs me,' George said, his voice very quiet, 'that you are using my home, my time and my resources to study for some sort of – scholarship?' The last word was spoken with distaste.

'Yes—'

George's head came up sharply, his eyes glinting perilously.

'Sir.' The word all but choked Liam.

'Why?'

Liam blinked. 'I'm sorry?'

'I said "why?" For what reason are you studying?' The man spoke slowly and insultingly patiently, as if speaking to a retarded child. 'What possible reason could there be for you to – study?' Again the heavy and exaggerated distaste.

'My teacher at school suggested it, Sir. He said—'

'I don't give a damn what some chalk-fingered do-gooder said. I asked "why?" You'll kindly answer the question.'

'So that I can stay on at school. I might even be able to go on to college—' Liam stopped. George Clough was shaking his head, very slowly and very deliberately.

'No.'

'What?'

'*No!*' It was a sudden roar.

Liam, despite himself, all but jumped from his skin. 'But why?'

Moving extremely fast for such a big man, George stepped forward and caught him by the front of his shirt, twisting his hand and yanking Liam close to him. 'Listen to me, boy. If you think that I'm going to subsidise a jumped-up Irish bastard with ideas above his station while he plays at being as good as his betters, you're wrong. You don't know how wrong you are! If I'd known what was going on I'd have stopped it sooner. How old are you, boy?'

'Fifteen.' Liam ground the word savagely, through clamped teeth.

George threw Liam from him, so violently that he had to grab the desk to prevent himself from falling. 'Then what the devil are you still doing at the Board School anyway? You should have left a year ago! Now you just listen to me, young man.' He shook a threatening finger in Liam's furious face. 'If you want charity you can look elsewhere

for it. In this house you pay your way, you hear me? Who
the hell do you think you are? Who the hell do you think
puts the food in your mouth, pays the bills that keep you
warm and dry? And you believe you can fart about playing
the young gentleman? I think not!'

'No! That isn't—'

'*Quiet!*' George was breathing heavily. He dropped his
voice a little. 'From now on you pay for your board. You
understand? Your mother earns her keep. Now you go
out and do the same. Or,' he added, sneering, 'were you
planning to live on her for the rest of your life? I wouldn't
put it past you, you snivelling little—'

He did not get the chance to finish. In a red rage Liam
had launched himself at George, taking him off guard. The
boy's broad, bony fist caught the bigger man square on
the nose. George reeled back, blood spurting. Liam, using
his shoulder, rammed hard into him, knocking him down.
George, roaring now, pulled himself up using the desk as
support. 'By Christ I'll have you in jail for this!'

Liam swung again, this time catching his already rocky
adversary on the side of the head. George went down
as if poleaxed. Liam did not wait to see if he was con-
scious or not; he turned tail and fled, slamming the door
behind him.

Already the house was in uproar. He flew up the stairs.
'Liam! What is it?' His mother came out on to the landing.
He ran past her and up to his room.

George was far from unconscious. The study door opened.
'You limb of Satan! I'll have the law on you, see if I don't!
Siobhan! Siobhan! Send for the police! Now! By God, I'll see
you whipped for this, boy!'

Liam was grabbing anything he could think of, or anything that readily presented itself, and stuffing it into a
battered bag.

'Liam!' Mary was at the door, her hand to her mouth.
'Liam – what have you done?'

'Something that should have been done long ago.' Liam

straightened, his face grim. 'Got to leave, Ma. He means it. He'll have me if I don't.'

'But, son – where will you go? What will you do?' Tears had begun to run down her face.

'Don't worry, Ma. I've somewhere to go.' He grabbed her hand and squeezed it, hastily kissing her wet cheek. 'Trust me. I'll be in touch somehow.' He brushed past her and scrambled down the steep attic stairs, raced across the landing below and down the next flight of stairs.

On the main landing George, his face a swollen and bloody mess, stepped forward to bar his way.

Liam was aware that Ned, eyes wide with astonishment and fright, was standing in the open door of Siobhan's sitting room. Liam did not hesitate; he simply charged like a maddened young bull straight at the man, shoving him as hard as he could. George, by no means steady on his feet to begin with, staggered backwards, arms thrown wide, and Liam was past him and down the stairs. At the bottom, hearing George start down after him, he grabbed at the Christmas tree and pulled with all his might. In a tinkle of smashing glass and falling needles the thing teetered, then crashed down across the bottom of the stairs.

In a moment Liam was out of the front door and running into the darkness as fast as his legs could carry him.

The last thing he heard over the sound of his own pounding feet on the pavement was Ned's young voice, high, clear and impassionedly desolate behind him.

'Liam! *Liam*, don't go! *Please* don't go!'

# *I*nterlude

## Ireland, 1932

The night was cold, starless and still. Dark waters lapped, soft and restive, against rock and sand. Liam McCarthy, the collar of his reefer jacket turned up about his ears, his hands jammed into his pockets, leaned in the deeper shadow of a massive boulder and waited, listening, his head turned towards the sea. A moment before he had fancied that he had heard something; he strained his ears, trying to distinguish between the gently rolling splash of the incoming tide and what might have been the quiet, regular sound of dipping oars. He narrowed his eyes; used to the darkness, he could just discern the glimmer of the breaking waves, the movement of the water. Then he heard it again; the faintest of creaks, the gentle splash of an oar. He did not, for the moment, move. He could now make out the dark shape of the little rowing boat that was inching inshore.

He picked up the small shuttered lantern that stood in the damp sand at his feet.

Click, click. Wait. Click, click.

Almost at once the signal flickered back, and was extinguished.

A figure jumped lightly into the shallow waters and waded ashore. The rowers did not wait. Oars flashed and glinted for a moment and the little boat slid back into darkness.

Liam stepped out from the shelter of the rock. 'It's dark tonight,' he said.

'But it will be bright in the morning.' The accent surprised him; cut-glass English public school, a quiet, well-modulated voice. He somehow had not expected that.

He turned. It was always dangerous to hang about at such moments. 'This way,' he said and, darkened lantern glinting, guided his charge towards the narrow path that led up the cliffs.

The German, equally versed in such things, followed him in silence.

'When, and where?' The speaker, a tall, thin man whose narrow face was shadowed by the peak of his cap, reached into his pocket for a packet of cigarettes.

The man Liam had collected from the beach smiled gently, and shook his head a little. He was a fair-haired, handsome man, sparely built and graceful in his movements. Even in waders and fisherman's jumper he exuded confidence and an air of command. 'There are things to be discussed first, I think?'

'We don't have time to bugger about!' Another of the group of men in the room slapped a sharp hand on the tabletop. 'The assignment's already late – we *need* the stuff! Now! I doubt we'll ever get another opportunity to hit this particular target again. You know better than most how important he is, and how well guarded – it's taken the best part of a year to infiltrate—' He stopped. Liam, standing forgotten by the door, had shifted from foot to foot. 'What's the kid still doing here?'

The tall man's eyes flickered to Liam. He jerked his capped head in a gesture of dismissal.

Liam left.

\*     \*     \*

It was a bright, clear day. In the village below the spot where Liam lay, flat on his belly and in the shelter of a stand of gorse, washing fluttered on the lines, dancing in the fresh breeze that brought the tang of peat smoke up the hillside. A group of women, shawled and aproned, gossiped by the pump. The sound of their laughter lifted clearly to the boy's ears. He shifted a little uneasily, glanced back at his charges: three powerful motorbikes, hidden in a gully and carefully camouflaged.

Below him a dog barked excitedly and was ordered to quiet. The women laughed. A child cried. It was a day like any other.

Liam stiffened. Far down the valley a black car had appeared, moving slowly on the rough track.

Liam closed his eyes. Despite the sun on his back there was no warmth in him; the sweat on his face was slick and cold. What was he doing here? How, in God's name, had he got involved with this? This wasn't running errands between nameless men, or cutting the odd telephone wire. The road beneath him, which wound up the picturesque hillside, was booby-trapped. The people in the black car that crawled so slowly and so unaware towards its nemesis would surely die. He began to tremble.

The babble of voices and laughter opened his eyes. A group of children had come from the tiny schoolhouse, a crocodile, hand in hand, with a young woman, obviously a teacher, bringing up the rear. They all carried bags or satchels. The young woman carried a basket. A scuffle broke out in the line. Good-temperedly the young teacher hauled the miscreants away from each other, repositioned them next to her. Then, in at least relative order, they moved off.

For a moment Liam did not realise the significance of what he was watching. His attention was still on the approaching car, on his own distressed misgivings. It was not until the little crocodile actually passed the last of the cottages and began to toil up the hillside road that the monstrous possibility of what might be going to happen hit him. Jesus, Mary and Joseph! The car had reached the village, was winding through the dusty street. The children—

He scrambled to his feet. His father was posted higher up, hidden behind rocks. He probably hadn't seen the children. He had probably already passed the message that the car was coming. Liam clawed his way up the hillside, making no attempt to hide. 'Pa!' He threw himself into his father's hiding place. 'Pa, there are kids down there!'

'*What in hell's name are you doing here?*' The handgun in Dermot McCarthy's hand dropped as he recognised his son. 'Get back to the bikes. Now.'

'*Pa!* There are children down there – you've got to stop them!'

'Too late.' The words were brusque. Liam had been wrong. Dermot had seen the children. He had still passed on the message about the car.

'*No!*' Liam turned, wildly. 'I'll go and tell them. They can't do it. They *can't!*' The first blow with the gun caught him square on the jaw, slamming him back against the rock. The next knocked him cold. He was opening his eyes groggily when the explosion came. He stared at the gun that was pointing unwaveringly at him. 'Jesus!' he said, his face crumpling to tears. 'Oh, Jesus!'

The blast hummed in the air, rock and stone clattered about them. There was an uncanny moment of silence. Then screams.

'Get back to the bikes,' his father said, coldly. 'Now. And quick about it, before the others get there. If O'Connor so much as suspects you of this, he'll cut you to small pieces and there'll be nothing I can do about it. *Go*, by damn, or I'll do it myself!'

Shaking and sobbing, the boy scrambled back down to the hidden motorcycles.

In the carnage of the road below a small child sat in the dirt beside his dead teacher and wept desolately for his mother.

# PART TWO

# Chapter Six

## London, 1936

'D' you think Joe's right when he says that Hitler's going to send help to Franco?' Emma Clough, standing on top of a small set of folding steps, ran a finger and an eye along a row of dusty books. 'I know I've seen the blasted thing somewhere,' she added, 'I could have sworn it was – ah,' she stretched up and took a battered volume from the shelf.

The young man she had spoken to, tall, thin and shabbily dressed, held out a hand to steady her as she scrambled off the steps, and took the book she offered, flicking through it quickly. 'That's the one. Thanks.' Then, shrugging, he added, 'Who knows? He might, I suppose. There's no knowing with that bloke. I wouldn't put it past him.'

'He's thinking of going, you know.' A faint, worried frown creased Emma's brow.

'Who, Hitler? Where?' The young man looked puzzled.

Despite herself, Emma laughed. 'No! Joe. To Spain.'

The young man shook his towhead gently. 'Don't worry, Em. We've all thought about it.' His grin was wry. 'And we're all still here.'

From the shop beyond the serried bookstacks where they stood came the warning jangle of a bell as someone opened the door. The sound of traffic rose, then died again as the door was closed.

'We aren't talking everybody else,' Emma said, a little gloomily. 'We're talking Joe.'

He laughed a little. 'That's true.' He held up the book. 'How much?'

She took it from him, flipped it open. 'One and six.' She hesitated, then threw him a quick grin. 'A shilling to you, Sir, seein' as 'ow I know you.'

His own smile widened. 'Joe's poor old dad isn't going to make his fortune with you working for him, is he?'

She laughed aloud, turned to walk out of the stack of shelves. 'Don't be daft. You know Mr Davies. He's worse than I am. He'd give the darned things away if he could. If he'd wanted to make a fortune I hardly think he'd have gone into the second-hand book trade, do you—' She stopped so suddenly that the young man almost cannoned into her.

The man who had come into the shop while they were talking stood a little awkwardly in the cluttered space between the shelves and the old desk that Emma used as a counter. He was tall, and broad-shouldered, his dark, curly hair neatly trimmed. He was dressed casually but with some style in flannels, an open-necked shirt and a sports jacket. Emma was staring at him in uncertain but growing delight.

'Liam?' she asked. Then, with a little shriek, 'It is, isn't it? *Liam!* What on earth are you doing here? It's been so long! How are you?'

His own smile was diffident. 'I'm grand. Grand. I'm living in rooms just around the corner from here. I've seen you a couple of times in the street, then realised you were working here. I just thought I'd pop in and pass the time of day – find out how you were—' He shrugged, spread his hands and left the sentence hanging. He was not himself exactly sure why he was here. Curiosity? Pride? A desire to show the Cloughs that he had survived – and more than survived – in a world harsher than any of them even knew existed?

For the first few years after he had left Holland Park his bitter hostility against George Clough had extended to all who were associated with him, unfair though Liam knew that to be. That his mother, in the first pain and shock of discovering that he had gone to his father, had obdurately cut herself off from him had made things worse. To the angry, embittered boy it had seemed that she had sided with the Cloughs against him; indeed, in his heart of hearts he still felt so. He had neither seen nor spoken to her for five years, and their last meeting had been a painful one. He was no green boy now, however; he was a man grown, both in years and in experience, who owed nothing to anyone and could very well take care of himself. Time had put the events of the past into perspective, and now, looking at the warmth in Emma's smiling brown eyes, he was suddenly glad he had yielded to the impulse that had brought him here.

The young man who was standing behind Emma cleared his throat. Emma laughed and stepped forward, drawing him with her. 'Charlie – this is a very old friend of mine, Liam McCarthy. We grew up together.' The words were open and unthinking, with not the slightest trace of irony. 'We haven't seen each other in – what is it?' She looked at Liam. 'Six years?'

'Something like that.' The two young men nodded acknowledgement of the introduction.

'Well, I'll take this and be off and leave you to it, then.' Charlie dug into his pocket and pulled out a handful of change, than handed Emma a shilling coin. 'Thanks, Em. Coming to the meeting tomorrow?'

'Probably. Papa's away, so it shouldn't be too difficult. Joe will certainly be there.'

He grinned, not unkindly. 'If he isn't in Spain.'

Emma's own smile was lopsided. 'If he isn't in Spain,' she

agreed. She watched him to the door before turning back to Liam. They stood for a mute moment looking at each other. 'First things first,' Emma said. 'Let's put the kettle on.'

Liam followed her into a chaotic storeroom. Books and papers were everywhere, stacked on rickety shelves and piled on the chocolate-brown, age-smoothed lino of the floor. A small, grimy window set beside an outside door let in no light at all. Emma clicked a switch on the wall as she passed. A bare bulb glared yellow above them. Expertly she negotiated the teetering piles of books to a grimy little sink and draining board in the far corner of the room. On the counter next to it stood a small gas ring. Liam propped himself on the edge of a table, leg swinging, as she filled a dented tin kettle at the tap, lit the ring and perched the kettle precariously on it. The warm, muggy smell of gas filled the air. She searched in a cupboard, produced two cups, a tiny teapot and a dirty tin. 'So,' Liam said, reaching into his pocket for his tobacco, 'how have you been?' The accent was still there, and still recognisable, but nowhere near as strong as she remembered it.

Emma straightened, a glowing smile lighting her face, and gestured to the cramped, grubby surroundings. 'Would you believe I'm as happy as a sandboy?' At eighteen she had not changed so very much from the child he remembered. She was of medium height, chunkily built, her natural expression sweet and solemn. Her dark eyes were large and soft and her short hair shone brown as new-peeled chestnuts.

He looked up from the cigarette he was rolling and regarded her with thoughtful eyes. 'Indeed I can believe it,' he said. 'But I find it hard to believe that your father allows it.'

The kettle was boiling busily. She turned from him, lifting it gingerly from the gas ring. 'He doesn't,' she said, unruffled. 'He doesn't know.' She threw a mischievous glance as she tipped a little water in to warm the teapot. 'It's—' she hesitated, 'a kind of conspiracy, I suppose you'd call it. He thinks I'm working in a posh antiquarian bookshop filling in time until I find a suitably rich middle-class husband.'

Liam pulled a questioning face and glanced about him.

'Quite.' With square, practical hands she made the tea, then she grinned. 'Not going to meet many of those here, am I?' She sounded not the least bit concerned about that. 'In fact,' she reached into the cupboard again and brought out a square tin, 'I suppose you could say it's all Aunt Pamela's fault, really. Good old Aunt Pamela. I always loved her to bits.'

He waited, the cigarette still unlit. She opened the tin, which was full of chocolate biscuits. She proffered it to him. He shook his head, smiling. She helped herself to two, thought about it and made it three. 'I know I shouldn't.' The words were cheerfully unapologetic. 'I just like them.'

'So,' he lit the cigarette, waved a hand to indicate their surroundings, 'how is this—' He hesitated. Her own informality had almost communicated itself to him. 'How is this Mrs Barker's doing?'

She shrugged, munching a biscuit as she poured black tea that looked strong enough to stand a spoon up in. 'Sorry, no milk, it's off. I forgot. Sugar's in that tin.' She handed him a cup. 'She convinced Mama that my interest in left-wing politics,' she emphasised the last three words heavily, rolling her eyes, 'wasn't a symptom of dementia or moral collapse.' She laughed a little. 'To be fair, I think that privately even she believes I'll grow out of it. I think she believes that in the end I'll come to my senses and settle into a nice, humdrum middle-class life with a nice, humdrum middle-class husband. Perhaps I will. But at least for now I'm here. And that's enough for me. To be honest, I don't think much about tomorrow.'

'But – your father?'

'I told you. He doesn't know. Christine works two or three days a week in a swish art gallery in Mayfair – she would, wouldn't she? – and we've managed to give him the impression that I'm doing much the same sort of thing. Except that, as you can see, I'm not.' Her tone expressed nothing so much as total and absolutely carefree satisfaction.

'We?'

'All of us, to a greater or lesser extent. Mama. Christine. Me. The Barkers. Everyone knows but Papa.' Her expression, which had been mischievous, suddenly sobered. She held his eyes with her own. 'He hasn't changed, Liam. Why would he? I don't think he's really interested in anything any of us does or thinks, as long as he believes that we're doing or thinking as we're told. Disobedience doesn't really occur to him. So he doesn't look for it. Which is all the better for me.' She smiled a small, subversive smile. 'We don't even have to lie, really. As long as we say, "Yes, Sir, no, Sir, three bags full, Sir," he doesn't challenge his own assumptions.' She shrugged. 'Not very brave, perhaps, but there you are – it works. Anyway, he's away a lot of the time on business, in America mostly. And he and Mama have bought a cottage in the country, down in Kent; Mama's nerves are not good, as you know. So it's all easy enough, really. In fact,' suddenly the laughter was back, 'I suppose that, to be honest, it's all part of the fun.'

He surveyed her with a growing and quizzical admiration. Of the two sisters Emma was the one who made the most unlikely rebel. Christine, with her fiery temper and challengingly outspoken ways, would seem to be the more obvious candidate for the role; yet here was little bookworm Emma openly flouting convention and her father, and obviously loving every moment of it. He shook his head a little in amused appreciation and took a sip of his tea.

Emma saw his expression. 'Sorry. I do make the most terrible tea. Always have.'

He ladled another two spoonfuls of sugar, then reached into his pocket. She grinned as she saw the flask. Wordlessly he offered it. Still smiling, she shook her head. He diluted his tea.

'So.' She eyed him over her cup. 'What about you? What

have you been doing to look so handsome and prosperous?'
There was not the faintest hint of flirtation in the words; her
guileless eyes were open and interested.

'Oh—' he hesitated, 'a bit of this, a bit of that, you know.
Did you say that Christine was working in an art gallery?'

She accepted the change of subject without question.
'Yes. Being terribly, terribly nice to the shit-rich clients.'
She laughed at his raised brows. 'I quote,' she said. 'And
that's the least offensive thing she says about them. Oh,
I think for her it's really just something to do to pass the
time. Something to relieve the boredom. Chris's problem
is that she doesn't know what she wants. She pops in here
sometimes – well, they all do, actually – but she's the one
who can cause the most havoc without even trying. She
doesn't change. Ned's still at school, of course.' Again for
a moment she sobered. She picked up her spoon and stirred
her tea, watching the black liquid as it swirled about the
cup. 'He's terribly unhappy. Hates it. Papa—' She took a
deep, controlling breath. 'Oh, never mind.' She lifted her
head to look at him. 'Ned was—' she paused, searching for
the word, all the light gone from her face, 'distraught about
what happened to you. We all were to a certain extent, but
Ned took it terribly badly. He was physically ill.'

'I'm sorry,' he said, automatically.

'Oh, don't be silly!' She was suddenly fierce. 'It was hardly
your fault!' Again she lifted her head. 'It was all so horrible.'
She hesitated. 'Where *did* you go?' she asked, softly.

Liam's face closed. 'To my father. Well – to an address my
father had given me. He came to join me when he heard I
was there. He had an – arrangement – with a lady.' His
smile was small and cynical.

'Your – father?' She could not hide her astonishment.

'My father,' he said, and then with caustic humour,
'Turned out I had one all along.' A memory stirred. *How
would you know?* 'You might tell your sister that next time
you see her.'

'No need.' The cool voice came from the doorway. Both

of them jumped. 'Honestly, Emma, anyone could clean this bloody shop out without your knowing it.' There was no way of telling from her tone how long Christine had been standing there or what she had heard.

'Don't be silly, there's nothing worth taking. Most of this stuff wouldn't sell at the nearest flea market.' Emma jumped cheerfully to her feet and went to Christine, kissing her cheek. 'Just look who's here.'

'I've looked. I've seen.' The words were light; amused and friendly. Christine sauntered into the room. She was still small. She was still fair. She had become vividly attractive. She held out a hand. 'Hello, Liam. How are you?'

Her hand was small and surprisingly firm in his, her blue eyes were wide and steady. 'Hello, Christine. I'm grand. Yourself?'

'I'm—' she hesitated, tilted her head a little, laughing at him. 'I'm grand too,' she said. 'Could I have my hand back, please?'

He dropped it like a hot brick.

This time they heard the shop bell tinkle. 'Shop?' a voice called.

'Coming!' Emma lowered her voice. 'That's the only problem with this place,' she observed happily, 'people have the cheek to think I'm here to serve them. Pour Chris a cup of tea, Liam, would you? I won't be long.' She disappeared into the shop.

'She doesn't mean that,' Christine said. 'About the customers, I mean, not about the tea.' She grinned. 'Mind you, knowing her tea—' She pulled a face, then nodded admiringly at the cup Liam still held. 'You're a brave man. Em's tea can ruin your tastebuds at a hundred paces.'

His grin matched hers. He slipped the flask from his pocket and held it up.

She looked at it reflectively for a moment. 'Ah,' she said, solemnly. 'Well – if you insist – maybe just half a cup: we can't go hurting her feelings, can we?'

He poured the tea, tipped a generous splash of whiskey

into it and handed it to her. 'Emma tells me you're working in an art gallery, in Mayfair, wasn't it?'

She nodded. 'For my sins.' She sipped the tea, pulled a face. 'You can hardly call it work, really. But it keeps me off the streets. Most of the time, anyway.' Her gaze was peaceful and apparently artless as she watched him over the rim of her cup, though there was a slight, flippantly challenging edge to the words.

'I assume you don't have to do it if you don't want to?'

She shrugged, lightly. 'What's the alternative? Real work?' She pulled a caustic, self-deprecating face. 'I ask you! Can you see it? Or of course I could always stay at home with Mama and stick to my embroidery and trips to the country. God, the very thought makes me feel quite queasy! No – I do well enough, I suppose. I meet a lot of people, and some of them aren't too bad. Though most of them are—' She pulled herself up.

'Shits,' Liam supplied for her, conversationally. 'Rich shits. Yes. Emma told me.'

This time, truly amused, she threw back her head and laughed. 'Papa thinks I'm going to marry one.'

'A rich shit?'

'Yes.'

'And are you?'

Suddenly the laughter was gone. Her face closed like a shutter. 'No. Not for a very long time at any rate, whatever Papa might think.' She wandered about the room for a moment, fidgeting, picking up books, flipping unseeingly through them, putting them down again. Then, aware of his eyes upon her, she turned. 'I had what Mama euphemistically describes as a Bad Experience. I made the mistake, a couple of years ago, of taking a bit of a shine to someone. A handsome someone with golden curls and a title. The world approved. The world positively slavered. With the world's gracious blessing we got engaged.' She fell silent.

'What happened?'

She lifted her head to look at him. 'What do you think? He

turned out to be as much of a shit as the rest.' Her voice was
completely unemotional. 'And not even a particularly rich
one at that. If he had been, perhaps I could have handed him
over to Lottie. She'd have shown him. She'd have chewed
him up and not even bothered to spit out the bones.' She
stood fiddling with her cup for a moment. 'Papa was keen,
of course – well, for one thing he'd be getting rid of a
none-too-docile daughter and for another he'd be buying
lords and ladies for in-laws. He liked that. He liked that
a lot. It took some doing to make him understand that I
wasn't actually for sale. I was rather surprised that no-one
seemed to have realised that before.' Her voice was light
and had the cutting edge of a fresh-honed blade. 'He still
reproaches me for it, on occasions. He's wildly disappointed
that he doesn't have an invitation to the party of the year.'
Liam looked puzzled. Christine laughed. 'The Coronation,'
she said. 'Lord, Liam, where have you been living? On the
moon?'

He shook his head.

She took a sip of tea, set the cup down on the table. 'God,
that is *terrible!*' She eyed him reflectively for a moment,
taking in the cut of his clothes, the shine on his expensive-
looking black leather shoes. 'So – where *have* you been?' she
repeated, quietly. Suddenly the cloud had lifted and she was
smiling again. 'Perfectly obviously you aren't working in
the docks or clocking on to a factory floor?'

There was a small silence as both remembered where she
had heard him speak of that. The shop door opened and
closed again, the sound of the traffic penetrated even to
them. The window was so grimy that it might as well have
been papered over. Ireland and the sea, the wild weather
and the mountains, seemed so far away as to be a part of
another, entirely different, world.

'No, I'm not,' he said, softly, reaching into his pocket for
his flask again. He offered it. The polished silver reflected
back the light from the bare bulb. She hesitated, then held
out her small hand.

'So – what are you doing?' There was real curiosity in her eyes. She took a sip from the flask, eyed it for a moment, and handed it back.

He hefted it in his hand for a second before taking a mouthful and slipping it back into his pocket. He had treated himself to that flask with his first really big win. Handling it never ceased to give him pleasure.

'Good Lord, you two – boozing at tea time? What is the world coming to?' Emma came cheerfully in from the shop, a pile of books in her arms, which she dumped on the table.

'Emma!' Christine's cross tone was only half-affected. 'I was just about to hear Liam's life story.'

Emma grinned with no contrition. 'No, you weren't. He doesn't want to tell us. Not yet.' She smiled her warm, friendly smile, her eyes on Liam. 'Do you?'

'Not a lot to tell,' he said, easily. 'Like I said before – a bit of this, a bit of that. I make out.' He turned to Christine. 'You mentioned Lottie. How is she? How are they all?'

At the mention of Lottie both sisters glanced at each other, their expressions a mirror image. 'After you,' Christine said, drily.

Emma shrugged. 'She's working as a secretary. She absolutely *hates* it—'

'So she makes up for it by behaving as badly as she possibly can and getting away with it,' Christine put in, crisply. 'That's about it, really.'

'She *wants* to go on the stage—'

'Or be a mannequin.'

'She has so many boyfriends—'

'—that she can't tell one from the other.'

'*Christine!* There's no need to be unkind!'

Christine laughed. 'Lottie wouldn't recognise unkindness if it came up and bit her.' There was no trace of malice in the words.

'Sure, that sounds like the Lottie I knew.' Liam, mischievously, ignored Christine's sharp look and the sudden climbing of her brows. 'And Alex?'

'Alex has taken articles with his father. He'll join the firm once he's qualified. He always was a bit dull, you have to admit.'

'Christine! There you go again. That isn't fair!'

Her sister lifted a shoulder. 'So the truth isn't always fair.' She was still watching Liam, a speculative look in her eyes.

Emma was at the sink slopping water carelessly into the cups and rubbing ineffectually at the brown tea stains with her fingers. Liam straightened, stubbing out his cigarette. 'Well—'

Before he could finish, the door leading to the yard outside was flung open and a young man came in, calling breezily, 'Emma? Emma – are you—? Oh.' He stopped, grinning, looking from face to face. 'I'm sorry. I didn't realise you were holding a conference. Can anyone come?'

Emma's face had flushed rosily. 'Don't be silly, Joe. This is an old friend of ours. We haven't seen him for years. Liam, this is Joe Davies – Joe, Liam McCarthy.'

Joe stepped forward, hand outstretched. He was a pleasant-faced and friendly-looking young man, slightly built and with an untidy shock of straight, fair hair. His smile was warm.

Christine's eyes flicked slyly to her sister. 'We were actually just leaving,' she said, 'weren't we, Liam?' As Liam glanced at her, Christine's eyebrows lifted and she gave a tiny but significant nod towards the other two.

Emma's eyes were on the newcomer; and her heart was in them.

Taking the hint, Liam nodded. 'We were indeed.'

'Oh, please—' Joe shook his head and held up a genuinely protesting hand. 'Don't let me break up the reunion.'

'No. Truly. We were going.' Christine planted a quick kiss on Emma's warm cheek. 'See you later, sweetie. Cheerio, Joe. Coming, Liam?'

Liam said his goodbyes, promised on Emma's insistence to drop in again and followed Christine from the shop.

Outside she turned to him. 'I'm sorry about that. It's

just that poor old Em doesn't get much chance to have Joe to herself. There's a bunch of them go around together – they're forever at deep and deedy meetings or rabbiting on about how to put the world to rights.'

'Do I gather that Em and Joe are—?' Liam let the question hang tactfully in the air.

Christine pulled a small, sympathetic face. 'I don't think they are, to be truthful, though not from want of trying on Em's part. I'm not sure Joe even knows how she feels about him. She's got a real crush, I'm afraid.' She laughed up at him as they turned to stroll down the busy street. 'The first is always the worst, isn't it?'

'If you say so.'

She smiled.

They strolled in silence for a moment. 'Emma said young Ned was unhappy at school?' Liam said.

Glancing up at him, she pulled an expressive face. 'Unhappy? The poor kid's nearly suicidal! He *detests* it.'

'Can't he leave? He must be – what? coming up sixteen, isn't he?'

'Leave? You're joking! Papa would have a fit! No, I'm afraid the poor little blighter's just going to have to stick it out.' She tucked her hands into the pockets of her jacket, hunching her shoulders a little, her face shadowed. 'He ran away. Twice. In the first year.'

'What happened?'

She grimaced. 'What do you think? Papa thrashed him and sent him back. And the second time he forbade Mama to visit Ned for the rest of the term. He didn't do it again.' There was a moment's silence before she cocked her head to look at him and asked, 'Are you really living with your father?'

He shook his head, amused by her shamelessly open curiosity. 'Not now. I've a place of my own. But at first, yes I did.'

'How did you find him? I always understood—' She stopped, and had the grace to blush a little.

'Remember the stranger in Ahakista?'

She blinked in astonishment. *'That* was your *father?'*

'Yes.'

'But – why didn't you tell us?'

He shrugged.

She grinned. 'Are you inferring that it was none of our business?' she asked in mock-indignation.

His long mouth twitched. They had come to a corner, and had stopped walking. 'I go this way.' Liam nodded his head towards the side road.

She tilted her head to look at him, her flower-blue eyes very bright and clear. 'Ned will be so pleased to hear we've found you again. We have, haven't we? You won't run away again? We all tend to drop in at the bookshop when we've time to spare. Mr Davies is a darling – he doesn't mind a bit. You will drop by again, won't you?'

He hesitated only for a moment. 'Sure,' he said.

'May I tell your mother that I've seen you?'

He shrugged. 'Of course.'

'She cried and cried when you left,' she said softly.

'So did I.' The words were almost expressionless. Almost, but not quite.

Christine put a quick hand on his arm. 'It's all past,' she said.

'I doubt your pa would think so.' His voice held a grim edge.

'What Papa doesn't know can't bother him,' she said, composedly. 'I'm not exactly suggesting you come calling at the house. Now – you promise? You will keep in touch?'

'Yes.'

There was a moment of silence and, as they stood looking at each other, for the briefest of instants neither made the least attempt to disguise an open, appreciative and speculative interest. Then, with a swift smile and no further farewell, Christine turned and walked away from him, her heels clicking briskly on the pavement. Liam watched the small, erect figure disappear into the crowds. She did not look back.

Eyes thoughtful, he reached for his tobacco tin.

# Chapter Seven

'Now *that*,' Lottie Barker said with wistful and undisguised envy, 'is what I'd *call* a holiday. Forget Mr Butlin and his plebeian holiday camps! First class to New York on the *Queen Mary* with the nobs – boy, I'd give my eye teeth to travel in such style!' She was sitting curled up in an armchair by the fire, her long, slim legs folded under her, flicking through a magazine. 'Just take a look at this, you two.' She held up the magazine, spread open to show several pictures of the opulent interior of the great liner. 'How the other half lives, eh?'

Emma glanced up from the hand of cards she was playing and smiled, non-committally. Rain drove in solid gusts against the window.

Alex was not to be distracted. 'I still say,' he said, surveying his own hand with mild exasperation, 'that if there were anything the government could actually do about unemployment, they'd do it. Damn it, Em, you've dealt me a hand like a foot here.'

Emma's grin this time was more substantial. Shaking her head, she tossed a couple of cards face down on the table. 'You're wrong, Alex. It's government policy that's caused the problem. It's not an accident, it's a design. A deliberate ploy to keep the workers down.'

The two had been wrangling amiably for the past ten minutes. Lottie heaved an ostentatiously noisy sigh and went back to her magazine.

Alex picked out two cards, hesitated, then shrugged and tossed them on top of Emma's. 'Your box. Me to do.'

They played to the end of the hand, then Alex spread his cards in front of him. 'OK, clever clogs. I can't make it and you don't even need your box.' He leaned to move Emma's peg to the winning hole on the board and sat back, stretching a little.

'That's sixpence you owe me,' Emma said, smartly.

He felt in his pocket and, laughing, tossed the small silver coin to her. She caught it deftly, then leaned her chin on her fist, watching him. 'Seriously, Alex, if something isn't done about it soon there'll be real trouble, I'm sure of it. Eighty per cent of the working people on Tyneside are unemployed. Eighty per cent! And there's so little help for them – some of them are literally starving!'

Alex picked up the cards and shuffled them, slowly and thoughtfully. 'According to the *Daily Telegraph*—' he began.

Emma shook her head, fiercely and impatiently. '*That* Tory rag! You can't believe *them*. I'll tell you what,' there was a sudden challenging enthusiasm in her voice, 'why not come and see for yourself? Actually *talk* to people who know what they're talking about – the marchers themselves. They're due to reach London on the thirty-first. There's to be a demonstration in Hyde Park. We're setting up a free bread and soup stall for them. Come and help: we are a pair of hands short—' She stopped abruptly, nibbling her lip.

Alex eyed her, sympathetically. 'Your young man?' he asked, gently.

'I keep telling you. He isn't my young man. But yes, it was Joe who thought of the idea. He would have been there if—' She did not finish.

'Any word?'

She shook her head. 'No. Not yet.'

'You saw the news in the papers this morning?'

'About the Germans? Yes. Joe always said Hitler would send bombers.'

'They won't bomb civilians, surely?'

'Don't bank on it – Mussolini did in Africa.'

'Oh, for goodness' sake, you two, *must* you? The weather's miserable enough without all this doom and gloom.' Lottie jumped to her feet, tossing the magazine to the floor, reached to take the cards from her brother's hand. 'Let's play pontoon. I'll beat the pants off both of you.' She pulled a chair up to the table and eyed Emma with a gleam of interest in her eyes as she expertly shuffled the cards. 'Talking of young men,' she said, 'have you seen Liam McCarthy again?'

Emma nodded. 'He dropped in to the shop again the other day.'

'Did you find out any more about him?'

Emma shook her head. 'I didn't try. I daresay he'll tell us if he wants to.'

Lottie raised her wide, pale eyes to the ceiling in exasperation. 'Emma Clough, I do sometimes despair of you! You've got about as much natural curiosity as – as this table!' She rapped the wood with her knuckles.

'She was probably standing behind you in the queue,' Alex said, grinning. 'You got so much of it there was none left for Em.'

Lottie stuck her tongue out at him.

'If you're that interested,' Emma said, peaceably, 'then why not ask him yourself? He's ordered a book. Said he'd pop in on Saturday morning for it. Why not come and see him?'

Lottie tossed an offended red head. 'I'm not *that* interested, thank you very much!' And then she laughed, an infectious and self-mocking sound that gave the lie to her words.

'I got a letter from Ned yesterday.' Emma slipped the book

she was holding into a brown paper bag and folded it neatly. 'He was really excited that we'd found you again. He spoke about you so often – was always speculating about where you were, what had happened to you. He's dying to see you again.' She handed the package to Liam with a smile. 'Perhaps when he can manage to come home for a couple of days we could arrange for you to get together? Would you mind?'

'Of course not.' Liam paid for the book, watched as Emma rattled a practical, square finger around the partitioned wooden drawer of the battered desk, sorting out the change. 'Does he get to come home often?'

Emma straightened, and the slightest of shadows fell across her usually bright and open face. 'No. No, he doesn't. Belfairs is—' she hesitated, 'well, a little strict about that kind of thing. In term time you have to have a specific request from a parent. And Papa—' She pulled a small, rueful face. 'Well, you know Papa.' She flushed suddenly as she realised what she had said, 'I'm sorry – I didn't mean—'

'Don't be silly. To be sure I know your father. As well as I want to, anyway.' A grin lit his eyes, easing the sting in the words.

'Papa will only allow strictly unavoidable breaks during term time – Ned has his heart check-up at the end of November, for instance; he'll have to come home for a couple of days then. I doubt he'll get a break before that. Mama visits, of course.' Emma's own eyes dropped and, again, her mouth quirked a little, wryly. 'And when she comes home she is immediately stricken with a migraine that fells her for days.' She lifted quick, placatory hands and her smile was apologetic. 'I'm sorry. I didn't really mean that. Mama's right. We all know it, apart from Papa – and it's more than likely that he knows it too, but simply doesn't care – or, worse, thinks it doesn't matter.' The straightforward honesty was typical of her. 'Ned is wretchedly miserable at Belfairs. I truly don't think he

should be there.' She shrugged. 'Poor Ned. It's his burden
that he was born the boy of the family. The son and heir.
Christine and I get away with far more than he will ever
manage.' Her grin was quick, and engagingly subversive.
'Not from indulgence, you understand, but from sheer lack
of interest. We both exploit that, in our own ways. Ned has
no such way out. He's under the spotlight, all the time. Papa
demands so much of him.'

'Does he still sing?'

'Yes. Beautifully.' Her soft brown eyes met his, rueful and
expressive. 'When Papa isn't about,' she added.

He lightened the moment. 'I can never hear "Once in Royal
David's City" without thinking of Ned. I truly thought I'd
wring his neck if I heard a note of it again.'

'I'll drink to that,' Lottie said. She was sitting on the desk,
legs neatly crossed at the ankles and very slightly swinging,
her eyes thoughtfully focused upon Liam's face.

Liam slid a bright look at her, and then, more soberly,
glanced back at Emma. 'Any news of Joe?' he asked, quietly.

Emma shook her head.

Liam watched her for a moment, his eyes unreadable.
'Don't worry. He'll be all right.'

The girl smiled, brightly. 'Yes. Of course he will. We all
know that. We all know Joe.'

Lottie, with a swift, attention-snagging movement, jumped
to the floor and smoothed her skirt with her hand. 'There's
a Lyons Corner House just up the road,' she said, her eyes
on Liam, her smile winning. 'You can buy me a cup of tea
and a bun if you want.'

'You have got a sauce, Lottie! You can just as easily have
a cup of tea here,' Emma pointed out, mildly.

Lottie strolled to her, pecked a kiss at her cheek. 'Darling,
I love you to bits, you know I do – but your tea?' She shook
her head, turned back to Liam. 'Well?'

Amused by her impudence and by no means immune to
her beguiling good looks, he laughed. 'Why not?'

'Your enthusiasm,' she said, undisturbed, slipping her

arm through his, 'is only exceeded by your good looks. 'Bye, Em. See you later. Oh—' Turning to leave, she stopped. 'I forgot to tell you. I told him he was mad, but Alex says he will come and help on the thirty-first. He says he'll pop in during the week to make arrangements. Lord knows what the snooty girlfriend will think of it, but – there you are. No skin off my nose.'

'Alex has a snooty girlfriend?' Liam asked as they left the shop and strolled up the street.

Lottie pursed bright-painted lips. 'He surely has. Her name is Beatrice and she's a receptionist at some swank practice in Harley Street. God, she's a pain. Toffee-nosed isn't in it.' She laughed a little. 'I'll bet Alex doesn't tell *her* that Emma's dragged him into doling out bread and soup to the Jarrow marchers.'

The tea room was busy with Saturday-morning shoppers. Settled at the table with the tea and toasted teacakes ordered, Lottie rested her chin on her hand and regarded him with an expectant, limpid gaze. 'Right—' she said.

He raised his brows in innocent question. 'Right? Right what?'

She spread the pointed fingers of a delicate hand. 'We have six years to catch up on. Who goes first?'

There was a moment's silence. Liam's eyes were amused. 'You do,' he said, gently.

She shrugged her slim shoulders. 'OK.' She was brisk, and not the least abashed. 'Let's see. I scraped through school doing as little as possible, just about managed my School Cert., went to secretarial college because, frankly, I couldn't think of anything else to do, got a job in a solicitor's office because the chief partner is a friend of Father's. I'm looking for someone rich and handsome to marry, but I'm really in love with the Prince of Wales – sorry, I suppose I should call him King Edward now. Anyway, since unfortunately he seems otherwise occupied, I'm doing my best to hide my broken heart by going to dances, parties and the pictures as often as possible.' She stopped, posing her head and sucking a carefully manicured thumbnail in a parody of thoughtfulness. 'That's about it, I think. Your turn.' Her smile was swift and mischievous.

Liam laughed aloud, shook his head. A waitress dressed in the black and white 'Nippy' uniform set the tea and a plate of toasted tea cakes before them. Lottie reached for the pot. 'You aren't to try to wriggle out of it, now,' she said. 'That wouldn't be at all fair.' Again she dimpled, mischievously. 'I showed you mine, now you've to show me yours. It's only fair,' she asserted again, virtuously, and poured the tea.

This time the silence was longer and more thoughtful. Lottie did not break it but sipped her tea, her eyes steady on his face.

'Sure – there's not a lot to tell.'

'Try me.' She was pleasantly remorseless.

He shrugged. 'Pa had given me an address, not far from White City. I had no money. Nowhere else to go. Pa came and took me back to Ireland for a bit, but there was a touch of trouble so we came back again.'

'What sort of trouble?'

He was stirring his tea, studying it as if it were the most absorbing thing in the world. 'Just – trouble,' he said, and flicked a brilliant, narrowed glance at her. 'Nothing like the Irish to make trouble where there should be none,' he observed, lightly.

'When did you come back?'

'Two or three years ago.'

'And?'

He had to smile at her persistence. 'And I drifted around for a while, did a bit of this, a bit of that. Then I met a pal of Pa's, a bookmaker, who took me on, first as a runner, then as his clerk.'

Lottie's eyes had widened. 'A bookmaker?' she asked, 'You mean – an *illegal* sort of bookmaker? The kind you read about in the papers?'

'That's the kind, all right.' He was amused.

She was intrigued. 'Did you make a lot of money at it?'

He laughed aloud at that. 'God, no! But I did find I had some kind of talent for picking a winner or two. So after a couple of lucky breaks I decided to become a punter myself.'

'A punter?' She was mystified.

'A gambler.' He set his elbows on the table, laced his hands together and surveyed her over them, finally giving up any attempt at prevarication. 'That's how I earn my living, Lottie. I gamble. I also own a couple of good dogs and one leg of a halfway decent racehorse. Now, is there anything else you'd care to know? Be sure to tell me if there is.' The sarcasm was gentle.

'Women,' she said.

'I beg your pardon?'

'Women,' she repeated composedly. 'You haven't mentioned women.'

This time he all but exploded into laughter. Nearby, an elderly lady with a repressive expression and feathers in her hat turned her head, tutting. 'Now there I do draw the line. Yes, there have been women. Unlike you, I'm not in love with your handsome new king and neither do I dance. So I have to do something to entertain meself.'

She laughed with him; leaned forward on her folded arms. 'Are you rich?' she asked, interestedly.

He grinned. 'Not rich enough for you, I'm afraid.'

'Oh. That's a pity. Ah, well, never mind. Let me know if you make it, won't you?'

'Indeed I will,' he agreed with a tranquil smile.

She reached to pour more tea. 'What happened to your father?'

'I don't know.' The laughter was gone; his face was suddenly expressionless. 'I haven't seen him for – oh, three or four years. I doubt I will again.'

'Oh?'

'We had – a falling out.'

'That seems a shame.'

'Doesn't it just?' His voice held a grim edge.

She opened her mouth. He held up a protesting hand, eyes glinting. 'To be sure, Miss Barker, do you not think you've wormed quite enough out of me for one day?'

She leaned back in her chair, eyeing him speculatively. Then, 'I don't suppose,' she said, with a sudden and quite dazzling smile, 'that you'd consider taking a girl to the pictures?'

Liam pointed a long finger at her plate. 'Will you eat your tea cake, woman, before it gets cold?' He watched her, smiling appreciatively, as she picked it up and bit into it. 'Well, now, you're the smart one,' he said after a moment. 'Would you be knowin' what's on?' He had strengthened his brogue, and his grin had widened. 'I have to admit I'm halfway partial to a decent Western meself.'

By the middle of the week, as the month of October drew to a close and winter approached, the bad weather that had plagued the hunger marchers as they toiled down from the north had closed in on London too. Alex, his collar turned up against the wind and rain, pushed open the bookshop door. Wind gusted in behind him. Bell jangling, he slammed the door against it, took off his hat, beating it against his leg to shake the rain off.

The shop was very quiet and apparently empty. Emma's desk was the usual untidy jumble of books and papers. 'Em?' he called, and then again, more loudly, 'Emma?'

'I'm here.' Emma's soft voice was hoarse. She stepped out of the shadow of the bookstacks. Her hair was tousled, her face red and swollen from weeping. She stood like a miserable and woebegone child, a crumpled handkerchief clutched in her hand. 'Hello, Alex.'

'Em! What's the matter? What's happened?'

She struggled for a moment, twisting the handkerchief around her fingers. 'Joe,' she said, simply, and her face crumpled to tears again.

The lash of rain against the shop window was loud in the quiet.

'Wounded?' Alex asked at last, carefully.

'No. He's dead.' The words were a flat whisper. Tears slicked her cheeks. 'Dead,' she repeated. 'Mr Davies telephoned this morning. He's in an awful state. Oh, Alex—' Suddenly she moved, running to him, burying her face in his shoulder, sobs racking her body.

He held her to him, rocking her gently, saying nothing for a long time. Gradually she quietened. At last she lifted her head, scrubbing at her eyes with her handkerchief. 'I'm sorry. I'm so sorry.'

'Don't be silly.' He put an arm about her shoulder and drew her towards the small storeroom. 'Come on. I'll make you a cup of tea. Wait—' He turned back to the door, shot the bolt across and turned the sign that hung in the window to 'Closed'.

Emma did not protest. Her breath still catching in her throat, she preceded him into the storeroom and dropped awkwardly into a chair, her elbows on the table, her head in her hands.

Alex filled the kettle. The rush of the water, the clank of the makeshift plumbing, was noisy and somehow desperately inappropriate. 'What happened? Do you know?'

She shrugged. 'They were fighting – in Toledo, Mr Davies said. Joe was killed trying to take a machine-gun post. He'd only been in action for a week. Oh, for God's sake! What did *Joe* have to do with *machine-gun* posts?' She covered her face with her hands, her shoulders shaking again.

Alex lit the gas ring, set the kettle upon it. The shop door rattled. Neither of them took any notice. 'There isn't any chance – I mean – there couldn't be any – any mistake?' Alex asked gently.

She shook her head. 'No. It's definite. He's dead. Poor Joe.' She tilted her head back and closed her swollen eyes tiredly. 'Poor Joe,' she repeated. 'He was such a dear. He was so – convinced. So full of life. He *cared* so much.'

Alex warmed the pot and spooned in the tea.

'I knew it could happen. Of course I did.' Emma was talking almost to herself. 'People who go to war get killed. Doesn't take much of a brain to understand that. For heaven's sake – if what people are saying is true, it could happen to any of us if things carry on as they are. But – I simply can't believe it. Not Joe. Not *Joe!*' She sniffed. There was a moment's silence. Then, 'I wrote to him yesterday,' she said. 'Just an ordinary letter. It's out there, on the desk. I was going to post it on the way home last night, but I forgot to take it. Funny, that, isn't it?' The words were too calm, and then, suddenly, she was struggling with tears again. 'I never did tell him—' She stopped, shaking her head miserably.

'Here. Drink your tea.' Alex put a cup in front of her. They drank in silence, Emma's eyes staring miserably into space, Alex's sympathetic but helpless upon her. At last he said quietly, 'I called in to make arrangements about Saturday, but I guess things have changed now?'

'Oh no! Of course not!' Emma's head came up sharply. 'That's the last thing Joe would have wanted. It was his idea. We must do it. For Joe's sake, we must do it. Of course we must!'

Alex held up a hand. 'Fine. I just thought—' Again the shop door rattled, impatiently. Emma sighed and pushed back her chair. 'I suppose I'd better—'

'No. You stay there. I'll go.' Happy to do something positive, Alex jumped to his feet and left the room.

Emma crossed her arms on the table, resting her forehead on them, huddled quite still, trying to find a defence against the onslaught of awful and unexpected death. The room was very quiet. After a moment she stood and walked to the sink, splashed water on her face. When Alex returned she turned to him, her voice calmer and more firm. 'I'm sorry. I really am. It was just such an awful shock.'

'Don't be silly.' Alex's own voice was warm, affectionate and altogether too understanding. She bit against the tears

she thought she had defeated. 'It's perfectly natural for you
to be upset. Now – is there anything I can do to help?'

Emma shook her head with sudden resolution. 'No, I
don't think there is. I promised Joe's father I'd ring the
others. I'll do that now. I can get hold of most of them
by phone.' She stood up.

'You're sure you wouldn't rather I did it?'

'No.' Her smile was watery, but firm. 'Thank you, but
no. I'll do it. And I'll see you on Saturday.' She stood on
tiptoe to kiss his cheek. 'Thank you.'

Alex squeezed her hand and picked up his hat from the
table. She followed him out into the shop. At the door he
turned. 'If you need anything—'

She nodded. 'I'll call.'

'Till Saturday, then.'

'Yes.'

He hesitated for a moment, then lifted a hand and was
gone.

Emma stood quite still for a long moment, looking after
him. Then she took a deep breath and reached for the
telephone.

'So – how did the snooty Lady Beatrice take to your paddling off in the pouring rain to feed the Five Thousand?'
Lottie extended her leg and surveyed her slender foot, the
toenails of which were freshly painted a startling scarlet.
'D'you reckon that's a bit bright?'

Her brother sighed. 'Yes, I do; though I don't for a
moment expect you to take it all off just because I said
so. It's taken you twenty minutes to put it on,' he added,
looking pointedly at his watch. The two were in his bedroom. Lottie was perched on the edge of his bed, the nail
polish balanced precariously beside her; he was sitting at a
table strewn with books and papers, before him the sheet
of untidily scrawled notes he had been writing when she
came in.

'Oh, don't be such an old fogey.' She picked up the polish

again, and its odd, almondy scent filled the room. 'Just one more coat, I think. Well?'

'Well what?'

'What did Her Ladyship make of your good works on Saturday?'

He gave in, pushing the notes away from him, leaning back in his chair and stretching. 'I can't truthfully say it went down very well, let's put it that way.'

'Can't say I blame her.' Lottie leaned forward intently, concentrating on the delicate task in hand. 'For once I'm on her side. I hope you took her somewhere nice in the evening?'

There was a small silence. Lottie glanced up. 'You did tell me, as I remember, that you were seeing her in the evening?'

'That's what didn't go down very well.' Alex was rueful. 'I didn't make it. There was so much to do – a gang of us went back to the shop, and then someone suggested fish and chips, and someone else went to the Off Licence for beer.' He shrugged, more than a little embarrassed.

Lottie's movements had stilled and she had lifted her head to stare at him, exaggeratedly open-mouthed. 'Oh, my Lord!' The words were spoken in a mixture of amused disbelief and admiration. 'You silly blighter! She must have been fit to be tied!'

'She was.'

Lottie leaned her elbow on her bent knee. Her face was bright with amusement. 'Well, be fair! You can hardly blame her. What happened?'

'She phoned Sunday morning. You're right – she was *furious*.' Alex winced at the memory.

'You mean – you didn't even talk to her on Saturday night? You didn't telephone to say you couldn't make it?'

He shook his head.

'My, my!' Lottie cocked her head to look at him, her voice quiet and her expression suddenly speculative. 'You *must* have been enjoying yourself! And here was I happily going

along with the accepted opinion that I'm the flighty one in
the family! Come on, now – 'fess up – what were you doing
that was so interesting?'

'We were talking politics.' He was faintly defensive.

She looked at him blankly. 'Talking politics,' she repeated
flatly, as if testing the meaning of the words. 'You spent
*Saturday night* talking politics and eating fish and *chips*?'
She rolled her eyes. 'Alex, Alex, what has got into you?
Even an evening with Miss Snooty must surely be better
than that?'

He had had enough of her teasing. 'As a matter of fact
I enjoyed it.' His voice was sharp. 'Emma's got some
really interesting friends. Intelligent friends.' He stopped
for a moment before saying, with a slight and meaningful
emphasis, 'Caring friends.'

'Ah.' Lottie had the grace to look as abashed as she could
manage. She nibbled her lip for a moment. 'Of course. How
is she?'

'There were some tears. And not just from Emma. Joe was
a very popular chap. But there was a lot of laughter, too.
A bit like a funeral, really.' Alex turned his head sharply
away, looked out into the dark evening beyond the window.
The lights in the street glowed warmly. A crowded red
bus trundled past, its windows steamed up. 'There won't
actually be a funeral, so that was the closest they could get
to one, I suppose. They all said Joe would much prefer a
good political argument to a funeral anyway.'

Lottie forbore to ask why there could be no funeral; why
ask a question to which she did not honestly want to know
the answer? 'Poor Em. Poor kid,' she said softly.

'Yes. I think the saddest thing is that they were only
just starting to find each other. Nothing had ever really
happened between them. Nothing personal, so to speak.
And now it never will. Eighteen and twenty-one years old.
You'd have thought they would have had all the time in
the world, wouldn't you? Anyway—' He took a breath
and turned back to her, forcing a small smile, lightening

the atmosphere. 'That was my Saturday, what did you do with yours? I don't seem to have seen much of you over the past couple of days.'

'Me? I went dancing at the Savoy with Liam. He lied to me. He said he couldn't dance. But he can. Very well, as a matter of fact.' Her voice was light, her long eyelashes, glinting marigold in the light, veiled her eyes. 'It was fun.' She suddenly became very busy with her toenails again, but aware of the quality of her brother's silence looked up, a little irritated. 'Well, what is it?'

'Nothing.'

She pulled a small exasperated face and kept her eyes on his.

He shrugged a little. 'It's just—'

'It's just that you think I'm leading him on,' she finished for him, with one of those quick flashes of perception that could be so very disconcerting. 'Well, I'm not. And if I am it's none of your business,' she added, smartly, reducing somewhat the effect of the swift denial. She straightened, swinging her legs off the bed and screwing the top on the bottle of bright polish. 'Look, Alex – Liam and I understand each other. He's fun. He's different. He's very good-looking and he may not be rolling in it, but – most of the time, anyway – he's got money in his pocket and he knows how to enjoy it. He's a charmer, and somehow a slightly dangerous one.' She grinned quickly. 'And they don't come any more charming than that, I can tell you. I'm stuck in that bloody boring office for most of the week – I want to go places, meet people – and Liam knows some surprisingly interesting people. He owns one leg of a racehorse, you know. What do you think about *that*?' She grinned, flippantly.

Alex picked up a pencil and began to fiddle with it, twisting it around and around in his fingers, his face sober.

Lottie's eyes softened as she watched her brother. 'Alex, dear Alex, don't worry so! Don't worry about me and don't worry about Liam. We can look after ourselves better than most. All right, you have my permission to worry about

Emma for a little while, but she'll be all right in the end. It's funny, isn't it,' she added, suddenly pensive, 'we've all known each other for so long it's sometimes hard to remember that we aren't actually related.' She was watching him closely; his narrow, dark-eyed face gave nothing away. 'I suppose we'll all drift away from each other eventually – fall in love – get married – have children – meet up for christenings and Sunday tea.' She pulled a laughing, childishly disgusted face, then stood up. He looked up at her. She smiled. 'Shall I let you in on a secret? A very private secret?' For a moment she reminded him of the child she had once been, vivid and beguiling.

Returning her smile, he nodded.

'I've quite made up my mind,' she said, 'never to fall in love with anyone. Too emotionally messy. Too trying altogether.'

He shook his head, still smiling. 'Never? You're sure?' he asked.

'Quite.' The word was serene. 'Oh – I shall get married, I expect. Every girl has to do that, I suppose. After all – *somebody's* got to look after me.' The words were light. Too light. 'But love? No. Leave love to Hollywood. Perhaps – brothers are best?' The words were playful. As she passed him she ruffled his hair, and flicked a finger at one of the open books. 'Don't work too hard,' she said over her shoulder, as she opened the door, and then, eyes to the ceiling, she added, quite audibly, 'What *am* I saying? This is *Alex* I'm talking to. Bless him.'

Alex watched as the door clicked shut behind her. 'And don't play too hard, Lottie,' he said, quietly, into the silence. 'Don't play too hard.'

# Chapter Eight

'Look – there he is – on the steps – that is him, isn't it? Gosh, isn't he *tall*? Liam! *Liam!*' His thick fair hair flopping wildly in the brisk November wind, Ned broke into a run and flew ahead of the others, racing to where Liam was standing, his head tilted back as he studied the great, glittering glass fantasy that was the Crystal Palace. '*Liam!*' Ned flung himself at the unprepared Liam, all but knocking him off balance in his enthusiasm. 'Liam, how are you? Where have you been? Why didn't you get in touch?'

Steadying himself, and laughing, Liam took the boy by the shoulders and held him a little way from him. 'Well, well. Little Ned. All grown up.'

Ned visibly straightened, smiling with pleasure. 'I was sixteen last week.'

'So Emma told me.' Emma had also told him that the reason for Ned's visit home was his annual heart check. The boy had certainly grown, but the narrow shoulders felt fragile beneath Liam's fingers, and despite the words that had obviously delighted Ned, the delicate face beneath the flopping wheat-coloured hair was still a child's, the long-lashed eyes, bright with pleasure and excitement now, the same forget-me-not blue as Christine's. He and his older sister were indeed in some ways still very much alike; both had inherited their mother's colouring and diminutive stature, both too her cast of feature, but in a strange way their very similarity to each other somehow emphasised the contrasts between them. Ned's skin was transparently pale, his slenderness spoke of frailty, his mouth was softer than his sister's, and less certain. The four or five years' difference in their ages was not enough entirely to explain why Christine's every quick movement exuded bright, sometimes impatient confidence, whilst the immediate impression her brother gave was of a faintly nervous diffidence. His eyes now, despite his obvious excitement, were searching Liam's face with a trace of anxiety, as if uncertain of his welcome. As the others joined them, Liam grinned and fisted Ned's chin.

'Hello, Liam.' Christine ran up the shallow stone steps to join them. 'You remember Tom and Josie Barker, don't you?'

'Indeed I do.' Liam took the square hand that Tom extended and shook it gravely. Both the younger Barker children had grown surprisingly tall, the boy – Liam guessed him to be fourteen or fifteen years old – topping his sister by a couple of inches. They were long-legged and athletic-looking, and still might be taken for twins.

'Right, you lot,' Christine said crisply. 'Do we eat first and visit the Palace later, or the other way round?'

'Eat first and visit later, please,' the two Barkers said, promptly and in all but the same breath. 'If that's all right with you,' Josie added, politely.

'It certainly suits me,' Liam said. 'I'm afraid I've only got a couple of hours – I've to meet a man this afternoon.'

'O-oh. Won't you come to the pictures with us? Christine is taking us to the cartoon show up the road after we've visited the Palace.' Ned could not disguise his disappointment.

'Now, Ned,' Christine's voice was sharp, 'that's enough. It was more than kind of Liam to take time out to meet us. I don't somehow think a cartoon show is his idea of sparkling entertainment.'

Liam laughed. 'I would have come with pleasure. But I do have an appointment. So – I'll tell you what – I noticed a rather swish restaurant just along the road. Why don't I treat us all to a slap-up lunch to celebrate Ned's birthday?'

Christine opened her mouth.

'Yes, please,' Ned said, hastily, before she could speak. 'That would be awfully kind.'

'I rather had the Palace Café in mind,' Christine said.

Ned's flashing smile transformed his face. 'I know you did,' he said. 'I think Liam's idea is much better.'

They walked through the rising, blustering wind. 'This really is kind of you,' Christine said, quietly, watching the three youngsters as they walked ahead. 'He's been so excited since I told him you'd agreed to meet us. I fear he'll probably talk you to death over lunch.'

Liam laughed.

There was a moment's silence, then Christine said something that was lost on the wind.

Liam bent his head to her. 'I'm sorry?'

'I said—' The wind had whipped bright colour into her cheeks. 'I said that I hear you've been seeing something of Lottie?'

'I'm seeing something of a lot of people,' he said, lightly, but his eyes were sharp.

She did not reply.

Liam hesitated. 'To be sure, you're the only one I don't get to—'

'Liam! Liam? Is that the restaurant – across the road there?'

'That's the one.'

'Gosh, it *is* posh. Are you sure you can afford it?'

'*Ned!*'

'Sorry, Chris. I only meant—'

'If you can eat it,' Liam said, 'I can afford it.'

'Mother says—' Josie began.

'—that we've got hollow legs,' her brother finished, and then stopped abruptly, tilting his head, looking up to the sky, his attention caught by the drone of an aeroplane engine. 'Look, Jose,' he pointed, 'a De Havilland.' He shaded his eyes with his hand, 'A DH86A. Heading for Croydon, I should think.' He watched the biplane across the sky, his expression intent.

Christine smiled faintly. 'Still dreaming, Tom?'

He glanced at her, quick and bright. 'Oh, it isn't dreaming. I'm going to fly. I don't know how, but I am.'

'He will,' said Josie.

Since lunch had, after all, become a belated birthday celebration in his honour, Ned saw no reason not to monopolise it. He questioned Liam eagerly and persistently about the past six years. Liam, answering what he could and deflecting what he couldn't, noticed with some amusement that Christine made no attempt to check her brother. Her curiosity, it seemed, was as great as his; she just wasn't going to admit to it.

'So what do you do now? For a living, I mean? Golly! Look at that!' Ned's eyes widened hugely as a waiter set a vast ice-cream sundae in front of him.

Liam flicked a glance at Christine's politely interested and entirely unhelpful face, and decided upon honesty. 'I gamble.'

'Gamble? What on?'

Liam shrugged. 'Dogs. Horses. Cards.'

'Two raindrops running down a window?' Christine suggested, sweetly.

He was untroubled. 'For sure. If someone will take the bet.'

'Do you make a lot of money at it?' Ned was demolishing his sundae delicately, colour by colour.

'Ned—' Christine began.

Liam laughed. 'I have me days,' he said, lightly. 'And then again—' He shrugged.

Ned lifted his head. 'What's it like at the dogs?' he asked, unexpectedly.

A little nonplussed, since to be truthful it had never occurred to him to analyse what it was like at the dogs, Liam said 'It's – noisy. It's exciting.'

'Would you take me? When I'm home for the Christmas hols, would you?'

'Honestly, Ned, you have got a cheek! Papa would never allow—'

'Papa needn't know.' Ned was quick as a flash. 'If you came with me, we could say we were going to the pictures. Please?' The appeal was addressed not to his sister, but to Liam. 'You took Lottie,' he said, his face innocent as an angel's.

'Did he indeed?' Christine's blue, interested eyes turned to Liam's.

'Yes. She told me.'

Josie's and Tom's dark heads nodded in unison.

'I think,' Christine said, folding her napkin precisely and laying it beside her plate, 'it's time to change the subject, don't you? Come on now, eat up, or we'll be here all afternoon.'

As they walked back across the spacious grounds of the Palace, Christine glanced up at Liam to ask, 'You see a fair amount of Emma, don't you?'

He nodded. 'I quite often drop in to the shop for a chat.'

'Is it my imagination or is she spending rather a lot of time with Alex?'

'He's often there, yes.'

She grinned. 'Oh, you don't have to be so cagey. I won't say anything. I just wondered, that's all. I hardly ever seem to see her lately. She's for ever off organising things, or attending meetings.' She sobered a little, and chewed her lip. The wind ruffled her hair beneath the small and becoming hat that perched on the side of her head. 'I worry about her. I do hope Papa doesn't find out what's going on. He'd be livid.'

He misunderstood. 'Oh, I don't think there's anything actually going on.'

She shook her head. 'I don't mean Alex. I mean this political business. She's getting deeper and deeper involved. And she's getting careless. She brings books home, and – oh, pamphlets and things. Leaves them all over the house. It's all right when Papa's away, but when he's home—' She shrugged. 'Oh, well. None of my business, I suppose.'

They had stopped at the foot of the wide flight of steps that ascended the terraces in front of the huge, intricate building. 'It's an amazing structure, isn't it?' Christine clamped a hand on her hat as she tilted her head back to look at the building. 'It's like a huge glass cathedral. I can't imagine how they actually managed to move it here from Hyde Park. What a job!'

'It cost a million and a half pounds to build.' Ned had joined them. 'And over there,' he pointed to one of the towers, 'that's where the television broadcasts come from. Are you going to come in for a little while?' he asked Liam.

Liam glanced at his watch. 'I really can't. I've someone waiting for me. I'll have to be on my way.'

'I've got to go back to school the day after tomorrow.' A shadow crossed the boy's face, 'But I'll be home for Christmas in a couple of weeks or so.'

Liam touched his shoulder. 'We'll meet then,' he said, and with a smile and a quick lift of his hand to the others he left them.

Ned watched him go. 'I do like Liam,' he said. 'He's – I don't know – different. Sort of exciting. Don't you think?'

Christine smiled a little. 'He's certainly different,' she conceded.

Her brother cast a quick, bright and surprisingly astute glance at her. 'He likes you,' he said. 'You can see that by the way he looks at you.' Then, before Christine could react to that, he said suddenly, 'Wait a sec. I won't be a minute. Liam! *Liam!*' He ran after the tall, striding figure.

Puzzled, Christine watched as Liam turned, waited for the boy, bent to speak to him. Then, straightening, he spread his hands and shook his head, evidently with regret. Ned pulled a small book from his pocket and handed it to him. Christine saw Liam laugh as he accepted it and scribbled something in it.

A moment later Ned was back. 'I got his address,' he said. 'I want to write to him from school.' He held up the little book, teasingly. 'Want it?' he grinned.

That was an impertinence too far. She gave him a small but none too gentle push. 'Don't be so cheeky. Now, come on – what do you want to see first?'

They did not get to the cinema until much later than they had planned; in fact Christine was for postponing it until another day, but the disappointment of her younger companions and Ned's not unreasonable plea that he would be leaving for school in a day or so persuaded her. She was tired, and the antics on the screen, whilst making Ned and Tom all but fall from their seats with laughter, did not hold her attention.

She dozed.

An hour or so later she was awoken by Ned's finger digging her in the ribs. 'Chris. Chris!'

The cinema was still dark, the cartoons were still rolling, but there was a buzz of conversation around her, a buzz of excitement. 'What's the matter?'

'They're saying the Palace is on fire!'

That shocked the sleep from her. '*What?*'

'Someone just said there's a fire, a really big one.' Ned's face was lit by the flicker from the screen. His eyes shone excitedly. 'Let's go and see.'

All around them people were leaving as the news spread. Others hissed and 'shushed' as the level of conversation grew louder.

'Can we?' Tom asked.

'Please?' Josie was bouncing on her seat with excitement.

Almost everyone around them was moving. Christine stood up. 'All right, then. Come on.'

The cinema foyer was full of people streaming towards the doors, beyond which could be seen an eerie, flickering glow. Now they could hear the bells of the fire engines, the excited sound of voices. Christine glanced at her watch. Ten past eight; yet the pavement outside was as crowded as noon, the road clogged with cars and bicycles. When they stepped out into the cold wind she saw why.

Incredibly, the Palace was already a roaring inferno. The great arch of the south transept stood stark and twisted against billowing smoke that was lit from below by the white-hot glow of the flames. Whipped by the wind, the fire was devouring the building at monstrous speed. The crash and crack of falling glass and ironwork were deafening; cascading sparks lit the night; the explosions as the gas mains shattered blasted the ears and sent fresh flames high into the sky. The transept twisted further. The watching throngs gasped. The efforts of the firefighters who had managed to reach the building, though brave, were obviously – if not to say pathetically – inadequate.

The jostling, excited crowds were becoming denser by the moment. Police were moving in to control them. Christine glanced around a little uneasily, leaned to shout into Ned's ear. 'Ned, I think we should go.'

Ned turned an entranced face to her. 'Go? No fear! Don't be daft! We *can't* go!'

'Cor, look at that!' Tom pointed. Several people craned their necks to look. A small plane was buzzing overhead, swooping and diving into the smoke. 'What's he doing?'

'Taking pictures for the newspapers,' the man next to him said, knowingly. 'You mark my words. That's what he's doing.'

'Rather him than me,' said the woman with him.

Tom could not take his eyes off the plane. Caught in the draught of the fire, it was being sucked down towards the burning building; there were cheers as the pilot succeeded in righting it and swooped upwards through the smoke to safety.

'Less than half an hour, so someone said,' the woman next to Christine spoke with the matey familiarity so often engendered by moments of crisis. 'Less than half an hour ago it started. And look at it! Who'd have believed it?'

Christine flinched as another huge explosion shook the doomed structure. The whole place was incandescent now, a shattered skeleton consumed by fire; streams of molten glass were pouring from it like lava from an erupting volcano; people who had ventured too close ran shrieking from them.

'There she goes,' said the man who had spoken before, an odd and grim satisfaction in his words.

With a crash the great transept finally fell, imploding in a rush of heat and throwing up a macabrely beautiful sheath of swirling sparks.

Christine looked at her brother again. He was spellbound. The fire-flicker lit the fragile planes of his face and reflected in his eyes. Sensing that she was watching him, he turned. 'Fireworks,' he said, with the sweetest of smiles, 'for my birthday.'

'Ned's back at school, then?' Pamela Barker watched as Siobhan poured tea into delicate china cups.

'Yes. He went back yesterday.' Siobhan handed her the cup.

Pamela took it, her eyes still on the other woman as she stirred it. 'How is he?'

Siobhan sighed and shook her head. 'Unhappy. He does hate that school so. And the place isn't good for him, I'm sure of that. He isn't strong. I wish—' Her voice died. She shrugged.

Pamela picked up the unspoken thought. 'Have you spoken to George about it?'

Siobhan pulled a face. 'I've tried. But he won't listen. He

thinks I spoil the boy. I think if George had his own way, the poor child wouldn't be allowed home at all.'

'What did the specialist say? About his heart?'

'Much the same as before. There is some little improvement, but not much. He said—' She stopped as the door burst open and Christine came into the room like a whirlwind. She was dressed in her working outfit of pale blue twinset and navy blue skirt and was waving a newspaper excitedly.

'Have you seen this?'

Both women looked at her blankly. 'Have we seen what?' her mother enquired. 'And, darling, do close the door. It's quite cold enough in here without your letting in a gale-force draught to freeze us to death.'

Impatiently Christine kicked the door shut behind her. 'The king,' she said. 'The rumours *are* true. He does want to marry that American woman.'

'Good Lord!' Pamela's eyes widened. 'You mean the divorced one?'

'That's the one. It's in *The Times*. Look—' She thrust the newspaper under her mother's nose. 'What fun!'

Siobhan ran her eyes over the piece that Christine indicated. Pamela put down her cup and came to bend over her friend's shoulder to read it with her. After a moment she whistled between her teeth. 'Phew! *That's* put the cat amongst the pigeons, and no mistake!'

Siobhan looked up at her. 'But he can't, can he? I mean – the Church won't allow them to marry, will it? And she certainly can't be Queen! A divorcée? The country wouldn't stand for it!'

'Christine pointed a well-manicured finger. 'That's what it says, look: "*a marriage incompatible with the throne*". But apparently he's dead-set on it. Oh, bother, bother, *bother*! I've *got* to go to work. Why don't you turn the wireless on and see what's going on? There'll be such a fuss, I'm sure! I'll bring home an evening paper later.' She turned and flew to the door. 'What a to-do!' She threw the words over her shoulder with happy relish. The door slammed behind her, bringing a billow of smoke from the hearth, and they heard her footsteps race fleetly across the landing and down the stairs.

A sudden recollection struck Siobhan. Tossing the paper to Pamela, she jumped up to follow her daughter. 'Christine!' she called. 'Christine, just a moment—' By the time she reached the top of the stairs, Christine had already thrown her coat on and was tying a bright scarf about her throat. She looked up enquiringly.

Siobhan pointed. 'Darling – would you do me a favour? There's a letter. On the hall table there. Ned left it for me to post when he left and I forgot. Will you pop it in the post box for me?'

Christine smiled quickly. 'Of course.' She took a small feathered hat from the stand, checked in the mirror as she perched it at a becomingly rakish angle, pulled on matching green leather gloves, then reached for the letter that lay on the table. 'Bye. See you later. Don't get too excited about our naughty king.'

She was outside and running down the steps to the street before she looked at the name and address on the envelope. For a second she checked, tapping the thing thoughtfully on the gloved palm of her hand. Then she tucked it into her pocket.

Of course she would post it.

Later.

The abdication crisis shook the nation. Everyone had an opinion about it, and discussions were hot and furious. As Prince of Wales, Edward had been quite extraordinarily popular; much was made of his rapport with the ordinary working man and it was, on the whole, the ordinary working man who supported him now in his bid to marry the woman he loved and keep the throne. Parliament, the Church and the Establishment, however, were implacably against him. A choice, they insisted, had to be made. He made it. On the tenth of December, a week after the news had been broken to a stunned and confused public, he abdicated. A few days later he had left the country of his birth – the country he had been bred to rule – for ever and his shy, stuttering brother the Duke of York had been thrown, unhappy and unprepared, to the lions of dedication and responsibility, which looked ready, at first, to swallow him whole.

'I reckon Edward's got the best of it.' The young man who spoke was sitting cross-legged on the bookshop floor, an untidy heap of folded leaflets beside him, a neatly stacked and even greater pile of unfolded ones in front of him. 'He gets to go off jollying around Paris while his poor sod of a brother is left to face us lot. If you ask me, young Edward just didn't fancy staying to preside over the end of our not-much-revered and – hopefully – soon-to-be-deposed monarchy. God bless 'em every one.' He sketched a mockingly ironic sign of the Cross and reached for his beer.

Alex, seated at Emma's desk, grinned a little, and took a swallow from a tumbler of red wine. 'Problem is he has to live with that terrifying woman. I think I'd rather face us.'

There was an appreciative snort of good-tempered laughter. There were six or seven young people seated either at the desk or on the floor, all busily folding pamphlets as they talked. Two bottles of the strong, dark wine had already been emptied, as had several quart bottles of beer. The blinds were down and the shop was lit by two electric light bulbs, their eye-aching glare exacerbated rather than softened by the utilitarian white glass lampshades that reflected downward, casting harsh shadows across the intent young faces. The battered two-bar electric fire barely took the chill off the air. Everyone was in outdoor clothes.

'Well, he must love her.' Emma came round from the back room carrying another large cardboard box of unfolded pamphlets, serenely ignoring the groans that greeted her –

or rather its – appearance. 'After all, he wouldn't give up absolutely everything for her if he didn't, would he?'

'Absolutely everything?' The young man who had spoken first gave a shout of sardonic laughter. 'Em! Do us all a favour!' He gestured with the folded paper he held. 'The man's personal fortune is probably enough to save every miner's job in Wales, every steel worker's in Sheffield and every bloody docker's in London a dozen times over and still have change. Has he given that up? Course he hasn't.' He flicked a quick look at Christine, who, well aware that he had been trying to gain her attention all evening, studiously ignored him. She picked up her glass and drained it; the wine was strong and a little sour. She was bored and ill-tempered. Brash young men, however bright their eyes, interested her not in the slightest. She had long ago given up trying to deny to herself why she had come in the first place, and the thought was making her more irritable by the moment. She folded another pamphlet, very precisely, and tossed it on to the growing pile in the middle of the desk. Emma had begun to collect and count them, making them into neat packets with elastic bands.

Christine turned her head to look at her sister. 'Didn't you say that Liam was supposed to be here this evening?' she asked, quietly, and as she spoke she knew, to her own exasperation, that the words did not sound as offhand as she had intended.

Emma nodded, her attention still on the conversation that was going on around her. 'Yes.'

'Oh, come on, Peter. Give the bloke his due.' Alex emptied his glass in a long swallow, and refilled first Christine's, then his own. 'It took some guts to do what he's done.'

'It'd have taken more guts not to.'

A babel of voices was raised, in protest, in agreement.

Christine gave up. 'Then where is he?' The old and familiar impatience was in her voice. She lifted her glass again.

Emma, distracted at last, stopped what she was doing

and looked at her sister. It had not been lost upon her that Christine's totally unexpected offer of help for this evening had come after Emma's own casual mention that the Irishman often came to lend a hand at such times. 'I don't know. We don't have a rota, you know. People just turn up. I expect he's busy.'

As I could have been. Christine took a long breath, irritatedly avoiding Peter's bright, interested and totally irrelevant glance, and reached for another pile of pamphlets.

Emma it was who, an hour or so later, heard over the eager ebb and flow of conversation the rattle of the door. By now most of the wine and all of the beer was gone. The pamphlets were folded and neatly packed into boxes. Inevitably the conversation had turned to the war in Spain.

'Madrid won't fall,' Peter was saying. 'They'll hold out, you'll see.'

'Doesn't that depend on how much help Franco's mates in Italy and Germany give him?' A girl with a bright, cherubic face and short dark hair who was sitting next to Christine shook her head as she spoke. 'The Republicans are getting so little help.'

Emma went to the door; as she unbolted and opened it, a gust of cold air lifted the papers on the desk. Liam stepped from the darkness; he was holding a large brown paper carrier bag. 'Thought you might have run low on supplies.' He grinned as he handed it to Emma. Glass chinked. He raised a hand in greeting to the gathering, nodded towards the stacks of folded pamphlets. 'Sure now, isn't that a shame? It looks as if I've missed all the fun. Wouldn't you say that was just my luck?' He took his hat off, tossed it on to the desk. His smile was graceless.

There was a chorus of friendly jeering. Peter reached up a hand to be shaken. The dark-haired girl jumped up to kiss him. Alex, laughing, stretched to take a glass from a shelf as Emma took the two quart bottles of beer from the bag Liam had given her and put them on the desk.

Christine said nothing. She knew Liam had seen her; she had noted the surprise in his eyes as he had included her in the general greeting. Was that all the notice he was going to take? She watched as he hitched himself on to the desk and reached into his breast pocket for his tobacco pouch. His hands were long, strong and well-shaped. He nodded, smiling his thanks, as Alex passed him a beer before refilling the others' glasses, emptying the two bottles in one round. The last of the wine he tipped into Christine's glass.

Peter came to his feet in a single, quick movement and took the chair that the dark-haired girl had vacated. 'Christine, isn't it?'

She picked up her glass. 'Yes.'

He cocked his head to look at her. 'You don't look like Emma's sister.'

'No. We've never been very alike.' Her tongue was as crisp and dismissive as her recent intake of wine would allow it to be.

Liam had rolled his cigarette. He flicked his lighter and bent his head to it, narrowing his eyes against the smoke, his profile sharp in the bright electric light.

Peter tried again. 'You haven't had a lot to say this evening. I hope we haven't overwhelmed you?'

She shot him a brief, scornful glance. 'Of course not! I'm just not particularly interested in politics, that's all.'

The party was breaking up. Alex and Emma were deep in conversation, while another group stood by the book-shelves, glasses in hand, laughing at something the dark-haired girl had said. Liam slipped from the desk and joined them. The girl put a light hand on his arm and said something that Christine didn't catch, and everyone laughed again.

'I'm sorry?' The young man, Peter, had spoken and she had missed what he said.

'I said that seems strange – your not being interested in politics, when Emma is so involved.'

'I told you. We aren't alike at all. I only came tonight because she said she needed a hand.' Her foot touched something under the table. She leaned back to see what it was, then bent to pick it up.

'Will you come again?'

Christine lifted a shoulder, barely politely. Her temper was becoming more precarious by the minute.

Emma was collecting glasses and tidying up. Christine jumped up to help her, then wished she hadn't as Peter promptly joined her. Crossly she began to clear the desk. Over the girl's shoulder Liam was looking at her; she thought she caught a flash of amusement in his eyes. Colour rose in her cheeks. She stashed the empty bottles back in the paper bag and carried them into the back room. Alex was washing up cups, saucers and glasses; Emma was wiping. As Peter followed Christine through the door, Emma, laughing, tossed him the tea towel. 'Here. Make yourself useful. I'll put things away.'

Someone called a farewell, and the doorbell jangled. Christine went back into the shop where Liam and the girl were collecting and stacking the boxes of pamphlets. As Christine came into the light from the shadows of the bookshelves she collided with Liam, sending the box he was carrying flying, the corner catching her a glancing but painful blow on her cheek. Ignoring the box, he caught her arms to steady her, his eyes bright and concerned. 'Christine! I'm sorry! Are you all right?'

Mortified, she wrenched away from him, all the obscure disappointments of the evening suddenly stretching her wine-fuelled temper to snapping point. 'Of course I'm not bloody all right, you clumsy idiot!' She had spoken much too loudly; she was aware of silence, of sudden, startled looks. The half-smiling concern faded from Liam's face. Wordlessly he turned away from her to gather the fallen pamphlets. The set of his shoulders spoke volumes.

Suddenly everyone was speaking at once, calling good-byes, making arrangements, trooping to the door.

The dark-haired girl bent to where Liam had dropped to one knee and was gathering up the fallen papers and kissed him lightly on the cheek. 'Cheerio, Irish. See you soon.' She did not speak to Christine.

As the door closed behind her, Liam straightened and put the box on the desk. They could hear the murmur of Emma's and Alex's voices in the back room. Everyone else had gone. Liam surveyed her for a long moment. Refusing to back down, she glared stubbornly at him. Her cheek throbbed hotly.

When he spoke, his voice was very quiet, almost pleasant. 'Christine Clough, d'you know I do believe you're the most ill-mannered, ill-tempered, self-centred vixen it's ever been me misfortune to meet – ah! No.' He raised a sharp finger, shaking his head. She had made a swift movement, which he had interpreted, quite correctly, as the beginning of an impulsive attempt to slap him. 'I think not,' he said, gently. He stepped back, his eyes still on hers, and raised his voice. 'I'll be off then, you two. Be seeing you.'

After a moment Emma put her head round the book-shelves, smiling cheerfully. 'Thanks for the beer.'

Liam flashed her a smile, settled his hat on his black, unruly curls, looked down at Christine. 'Be seeing you, Miss Clough,' he said, softly and pleasantly.

Christine's lips tightened.

The doorbell jangled as he shut it behind him.

Emma had not observed the exchange. She smiled at her sister. 'Be with you in ten minutes or so. We always like to make sure we tidy up properly. It's so kind of Mr D. to let us use the shop like this, I don't like him to feel we're taking advantage. We'll just finish out the back, then take these boxes to one of the upstairs storerooms, out of the way.' She disappeared.

Christine walked to the desk, stood leaning on it, looking into the distance, her face pensive. Minutes passed.

Stupid. How stupid.

She slipped her hand into her pocket, brought out a small, square object, which she set very carefully on the desk. The light glinted on the worn silver. She looked at it expressionlessly for a very long time. Then with a sudden, decisive movement she picked it up, folding her small fingers about it. The metal warmed in her hand.

Emma was wiping the table in the back room. She looked up when Christine came to the door, and for the first time noticed the bruise on her cheek. 'Christine? What have you done to your face?'

Christine shook her head. 'Nothing. Banged it on a box, that's all. Look – I've found this.' She opened her hand. 'Liam's lighter. It was under the table.' That was no lie. 'He must have dropped it.'

Emma held out a hand. 'Best give it to me. I'll put it in the desk drawer. He'll come back for it, I daresay.'

'No.' The word was quick. Christine smiled a little, put a hand to her head. 'To tell the truth I think I've had just a tad too much of that quite awful wine of yours. I could do with some fresh air. He only lives around the corner – it's virtually on the way home – I'll drop it in to him.' She crossed the room to kiss her sister's cheek. 'I'll see you later. Don't forget to have a good story ready when you come home tonight. Papa's home, remember.' She lifted a hand. 'Bye, Alex.'

It was a minute or so after she had left that Emma said suddenly, frowning a little, 'Alex – do *you* know exactly where Liam lives?'

He shook his head. 'No.'

'Neither do I.' The words were very thoughtful, and – for Emma – a shade inquisitive.

He watched her with smiling affection. 'None of our business.'

'No. Of course not.' She turned and caught his eyes upon her, and for a moment the open tenderness in them took her breath away. Her always rosy face became suddenly rosier;

with a flustered little laugh she started to turn away. He put out a hand to bring her back to him. She stood, awkwardly, the damp, tattered cloth she had been using on the table still in her hand.

And then, gently, very carefully and for the first time, he kissed her.

# Chapter Nine

Christine stood on the dark landing outside the door marked '5A', and wished with all her heart that she had not come; it was not just the climb up two steep flights of dimly lit stairs that made her heart thump and her breath short. She was tempted – more than tempted – to change her mind and leave. But before she could move the door opened with a suddenness that almost made her jump from her skin and Liam's tall, broad-shouldered figure was etched in the doorframe against the light of the room behind him. He was in his shirtsleeves and had taken off the tie he had been wearing earlier.

'Christine?' There was enquiry rather than surprise in the word.

She took a small step backwards. 'I'm – I'm sorry to disturb you.' She put a hand in her pocket and brought out the lighter. 'I found this – you must have dropped it – it was under the table.'

He smiled and stood aside, waving her past him. She hesitated for a moment, then lifted her chin and walked into the room. It was surprisingly big, and surprisingly comfortable-looking. Bookshelves lined one wall, a fire blazed in the wide, cast-iron fireplace and a big old three-piece suite sported several large, plumped-up cushions in deep, masculine colours that matched the heavy curtains that were closed against the dark. In one corner stood a table with four dining chairs tucked tidily up to it. On the table stood a whiskey bottle and two glasses, both half-full. Startled, she looked around. 'I'm sorry – you're expecting someone.'

'Yes.'

She put the lighter on the table. Her cheeks were hot with embarrassment. Why hadn't she thought of that? 'I'll be off, then.' She turned back towards the door.

'You,' he said.

She stopped. There was a moment's silence. She neither moved nor looked at him. 'I – beg your pardon?'

'I said, yes, I was expecting someone, Miss Clough. And the someone was you.' His voice was patiently tranquil.

She spun to face him. 'Will you for *heaven's* sake stop calling me that?'

He grinned.

She glared at him.

He picked up the glasses, offered one to her.

For a moment she did not take it. 'What do you mean that you were expecting me?'

'Exactly what I say. D'you want this or will I be drinking it myself?'

Eyeing him warily, she took it.

He picked up the lighter, tossed it into the air, caught it deftly, held it up between long fingers. 'I saw you pick it up.' The teasing laughter was gone. His tone was almost gentle.

If the floor at that moment had opened up and swallowed her whole, Christine would have been more than grateful. She cleared her throat. 'Why didn't you say anything?'

'I wanted to see what you were up to.'

'And what am I – up to?'

'I don't know. You tell me.'

She stood for a long time looking down into her drink.

Then she lifted her eyes to his and shrugged. 'I can't. I don't know myself.'

'Then why don't you take your coat off, sit down and see if we can find out?' He caught the sudden caution in her eyes and laughed, softly. 'It's all right. I won't—' he hesitated, amused, 'bite you. I promise.'

She slipped her coat off and handed it to him. He laid it over the chair, watched as she took off her hat and shook her hair free. 'You've grown your hair,' he said. 'It suits you.'

'Thank you.' She picked up her drink again, went to stand with her back to the fire. She was wearing a red woollen dress, demurely high-necked, long-sleeved and trimly fitting with matching high-heeled shoes. She carried herself – as he had often noticed that she did – as if she were taller than she actually was. Her gaze was direct. 'I'm sorry,' she said.

His sudden, delighted grin lit his face. 'Trust you to say the one thing I wasn't expecting! What are you sorry for?'

'I was very rude to you. This evening, back at the shop.'

'Sure – you've been rude to me before, haven't you now?' Liam was making no attempt to disguise the fact that he was thoroughly enjoying himself.

She shrugged slim shoulders. 'Not as rude as that, and not in front of other people. I really am sorry. I behaved terribly and I'm ashamed of myself.' She lifted her chin in a characteristic gesture, as if defying him to deny it.

That brought outright laughter. 'I must say, M—' he stopped himself in time as her eyes flashed a warning, 'Christine, you don't look it. You don't look it at all.'

She clung to her dignity for a moment longer before letting out a sudden giggle. 'You should have told me,' she said, 'that you'd seen me pick the damned thing up. Fancy letting me make such a fool of myself! I'll never forgive you, Liam McCarthy.' The laughter was getting the better of her. 'Never!'

'You haven't made a fool of yourself. Don't think it.' His face was still bright with laughter, but his voice was soft.

She took a breath to control her giggles. Their eyes locked; a slightly odd silence fell suddenly between them. It was Liam who broke it. 'Will you drink your whiskey, woman! It's been waiting twelve long years for this moment, it doesn't seem fair to make it wait longer.' The lightness of the words, however, was at odds with the tone of his voice and the expression in the intense blue eyes, which seemed somehow to have darkened. Christine could see a pulse beating, regularly and powerfully, in the hollow of his throat. All at once she was aware of the sheer size and strength of him. The raw-boned boy she remembered had become a man with a daunting and vibrant physical presence. She ducked her head, took a sip of her drink; nearly choked.

The moment was gone. Grinning, he watched her trying to control the spasm. Scarlet, she managed it. Liam took her by the shoulders and directed her to the big sofa. 'Come on, now, sit down. Tell you what – I've eggs and bacon in the kitchen. Baked beans, too. How d'you fancy breakfast?'

'Breakfast?' Surprise and laughter started her coughing again. 'At,' she consulted her watch, 'ten o'clock at night?'

'Sure, what better time for an Irishman to eat breakfast?' he enquired.

She hesitated. 'I ought to go, really.'

'About to turn into a pumpkin?'

She shook her head. 'No. Well – not until twelve o'clock, anyway.'

'Then we've plenty of time.' He moved easily to a doorway on the far side of the room that was curtained with the same heavy material as hung at the window. As he drew it back Christine caught sight of a long, narrow kitchen. In the doorway he turned, grinning at her over his shoulder. 'We've yet to discover what gave you the urge to snitch my lighter,' he said, affably.

'I did *not*—' She took a breath and stopped herself,

wrinkling her nose and sticking out her tongue at him.
'Go and make the breakfast.'

'Yes, Ma'am.' She could hear his laughter over the clattering of a pan.

Still nursing her drink, she got up and wandered about
the room, unabashedly curious. The bookshelves were interesting. The books were obviously all second-hand; some
indeed were so battered that they could easily be third- or
fourth-hand. They were an eclectic mix; politics and fishing,
art and travel, history, shooting, mathematics, archaeology.
A set of well-thumbed encyclopaedias had one volume
missing and the spines were broken. There were novels,
too; Sir Walter Scott sat beside a couple of cheap editions of
William Faulkner, Baroness Orczy rubbed covers with T.S.
Eliot and John Buchan, Somerset Maugham with Agatha
Christie. Anthologies of poetry were tucked in amongst
practical aids to self-education. Rupert Brooke was flanked
by *Paradise Lost*.

'Have you read all these?' she called, above the sound of
bacon spitting and sizzling.

Liam appeared in the curtained doorway, a kitchen slice
in his hand. 'Most of them, yes. How do you like your
eggs?'

'As runny as possible. Are they all yours or did they come
with the gaff?'

'They're mine.'

She turned, studying him for a moment. 'Did you ever
take that scholarship you were studying for?'

He turned back into the kitchen. 'No. Your father made
sure of that.'

She went to the doorway, leaned on it, watching him.
'I'm sorry.'

He shook his head, broke an egg, sizzling, into the pan.
'Not your fault.'

'It was. Yes, it was.'

Another egg joined the first, and then two more. 'It all
turned out for the best in the end.'

'You can't know that. Which one of those is mine? They're getting rather well done.'

He grinned. 'None of them. They're mine. I'll do yours separately. How many do you want?'

'One will be plenty, thank you.'

'I'll do you two. Would you like to lay the table? There's cutlery in the drawer under the bookcase, and plates in the cupboard.'

She busied herself with the table, carried the plates into the kitchen. 'Salt? Pepper?'

'In the cupboard there.' He jerked his head. 'And the ketchup. Don't forget that. Breakfast isn't breakfast without ketchup.'

'Ketchup!' she laughed delightedly.

Liam looked a little startled. 'What's funny about that?'

'Papa would have a fit! He doesn't allow the stuff in the house!'

'More fool him.' Liam slid the eggs on to the plates, spooned out the beans. 'Has it occurred to you that your father would have a fit if he could see you now anyway? And for reasons that haven't a lot to do with a bottle of tomato ketchup?'

'Of course.' The words were prompt and unworried. 'But he can't, so where's the problem? Thanks.' She took the plates he proffered and carried them to the table. 'Where shall I sit?'

'Please yourself.' Liam followed with bread, butter and the whiskey bottle. 'Sorry – I haven't got any wine.'

'I thought this was supposed to be breakfast?'

'Irish breakfast,' he said with a grin. 'Tuck in. Here,' he handed her the ketchup bottle, 'take the chance while you can.'

They ate in silence for a moment. 'Mm. Lovely,' Christine said, appreciatively, sipping her whiskey.

Liam was watching her. 'How do you get on with your father?'

She thought about that for a moment, a piece of bacon

poised on her fork. 'All right, I suppose,' she said. 'He spends so much time in the States lately that we don't get to see a lot of him really.'

'He's expanded the business?'

'Yes, he has. But it isn't just business that keeps him away, we all know that. He has a mistress. He keeps her in a house in Hampstead, I believe. I rather like Hampstead,' she added, inconsequentially. 'Gosh, these eggs are lovely – just how I like them.' She suddenly noticed his silence and looked up. 'What's the matter? You aren't surprised, are you?'

'I suppose I am, yes.'

'I can't see why? A lot of men in Papa's position have mistresses, don't they?'

'That isn't what surprises me.' He hesitated. 'Don't you mind?' There was real curiosity in the words.

Christine shrugged. 'Why should I? If Mama doesn't – and she doesn't – then what has it to do with me? Anything or anyone that keeps Papa happy and occupied, and distracts his attention from what we're all doing, is fine by us, I can tell you. When the last one left him he was like a bear with a sore head for weeks, and poor Mama almost faded away.' Suddenly aware of what she had said she blushed hotly, then laughed a little. 'What a thing to say! Are you making me drunk?'

His grin was easy. 'I rather hope so.' He wiped his plate clean with a slice of bread, then pushed it away from him.

Delightedly Christine followed suit. 'This is something else that isn't allowed at home,' she said. 'Thank you. That was lovely.'

'My pleasure.' He put his elbows on the table, his hands nursing his glass. 'I assume you got my address from Ned?'

'Sort of. I posted the letter he wrote you. I took the address from that.'

'Why?'

'I don't know. Curiosity, I suppose.'

He let that pass without open comment, though the quizzical look he sent her was eloquent. 'That isn't the only letter I've had. There have been three in a week.'

She sighed. 'Poor Ned.'

'He isn't exactly what you could call happy, is he?'

'He's utterly miserable. The school doesn't suit him at all. I think he gets bullied. I wish Papa would let him come home and go to day school, like the Barkers do. That's what Ned wants, what would be best for him, I'm sure. But Papa won't hear of it, of course. Belfairs is his old school, you know. He always says it was the making of him.'

Liam's laughter this time was harsh.

Christine frowned. 'He isn't that bad, you know. Oh, I know he was horrible to you, and I understand you don't like him much.'

'An understatement,' he said, softly, and tossed back his drink. 'What amused me was the thought that anyone could possibly believe that a school that was "the making" of George Clough could be anything but the breaking of his son.'

'Oh, come on,' she was uneasy. 'It can't be that bad. Can it?'

He stood up, walked to the bookcase and took down a couple of envelopes. 'Here. Read them for yourself.' He dropped them in front of her.

While she read Ned's letters he shovelled coal on to the fire, took a tin from the mantelpiece and rolled a cigarette, lighting it from a spill. Then he turned, watching her.

'Oh, Lord,' she said.

'The lad's desperate.' Liam came back to the table, picked up the letters and glanced at them before tucking them back into the envelopes. 'As long as I live I'll never understand the English habit of giving their sons into the charge of sadists.'

'He's been more open with you than he ever has with me. Or with Emma or Mama, so far as I know.'

Liam shrugged. 'I'm an outsider. It's sometimes easier to confide in a stranger.'

'He's very fond of you, I know. Liam,' she leaned eagerly to put a hand on his arm, 'couldn't you help him?'

He looked at her in surprise. 'Me? How could I help him?'

'Talk to him. Teach him to look after himself. Show him how to survive this.'

'Just like that?'

She shook her head impatiently. 'Oh, don't be silly. I know it isn't that easy. But you're so good at looking after yourself, surely you could rub a *bit* of it off on to poor Ned?'

'And what in the world makes you think I'm so good at looking after myself?'

She brushed that aside. 'You're being silly again. *And* fishing for compliments. I'm surprised at you. But, Liam – seriously – would you at least try? He'll be home for Christmas soon. At least talk to him?'

'Well, of course I will, if you think it might help.'

'Thank you.' Christine jumped to her feet. 'Now, I really must be going. I'm trying to keep in Papa's good books at the moment. He's promised to buy me a car for my twenty-first. I'm not putting *that* at risk, I can tell you.' She reached for her coat, but he got to it first, shook it out and held it for her. She slipped her arms into the sleeves, turned and found herself trapped in his arms. She made an automatic effort to free herself, then stood very still, watching him.

'You've got eyes like saucers,' he said, softly. 'Did you know that? Great big blue saucers.'

'How very romantic,' she said, as tartly as she could manage.

His arms tightened. 'I don't believe we've established, Miss Clough,' his smiling mouth was very close to hers, 'why you came to see me in the first place?'

'I can't remember,' she said.

'Try this.' The words were gentle. His kiss was not. It was long, and just a little rough, as if he expected her to resist him.

She did not. When she stepped back at last the chin came up again, challenging as ever. 'You've done that before,' she said.

He nodded, smiling. 'So have you.'

'Once or twice.' No amount of assumed nonchalance could keep the husky edge of excitement from her voice.

'Was I right?'

'What about?'

'Was that why you came?'

She studied him. 'I don't know. Try again, and I'll tell you.'

This time he was less fierce, and when he lifted his head he kept his arms tight about her, her curly head tucked beneath his chin. 'Well?'

She snuggled closer to him. It was hard to tell which of them was trembling the most. She tilted her head to look up at him. 'Well, if it wasn't this time,' she said, 'it almost certainly will be next. If I'm invited, of course.'

'You're invited.'

'I'd better go.' The words were not convincing. She tucked her head back under his chin and closed her eyes.

'Yes, you had. No point in buggering up your chance of a decent birthday present.' Liam put her from him. 'Come on – I'll walk you home.'

'You don't have to.' That was even less convincing.

Liam grinned. 'Stop play-acting. It doesn't become you.'

She gurgled with laughter. 'I'm not very good at it, am I?'

For a moment he surveyed her; all at once his eyes were serious. 'I mean it, Christine. Let's get something straight from the start. Don't ever pretend with me. Don't ever act. Don't ever lie.'

'I don't!' she said, indignantly, then added, flushing a little, 'Well – not often.'

'I don't give a damn what you do with other people. Just never do it with me.'

'You too?'

'Me too.'

'Even if it means hurting each other?'

'Even then.'

There was a small, intent moment of silence. 'All right,' she said, not lightly. 'Now, I'm sorry, but I really do have to go. Papa—'

'I know, I know.' He buttoned her coat, handed her her hat, took her hand. 'Something tells me,' he said, towing her towards the door, 'that you're going to be a bloody little nuisance, do you know that?'

They walked the couple of miles to Holland Park almost in silence. It was freezing cold and there was sleet in the air. People hurried past them, collars turned up, scarves flapping, heads down into the wind. Traffic was heavy and the buses were crowded, their windows steamed up. Couples kissed in darkened shop doorways, and cats slunk and skittered around dustbins.

'I'll come no further. You'll be safe from here.' Liam stopped on the corner of the familiar, elegant crescent, drew her to him and kissed her, then gave her a small push. 'Off with you. It's getting late.'

She hesitated for a moment, then after standing on tiptoe to kiss him again, lightly, she turned and hurried into the lamp-lit darkness. She did not look back.

Liam looked after her, hand automatically reaching into his pocket for the makings of a cigarette. After he had lit it, and when he had seen her run swiftly up the steps of the house and let herself in, he turned and strolled, slowly and thoughtfully, into the buffeting wind, back the way he had come.

It was not until she was slipping between the cool linen sheets of her bed that Christine realised that they had not made arrangements to meet again. She smiled into the darkness. They would. Of course they would. If worse came to worst she could always steal his lighter again.

It was a very long time before she slept.

\*       \*       \*

'I saw Liam the other day.' Ned Clough was sitting on the kitchen table, legs swinging, a large slice of cake in his hand. 'He sent his love.' Liam hadn't, in fact, done any such thing, but it seemed only polite to say he had. And Mary just might say something interesting; Ned was very good at seeking out and storing the small snippets of information that could be gleaned from general conversation.

Mary McCarthy neatly folded a freshly-ironed shirt and added it to a growing pile. She did not reply. She knew Ned. And she knew Liam. All too well. There was little likelihood he had sent any such message.

Ned put his head on one side, watching her. 'Why don't you go and see him? I'm sure he'd like you to.'

'I'll go when I'm invited.' The words were composed.

Ned took a mouthful of the cake he had cadged from Turner. 'I mean, he can't come here, can he? Papa would have a fit.'

'Liam will do as he wishes, Ned, that's for sure. Now,' she added before he could answer, 'will you do me a favour and take these,' she laid a pile of freshly-ironed clothes into a small basket, 'up to Emma's room for me? My poor feet are hurting like the devil again. Lord blast young Spencer for walking out on us just before Christmas! Just leave them on the bed; Emma prefers to put her own things away.'

'Of course.' He jumped from the table, crammed the rest of the cake in his mouth. 'Sort out the rest and I'll come back for them. Thanks for the cake, Turner,' he added. The cook nodded distractedly.

He climbed the stairs with the basket. The house was decked for the Christmas celebrations, and the air smelled of pine from the huge tree in the hall. It was very quiet. Chill winter sunlight lit the rooms and dazzled upon the polished floors. Emma's bedroom was next to his own, on the second floor. He pushed the door open, lugged the basket across the room and dropped it beside the bed. As he bent to lift the clothes out, he caught a glimpse of something under the bed. He pushed the basket away, dropped to his knees and lifted up the valance to peer underneath. A couple of scruffy and bulging brown paper carrier bags had been pushed out of sight, close to the wall. The temptation was irresistible; he reached in, hauled one out and opened it. A little disappointingly it was full of nothing but folded pamphlets. Ned took one, and sat back on his heels to read it; and as he did so a door downstairs slammed and quick footsteps came across the landing and to the bottom of the stairs. Hastily he shoved the bag back where he had found it and scrambled to his feet, straightening the bed. He could hear Christine humming as she came up the stairs. As she passed the open door she glanced in and caught sight of him. 'Ned? What are you doing in Emma's room?' Christine knew her young brother well enough to feel the stirring of suspicion.

He indicated the basket. 'I'm delivering the laundry for Mary. Her bunions are playing her up again.' The pamphlet crackled in his pocket as he bent to retrieve the basket.

She stood by the door, waiting for him to leave. She had once caught him going through the drawer of her little writing table; Ned knew that the thought was in her mind, and he found himself flushing uncomfortably. With an air of injured innocence he stalked past her and down the stairs.

He read the pamphlet, later, in his own room, running his eyes over it swiftly, then again, more slowly, grimacing a little. '*Workers, unite! Unite against vile Oppression! Unite against Injustice! Unite against the canker of Racial Hatred! A Labour Movement Rally will be held in Hyde Park on the 6th of January, at 3.00 p.m. Support us! We need your voice! We need your marching feet! The Fascists must be opposed! Support your brothers in Spain and let the world know that Mosley's Blackshirts Shall Not Pass!*' Golly. That's a bit strong.' He read the thing again, then, about to screw it up, he stopped, shrugged and bent to tuck it into the book he was reading, which lay beside his bed.

It was against his nature to throw something of this

kind away; in his experience there was never any knowing whether it might come in handy.

In the event he regretted keeping it, and he regretted it bitterly.

Two days later, curled in an armchair in front of the drawing-room fire, he failed to hear his father enter the room. When he finally sensed his presence Ned snapped shut the book he was reading and scrambled to his feet. 'Good afternoon, Papa.'

'Good afternoon, Edward.' George Clough was in a benign mood. His morning assignation at the little house in Hampstead had been especially gratifying. Really, young Deirdre was becoming delightfully inventive. He would have to buy her a little something in reward. 'What's keeping you so quiet?' He was almost jovial.

'I'm r-reading, Papa.'

George suppressed the sudden lift of irritation. 'I can see that, boy. I mean *what* are you reading?' he asked with heavy, almost playful patience. He held out his hand.

Ned froze. 'It's—' His treacherous tongue betrayed him entirely. 'It's a J-J-J—' He bit his lip.

George glowered and snapped his fingers. Edward handed him the book. His father flicked open the front cover. 'John Buchan, eh? *Greenmantle.* Don't think I've ever got round to reading this one. Is it any good?' He riffled through the pages. Ned watched, frozen, as – as if in slow motion – the inevitable happened. The pamphlet fell to the floor. His father picked it up. Glanced at it. Then looked again.

The thunderous silence lasted for perhaps thirty seconds; it was the longest thirty seconds Ned had ever endured.

His father's eyes lifted to Ned's. All traces of benevolence had left his face. 'Is this some kind of joke?' His voice was as cold as his eyes, and promised retribution of the severest kind, whatever the answer to the question. 'What is this filthy, rabble-rousing nonsense doing in my house?' The very softness of the words was terrifying.

Ned swallowed. He stared at his father as if hypnotised. 'I – found it.'

'You found it,' his father repeated. 'Where did you find it? In the street, perhaps?'

'Y-yes.' Eagerly Ned grasped at the straw. 'Yes, that's right. In the s-s—' He drew a long breath, trying desperately to gain some kind of control over himself. 'In the street.'

'And when was that? Today? Yesterday?' George was playing him like a fish. The quiet voice was steely.

Ned was paralysed with fright. 'Yesterday,' he said. 'It was y-yesterday.'

His father lifted the pristine pamphlet and examined it, interestedly. Then he looked back at Ned, and Ned flinched. 'Strange. It must have been a remarkably well-sheltered street. As I remember, it rained yesterday. All day. But,' he held up a quick hand as Ned opened his mouth to speak; his voice now was almost gentle, 'let that pass. Tell me; once you had "found" it,' there was a heavy, almost mocking, emphasis on the word, 'why did you keep it?'

Ned stared at him and said nothing.

'Well?'

Panic had deadened Ned's brain. Tears welled and the soft mouth trembled.

'*Why did you keep it? Answer me!*'

Numbly Ned shook his head.

'Could it be that you are thinking of attending this ill-begotten circus? Could it be that a son of mine could be so misguided, so *perfidious*, as to have embraced this,' he thrust the pamphlet into Ned's face, 'this absurd rot?'

'No!'

'Then why did you keep it? *Tell me!*'

Ned broke. 'It's n-not mine! It's Emma's.' Tears streamed down his face. 'I f-found it in her room. Sh-she's got hundreds of them. Hidden under her b-bed.'

George's eyes narrowed. He studied his sobbing son in silence. Then, very quietly, he said, 'You'd better not be lying, boy.'

'I'm not. I'm not!'

George stepped back. 'Then show me.' He strode towards the door, and was through it before he added, witheringly, 'And for God's sake stop blubbering.'

Emma was sitting at her desk, cataloguing a pile of books, when the door crashed open. Though still early, the December afternoon had darkened to dusk and, despite the little electric fire, her booted feet, tucked under the desk, were cold. Her father slammed the door behind him. The bell jangled convulsively. One contemptuous glance took in the surroundings before he strode to the desk. 'Emma. Get your coat. You're coming home.'

'Papa?' Flabbergasted and all but frozen with shock, she came to her feet. 'Papa? How on earth—? Is something wrong? Has something happened?'

'Yes,' he said, heavily. 'Something has happened.'

'Mama? Is there something wrong with Mama?'

'Apart from the fact that she, like you, has deceived me, then so far as I know there is nothing whatsoever wrong with your mother. Get your coat. Now.'

Emma's heart had begun to beat like a drum. 'Why?'

'Stop asking questions. *Get your coat!*'

Emma shook her head. 'Not until you tell me—'

'Emma? Is something the matter?' Mr Davies had appeared around the bookshelves. He was a tall, thin man with stooped shoulders and a sharp, thin nose. His eyes were mild behind the wire-rimmed spectacles.

'Mr D., this is my father—' Emma's voice trailed off.

Mr Davies nodded, manifestly and ingenuously unimpressed. 'How do you do?' he said, politely.

George Clough's face was black with rage. He did not acknowledge the greeting. 'Emma. Get your coat. Immediately. I'm taking you home.'

Emma took a steadying breath. 'No,' she said, and was amazed at how calm the word sounded. 'I'm sorry – I don't know how you found this place, and I know it isn't what we – I—' she hesitated, searching for the word, 'implied it was. But this is where I work, and I love it. I don't think you have the right—'

'The right?' her father interrupted, tightly. 'You dare to speak to me of *rights*? Get your coat, child. I've no intention of talking in front of a stranger. I'll deal with you at home.'

'Mr D. is not a stranger. He's a friend. A good friend.'

'Is he indeed?' George glared, first at Joe's father, then at Emma. 'So does he perhaps have something to do with this?' He tossed the pamphlet on the desk.

Emma picked it up. She had no need to read it. 'I see.'

Her father stabbed a finger. 'No, my girl, you don't see. You don't see at all. *Get your coat!*'

'No.' Emma was suddenly perfectly calm. Somewhere in her heart she had known this was going to happen. Somewhere in her heart she had already made her decision.

'Perhaps you should go, Emma,' Mr Davies said, gently.

'No!' Emma tilted her head in a manner not unreminiscent of her fiery sister. She even managed to smile at him, albeit none too certainly. 'I finish work at six. That's when I'll leave.'

'You'll come now,' her father said, ominously, 'or you'll not come at all. I want an explanation of that—' he pointed a finger, 'that ill-conceived nonsense. And I want an assurance that no child of mine is involved with it.'

'I can't give you that,' she said, composedly.

He stepped forward. For a moment she thought he might strike her. Mr Davies moved, lifting both hands in quick protest. Emma steeled herself to hold her father's eyes. 'You have no right to tell me what to think,' she said, quietly.

'I have a right – a duty! – to protect you from yourself and from others who lead you astray!'

'No.'

He glowered, unexpectedly nonplussed by her calmness.

'I'm sorry, Papa. Truly sorry. But I know my own mind. If you can't accept that, then so be it. I've had a privileged upbringing, a privileged life. I know it. And I thank you for it. But I see what's happening around me. I want to *help*!' To her own astonishment, to say nothing of her father's, on that last word her flat hand hit the desktop. 'It isn't fair. What's happening isn't fair! I shouldn't live in luxury while others starve. Men shouldn't be working underground for a week in killing conditions for what it costs us to go to the theatre, or have a swank night out at the Savoy! Women shouldn't be working on sweatshop wages while their children wait at home to be fed! And those children should have the right to be educated as I was educated.'

'They have it,' her father said, harshly.

'*They do not!* I'm not stupid! I see, and I listen. They don't.' She was calm again. Oddly, through all the emotion, she knew what she was doing. Oddly, she was prepared for it. Even more oddly, she was almost relieved. She shook her head. 'I won't come home with you,' she said, quietly.

'Then you needn't bother to come home at all,' he said flatly, and with the air of one who had won the game.

She faced that bravely enough. 'I'll have to pick up my belongings.'

He concealed his anger and astonishment. 'Not while I'm there.'

'I'm sure that can be arranged.'

He stood for a long moment, watching her. 'You've taken leave of your senses.'

'Possibly. We'll see.'

'Don't come to me when you find you're wrong.'

'I won't.'

'I mean it, Emma. If you don't come with me now, you are no longer my daughter.'

'I know you mean it. But, oddly enough, I will always be your daughter. You're the one who is going to have to remember that.'

He stared at her.

'One thing,' she said, 'Just one thing – don't blame Mama. She had nothing to do with any of this.'

Still he stared.

Very composedly she sat down, then pulled the book she had been working on towards her.

Bizarrely, the door jangled again and a young man in an old trench coat and moth-eaten woollen scarf came in, saluted them all casually and disappeared into the book stacks.

'Emma,' George said, very quietly. 'Get your coat.'

She lifted her head. Her usually rosy face was pale as death. 'No.'

For the space of a few heartbeats he stood, every last ounce of his powerful personality focused upon her.

She outfaced him.

He spun on his heels and left.

As the door slammed noisily behind him she closed her eyes and bowed her head. Joe's father moved towards her. She shook her head. 'I'm all right. Honestly.'

The young man had emerged from the shelves holding a book and was standing uncertainly a few feet away. Emma smiled at him, very brightly. 'May I help?'

He proffered the book. She put it in a brown paper bag. 'That will be one and threepence, please.'

After he had gone she asked, very quietly, 'Would you mind if I used the telephone, please, Mr D.?'

'Of course not, my dear.' He was watching her concernedly.

'I need to talk to Mama before he gets home. To warn her. He's bound to take it out on her. And,' she spread her hands a little helplessly, 'I need to make some kind of arrangement – find somewhere to go – the Barkers. Aunt Pamela. They'll help, I'm sure.' She was aware that she was speaking all but incoherently. She was aware too that suddenly she was trembling with reaction and shock.

'Make as many calls as you like, my dear. But—' Mr Davis hesitated, 'do you really think it necessary? He surely didn't mean what he said? After all, he is your father.'

Emma knuckled her eyes before lifting her head. Her small smile was grim. 'Oh, he meant it all right, Mr D. Make no mistake about that. He meant it.'

# Chapter Ten

The pitiless bombing by forty German aircraft of the little Spanish market town of Guernica in April 1937 horrified the world and sent the most terrifying of messages to the watching nations of Europe. These, after all, were not fighting forces being maimed, blasted, mown down by machine-gun fire as they ran in panic from their flaming homes; these were civilians: men, women and – even more horrifyingly – children, going about their legitimate, every-day business in an undefended town more than twenty miles from the fighting front. The little Basque town with its burning streets and thousand slaughtered innocents overnight became not just a symbol of the brutality of modern warfare, but for many a fearful prediction of what might be in store for Europe if a wider conflict should break out. Prime Minister Stanley Baldwin had famously warned his people that 'the bomber would always get through' – and here, for many, was proof of that. What defence was there against wave after systematic wave of bombers carrying high-explosive and incendiary weapons? Where would there be to hide from the raging inferno that would surely ensue? How could men be persuaded to fight if they knew their defenceless loved ones were being slaughtered in their homes? Whilst the martyrdom of Guernica produced an enormous and spontaneous wave of sympathy for the suffering Spanish people, it also – as almost certainly it had been intended to do – instilled a nervous dread of war into a large part of the populations of Europe, and for a while at any rate strengthened the hand of the appeasers in government who were ready to go to almost any lengths to prevent an outbreak of hostilities.

On a more personal level, it brought back the worst of Siobhan Clough's nightmares.

She had been a sensitive, highly imaginative child of ten when her parents had died in the earthquake that had all but destroyed San Francisco in 1906. She had studied the pictures of the collapsed and burning buildings with the morbid intensity of grief and terror. She had read the harrowing accounts of survivors and of rescuers. For years the horror of it had haunted her subconscious and ambushed her dreams. The nightmares were always the same: always buildings were collapsing around her, always she was trapped, always there was fire. Always there were screams. Always she was alone.

And now it could happen. To her. To her children.

She could not bear the thought.

'Darling, please stop worrying so. You'll make yourself ill.' Pamela regarded her friend with worried eyes. 'And it doesn't do any good.'

'I know. I know! I just can't seem to help it.' Siobhan's fair skin was even paler than usual. Dark rings of sleeplessness marked her face like bruises. 'I can't sleep. I'm *afraid* to sleep.' She twisted her hands nervily. 'It makes George so angry.'

With an effort Pamela forbore to ask what did not make George angry lately. 'Why don't you see the doctor? Perhaps he could give you something to help you sleep?'

Siobhan shook her head. 'What good would that do? It wouldn't stop the nightmares, would it?' She sighed. 'What do you think, Pamela? Will there be a war?'

Pamela shrugged a little. 'Who knows? I hope and pray

not.' Unbidden, a picture of Alex rose in her mind: tall, slim, soft of voice and with a smile that would melt any mother's heart. The thought of him with a gun in his hand physically sickened her. She shook her head sharply. 'It's worrying, I grant you – I heard a talk on the wireless the other day about German rearmament. Who knows what they're up to? But worrying about it – making yourself ill – won't help, will it?'

'No. I know.'

'Go to the doctor. See what he says. Please?'

Smiling faintly, Siobhan nodded. 'All right.'

'Promise?'

'Promise.'

'More sherry?'

'Just a small one. Thank you.'

Pamela picked up the decanter. 'Does George know you're here?'

Siobhan shot her a slightly guilty look. 'No.'

'Ah. So we're still in the doghouse, are we?'

'I'm afraid so.'

'Oh, for heaven's sake!' The words were exasperated. 'What on earth did he expect us to do? Did he truly believe we'd throw poor Emma out on the street, like he did? I'm sorry – I'm sorry!' She held up her spread hand in automatic apology as Siobhan opened her mouth. 'I know we agreed not to talk about it, but honestly, George does make my blood boil sometimes. Have you been to her new home?'

A smile flitted across Siobhan's face. 'Yes. Wasn't it kind of Mr Davies to offer it? She absolutely loves it. She's scrubbing and painting and buying second-hand furniture – I'd no idea she was so domesticated! Or so independent.'

'Oh, she's that, all right. And good for her, I say.' Pamela sipped her sherry, than slid a sly, sideways glance at her friend. 'Have you noticed that she has a ready pair of hands helping her?'

Their glances held for a moment. 'I have,' Siobhan said.

'And – do you mind?'

There could be no mistaking the genuine warmth in Siobhan's smile. 'Why should I mind? Alex has always been like a son to me.' The smile faded a little. 'I don't know if George would.'

'Sod George,' Pamela said, with a calm and startling frankness that brought surprised laughter from her guest. 'If he's done nothing else, he's abrogated the right to approve or disapprove of anything that Emma does. Tell me – does he really know her so little? Did he really think she'd cave in and come home? How little he knows her.'

The smile disappeared from Siobhan's face. 'How little he knows anyone,' she said, quietly.

'Emma?' Alex's voice echoed up the narrow stairs.

Emma pushed her hair away from her forehead with a distemper-covered hand. 'Yes?'

'Fancy a cuppa?'

'Oh, yes, *please!*' She stepped back and surveyed the wall she had been painting. The main room of the little flat above the bookshop, once cleared of the clutter accumulated from being used as a storeroom for twenty years, had proved to be surprisingly big. It was at the back of the building and so looked out upon the long, narrow gardens of the houses in the street behind it. A large tree grew not far from the window; a chestnut, its new spring growth bright in the sunshine. In the Sunday quiet Emma heard a blackbird's trill. She walked to the window, threw open the sash and watched the bird for a moment as, with head thrown back, it poured its music into the still air. She heard Alex's feet on the stairs and turned, smiling, as he entered the room.

He grinned as he saw the state of her. 'You're supposed to be painting the walls, not yourself,' he observed, teasingly, as he bent his head to kiss her. 'Kettle's on.'

Still holding the distemper brush, she reached her arms about his neck. In the moment's silence that followed, the bird's song filled the room as if with sunlight. She stepped back, gesturing. 'What do you think?'

Alex looked around in genuine surprise and admiration. 'Good God – whatever time did you get up this morning?'

Emma laughed. 'Four o'clock,' she admitted. 'It was such a lovely morning, and I so much wanted to get on.'

'You've certainly done that. It's looking great!'

'If we can get this room finished, then we can take our time about the rest.'

'I'll believe that when I see it.'

She grinned at his interruption. 'Mama's offered to pay for some curtains. And I've found a smashing old three-piece suite in the second-hand shop down the road. It's really comfortable. I've put down a deposit and the man says he'll keep it for me until we're ready for it. And Mr D.'s found me some bookshelves that will just fit that wall.' She pointed. 'I thought I'd look for a little table and a couple of chairs for that corner. We can have checked tablecloths and candles in bottles and pretend we're living in an attic in Paris.' The enthusiastic rush of words stopped and she blushed suddenly as she realised the implication of what she had said.

He put his arms about her and rested his cheek on her shining hair. There was a moment of silence. Then, 'Alex?' she asked, very quietly.

'Yes?'

'Did you – did you really mean what you said last night?'

'Yes.' His arms tightened.

'You really do love me?'

He smiled into her hair. 'I do. Why should you doubt it? I've always loved you.'

'But this is different.'

She felt his movement as he nodded. 'Yes. This is different.' His voice was tender.

Emma tilted her head to look at him. 'That was the real reason I got up so early,' she admitted softly. 'I couldn't sleep. I couldn't sleep for loving you.'

He laughed aloud. 'So being the good, practical little thing you are, you dismissed the idea of writing a poem and picked up a paintbrush!'

'Something like that.' She turned in his arms, leaned back against him, looking out into the sunshine. 'I'm so happy I feel almost guilty.'

He squeezed her to him. 'Idiot! Why should you feel guilty?'

She shrugged a little. 'So many awful things happening. Spain. Those poor souls on the *Hindenburg*.' She shuddered. 'That must have been just awful.' The airship *Hindenburg* had exploded like a firebomb two days before as it was mooring after a transatlantic flight from Frankfurt; the trag-edy made somehow worse by the fact that a live broadcast had been going out at the time, so the horrified world had heard a blow-by-blow account of the disaster as it had happened.

Firmly he turned her to face him. 'Awful, but hardly our fault,' he said. 'If it teaches us anything, let it teach us to enjoy what we've got while we've got it. Now – tea and buns?'

Her face lit up delightedly. 'Buns? Sticky buns?'

'The stickiest I could find,' he assured her. 'I'll go and make the tea.' At the door he paused. 'Mother asked if you'd like to come over for Sunday lunch, by the way. I think she thinks you're starving in a garret or something.'

'I'd love to. Then perhaps we could come back and—'

'Then,' he said, very firmly, 'we'll go for a stroll around town and look at the Coronation decorations. You know what all work and no play does for a girl! Take the afternoon off. Bond Street and Regent Street look absolutely splendid. Selfridges looks fantastic! They're running in charabancs from the suburbs just to see them.' His warm smile lit up his narrow face and her heart turned over. 'So, put on your best bib and tucker; I'm taking my girl out on the town.'

She pulled a comic face and spread bright blue fingers. 'Distemper and all?'

'Distemper and all,' he said. 'Wear a white dress and carry a red handkerchief and you'll blend in beautifully with the patriotic show.'

'The parents are being a bit of a pain about this Coronation thing tomorrow.' Lottie was sitting on Liam's table, slim legs crossed and swinging. She was dressed in pale green and white; a polka-dotted flare-skirted dress with white leather shoes, wrist-length white gloves, a cheeky beret perched at a gravity-defying angle on her red curls, a wide belt cinching her tiny waist. She looked stunning, and knew it.

'Oh?' Liam splashed whiskey into a couple of glasses and handed her one. 'How's that?'

'They're insisting we all go to the Cloughs' party. Because of the business over Emma, you know. Mother and Aunt Siobhan have been trying to negotiate a truce for ages. So when the invitation did come, Mother insisted that we accept it. What a bore! Bunch of old fogies talking business, getting pie-eyed and trying to pinch my bottom.'

Liam threw himself on to the sofa, grinning. 'Sounds fun.'

Lottie tossed an airy head. 'Oh, I'll get out of it somehow. I've got other plans.' She eyed him, waiting for him to ask. Knowing he would hear anyway, he sipped his drink placidly, dark eyebrows raised. She wrinkled her nose at him, then grinned like a mischievous elf. 'Quaglino's!' she said, lifting her glass as if toasting him. 'What do you think of that?'

He laughed. 'Why am I supposed to think anything?'

'Oh, come on!' She, too, was laughing. 'Be at least a little impressed.'

'I'm impressed,' he assured her with obvious and friendly insincerity.

'So you should be. There's dancing and a cabaret, and a special Coronation dinner. And I've been invited by the

most charming, handsome, rich—' She paused, looking for
another adjective.

'—married?' Liam suggested.

'—well, of course.' She was exasperated. 'But if she's
stupid enough to prefer to stay in Yorkshire, striding across
moors and shooting things, what's the poor lamb supposed
to do? Live like a hermit?'

Liam tossed back his drink. 'Lottie, you're priceless.'

In typical fashion she took that as a compliment. 'Thank
you. So,' she shook her head as he offered the bottle,
watched as he poured himself another drink, 'what are
you doing?'

'Doing?'

'For the Coronation. Everyone's doing *something*.'

Liam shrugged. 'Working. There'll be a lot of money
around tomorrow night. No reason why some of it shouldn't
finish up in my pocket.'

'How boring.' Lottie jumped from the table, set down
her empty glass. 'The biggest party in London for nearly
thirty years and you're going to be stuck in some smoke-
filled room playing cards! What a waste of a good pair of
dancing feet!' She twirled towards him, skirt flaring about
her knees.

He smiled as she caught his hand and pulled him upright.
'I daresay I'll manage the odd waltz or two,' he said. 'After
I've cleaned out a couple of wallets.'

Lottie cast her eyes to the ceiling. '*You* and *money*!'
she exclaimed exasperatedly. 'Honestly, Liam, you could
be really great fun, if only you wouldn't keep on about
*money*!'

He smiled lopsidedly. 'Come back when I'm rich.'

That truly amused her. 'Oh, I intend to!' she laughed,
delightedly. 'I told you that. Mind you,' her green eyes
were sly, 'I think Christine might have a word or so to say
about it if I did.' She dodged away from him as he reached
for her and ran to the door. 'Don't forget – if you want a bit
of cheek-to-cheek I'll be at Quaglino's.' She slipped through

the door and, as she ran down the stairs without bothering
to close it behind her, Liam could hear her laughter echoing
up the dark stairwell.

For the first time since the row with her father Emma
Clough was honest enough to admit to herself on the
day of the Coronation that on this occasion she did miss
being at home. With the world, his wife and his children
celebrating together it was hard to be alone. Even Mr
Davies had gone with his brother and sister-in-law to stake
a place overnight in Pall Mall to watch the procession. They
had offered to have her join them but, though touched,
she had declined. Strangers, no matter how kindly, were
no substitute for family, and never could be, however
strained relationships might be. She opted instead to help
out at the children's street party that the local residents and
shopkeepers had organised and thus spent the best part
of the day handing out paper hats and streamers, passing
round cream cakes, pouring tea and lemonade, mopping
up spillages, settling disputes and keeping a wary eye on
the minority of small boys intent upon mayhem. There was
a show in the afternoon, put on by the children themselves;
an upright piano on a somewhat rickety makeshift stage
provided the music, the girls of Miss Jay's School of Dance
trod the boards with commendable grace, several small
boys told jokes and almost everybody sang. After tea the
tables were cleared back to the pavements to make room
for party games. Bottles of beer and sherry, which had been
around discreetly all day, appeared openly on the tables as
the adults watched and clapped their offspring's efforts.
Musical Chairs, Blind Man's Buff, Pass the Parcel – in the
excitement the pretty party dresses and the smart suits
became dishevelled and dirty, knees were scraped, heads
bumped; there were squeals of laughter, occasional tears.
Emma was refereeing a dispute over a small, patri-
otically dressed knitted teddy bear that looked unlikely
to survive the battle it had innocently provoked, when

she looked up suddenly to find Alex, a little posy of red, white and blue flowers in his hand, watching her, smiling.

'Alex!' She straightened, her face alight at the sight of him. 'What are you doing here? I thought—'

He kissed her lightly, stopping the words. 'Mama agreed that I'd done my duty and sent me on leave to you. Mind you, I suspect she knew that if she hadn't, I'd have gone AWOL anyway.' He presented the flowers to her with a flourish, then grinned. 'Lottie having already done so,' he added.

'Done what?'

'Gone AWOL.' Alex's grin widened. 'She's been as good as gold all day – watched the ceremony on the hired television, discussed the outfits, helped Christine serve drinks and tea, charmed all and sundry – especially the older male sundry – and then, cool as a cucumber, politely kissed everyone goodbye and said she was off.' He was laughing at the recollection. 'She really has got the cheek of the devil. There was no way, short of tying her down, that anyone was going to stop her and she knew it. So she simply smiled and left.'

Emma too was laughing. 'I don't know how she gets away with it, truly I don't.'

'Christine's fit to be tied. For two pins she'd have come with me. But she's taking her driving test next week, and she's desperate for the car her father said he'd buy her, so she's had to toe the line and stay behind like a good little girl.'

'Which is a pity for her,' Emma said, 'but not for us.'

'Quite.' He linked his arm in hers. All around them was talk and laughter. Someone had started to play the piano. People gathered round and began to sing. 'Come on.' Gently he drew her away from the crowd and down the street to the bookshop. 'Everyone's well amused now. They won't miss you. I've a surprise for you.'

He pushed open the shop door, led her through it. 'I had

a word with Mary. Who had a word with Turner. She was very obliging.'

On the desk stood a very large picnic basket, its lid propped open.

'Alex! My goodness – a feast! And champagne! Oh, darling, what a lovely surprise!' Emma, blinking, threw her arms about him, almost knocking him off balance. 'I didn't expect anything like this!'

'Your very own Coronation feast. There's smoked salmon and cold chicken and – oh, all sorts of good things. Come on, help me up the stairs with it.'

She giggled. 'However did you get it here?'

'An obliging taxi driver. Oh, and just a minute,' he bent and kissed her, hard, 'your mother sent that. She made me promise to deliver it.'

Emma's eyes widened.

Alex, who had already spent a large part of the day drinking champagne, gave a stage wink. 'I think she may suspect something,' he said, darkly.

Emma picked up the huge bottle of champagne. 'I'm sure I don't know what you're talking about,' she said, primly, and then, her eyes softening and her laughter fading, she stood for a moment studying his face. 'Oh, Alex, I am so very glad you've come.'

'You'd jolly well better be. Or I'll take this lot back.'

'Over my dead body.' She set off towards the stairs.

The crowds outside sang and danced as the evening wore to dusk and then to darkness. The street lamps came on, lanterns strung upon the red, white and blue bunting were lit. Alex and Emma, sitting in the candlelit sitting room at the little folding card table, which was all that Emma had for the moment, listened, smiling, to the sounds of laughter. Someone had lit a bonfire in one of the gardens beyond the window; there had been fireworks as they sipped their champagne. Now Alex emptied the bottle into Emma's tumbler and lifted his own glass in a toast.

'Here's to the new king.'

Emma nodded. 'And to the old one,' she added. 'Please God he'll never regret the choice he's made.' She sipped her wine, then sat looking thoughtfully into the glass, watching the bubbles fizz to the surface. 'He must love her very much.'

'I know the feeling.'

Her head came up and, slowly and sweetly, she smiled.

Alex stood up. Held out his hand. She took it, let him draw her to her feet. In the street the pianist had been joined by a trumpet player, who had swung into a more than competent rendition of 'Begin the Beguine'. Alex pulled her close to him and wordlessly, eyes closed, they swayed to the music, feet hardly moving.

Outside the fireworks glittered again.

'I love you,' Emma said, very softly.

His arms tightened about her. She lifted her face for his kiss; and suddenly they were both fierce with the need for each other. Alex's fingers fumbled with the buttons of her blouse, slipped it from her shoulders and then unclipped the catch of her brassière. His hands were warm, and firm. He dropped to his knees, his mouth at her breasts. Emma gasped, clasped his head to her.

Moments later he pulled away from her, very suddenly, grabbing at the fallen blouse. 'Emma – I'm sorry – darling, I'm sorry!' He scrambled to his feet, put the blouse about her shoulders. His dark eyes glittered in the candlelight. 'I can't think what came over me.'

Emma shook her head. She made no effort to put the blouse back on. 'Don't be sorry,' she said.

'But – you must think—'

'I think you love me.' Despite the calmness of her voice she was trembling uncontrollably. 'And I know I love you.' She shrugged the blouse from her shoulders and stood before him, naked to the waist. 'I want you to make love to me,' she said.

He was very still, his face in shadow. For a moment the

noise in the street seemed to recede, leaving them isolated in an intimate quiet. He shook his head.

'Please,' she said.

'Emma—' Alex too was shaking. He reached a hand to her, cupped her breast gently. 'Oh, Emma!' The words were almost a groan.

'Don't you want me?'

He caught his breath. 'Of *course* I do! How can you ask?'

'Well then—'

He pulled her to him, running his hands up and down the curve of her back, her young skin smooth and warm to his touch. 'I can't,' he said, into her hair, 'I won't risk it.'

'There isn't any risk. Not much, anyway.' She pulled away from him to look into his face, glad that in the flickering light he could not see the colour mounting in hers as she spoke. 'I – found a book. About contraception. About – times of the month and things. And it's all right. Tonight's all right.' She stood very still within his arms, watching him steadily, waiting for him to understand not only what she had said but the implications behind it.

Very, very tenderly he kissed her. 'You're sure?'

'I'm sure.'

She took his hand and led him into the bedroom. The crowds in the street outside had reached the noisy 'knees-up' stage of the celebrations.

They smiled at each other as they undressed and slipped into Emma's narrow bed.

Liam had had a good evening. A very good evening indeed. He had also drunk a large amount of whiskey. As he wandered along the street towards home he hummed to himself; in his hand he held a bottle of champagne, the provenance of which he could not quite, for the moment at least, remember. He remembered the game. He smiled as he recalled it. He remembered the party. That brought another smile. It had been a very good party indeed. He remembered a girl in a red, white and blue dress. A very pretty and amenable girl. Perhaps that was where the champagne had come from?

He shrugged as, still humming to himself, he turned into the dark doorway of his apartment house and switched on the light. Nothing happened. 'Bloody bulb. I swear that harridan landlady uses second-hand ones.' Grinning a little at the thought, he started up the stairs.

The movement on the stairs above him stopped him short. In a moment adrenaline had cleared his head; he stood, still and alert. Very quietly he reversed his hold on the bottle. 'Who's there?'

Another faint movement. Now he could hear breathing. 'Who's there, I say?' he repeated sharply.

'L-Liam. It's m-me—'

Liam stood, thunderstruck. 'Ned? Jesus, Mary and Joseph! What the—?' He ran on up the stairs, nearly fell over the hunched figure who sat, shivering, on the landing outside his door. Ned's shoulders were shaking. 'Wait,' Liam said. 'I'll get some light.' He fumbled for his key, threw open the door, switched on the light.

Ned stumbled after him. He was wearing grey flannels, a grubby white shirt and a blazer with an obviously new rent in the elbow. His face was haggard and wet with tears. His blue eyes were bleak with misery. 'I'm n-not going b-back, Liam. P-Please – you've got to help me – p-please!'

Liam took Ned by the arm, drew him to the large sofa and sat him down. 'Just hold on a minute.' He went to the table, poured two large whiskies, then joined the boy on the sofa. 'Here. Sip it. Slowly.'

Obediently, cupping the glass in both hands, Ned sipped, struggled for a moment, coughed, then sipped again. His hands were shaking violently.

Liam gave him a chance to compose himself, then, 'Now, perhaps you'd best tell me exactly what's going on?' he asked quietly.

# Chapter Eleven

Emma was only half-awake when the telephone rang in the shop downstairs. In her sleepy state and with some diehard revellers still singing outside her window, it took a couple of moments for the sound to register properly.

Alex. It must surely be Alex ringing to say goodnight again?

Suddenly wide awake, she threw on her dressing gown and flew down the stairs. 'Hello?'

There came the harsh rattle of coins into a call box. 'Emma?'

There was a moment's startled silence. Then, 'Yes,' she said. 'Who's that?'

'It's Liam.'

'Liam? What on earth – it's gone one o'clock.'

'I know. I'm sorry. Em, listen. I've only a couple of coppers left. I've got Ned with me.'

'Ned?'

'Yes.'

'But he's supposed to be – oh, no! He hasn't run away again?'

'Yes. In fact – well, it seems it could be rather worse than that.'

'What do you mean?'

'There's been a fire – at the school.'

There was a very long silence.

'Emma?'

'I'm here. Liam, you aren't saying that Ned – that Ned had something to do with this fire?'

'I don't know. He swears not. But it seems that others think differently. Look, Emma, I'm really sorry, but I couldn't think of anyone else to contact – can I bring the lad over to you? He's in an awful state and at the moment won't hear of being taken home.'

'Where are you ringing from?'

'The phone box outside my rooms. I've left Ned upstairs. I don't want to leave him alone for long. Can we come to you?'

'Of course. But, Liam, I'll have to ring Mama. The school will surely have got in touch with her by now – she'll be frantic.'

'The lad thinks it unlikely he'll be missed before morning. He was locked in his room for the night until they could fully investigate what happened. He climbed out of the window. But you must do as you think best. We'll be with you in ten minutes or so. I'll have to go. I'm running out of—' The telephone beeped and went dead.

Emma put the receiver down and stood staring at it, blankly. And then, before she could move, it rang again. She snatched it up.

'Hello?'

'Were you sitting on the telephone?' Alex sounded amused and surprised.

'Alex! Thank goodness.'

'Emma? Is something wrong? I just rang to say goodnight – to tell you I love you.'

'Darling, darling Alex, I love you too. But yes, there is something wrong. Tell me – are your parents home from the party?'

'No. I'm not expecting them for an hour or so yet.' Alex's voice was becoming increasingly concerned. 'Emma, what is it?'

'Darling, would you do something for me? Would you ring and speak as privately as possible to your mother – ask her to warn Mama that Ned's run away from school again, but to tell her he's quite safe. He's gone to Liam. Liam found him on his doorstep. He's bringing him round here – though I'd rather no-one knew that just yet. I just don't want Mama to worry. The school is bound to ring when they find him gone.'

'Oh, Lord!'

'Quite. Liam says he's refusing to go home. I want to talk to Ned, try to persuade him—'

'Your father's going to hit the roof,' Alex put in, uneasily.

'I know.' Emma's voice was grim. 'And presumably so does Ned. That's why he won't go home, of course. But Papa's going to be even more furious if he finds out who he ran to! And that's not all – Liam said something about a fire at the school – oh, what a horrible *muddle!*'

'A fire?'

'Yes. Look, Alex, I'll have to go and get dressed. I'll ring you tomorrow.'

'You're sure you don't want me to come back now?'

Her voice softened. 'Thank you, my love, but no – I can manage. We just need some time to calm Ned down, make him see sense. He'll have to go home sooner or later; the longer he leaves it, the worse it will be.'

'I suppose so.' Alex did not, in fact sound too convinced about that. 'All right, then. I'll ring Mother and tell her. What do we do about your father?'

'I suppose we'd better leave that to your mother; but quite honestly I'd rather no-one told him just yet. If I can persuade Ned to go home, he need never know it was Liam he ran to, or that he came here. It'll only make it worse for Ned if Papa finds that out. You know what he's like.'

'Yes.'

'Once the school rings, Papa's going to turn the world upside down to find him. It'll be much better for Ned to go home of his own accord, as if he went straight there.'

'I hope you can persuade Ned of that.'

'So do I. Darling – I have to go. I love you. I'm going to love you for ever.'

'That's a long time.' His voice was gentle.

'Yes. I know. Goodnight.'

'Goodnight, my love. Try not to worry.'

'I'll try.' She stood for a moment, reluctant to put down the phone, to break the link between them. 'Goodnight,' she said again, very softly, and replaced the receiver before she went to the door, unlocked it, then went into the kitchen to put on the kettle. She was tired, and just a little sore. All she really wanted to do was to curl up in a bed that was still warm from their lovemaking and relive the evening she had just spent with Alex.

Sighing, she plodded upstairs to get dressed.

She suspected it might turn into a very long night.

'He'll kill me,' Ned said again, miserably and for about the hundredth time. 'You know he will.'

Emma and Liam exchanged weary glances. Stubble rasped, as Liam rubbed tiredly at his face with his open hands.

'Not if you haven't done anything,' Emma said, stubbornly. 'If they were going to punish you for something you didn't do, then he can't get that mad at you for running away. Can he?' The words were almost pleading. 'Ned – you didn't do it, did you? Set the fire?'

Not for the first time the drowned, flower-blue eyes dropped from hers. 'No.'

Liam reached for the makings of a cigarette.

Outside, the faintest of light was beginning to wash into the sky.

Emma had seen that look on her brother's face before. Her heart sank. 'Then, Ned, why do they think you did?'

His head came up fiercely. 'Because the Head's got it in for me, that's why! He always has. He'll always believe anyone but me—' Ned stopped abruptly.

'And – is there an "anyone" in this case who they might

believe?' Liam asked, very quietly, into the silence that followed.

Ned's soft mouth tightened for a moment, then he muttered, miserably defiant, 'Denby Major.'

'And will you tell us just what this Denby Major might have to say?' Liam pressed.

'A lie. A huge, huge *lie!*' The tears were beginning to run again.

'You might as well tell us, Ned,' Emma said, tiredly. 'We'll find out in the end, you know we will.'

Ned dropped his head, muttering something.

'What?'

'*I said: he says he saw me!*' Ned suddenly lost control completely. 'He's lying! He's *lying!*' He flung himself sideways on Emma's bed, where he was sitting, crying hysterically again.

'Jesus, Mary and Joseph,' Liam said, tiredly conversational.

Emma closed her eyes for a moment. 'Oh, Ned.'

'I didn't do it! I *didn't!*'

'Why would this boy say such a thing if it weren't true?'

'Because he hates me. They all hate me! Emma, don't make me go home! *Please* don't make me go home!'

Liam hunkered down beside him and rested a hand on the tousled head. 'You can't run away for ever, lad,' he said, not unsympathetically. 'You must know that. We've got to get this thing sorted out, and the only way to do so is for you to go home and face it. Emma's right. The longer you stay away, the harder it will be.'

The boy's shoulders heaved.

'Think of Mama, Ned,' Emma said. 'Think how worried she'll be. She hasn't been at all well.'

An all-night reveller shouted in the street outside.

Ned sat up, looked at his sister, then at Liam. 'You don't believe me, do you?'

'Of course we do.' Emma's reply was too quick. Liam said nothing.

Ned watched him. 'If you don't believe me,' he said, 'then no-one will.'

'I believe you,' Liam lied. 'But I also believe that the only thing you can do is go home and face it.'

'That's what you'd do, isn't it?'

'Yes.'

'Once they know you're gone they'll find you, Ned. You know it. We can't hide you for ever.' Emma herself was on the verge of tears.

There was a long moment of hesitation. Then Ned took a deep breath; he was trembling visibly. 'I – suppose you're right,' he whispered. He seemed almost not to realise that he was still crying.

'I'll come with you. As far as the end of the road,' Liam said, gently.

'Thank you.' Ned stood up, like a frightened and obedient child.

Emma put her arms about him and hugged him hard. Long and adolescently lank, he was a good head taller than her. 'Call me if you need me.'

'I will.'

'Come on, lad.' Liam put an arm about his shoulders. 'Let's get it over with.'

They walked through the pale light of the breaking dawn in silence. The streets, full of the tattered detritus of celebration, looked slovenly. Red, white and blue streamers and favours littered the gutters and pavements. Half-deflated balloons drifted along the pavements and hung tangled in the branches of the trees. A noisy crowd of youngsters was singing and dancing in a small park; a man in evening dress snoozed in a doorway. At the corner of the crescent where the Cloughs lived they stopped. There were still lights on in the house, though it was impossible to tell if that were simply because of the celebrations of the previous night or because news of the runaway had already arrived.

Ned stood numbly for a moment, breathing hard, his lips trembling.

Liam extended a hand. 'Good luck.'

'Thanks.' The word was whispered. The hand that shook Liam's was soft, and slick with sweat.

'Come and see me whenever you want,' Liam said.

The boy nodded.

'And Ned—' Liam paused. Ned waited. 'Don't let him bully you. Try to stand up to him. Whatever you have or haven't done, whatever happens, try to do that.'

Tears were running down the thin, fair face again. With no further word Ned turned from him and walked quickly away. Liam watched as he reached the foot of the steps, hesitated for a moment, then ran up them and rang the doorbell. Drawing back in the shadows, Liam waited until the door had opened and the boy had disappeared inside; then, scowling blackly and with his hands bunched into fists in his pocket, he turned and walked away.

It was three days before Liam learned what happened in the Clough household that morning.

In the past months, since the incident with the lighter, he and Christine had taken to meeting on an *ad hoc* basis at the bookshop, and from there going on, perhaps to the pictures or a pub or, very occasionally – and, in a sense, rather more dangerously – back to his rooms around the corner. Their relationship – if it could truly yet be called such – was an odd but stimulating mixture of challenge and friendship, of mutual sexual attraction and a certain stubborn insistence on denying, or at least resisting, that attraction. They were two independent and overly headstrong individuals, each believing themselves to be well aware of what was at stake; neither was ready to give in to the other; both, rightly or wrongly, believed that that was what the other would demand. They quarrelled almost as frequently as they laughed, often in public, sometimes just for the sake of it and on a precarious scale of severity that ranged from mild and teasing malice through impatient and provocative scorn to a sometimes quite spectacular flare-up of temper that bordered on verbal, if not physical, violence. Both were wary, both quick to take offence; yet over the months the fascination between them had grown steadily. On many an occasion an exasperated Liam had told himself to pull himself together and find himself a girl less likely to cause mayhem in his life; on even more occasions Christine had stalked away, determined never to see or speak to him again. But always they met again, even if sometimes they did pretend it to be by accident.

On the Sunday after the Coronation, however, Christine's visit had been surreptitiously arranged over the telephone, and Emma, at Christine's request, had sent a note round to Liam's lodgings. Christine herself was strained and sub-dued. She, Liam, Alex and Emma sat on Emma's newly-acquired three-piece suite in a room that smelt of paint and distemper, drinking the tart red wine that an Off Licence in the next street dispensed from barrels, and which was all that Emma could afford.

'So – how is it at home?' Emma asked, with some trepi-dation. She was so unused to seeing her usually vivacious and confident sister in a mood like this that she found it positively unnerving.

'Awful.' Even Christine's voice was tired. 'Just awful.' She sat looking into her glass for a moment.

Alex opened his mouth to speak. Emma caught his eye and shook her head a little, gently.

'The school insists that it has irrefutable evidence that Ned set the fire. They won't take him back.' Christine's mouth twisted in the faintest shadow of a totally humour-less smile. 'They have resisted Papa's every threat and blandishment. For once, he isn't going to get his way. Ned's expelled for good.' She took a deep breath, exhaled slowly. 'Apparently this isn't the first time he's caused trouble – though it's certainly the worst.'

'Then why didn't they say something?' Emma could not restrain her indignation. 'Why didn't they tell us?'

Her sister turned a weary face to her. 'Apparently they

did. They telephoned, several times. On each occasion it was Mama who took the call, Mama who went to the school and smoothed things over. You know how often Papa has been away these last couple of years.'

'You mean – she didn't tell him?' Emma was aghast.

Christine shook her head. 'No.'

'Oh, Lord,' Alex said very quietly.

Liam, leaning forward in his chair, his elbows on his knees, head bent, looking at no-one, his face set and inscrutable, said nothing.

'What – what did Papa do?' Emma asked.

For a moment Christine did not speak. When she did her voice was flat, almost entirely devoid of expression. 'He took a strap to Ned. It was awful. Brutal. I've never heard anything so—' She stopped abruptly, squeezing her eyes fiercely shut, obviously controlling tears. It seemed like a long time before she went on, 'Then Papa locked him in his room.'

A muscle was throbbing in Liam's jaw.

'None of us has been allowed to see or speak to him since.' She took a very large and slightly clumsy mouthful of her wine. The room was quiet as the grave. Christine took a deep breath. 'Then, of course, he started on Mama. Oh – not physically. He didn't have to. There are more ways than one to tear someone apart. And he knows them all. He shouldn't do it!' Her voice was suddenly passionate. 'She can't help the way she is! She isn't well! I tried to tell him, *tried* to stop him.' She stopped again, shook her head tiredly. 'He threw me from the room. Locked the door. There was nothing I could do.'

Liam lifted his head. The blue gleam of his eyes was very cold. 'Sure, wouldn't you say he's a brave man, that father of yours?' he asked quietly, with all the singing accent of Ireland suddenly stronger than ever in his voice.

Emma's eyes had filled with tears. Alex put out a hand and took hers, pressing it reassuringly. 'What's going to happen now?' he asked.

'I'm not sure. Mama seems to have collapsed completely. I truly fear she's having some kind of breakdown. She cries all the time. She won't eat. Won't leave her bed.' Christine glanced at Liam with a tired but warmer smile. 'Your mother has been wonderful. I don't know how she's done it, but she's stood up to Papa and somehow talked him into letting her look after Mama.'

'And Ned?' Liam asked.

Christine shook her head. 'I don't know. Papa has the keys to his room. I called through the door, but Ned won't answer.' Suddenly she dropped her head into her hand, pressing hard against her forehead as if to wipe out a thought. 'Papa did beat him horribly,' she whispered. 'I think he might need a doctor. I don't know what to do.'

Without a word Liam, moving abruptly, stood up, reached for his jacket, slung it across one shoulder and strode to the door.

Christine's head came up sharply. 'Liam? Where are you going?'

'I'm going to Holland Park.' His voice was cold and sharp as flint, the words, though quiet, ground out through fury. 'I'm going to break down that bloody door. And if your bloody father gets in my bloody way, I'm going to break his bloody neck.' He turned.

'No!' It was Alex who reached him first, though Christine too had jumped from her seat. Despite the flare of danger in Liam's eyes, Alex barred the doorway with his arm. 'Liam, no! Think!' His voice was urgent. 'What good would that do? Who will suffer in the end? Ned himself, most likely. Possibly Christine. Certainly your own mother, and through her Aunt Siobhan.'

In his outrage and anger Liam had not made that connection. He scowled.

'You aren't supposed to have anything to do with the household, remember? If you turn up there raging and lashing out, the first thing George is going to want to know is where the hell you came from and how you knew what was going on.'

'*I sent the boy back there!*'

'No.' It was Emma who spoke, as urgently as Alex. 'We sent him back. You and I. And in the same circumstances we would have to do it again. There wasn't anything else to do. But Alex is right. Storming in there and breaking Papa's neck – however satisfying it might be to do it,' the words were grim, 'won't solve anything and will very probably make things worse. If Papa thinks your mother told you he might send her away, and if—' she hesitated, shook her head, 'if he finds out that Christine or Ned has had anything to do with you—' She lifted her shoulders in an expressive shrug.

Liam stood for a moment, fists bunched, tense as a coiled spring. Alex did not remove the arm that barred his way. Then, with an audible exhalation, Liam tossed his jacket back over the arm of the chair and turned to walk to the window, where he stood with his arms tightly crossed and his back to the room. There was a long silence.

It was Christine who broke it. 'Liam's right in one way,' she said, 'we can't do *nothing*.'

Emma shook her head helplessly. 'What can we do?'

Liam turned, a sudden gleam in his eye. 'It would help, wouldn't it,' he asked slowly, 'if you could get in to see the lad?'

'Well, yes, of course it would. But I told you – Papa has both the keys. He took Mary's from her, too. There's no way to get to him.'

Liam's expression had relaxed a little; there was something close to a smile in his narrowed eyes. 'Oh, but there is,' he said, and held out a hand to pull her from the chair. 'Come on.' He reached again for his jacket.

'Where to?' Christine was puzzled.

This time he really did smile. 'My place,' he said.

'What for?'

'Woman, will you never stop asking questions?' The grim

smile widened. 'You're about to discover one of the benefits of a misspent youth.'

'That's the way. Feel for it. You're nearly there – gently, gently.'

'Got it!' Christine was kneeling on the floor in front of the door to Liam's rooms. 'I felt it – there!' With a soft snick the lock released. She turned the handle; the door opened. 'I did it! I did it!' She looked up excitedly at Liam.

'Ah-ah.' He put up a warning hand. 'You've got to lock it again now, remember.' He leaned forward and pulled the door closed. 'Off you go – no, no cheating.' Christine had folded her fingers around the handles of the skeleton keys she had been manoeuvring in the lock. 'Take them out and start again.' He watched her as, face intent, her fingers sensitive on the keys, head turned a little as she listened to what she was doing, she manipulated the things again.

Again the lock clicked. 'There!' Pushing her hair back from her face, she sat back on her heels, triumphant.

'Sure, you'd make a wonderful cat burglar,' he said, softly.

She grinned like a child, jingled the keys in her hand.

'Now the other one,' Liam said.

'What?'

'The bedroom door.' Liam pointed. 'Try that one.'

'But—'

He shook his head. 'You've got to practice finding which keys fit which lock. Try the bedroom.' He reached a hand to pull her to her feet. She came fluently and with no resistance; so much so that he found he had pulled her towards him and they were standing, hand in hand, bodies touching.

She lifted her head to look into his face. 'Is that an invitation?' she asked, eyes innocent and wide.

'Behave yourself.' He did not move.

Christine raised her sharp, fair eyebrows, wrinkled her nose mischievously, stepped away from him.

For a moment Liam veiled his eyes with the curled sweep of his lashes, but she saw and understood the look and laughed delightedly. 'You pour the whiskey,' she said, with brisk confidence, 'I'll pick the lock.'

And, at a speed commendable for a novice, she did. Liam watched her as she scrambled to her feet and fitted the normal key back into the lock. 'There,' she said proudly, 'how's that?'

'If you ever fall on hard times,' he said, straight-faced, 'then you've a skill at your fingertips that'll make good and sure you don't starve.'

'Speaking of which—' She sauntered to the table, laid the keys upon it and picked up her glass. Her eyes were thoughtful upon his face. 'Would it be impertinent to ask just how *you* came to acquire such a skill?'

'Yes,' he said, tranquilly, 'it would.'

'I thought it might, somehow.' She sipped her drink, her eyes not leaving his. 'But then – I'm an impertinent kind of person, aren't I?'

'Ask away.' His tone had not changed, his smile was bland.

'Would you answer me?'

'No.'

She hitched herself up on to the table, sat nursing her drink, feet swinging. 'Not much point then, is there?' She tried to keep up the bantering tone, but Liam could almost feel the sudden mood swing that shortened her voice.

He reached out a hand and touched her arm. The eyes that lifted to his were dark with worry. 'This will help a little, won't it?' she asked, doubtfully. 'If we can get in to see him, cheer him up a bit—' She trailed off, biting her lip.

'It can't go on for ever,' he said, reassuringly. 'Your father can't treat him like this for long.'

'He's trying to make him admit that he set the fire.'

'And Ned won't?'

'No.'

'Perhaps he didn't?'

She did not reply, but the flick of her glance was telling enough.

'Surely he would have admitted it if he had? He has nothing to gain now, has he, by denying it?'

She shook her head. 'It's not that. It's – a sort of stubbornness. And a—' she hesitated, searching for words, 'a kind of self-deception, too, I think. I wouldn't be at all surprised if he hadn't convinced himself that he *hadn't* started the fire. Because that would make him the victim of a cruel injustice, rather than a naughty boy who doesn't know how to behave. Oh, Papa shouldn't have beaten him like that. He shouldn't! But if Ned *has* been behaving so badly – badly enough to get himself expelled, wickedly enough to put people's lives at risk – then he does deserve *some* kind of punishment. But he can't accept that. He won't accept it. He thinks he can do as he likes; it comes hard to him to discover that he can't. I sometimes wonder—'

'What?' he prompted.

She cocked her head to look at him. 'I sometimes wonder,' she said, soberly, 'if Ned can actually tell right from wrong.'

He shook his head. 'Too deep for me.'

'Perhaps I'm wrong.' She drained her glass, jumped from the table, picked up the keys. 'I hope I am.' She lifted her face to him and smiled, briefly. There was something so valiant in the way that she stood, small and straight, the keys in her hand, that suddenly, and to his own astonishment, Liam was overwhelmed by a wave of tenderness.

Very carefully he cupped her face in his hands, bent his mouth to hers, kissed her very gently and for a long time. Then, equally gently, he folded his arms about her, holding her against him. For the briefest of moments, eyes closed, she rested her head on his chest. He could feel the tension in her. 'It'll be all right,' he said, into her hair.

'Of course it will.' She stepped away from him. Her eyes were suspiciously bright. 'I'd better go.'

'Sure.' He saw her to the door, opened it and kissed her lightly before she stepped through it. 'Just one thing—'

'Yes?'

'The keys. When you've done with them, I'll be having them back, if you please.'

That brought a real smile. 'Afraid I'll use them for nefarious purposes?'

'I wouldn't put anything past you,' he said.

And meant it.

At least she left laughing.

# *Chapter Twelve*

Six weeks after her son was expelled from school Siobhan Clough was admitted to a private mental institution in Croydon, south London. A few weeks' complete rest was the specialist's recommendation; she was to be allowed neither telephone calls nor visitors. Her breakdown came as no surprise to anyone; Siobhan had never been particularly strong, and the strain of coping with what had happened – and with her husband's reaction to it – had simply, and perhaps predictably, proved too much for her.

'For once I have to say that I think Papa is right,' Christine told Liam. 'She needs help. It seems odd at home without her, though.'

'How's Ned coping?' They were strolling through Hyde Park on a warm July day. Office workers in their dinner breaks were taking advantage of the good weather, sitting on benches or sprawled on the grass, their pale, city faces turned to the sun.

'Better than I expected, actually. You know Ned – if he gets his own way he's happy – regardless of what's going on in anyone else's life, even Mama's. And that, really, is what's happened. He's got out of Belfairs. He's enrolled in the day school that Josie and Tom go to, to finish studying for his Matric. and School Cert. – which is what he has always wanted. He's even singing in the school choir; he loves that. And Papa is spending more time than ever away from home – in Hampstead, I assume – so really we get to do more or less what we like.'

'How are Ned and your father getting along?'

Christine shrugged. 'Ned keeps his head down and does as he's told. To be honest, I get the feeling that Papa is a bit ashamed of what happened – the beating, I mean. And, as I say, he's hardly ever at home anyway. He's off to America again in a couple of days.' She walked on in silence for a moment, her face pensive. 'I do hope Mama is going to be all right,' she added.

Touched by the sudden uncertainty in her voice, Liam took her hand. 'She will. To be sure, she will.'

Christine smiled a little. 'That's exactly what your mother said.' She cocked her head to look up at him. 'Liam, why don't you come and see her? I told you – Papa's going away, and I know Mary would be pleased to see you.'

Liam was shaking his head. 'I've not been invited,' he said, gently.

'Yes, you have. I just invited you.'

'You know what I mean.'

'But why? Why be so stubborn? Mary's done nothing to you.'

'It isn't what she's done to me, it's what I did to her. I broke a solemn promise.'

'Then for goodness' sake, come and see her. Talk to her.'

'She'll let me know when she wants to see me.'

Christine stopped, shaking her head exasperatedly. 'If you aren't the most obstinate pair I've ever come across—'

He bent to kiss her, lightly, stopping the words on her lips. 'Got time for a quick drink?'

She grinned at the unsubtle change of subject, but shook her head reluctantly. 'I'd better get back to work. We've got some Americans coming this afternoon, and I'm supposed to be looking after them.'

'Lucky Americans. Come on. I'll walk you back.'

*    *    *

Of all the people who were close to Siobhan it was perhaps Pamela Barker who missed her the most. For years they had seen or spoken to each other virtually every day; they were as much like sisters as friends. She hated the thought of Siobhan being alone amongst strangers, fretted at what might be happening to her.

'I don't understand why she can't have visitors,' she said for perhaps the dozenth time to her husband. 'It doesn't seem right to isolate her so. I've a good mind to go anyway – they surely wouldn't turn me away?'

'I think they probably would, my love. Not even George is allowed to see her for a while. It's part of the treatment, so he said. She is to be kept absolutely quiet.'

'But—'

David shook his head. 'They must know what they're doing. And she did agree to go, remember. She wasn't forced against her will.'

Pamela sighed. 'I know. I know. I just wish I could talk to her. I wonder how long they'll keep her there?'

'Emma said at least a month.' Alex unfolded his long frame from the chair in which he had been sitting and stretched. 'Gosh, I'm hungry. Isn't it time to eat yet?'

His mother smiled. 'You're always hungry! Supper's a little late tonight. I'm waiting for the others.'

'What are they up to?'

'It's Tom's Flying Corps night, Josie's stopped off at a friend's house and Lottie's doing something mysterious.'

'Oh? How mysterious?'

'I've no idea.' Pamela spread her hands expressively. 'You know Lottie. She just said she'd be home for supper, but she'd be a bit late.'

David had folded his paper and walked to the window, looking out at the street. 'Here she comes now. Whatever she's been doing, it looks as though she enjoyed it. She looks remarkably pleased with herself.'

Lottie was indeed pleased with herself. She positively

danced into the house. 'Hello, everyone. Guess what?' She stopped, smiling mischievously, enjoying being the centre of attention, her great, pale eyes sparkling.

Pamela indulged her. 'What?'

'I—' Lottie performed a small twirl in the centre of the room and her skirt lifted, swirling about her slim legs, 'I have got a new job.'

Alex blinked. 'A *job*? I thought the way you were carrying on you must at least have won the pools! You don't like jobs!'

'I like this one.'

Her father smiled affectionately at her. 'What makes this one so special?'

'It's with *Patrick Hampton*!' Lottie paused for dramatic effect, only to be met by three completely blank stares. 'The society photographer! *The* society photographer!' she corrected herself. 'I met him at a party a little while ago. He said he was looking for a receptionist-cum-assistant. I applied. And hey presto! I got it. What do you think of that?'

'It sounds very nice, dear,' said Pamela.

'Oh, *Mother*! Very *nice*? It's absolutely *swagger*!'

'Darling, I do wish you wouldn't use that slang.' The reproach was mild.

Lottie turned her eyes to the ceiling.

'Is the pay good?' David asked, cautiously.

Lottie tossed her handbag on to a chair, then walked to the mirror over the mantelpiece to smooth her bright lipstick with the tip of her little finger. 'It's OK. But that's not it. Just imagine who I'm going to *meet*! Patrick photographs just anyone who's anyone. He knows the Prince of Wales – sorry, the ex-king, or whatever he is now. Patrick took Wallis Simpson's photograph, in Paris, before they got married. He knows absolutely *everyone*. And everyone who knows *me* is going to just *die* of envy. You should see the studio. It's gorgeous. Very swish. I'm to have a clothes allowance.'

Pamela was eyeing her now with just the slightest alarm. 'Is this gentleman married?' she asked.

'Oh, *Mother!*' Lottie twirled again. 'When's supper?'

'When the two youngsters get in. Half an hour or so.'

'Right. That gives me time to have a bath. I'm going dancing with Richard later.' She was gone, a slender, perfumed whirlwind of quick laughter and exaggerated gestures.

'Who's Richard?' David asked a little bemusedly into the silence.

'Search me.' Alex grinned. 'You'd need a memory like an elephant's to keep up with Lottie's boyfriends.'

Later that evening he was in the kitchen with his mother, wiping the supper plates as she washed them. Pamela eyed him. 'You're very quiet all at once?'

Alex pulled a small, rueful face. 'I wanted to talk to you. And now I don't know where to start.'

Pamela raised her brows in mild amusement. 'I wondered what was behind the unusual eagerness to wipe up. Oh, don't be silly,' she added quickly as he opened his mouth to protest, 'I'm only joking. Tell you what,' she smiled a little slyly, 'shall I start for you?'

He sucked his lip.

'Emma?' she suggested, gently.

He nodded.

'Is something wrong?'

'No. Oh, no.' The words were quick. 'Far from it. It's just—' He shrugged, let the words trail off.

Pamela took the tea towel from him and dried her hands on it. 'Come and sit down for a minute.' She guided him to the kitchen table, pulled out a chair for him and then went to sit opposite him, her elbows on the table, her chin in her hands, waiting.

Alex looked down at his own hands, loosely linked before him. 'I love her,' he said, quietly.

'I know you do.'

'And she loves me.'

'I know that too.'

His head came up very suddenly. 'Mother – what are we going to *do*?'

She shook her head. 'At the moment there's nothing you can do.' The words were practical, but her eyes were sympathetic. 'Marriage is out of the question. Emma is under twenty-one. And, the way things are at the moment, it's most unlikely that George would give his consent.'

'We both know that.' He was clicking his thumbnails together, the nervy, rhythmic clicking loud in the quiet room.

'Darling, you'll just have to wait. In eighteen months or so Emma will come of age. Then she doesn't need her parents' consent.'

He lifted his head again, looking at her. 'What about you?' he asked.

She was silent for a moment. 'I already think of Emma as a daughter,' she began.

'That isn't what I mean.' He shook his head stubbornly. The line of his mouth was unhappy. 'I know how you feel about Aunt Siobhan. I know how much she needs you. If Emma and I defy her father – and we both know he'll be against our marrying, even after she doesn't need his permission – then he might come between you two. Oh, heck!' he muttered. 'Why do people have to complicate things so?'

'George,' Pamela commented drily, 'in my view has always managed to complicate things just by being there. Are you so sure he wouldn't approve?'

'Emma is. She knows him better than most. Whether she stays where she is, or gives in and goes back, he'd stand against what she wanted, just to punish her.'

'Is she thinking of going back?'

'No. Of course not. She loves it at the shop. She loves being independent. The only reason she would even consider going home is if she thought there was a hope in hell

– sorry – any hope at all that she could persuade her father to let us marry. I'd be willing to wait until I'd qualified. I'd be willing to do almost *anything* – but it won't make any difference. Emma and I have talked and talked about it. I'm sure she's right. He'll stick out against us, just for the sake of it. It wouldn't matter if it weren't for you and Aunt Siobhan. Emma's so worried about her mother. And I'd hate to do anything to hurt you.'

Pamela stood up and came around the table to him. He lifted a worried face to her; to his mother's eye, Alex suddenly looked quite heartbreakingly young. She put an arm about his shoulders, laid her face on his dark hair for a moment. 'When it comes to it, you must do what's best for you and for Emma. You have your lives ahead of you. We'll take care of ourselves. But meanwhile worrying about it isn't doing any good. You never know what's around the corner. Perhaps things will change. And whatever happens, the year after next you can marry, with or without George's permission.' She hesitated before adding gently, 'Perhaps it's not such a bad thing to give yourselves a breathing space anyway, you know.'

It took a moment for that to sink in. Then he pulled away from her, shaking his head fiercely. 'We won't change our minds. We won't!'

She dropped a quick kiss on to his head. 'Then eighteen months won't make that much of a difference, will it?'

'It seems like a lifetime!' he said, gloomily.

She laughed a little. 'The impatience of the young!'

He shook his head again, pushed the chair away from the table and stood up. His face was suddenly very serious, the youth that had so touched her a few moments before entirely gone, overlaid by a purely adult gravity. 'You said it yourself. Perhaps things will change. Perhaps they will. Perhaps there'll be a war.'

'Alex! Don't say such things!'

'You have to face it, Mother. It could happen. Then

perhaps eighteen months is going to seem like a long time to everyone.'

She gave him a little push. 'Oh, don't be such an old down-in-the-mouth! Go on – off you go. Go and listen to the wireless with your father. I'll finish up in here.'

He bent to kiss her cheek. 'Thanks.'

After he had gone she stood leaning against the table for a long moment, her eyes distant.

*Perhaps there'll be a war. Then perhaps eighteen months is going to seem like a long time to everyone.*

Out of the mouths of babes—

'No,' she said aloud, as if her very determination could make it so. 'No, no, no!' and she went back to finish the washing up, very noisily.

'I could always get pregnant,' Emma said, yawning. 'That'd put the cat among the pigeons, wouldn't it?'

Alex tucked his head more comfortably upon her shoulder. 'Don't be daft.' The words were fond. He rested a hand upon her breast, stroking the nipple gently. 'You're still under-age, your father could still refuse permission, and Lord only knows what might happen then. No. Mother's right. We'll wait until you're twenty-one and then we'll do things properly.' He turned his head to kiss her. 'I love you. That's all that matters.'

She smiled a little sleepily. 'How many children shall we have?'

'Oh, at least a dozen.'

'And where shall we live?'

He looked at her, mildly surprised. 'I can't say I'd thought about that.'

'I have. Once you're qualified we could live anywhere, couldn't we? You could set up your own practice in a little country town somewhere. Somewhere pretty, and quiet. Somewhere with hills and woods. Or perhaps by the sea. Somewhere we can have dogs, and ponies – what are you laughing at?'

'You.' He leaned on his elbows and kissed the tip of her nose. 'I didn't realise what an old romantic you are.'

'I'm not being romantic. I'm being very practical.' She wound her arms about his neck and pulled him to her, nibbling his ear. 'Think on. With all those children about, we're going to need a lot of space.'

Mary McCarthy turned up at Liam's rooms on a sultry August evening that gave warning of storms to come. Liam was so surprised when he opened the door to her knock that he stood for a moment, speechless. Then, 'Ma?' he said. She was smaller, and dumpier, than he remembered. Her long hair, greying a little now, had been cut short, and was fashionably – and severely – permanently waved.

'To be sure,' she said, composedly and as if they had last seen each other the day before, 'Christine and I had a little chat. Mahomet and the mountain were mentioned. Are you not going to invite me in?'

'Of course.' He stepped back, waving a hand, a sudden smile lighting his face. He had been getting ready to go out; he was in his shirtsleeves, and a tie dangled from his fingers.

She walked past him, angled her cheek for his kiss. He bent to her and obliged. She smelled of rose-water, as she always did. She stood looking about the room.

'Sit down, sit down.' Ridiculously Liam suddenly found himself nervous, almost tongue-tied. 'Will I get you something? Tea?'

She smiled. 'I won't be keeping you. I can see you're going out. I just wanted—' she hesitated, shrugged a little, 'I just felt it was time to break the ice between us. Christine is right. This is no way for mother and son to behave.' She studied his face for a moment. 'She's right about something else, too. You've grown into a fine man,' she said, softly.

Liam tossed the tie on to a chair. 'Sit you down,' he said. 'I'll make the tea. We've a lot to catch up on.'

'Are you not going out?'

'Later.' He kissed her again, very lightly, on the cheek. 'I've all the time in the world.'

'So. 'Tis a gambler you are.' Mary set her empty cup on the table. 'I suppose I shouldn't be surprised, given your bloodline.'

'Do you mind?'

She shrugged. ''Tis none of my business. You're a man grown, and you'll do as you wish.' She glanced around the room. 'At least you don't seem to be doing too badly from it.'

'Oh, I've me fingers in a fair few pies.' Liam was amused to realise that, talking to his mother, his own accent had deepened. 'I've a couple of greyhounds, and a share in a promising horse.' In consideration of his mother's peace of mind he thought it best to omit any mention of his even more profitable interest in an illegal gambling club in Soho. Broad-minded she might be, but he somehow doubted her broad-mindedness would stretch that far. He sipped his drink, and decided a change of subject might be diplomatic. 'How's Mrs Clough?'

A shadow flickered in his mother's eyes. 'She's having visitors now at least. I went to see her yesterday. I hate that place. Oh, 'tis posh enough, and comfortable. But Jesus only knows what they've been doing to the poor lamb. I want her out of there. I've suggested we might go down to the cottage for a few weeks. She can rest just as well down there, with me to care for her. God forgive that husband of hers for what he's done to her,' she added. The words, to Liam's surprise, contained more of venom than of piety. He had never heard her speak so openly bitterly of George before, though he had always known of her dislike of the man.

'To say nothing of what he did to Ned,' he put in, quietly.

'The man's a barbarian.' Mary stood up, her face bright with indignation. 'And no amount of money and fancy manners can disguise the fact. He should be horsewhipped for what he did to that lad.'

Liam, too, stood up. 'Perhaps it can be arranged,' he said, smiling a little grimly.

'Ah!' His mother lifted a sharp, warning finger, shook her head. 'You stay away from him. Get anywhere near him and he'll cause you nothing but grief.'

Liam grinned. 'Not here two minutes, Ma, and you're ordering me about already?'

She refused to be drawn to laughter. 'I mean it, Liam. Stay away from him. He's done enough damage. Don't be giving him a chance to do more.' She hesitated. He waited, guessing what might be coming. 'If I had my way,' his mother said at last, her eyes very steady on his, 'you'd stay away from the whole family.'

Liam shook his head. 'Why should I? They're my friends.'

'Friends, is it?' she asked, softly.

He felt a slight colour rise in his cheeks. The night before he had taken Christine out to dinner and they had come back to this very room for a nightcap. The evening had been an interesting one. 'Of course,' he said, trying not to remember the softness of her mouth, the smoothness of her skin.

His mother might have read his mind. She walked to the door. Somewhere in the distance, thunder rumbled. At the door she turned. 'You're out with Christine at the weekend, I hear,' she said, 'in the new car.'

'Yes.'

This time she did smile. 'I wish you luck,' she said, and shook her neatly permed head, laughing at his enquiring look. 'You'll find out for yourself. Now – in the name of the saints, is your old mother not to have a kiss before she leaves?'

On Saturday morning he did indeed discover for himself the meaning of Mary's words. Christine drove like a maniac, apparently blithely oblivious to all other traffic. She drove her little Austin 7 through the streets of London as if she were practising for a Keystone Kops car chase, an impatient hand never far from the horn. Even once out on the open road and heading into the Kentish countryside she could not, apparently, see a car ahead of her without trying to overtake it.

'Are we in a hurry?' Liam asked at last as she swerved around a haycart and accelerated off again. 'Do we have an appointment to keep? I thought this was going to be a quiet day out in the country?'

'It is.' She glanced at him, looking genuinely surprised. 'But we've got to get there, haven't we? What's the matter?'

He shook his head, half-laughing. 'Nothing. Nothing at all. Where are we going?'

'I thought you might like to see the cottage.' She slammed a foot on the brake barely feet before they reached a junction. 'It's really nice and in a very pretty spot. Light me a cigarette, would you?'

In a slightly wary silence he took her cigarettes from the glove compartment, lit one and handed it to her. 'Is that a good idea?'

'What?'

'The cottage. Your parents.'

She shook her head. 'I told you – Papa's away. And Mama – well, I just told her I was going to take a spin out with a friend to give the place an airing ready for her and Mary. She was quite happy about it.'

'But you omitted to explain that I was the friend?'

'Yes.'

Liam, rolling a cigarette, said nothing.

She glanced at him. 'Do you mind?'

'Mind?'

'Being the world's best-kept secret, so to speak.'

He shrugged. 'Why should I mind?' But the words were neither light nor particularly convincing.

She reached a hand to touch his knee. 'Wait,' she said. 'Let's just wait and see what happens. Meanwhile we've got today. And a glorious day it is. Mary's packed us lots of goodies. Now, there's a lane along here somewhere – ah! – there it is.' She executed another bumper-car turn into a narrow lane. 'Through the village, up the hill, and we're there.'

The cottage was indeed very pretty, and in an idyllic setting. It was long and low and tile-hung in the Kentish manner, with three tall brick chimneys. The walls were a riot of climbers, and tall trees dwarfed the building. The little garden was laid out on the slight slope of the hillside and the views were breathtaking.

'Nice, isn't it?' Christine asked, casually, as she fitted the key into the lock of the back door.

'Sure, and isn't that the English understatement of the year?' Liam said quietly. He was standing looking out over the valley, eyes narrowed against the smoke of his cigarette, hat tipped to the back of his head. He had an odd and idiosyncratic way of standing at such moments, his weight settled relaxedly on to his left leg, narrow hips slightly askew.

Christine turned to look, not at the view, but at him. She watched him for a long moment and then, very quickly, turned back and pushed open the door. 'Come on. Let's get the windows open.'

The interior was spacious yet somehow cosy, with big open fireplaces, polished wooden floors, leaded windows. The kitchen was flagged and big enough to give space to two large, squashy armchairs next to the fireplace, as well as a range and a pine table and chairs. The rest of the house was furnished simply but very comfortably; Liam could see why Siobhan loved it so.

'Do you like it?' Christine asked, as she flung open the long French doors of the sitting room, which opened out on to the pretty garden and the view of the valley.

'Very much.' He watched as she stepped through the doors and shaded her eyes to look across the valley. A wide river wound a lazy, willow-lined path through verdant pastures that were dotted with great stands of trees: oak,

elm and chestnut. The cattle looked like toys on a child's
model farm. On the far side of the river the hop gardens
glimmered in the sunshine, their rows of bines orderly as
a green regiment of guards. 'I can see why Ma wants to
bring your mother here. It'll do her good, I should think.'

'Yes.' Christine turned with that quick, bright smile that
lit her face like sunshine. 'I'm so pleased she's out of that
horrible place. She'll be much better off down here with
Mary, I'm sure. Now – shall we eat? Then, if you'd like,
we can go for a walk. There's a footpath just a little way
up the road. It goes on up to the top of the hill. The view's
even better from there. You fetch the hamper, I'll get the
crockery and things.'

They ate in the garden at a rickety table set under a
tree. Mary had packed sandwiches, hard-boiled eggs, cakes,
lemonade and wine.

'Why does food always taste better outdoors?' Christine
asked, munching her egg.

He shook his head, smiling, and sipped his wine. 'You
asked me that once before, remember?'

'Why, so I did!' Her eyes were bright at the recollection.
'At Ahakista! Lovely, lovely Ahakista! I think of it often.
Shall we go there again one day, do you think?

He smiled, but said nothing. A bird sang, clear and
beautiful in the sheltering tree.

Christine turned her head to listen, smiled her warm
smile. She reached across the table to take his hand. 'Isn't
it funny how some moments are – just perfect?' she asked,
quietly.

In answer he lifted her fingertips to his lips and touched
them, very gently, with his tongue.

She shivered.

He emptied his glass. 'Come on. Let's clear this lot up
and go find your hilltop.'

They walked the wooded path hand in hand. Squirrels
skittered through the leaves and the air rang with birdsong.
Somewhere, far away, there was a rumble of thunder. The

air was very warm and very still. Hot and a little breathless, they emerged at last on to the hilltop and stood gazing at the panorama that spread before them.

'It's like the very essence of England, isn't it?' Christine asked softly. 'All laid out in miniature beneath us. Look – there's the village we came through. And see that lovely farmhouse over there – it looks like a doll's house. And it's all so very green.' As she spoke there was another faint growl of thunder.

Liam had thrown himself down on the grass, leaning on one elbow, long legs sprawling. His curly hair was tangled and damp in the heat. He plucked a long, juicy stem of grass and chewed on it, his eyes half-closed against the brightness of the sky.

Christine dropped down beside him, half-leaning on him. Liam let himself collapse on his back, lay with his eyes closed, felt her lips very lightly on his, trapped her head before she could lift it and kissed her soundly, without opening his eyes. She laughed delightedly when he finally released her. He felt the tickle of grass on his face. 'Would you miss me,' she asked, 'if I went to America?'

That opened his eyes. She laughed again at the expression in them. '*America?*' he asked. 'Since when are you going to America?'

Still laughing, she brushed his face again with the frond of grass she had picked. 'I'm only teasing. I've no intention of actually going.' She leaned to kiss him again. 'I'm having far too much fun here.'

Liam was still staring at her. 'But – why would you even think of it?'

'Didn't I tell you?' She sat up, pulled up her knees, wrapping her arms about them and looking out over the valley. 'John Waters, at the gallery, is thinking of opening a branch in New York. Just a small one – more for the prestige than anything else. Those Yanks who came over, remember? That was what they were here to talk about. It seems,' she directed a slanting, laughing glance down at him, 'that they were rather taken with me. It seems that I'm the perfect English rose,' she affected a not-very-good western twang, 'so John half-suggested that I might like to go for six months or so.'

'And will you?' Liam still had not smiled.

She appeared to realise only then that his mood was suddenly not as light as hers. She turned, quickly. 'No! Of course not! Don't be silly. I told you – I've no intention of going. I'm not even sure if he really meant it. Hey!' She lifted her head. 'Listen to that thunder.' Inky clouds were building up behind them and, even as she spoke, they suddenly smothered the sun. The air became instantly cooler and the hillside darkened, though the river in the distance still sparkled in sunshine. She jumped to her feet, extended her hand. 'Come on. We don't want to drown!'

They hurried back down through the now-gloomy woodland. Halfway back to the house huge spots of rain began to patter through the leaves. A sudden lightning flash crackled in the sky. A few seconds later the thunder crashed again.

'We're going to have to run for it,' Liam said.

They almost made it; almost, but not quite. Breathless and laughing they threw themselves through the back door into the kitchen. 'The French doors,' Christine gasped. 'I left them open. Come on – give me a hand.' They flew around the house shutting the windows. By now the storm had broken with a vengeance, thunder and lightning crashing in unison, rain pouring in sheets from a sky that was black as night. Liam re-entered the kitchen to find Christine rubbing at her wet hair with a towel. Beyond the open door the rain thundered and streamed.

'My goodness!' Christine emerged from under the towel. Her eyes were bright and laughing. 'Reminds me of my days in the tropics with my good friend Somerset Maugham! Here – let me do you. You're soaked!'

Obediently he went to her, bent his head to let her rub his hair. That operation did not last long; Liam's arms went about her, his mouth closed on hers. Her dress was damp, her skin was wet. She smelled of the rain. She leaned back to look at him. There was a very long moment of silence, broken only by the sounds of the storm. A sudden wind had gusted; the trees swayed, branches lashed. Liam's long lashes half-veiled his eyes, the bones of his wet face gleamed in the dimness. Christine opened her mouth as if to speak, then, oddly uncertain, shut it again, swallowed.

Liam said it for her. 'I love you,' he said, gently. 'You're the most stubborn, exasperating, high-handed, self-opinionated person I know, and I love you.'

'That's just exactly what I was going to say.'

'I know. You're also the most beautiful, exciting, desirable—'

'Intelligent,' she put in, helpfully.

'—intelligent,' he conceded, 'funny—' There was a huge crash of thunder. Christine jumped a little. '—scaredy-cat, warm-hearted and lovable person I know, and I love you for that, too.'

'That's what I was going to say next.'

'I thought you might. Will you see how good I am to you? I even save you breath.' He drew her with him to one of the big armchairs, dropped into it and pulled her on to his lap. She curled there like a child, her wet head tucked beneath his chin. His hands stroked gently the curve of her back, and her damp hair tickled his face. She guided his hand to her breast. 'Do what you did the other night,' she breathed. 'And show me what pleases you.'

The thunder growled round the valley, and the lightning flickered like faerie fire.

'We ought to go.' Christine was lying, naked except for her knickers, on her stomach on the narrow single bed in the little spare room in the attics of the house. Liam had pulled on his trousers and was leaning by the open dormer window, smoking.

He glinted a smile over his shoulder. 'Yes.'

The storm still rumbled in the distance, its fury now lulled. Rain still pattered through the leaves outside.

Christine reached for her own cigarettes. 'May I have a light, please?'

'Of course.' He came to her, perched on the edge of the bed. After he had lit her cigarette he regarded her for a long moment, his fingertip tracing the line of her bare back. 'May I ask you a question? A personal question? An impertinent personal question, I suppose.'

'Ask away.'

'You were engaged to be married?'

'Yes.' She sounded disinterested.

'Did you and your fiancé ever make love? I mean – really make love?'

She turned her head, startled. 'Good God, no!'

He grinned, a little crookedly, already half-regretting having spoken. 'Too well bred?'

Her laugh was sharp. 'No. Oh, no. He wanted to all right. But I wouldn't let him. As I have never let anyone else. Because I truly believe,' she blew out a cloud of smoke and watched pensively as it drifted in the draught from the window, 'I do truly believe that that last act is—' she hesitated, shrugged a little self-consciously, 'well, sacred, I suppose. Weird word for me to use, I know. Especially under such circumstances. But I can't think of a better one. Oh, I'm not talking God, church, bride-in-white sort of sacred. It's just – an instinct. Self-respect, perhaps. Self-preservation? I don't know. All I do know is that I don't want to make a mistake. I don't want to wake up one morning hating myself because I've squandered on one what might be – treasured—' she hesitated upon the word, 'by another.' She pulled a face at him over a small, hunched shoulder. 'Oh, you've *muddled* me now! I'm not making any sense.'

'As it happens, I think you're probably making better sense than I deserve for asking.' He dropped a gentle kiss on her shoulder, then slapped her bottom briskly. 'Come on, up with you. Time you took me home.'

She smiled at his own self-mockery. 'I do love you.'

'After what you've just put me through, you'd better.' Grinning, he reached for his still-damp shirt. 'You always were a pain in the neck.'

# Chapter Thirteen

Fresh as a daisy in crisp navy and white, Lottie Barker eyed the grubby disorder of Liam's living room with critically arched brows. 'God, it smells like a brewery in here! Heavy night last night?'

Liam, groggy-eyed and tousled, barefoot and dressed in a hastily thrown-on dressing gown, yawned, rubbed at his unshaven face and ran his fingers through already wild hair. 'Very,' he said.

She watched with a blithe lack of sympathy as, slightly distractedly, he set about tidying the room, picking up bottles and glasses, emptying ashtrays, collecting and sorting the packs of playing cards that lay on the table. 'Profitable?'

Faintly, he grinned. 'Very,' he said again.

'Well, that's all right, then.' Lottie had already dropped her gloves and hat on to the settee, now she followed them with her handbag and the large square envelope she was carrying and slipped out of her smart coat. Liam sighed a little; much as he liked her, he was not exactly entranced at the thought that she obviously intended to stay, mess or no mess. Lottie, perfectly aware of that, composedly chose to ignore it. 'You look as if you could do with some coffee.'

'Do with it?' Liam winced as he moved his head too sharply. 'Sure, I'd murder for it.'

'No need to go that far.' She patted him cheerily on the cheek as she passed him. He flinched again. She laughed. 'I'll make some.' At the kitchen door she paused, wrinkling her nose. 'Oh, *Liam!* Honestly!'

'I know, I know. 'Tis a bit of a mess.'

'A *bit* of a mess? I'd like to know what you call a proper one!' Lottie picked her way across the dirty floor, threw open a window. The coolness of autumn drifted through it. Sunday-morning quiet had settled upon the usually busy streets; there was a faint savoury smell of cooking on the air. She filled the kettle and set it on the hob, then went back to lean in the doorway as she waited for it to boil. Grinned again as she watched Liam amble at a snail's pace from table to fireplace, emptying ashtrays.

'For God's sake, woman,' he said, with amiable asperity, 'will you shut that bloody window? A chap could catch his death of cold!'

'Better than suffocating,' she said, cheerfully. 'Boy, I reckon you could catch something just breathing this air.'

'I think I already have.' The words were doleful.

'It's called a hangover. And knowing you,' she pointed a slender, scarlet-tipped finger, 'it must have been one hell of a party to get *you* into this state?'

He shrugged, picked up an empty whiskey bottle, eyed it as if he had no idea what to do with it, then put it down again. 'Just a few friends.'

'Here—' She took a large cardboard box from the kitchen table and carried it into the living room. 'Put the empty bottles in this. You can cart them down to the dustbin later.'

'Thanks.' Still moving carefully enough to make her laugh outright, he began collecting bottles. 'So – to what do I owe this pleasure? You haven't been around for quite a while.'

'Been busy.' Lottie picked up a couple of glasses, took them into the kitchen.

'The new job?'

'Yes.' She clattered the glasses into the sink, reached for cups as the kettle began to sing, banged a couple of cupboard doors. 'Camp OK?'

'It's all I've got.'

'That rather settles that, then, doesn't it?'

'Enjoying the job?'

'It's wonderful. Wonderful, wonderful, wonderful! Better even than I thought it would be. Would you believe I actually look forward to Monday mornings?' She brought two steaming cups into the room and deposited them carefully upon the partially cleared table. 'There. Get that into you.'

'Thanks.' Liam reached for a half-full whiskey bottle and tipped a generous shot into his coffee. 'Hair of the dog.' He held out the bottle. 'You?'

She shook her head, laughing. 'Anyway, I was actually on my way round to Emma's. They've invited me to lunch with a couple of their loony but likeable friends. Thought I'd just drop in on the way – see what you've been getting up to.'

'They?' Liam picked up on the word. 'Alex and Emma?' Christine had wondered aloud more than once about what was actually going on in the little flat above the bookshop.

'Yes.' She was breezy. 'They're virtually living together. Terribly Bohemian and romantic, isn't it? I would never have thought that my conventional big brother had it in him.' She raised a slightly sly eyebrow. 'You haven't been round there much recently, then? I had rather gathered that you, too, have been – otherwise occupied?' The bright and undisguised interest in her eyes entirely belied her claim to have dropped in on the spur of the moment. Lottie Barker was curious, and she intended to have her curiosity satisfied.

Liam sipped his coffee and stuck firmly to the subject. 'Don't your parents mind?'

She hesitated a moment, a small half-smile acknowledging the tactic. Then, for the moment at least, she gave in.

'About Alex and Emma? Well, obviously the situation isn't ideal. But they're both extremely fond of Emma – we all are – and at the moment there doesn't seem to be any other way for them. They intend to marry when Emma comes of age.'

'Isn't there anything they can do?'

'They could go to a magistrate's court, apparently – try to prove that George is being unreasonable,' she waved a vague hand, 'something like that, anyway. But they don't want to do that, for the moment at any rate, because everyone is worried about what effect another epic family row – and there would be one, with knobs on! – might have on Aunt Siobhan. George would be livid if he found out what was going on. And he'd fight it to the death.'

'Will he not be livid anyway, sooner or later?'

'Of course. But at least he won't be able to do anything about it.' For a moment her bright face was shadowed. 'It really is a muddle. You'd heard, I expect, that Emma went to visit her mother a couple of weeks ago and George came home unexpectedly? There was a hell of a row. He virtually threw her out of the house.'

'Yes. I had heard.' The words were short.

'Christine told you, I expect?' She smiled suddenly, all sweet innocence.

He surrendered. 'Yes, Lottie. Christine told me. And so did Ned.'

'Ah. Good old Ned. He does love a good gossip, that boy.' The curly lashes lifted. A short, speculative silence fell.

Liam waited. Over the past couple of months – since the trip to the cottage – he and Christine had spent every available moment together. At first it had seemed as if that day had been a turning point; on the way home – in between a few nerve-racked silences on Liam's part as Christine had practised for Silverstone – they had discussed not the future but the present. The future, they had agreed, was too complicated, too delicate, perhaps even too dangerous a place for them to contemplate for now; best to take the relationship day by day, enjoying, learning, giving, taking; and it had seemed to work. They had laughed a lot, argued but never quarrelled or mocked, and had become intimately at ease with each other's bodies – for although Liam respected Christine's wishes about making love, there were many other ways to give each other pleasure, and they had discovered most of them. All in all it had been a quite extraordinarily happy time, even the fact that they had to meet more or less clandestinely somehow enhancing the romance rather than detracting from it.

Until three days ago, that was. Three days before, the inevitable and spectacular quarrel had blown up – for the life of him Liam could not remember what had started it, and he doubted if Christine could, either – and she had stormed off declaring that she hated him and never intended to see or speak to him again. The anvil in his head at this moment was testament as to how well he had taken that. He was still not sure whether pain, anger or a racking longing was predominant among his emotions.

'Ned says that you and Christine are—' Lottie paused, then continued delicately, 'seeing each other.'

'Does he indeed?' Liam drained his coffee, poured a drop more whiskey in the cup and knocked that back for good measure. 'Well, as it happens, young master Ned is this time a tad behind the times.'

'Oh?' She waited expectantly.

Liam said nothing.

'Oh, come on, Liam. Do tell.'

'Nothing to tell.' He stood up, started to clear the table again. 'We were seeing each other. Now we're not. That's it.'

She watched him, and this time there was real sympathy in her eyes. 'You do like to live dangerously, don't you?' She hesitated. 'Do you love her?' she asked, softly.

Liam had his back to her. 'No, of course I don't,' he said, bitterly self-mocking. 'I just want to take another swipe at her father.' He heard himself say it, knew that it had not sounded as he had intended it. But he could not bring himself to take it back. He scrubbed the heel of his hand into his aching eyes.

'Liam!' Even easy-going Lottie was shocked at that.

'Look—' He swung on her more angrily than he had intended. 'Let's just leave it, shall we? Let's talk about something else. Oh, and next time you see young Ned, tell him I'm going to wring his neck like a chicken's.' His anger had died as quickly as it had flared. The threat had no bite. He carried a clutch of dirty glasses into the kitchen.

Lottie followed him, still carrying her cup. 'Do you see much of him?'

'Ned?' Liam had recovered his equilibrium. 'Quite a bit, yes.' He quirked a small smile. 'He comes as much to play with the keys as to see me, I suspect.'

'Keys?'

'The skeleton keys. He was very impressed when Christine got in to see him after his father belted him. He pestered me to show him how to do it.'

Lottie looked thoughtful, but said nothing.

'So,' Liam turned the tap on the geyser; the gas popped and water trickled steamily into the sink, 'tell me more about this job of yours. What is it you actually do?'

'All sorts of things. Never a dull moment. I receive the great and the good,' she grinned, 'and the not-so-good, if you listen to half the gossip, which of course I do. I help Patrick set up the shots. Sometimes sit in for the sitter, so everything's set up when he or she arrives. Do a bit of secretarial work – it all really is great fun.' She went back into the living room and picked up the envelope she had dropped on to the sofa. 'Patrick took a few photographs of me the other day.' She slipped them from the envelope and spread them on the table, carefully avoiding the more insalubrious stains that marked it. 'He was using a new lighting technique, so he thought he'd better try it on me before he tried it on his clients.'

Liam looked at the pictures in genuine interest. Lottie

was, in fact, very photogenic indeed, and the technique the photographer had employed had enhanced that. She smiled out of the photographs with the total lack of self-consciousness of a natural performer, skin flawless, eyes mischievous and laughing, the delicate bones of her face lit to a beauty too perfect for mere life to imitate.

'Good, aren't they?' she asked, modestly.

'They certainly are.' He grinned as he gathered them up and handed them back to her. 'Sure an' if they don't make you look like a proper filum star, Miss,' he said, in his thickest accent.

She giggled, tossed one of the pictures back on to the table. 'You can have one if you like. Here,' she had picked up a pen from the cluttered dresser, bent to scrawl on the picture, 'when I'm rich and famous you can stick it on your mantelpiece and boast about it.' She straightened. 'I suppose I'd better go.' With one of those sudden whirlwinds of energy that were so typical of her, she was in the sitting room, slipping her coat on before he could get around to helping her, settling her small brimmed hat expertly upon her curls, pulling on gloves, checking the seams of her stockings, standing on tiptoe to kiss him, lightly. 'Golly, what bristles!' She rubbed at the soft skin of her face with a laughing grimace. 'Whenever did you last shave? You look like Desperate Dan – see you soon. Bye.'

He stood at the door, listened to her humming to herself as she sped down the stairs, raised a hand as she waved before she disappeared out of sight.

When *had* he last shaved?

He went into the bedroom, stared at himself in the mirror. Eyes bloodshot, at least two days of dark beard shadowing his jaw, he looked like a down-and-out. If he were going to the club tonight, he'd better sort himself out. And he was going to the club tonight. Because he had a living to earn. And because he had nothing better to do.

It was Emma who, in the end, a few weeks later, brought

Christine and Liam back together again. 'Honestly, Liam, the pair of you are as bad as one another! Stubborn as mules and daft as brushes! Ring her, for heaven's sake! At the gallery, if you don't want to ring home – oh, do stop that!' she added, truly cross. Liam, perched on her desk in the shop, had shaken his head. 'You're like a couple of silly children squabbling in the playground! You're miserable. She's miserable. What good's that doing either of you? Talk to her! Do you know – she can't even remember what started the quarrel?' She eyed him for a moment. 'Can you?'

He said nothing. Inspected the toe of his shoe as if it were the most interesting object in the room.

'Exactly!' Exasperated, Emma thumped the books she was carrying on to the desk. 'Liam, life's too short for this kind of stupidity.' She planted herself in front of him, four-square, her round brown eyes on a level with his. 'I know it's none of my business, but I'm going to ask all the same. Do you care for her at all?'

'Emma!'

'Do you?'

'Well, of course I bloody do, but—'

'Right.' She marched past him to the telephone.

'Emma!'

Emma ignored him. She lifted the handset, asked crisply for the number, turned to watch him as she waited for the phone to be answered. 'Chris? It's Emma. Fine, thanks, yes. Listen, I've got someone here who'd like a word with you.' Smiling beatifically, she held out the phone.

Liam took it. 'Christine?' There was a moment of silence, and for an instant he wondered if she might put the phone down.

'Yes.'

Now what, for God's sake? He said the first thing that came into his head. 'Your sister's just been giving me a bit of a rollicking.'

The silence this time was of a different quality. 'No doubt

you deserved it,' Christine said, the words tart but far from hostile.

'No doubt I did.'

Another silence.

'How are you?' she asked.

'I'm well. Yourself?'

'Fine. I'm fine.'

He could hear a clicking sound, as if she were nervously tapping a fingernail against the receiver. 'Chris—'

'Yes?'

'Would you feel like having a bit of a talk?'

She was not giving in that easily. 'What about?'

'Oh, don't be so damned awkward, woman! You know very well what about!'

Emma who had discreetly withdrawn to the book stacks indulged in a small, satisfied smile.

'Well?'

'I'm thinking about it.'

'Think about it tonight. At my place.'

'I'd rather think about it at Brown's, over dinner.' Her voice was still deliberately cool, but she could not quite disguise the edge of happiness in it.

'Done. Eight o'clock?'

'Eight o'clock. Sorry, I'll have to go. Someone's come in. I'll see you at eight.' The receiver clicked down.

'There.' Like a rabbit popping out of a hat Emma appeared, beaming, from behind the shelves. 'That wasn't so hard, was it?'

Liam replaced the handset. 'Neither's breaking a leg,' he said, a little caustically, 'but I wouldn't want to do it too often.'

'I'm sorry,' Christine said again.

Liam said nothing.

Christine toyed with the food on her plate for a moment, then put down her knife and fork and raised her eyes to his. 'I was angry. So angry. And miserable. When I realised they

were serious – well – it seemed like a good idea, a chance
to get away for a while.'

'From me?'

That brought a quick spark. 'There wasn't any "you"!
That was the whole point! You didn't get in touch.'

'Neither did you.'

'Oh, for goodness' sake! Don't let's go through *that* again!'
She reached a hand to him across the table. After only a
moment's hesitation he took it. 'Look, I'm not going for
ages yet – not until next summer. And then it'll only be
for six months or so. Honestly, Liam, you must admit it's
a terrific opportunity.' She sighed, a little helplessly. 'I'm
sorry,' she added again.

His fingers tightened on hers. 'Will you stop saying that,'
he said, suddenly gentle. 'Of course it's a grand opportunity
for you, and of course you should take it. It was just a bit
of a shock, that's all.' He studied her for a long moment.
'Sure, it's proud of you I should be. You must be very good
at what you do.'

She shrugged deprecatingly, but her smile betrayed her
pleasure. 'I'm a good organiser, that's all. And I've learned
quite a bit in the time I've worked at the gallery. I know a
good painting from a dud, at least, and that's something.'

'How do your family feel about it?'

'Mama is anxious and trying not to show it. Papa is
flabbergasted and doesn't bother to hide it. Ned and Lottie
are both green with envy. Emma's too wrapped up in Alex
even to think about it.' She reached for her wine glass and
raised it to him. 'But as I say, New York is months away
yet. What matters now is you and me.'

The glasses chinked gently together. Their eyes held.
Liam it was who broke the silence at last. 'By the way,'
he said, 'what the hell *was* that bloody row about?'

She shook her head. 'Damned if I know,' she said, with
a sudden, flashing grin, 'but I'll bet it was your fault.'

Rumours of war – and fear of war – were ever-present

during that winter; for some people the announcement, on the third of January 1938, that all British schoolchildren were to be given gas masks brought a step closer the fulfilment of their most gloomy prophesies. In the East, Japan had invaded China and had bombed Shanghai: in Africa, Fascist Italy had overrun Abyssinia: suffering Spain was still in flames. And Nazi Germany strutted the European stage, confident, rearmed and hungry for a return to her former power. War, said some, was inevitable. Yet to others, still bearing the scars and losses of that other, terrible conflict of twenty years earlier, the idea was not to be contemplated. Anything – *anything* – must surely be better than a return to such barbarism? The belief that there could be no winning of a modern war, that cities would be razed to the ground, and whole civilian populations wiped out, was strong. Civilisation must be defended at all costs; those who suggested that, in the end, defence would have to take the form of force, or at the very least resistance, were labelled, by many, warmongers. Even when Hitler's jackbooted troops marched into Austria in March of that year, there were intelligent people still ready to fool themselves into believing that his cynical machinations would stop there. When the British government, in that same month, broadcast an appeal for people to join the new Air Raid Precautions Services, those who came forward were regarded with suspicion by some of their fellow citizens. Did these people actually *want* a war?

'Some people just can't see beyond the end of their noses,' Alex said, stretching his long legs out to the fire. 'How you can equate being ready to defend yourself with actually wanting to go to war is beyond me. If you bar the door at night, it isn't because you want someone to come in and pinch the family silver, is it?'

'To be honest with you, I don't really want to think about it.' Emma was laying the table for tea. It was a blustery Sunday in April; every now and again rain rattled against the window panes and the trees outside tossed in the wind.

The room, however, was quiet, cosy and warm. Over the winter a considerable amount of effort and a lot of loving care had gone into transforming the shabby rooms over the bookshop into a comfortable home. There were prints on the walls, rugs on the floor, books on the shelves. Alex had a small desk set under the window, neatly stacked with books and papers. A rather splendid modern clock featuring a languid and elegant young woman leading a pair of equally languid and elegant Borzoi hounds ticked upon the mantelpiece, a Christmas present from Siobhan, whose generosity had also supplied the pretty china tea service that Emma was setting out upon the table.

Alex leaned forward, elbows on knees, looking pensively into the fire. 'I wonder what *is* going to happen? I wonder – if there is a war – what it'll be like.'

'Alex, for heaven's sake! I said, I don't want to think about it!' Emma's voice was, for her, so sharp that he turned to look at her in surprise. She was leaning with both hands flat on the table. She was very pale.

'Emma? Em, what is it?' Concerned, he scrambled from the chair and went to her, putting an arm about her.

She stood for a moment, shivering against him, then, without a word, she pulled suddenly away from him and fled from the room. He heard the bathroom door slam, and the sound of violent retching. Truly worried now, he tapped on the door. 'Em? What's the matter, love?'

There was a moment's silence. Then, 'Just a sec,' she said.

He heard the water run. A moment later Emma opened the door. She was still pale, there was a faint sheen of sweat on her brow and dark rings under her eyes. 'Trust me,' she said, a little shakily, 'to get it wrong. That's supposed to happen in the mornings, I believe.'

He stared at her. 'You're ill?' he asked. 'Darling – are you ill?' He stopped, the words only just registering. 'You mean – oh, my God!' he said, faintly.

'I'm sorry.' Her voice was very quiet. Sudden tears had welled in her eyes. 'I'm sorry,' she whispered again.

Alex was staring at her. 'A baby?' he said. You mean you're – we're – expecting a *baby*?'

Emma sniffed. 'Yes.'

'But – that's wonderful! A *baby*! Why didn't you tell me? A *baby*! *Our* baby! Sweetheart, come and sit down. Put your feet up. I'll make a cup of tea. Oh, Emma, darling, don't cry, please don't. Everything's going to be fine, I promise you.'

'I – thought you might be cross.'

'Cross? *Cross?*' He had caught both her hands in his. 'Why on earth would I be cross? Can't you see – he'll have to let us get married now. I'm sick to death of this hole-in-the-corner living. I have been for a long time. I just didn't want to force the issue, because I didn't want to upset you. Well, the issue is well and truly forced now, isn't it? And there's nothing anyone can do about it.' His lean face was alight with love and excitement. 'Darling, darling Emma – will you marry me?'

She was laughing and crying at once. 'Yes. Oh, yes! But – what if Father still refuses his permission? I'm still not twenty-one until next year.'

'We'll run away to Gretna Green. Perhaps we should have done that anyway. Oh, Em!' He held her to him, resting his cheek on her smooth, shining hair. 'I'll look after you. I promise. For ever and ever. Nothing will ever hurt you again. You mustn't worry. And you must be careful. Whatever happens, you must look after yourself and our baby.'

'Our baby,' she repeated, then, for the briefest of moments, closed her eyes.

'You aren't frightened, are you?' he asked, gently and a little anxiously.

'Of having the baby? Or of facing my father?'

'Either. Both?'

She shook her head, her face still concealed in his shoulder. 'No,' she lied, on both counts, 'of course I'm not.'

\*      \*      \*

'You, Sir,' George Clough said quietly, 'are a young black-guard. You have abused my hospitality and my trust. You have disgraced your own family and mine.'

Alex stood, pale and tight-lipped. 'I love Emma, Sir. I wouldn't do anything to hurt her.'

'Love? *Love?* What do you know of love, you irresponsible puppy? Will it put bread on your table? Will it clothe and feed your children? Will it put a roof over your head? Hurt her? You treat her like a whore, drag her good name in the dirt, get her with a bastard child and then have the gall to say you wouldn't do anything to hurt her?'

'Papa – please!' Tears were streaming down Emma's face, which had grown thin and drawn in the past weeks.

George turned on her, sharply, yet still did not raise his voice, a fact that for some reason she found more, rather than less, disturbing. 'You'll keep a still tongue, Miss. I'll deal with you in a moment.' He turned back to Alex. 'I will make one thing quite clear. She comes to you in the clothes she stands up in. You'll get nothing, not one penny, from me, neither of you. You hear me? Not – one – penny. Ever.'

'But – you will sign the forms, Sir?'

George made him wait for a long, tense moment. 'I'll sign the forms,' he said. 'I'll sign because her mother has asked – begged – me to. And because she can at least no longer disgrace my good name if she no longer bears it.' His eyes went back to Emma. A finger stabbed the air. 'But understand this, young woman, and understand it well. You've made your bed, and now you'll lie in it. I no longer consider you to be my daughter. This is no longer your family. If you choose to behave like a slut, then at least have the decency not to tarnish the rest of us with your gutter behaviour.'

'Mr Clough, I really must protest!' Alex's paper-white face had paled further.

'You? *Protest?* The best thing you can do is to shut your

mouth. Now – get out of here, the pair of you. I never intend to see or speak to either of you again. Go.'

Emma was crying openly now. Alex put his arm about her shoulder and led her to the door. Once there, he paused, opened his mouth to speak.

'Go!' George Clough barked.

Alex opened the door. Ned, stepping back silently, made no effort to disguise the fact that he had been eavesdropping. His blue eyes were very wide, fixed on his sister's face. 'A baby?' he whispered. 'You're having a *baby*?'

'Yes.' Emma walked to the top of the stairs. Her mother was waiting in the hall below. She, too, had been crying. Emma started slowly down to her.

'A baby!' Ned said again, softly, from behind her. 'My sainted aunt! There's a turn-up!'

'Mama—' Emma walked into her mother's arms, sobbing. They hugged for a moment, with Alex standing awkwardly by, watching them.

'Did he agree?' Siobhan asked at last.

'Yes.' Emma passed a tired hand across her face. 'He'll sign. We can marry before the baby comes.'

'Siobhan, get away from her. You two – I told you to go. Get out of this house. Now.' George Clough had appeared like an avenging angel on the landing above.

Emma hardly glanced up at him. She stepped back, her eyes on her mother's face. 'I love you,' she said, and took Alex's hand. 'Make sure you take good care of yourself.'

Tears were brimming again. 'And you, my Emma,' Siobhan said.

Emma's chin came up. 'Alex will do that,' she replied, firmly. And hand in hand they walked into the street. Emma did not look back.

'Papa didn't even raise his voice. *That's* how bad it was,' Ned said. 'Emma cried and Mama cried. I even thought Alex might at one point, but he didn't.'

'Your father is inclined to have that effect on people,' Liam called from the kitchen, his words wry.

'It's caused terrible trouble of course,' the boy said, cheerfully. He was wandering around the living room, inspecting the bookshelves, looking at pictures and prints, his bright, sharp eyes everywhere. 'Papa went round to the Barkers and caused a terrible row. He's forbidden any of us – even Mama – to mention Emma's name in the house.' He stopped, his interest caught. Quietly careful, he prised something from between two books. A photograph. A photograph of Lottie Barker, signed with a flamboyant scrawl: *To Liam, loads of love and kisses. Lottie.* He looked at it pensively for a moment. 'Fancy *Emma* being *pregnant*,' he said, absently.

'It happens,' Christine said, drily.

Ned wandered to the kitchen door, still holding the photograph, stood for a moment watching as Liam made tea and Christine buttered toasted tea cakes. 'Lottie really is very pretty, isn't she?' he said after a moment, lifting wide and artless eyes. 'This is a jolly good picture, Liam. Where did you get it?'

'She gave it to me,' Liam said shortly, and held out his hand for the photograph, but Christine was quicker. Ned did not stop her from taking it.

'Did she indeed?' Christine said sweetly, as, having glanced at it and taken note of the message, she passed it on to Liam. 'You'd best look after it, then, hadn't you?'

That Ned's typical piece of mischief – for that was undoubtedly what it had been – should blow up into a quarrel of major proportions was, ironically, the result not so much of the boy's trouble-making as of Lottie's true fondness for Christine. When the ever-impulsive Christine mentioned the photograph to Lottie, it brought back sharply the memory of the conversation she had had with Liam that Sunday morning; a conversation that she had found uncomfortable at the time and which she had not been able to put entirely from her mind ever since. Christine, sensing her unease, questioned her. Lottie, fond though she was of Liam, regarded Christine as much as a sister as a friend, and was worried for her. She answered her questions.

'Did you say that?' Christine asked, quietly. 'Did you say that you didn't care for me, but that you wanted to take another swipe at my father?'

'I—' Liam gestured helplessly.

*'Did you say it?'*

'I didn't mean it! Not the way it sounded! Chris, you'd gone, left me – I'd drunk a terrible amount the night before – I was hung over – I didn't know *what* I was saying.'

'How dare you?' Her control was worse than a screaming temper would have been. 'How dare you say such a thing? To Lottie? To anyone? *How dare you?'*

'Will you listen to me? I'm telling you – yes, I can't deny I said it, or something like it. And yes, it was an unforgivable thing to say. But, Christine, I swear I didn't mean it! I promise you! I was hurt and unhappy and I didn't want Lottie's pity.'

Christine turned away from him, her arms hugged across her breasts, her shoulders hunched as if against pain. 'You said it,' she repeated, her voice expressionless. 'So it was there in your mind.'

'Chris, I was still drunk.' He stopped as she swung to confront him, her face fierce, her cheeks wet. But despite the tears her eyes were absolutely steady.

'*In vino veritas*, Liam,' she said, very quietly. 'And in case you haven't noticed, you aren't the only one with pride.' And she turned on her heel and left him to curse himself long, and inventively, and to no avail whatsoever. He knew that this time she would not come back.

That night he shed tears of his own, for the first time in a very long while.

Ten days later, with no word of farewell, Christine left for New York.

# $C$hapter $F$ourteen

It was not lost on Pamela Barker that under different circumstances the marriage of her son to Siobhan's daughter would have been an occasion of much joyful – and personal – celebration for both of them. As it was, the short, rather dull ceremony, which took place in a register office that reminded her of nothing so much as a grubby waiting room on a rundown railway station, was something of an anticlimax. No-one from Emma's family was there – Christine being in New York and George having absolutely forbidden either Siobhan or Ned to attend. The lovely flowers that Emma carried, however, a vibrant splash of colour in these drab surroundings, had arrived at the bookshop that morning with a brief but loving message from her mother. In contrast, the Barkers had turned up in force; Lottie attending Emma as an unofficial bridesmaid. Liam, too, was there, looking tired and, Pamela thought, mildly but not unattractively dissipated; something she noted, with a mother's sharp eye, that Lottie had obviously also observed. Puzzlingly there seemed to be some strain between these two; Pamela had been surprised at Liam's brusqueness when Lottie had greeted him, though she had received the distinct impression that her daughter had not. Another surprise had been the fact that this was far from the quiet affair she had expected. A large number of the young couple's friends had turned up; cheerful young men in flannels and sports jackets, talkative girls in everyday jumpers and skirts, none of them, apparently, in the least bit disconcerted by the unconventional circumstances of the occasion.

One thing, though, was certain; however matter-of-fact the ceremony, however dour the surroundings, nothing could tarnish the obvious happiness of the bride and groom. Emma, dressed in a cream suit with a tiny veiled hat, the pallor and distress of the past few weeks entirely gone, fairly glowed as Alex slipped the ring on her finger, and the look on her son's face as he bent gently to kiss his new wife brought sudden tears to Pamela's eyes. It may not have been quite the wedding she might once have envisaged for a son of hers, but it was none the less moving for that; Pamela's heart ached for Siobhan. She herself could not envisage, or even indeed contemplate, not being allowed to witness the marriage of one of her children. As she hugged Emma and kissed Alex, she could not help but wonder if George Clough did not somewhere in his father's heart regret taking such a fierce stand against the youngsters. He had after all closed the door not only on his daughter, but on his first grandchild.

The wedding breakfast was held at the bookshop, which Mr Davies had readily closed for the day; he had himself pointed out that since most of the customers and all of the staff, including himself, were at the wedding, it would hardly cause offence to do so. Desks and shelves had been moved, tables set up and later, after the food and the speeches, Emma's battered wind-up gramophone was brought downstairs for the dancing. Though Pamela and David had offered to pay for one, there was to be no honeymoon. With little income and a child on the way the newly-weds had sensibly opted to spend the money turning the little second bedroom into a nursery. Eventually, once Alex qualified, they should be financially secure; for now neither cared in the least that the rooms over the shop, with their shabby second-hand furniture and worn rugs, were not the height of fashionable luxury. They were home, and that was all that mattered.

'I don't think I've ever seen Emma look so pretty or so happy,' Lottie spoke quietly. 'I know brides are supposed to be radiant and all that, but she's being positively indecent about it, don't you think?' She had come up behind Liam, who was leaning on the corner of a table, long legs crossed, watching the dancers, a glass of beer untouched in his hand.

Liam glanced at her, then looked away without speaking.

'You always could scowl,' she said, collectedly. 'You look just like you used to when you were little and one of us got on your nerves.'

'Take a hint.' The words were blunt.

She was quiet for a moment; he was aware of her eyes steady upon him. 'Liam – I want to apologise. I'm sorry I told Christine what you said. With hindsight I can see that I shouldn't have done. In fact almost as soon as I'd done it I realised that I shouldn't have done. It's just – well, you *did* say it. And I was worried for her. I didn't want her hurt.'

He laughed, entirely without humour, and took a swig of his beer.

'Have you heard from her?'

He shook his head, his eyes still on the chattering crowd.

'Have you written to her?'

Again the shaken head. 'No point.'

'Would you answer a question?'

He shrugged.

'Did you mean it? What you said about taking another swipe at her father?'

'No.' He grinned a little grimly. 'Not that I wouldn't, mind, given the chance. But no, I didn't mean it the way I assume I must have said it.'

She put a small hand on his arm. 'I'm sorry,' she said, softly, 'Honestly I am. I should have known.'

Liam let out a long breath and at last looked at her. 'It's not your fault. Not really. You're right – I did say it. And it was an inexcusable thing to say, whatever the circumstances. Anyway, if it hadn't been that, it would no doubt have been something else. We're cat and dog. Always will be, I shouldn't wonder.'

'I've known cats and dogs that have got on very well. Leave it for a while. She'll cool down, I'm sure.'

He shrugged. 'Not a lot else to do, is there? She'll probably come back with some rich Yank in tow.'

She shook her head, smiling. The music had stopped. Someone was changing the record, winding away at the gramophone. The needle thumped and crackled on scratched wax; Crosby crooned about pennies from heaven.

'Liam?'

He looked at her enquiringly.

'Can we be friends again? Please?'

It was hard to nurse resentment in the face of such disarming straightforwardness. With a half-smile, Liam gave in. What was to be gained by prolonging hostilities? 'To be sure, we can.'

She held out her hand. 'Then come and dance with me?'

'It looks as though Lottie and Liam have made it up,' Pamela commented, watching them as they joined the crowd.

'Oh? Was there a problem?' her husband asked abstractedly. He had taken a book from a shelf and was leafing through it interestedly. Pamela regarded him with affectionately exasperated eyes. 'David Barker!' she said, taking the book from him and snapping it shut. 'It's your son's wedding day. The very least you can do is to dance with his mother!'

'What a lovely, lovely day!' Emma yawned sleepily, stretched a little, snuggled her head into her new husband's shoulder. 'I'll never forget it. Never.'

He cupped a hand about her smooth head, stroked her cheek with his thumb. 'You're sure? It wasn't a disappointment?'

'Oh, don't be silly. How could it be? Of course it was horrid that Mama and the others couldn't be there – but I knew all along that they wouldn't be, so it was hardly a disappointment. I never did fancy that princess-for-a-day-white-satin-and-pearls stuff anyway. We're just as married, aren't we?'

He smiled into the darkness. 'Yes, Mrs Barker, we are just as married.'

She giggled a little. 'It was a lovely party, wasn't it?'

'It certainly was.'

She guided his hand to her soft, rounded stomach. 'He enjoyed it,' she said.

'He?' Alex asked, amused.

'Oh, yes. Beatrice assured me it's a "he". She says she's never wrong. She predicted the sex of all her sisters' babies, apparently.' She yawned again. 'Oh dear, I do believe I'm a little bit tiddly.'

He leaned on his elbow above her, watching her in the light of the street lamp that fell through the window. 'Well, personally I'd prefer a "she". A brave "she" with dark hair and shiny chestnut eyes, just like her lovely mother.'

She smiled sleepily. 'Now you are being silly.'

'Are you really tiddly?'

'\'Fraid so.'

'Too tiddly to make love?'

The bright eyes opened. Emma lifted a tender finger to his face. 'Never too tiddly for that,' she said.

In the event Emma's prescient friend Beatrice was right; nearly six months later, on a cold November night, Charles David Barker entered the world, red-faced and screaming. In the intervening months almost all resistance to Franco

in Spain had collapsed and Europe had teetered on the
brink of war over Hitler's proclaimed intention to invade
Czechoslovakia, a war averted – and a country sacrificed
– by the shameful and shameless appeasement of the Nazi
leader by Britain's Prime Minister Neville Chamberlain. Yet
the euphoria engendered by the infamous agreement with
Hitler and the promise of 'peace for our time' did not last
long. Air-raid precautions were stepped up, 'black-outs'
were tested and plans were drawn up for the evacuation
of children from the cities. The world into which Charles
David made his noisy appearance was becoming more
unstable with every passing day. There were not many
who were optimistic enough to believe that war would
not, sooner or later, break out.

'What if it does? It's about time *somethin'* excitin' 'appened
around 'ere.' The girl who spoke giggled a little as she
draped an arm about Liam's neck. 'Somethin' apart from
you, o' course, darlin'. I'm not infer—' she hiccoughed a
little, 'inferrin' *you're* not excitin'.'

'It's glad I am to hear that.' Liam unwrapped the arm
and put a supporting hand under her elbow. His plans
for the rest of the evening did not include his companion
measuring her considerable length on the pavement. She
was a tall, leggy brunette with blue eyes and a smoky voice.
Her name, she had informed him, was Dorothy, 'But you
can call me Dol, darlin' – everybody does.'

'Bloody 'Itler,' she was saying now. 'Bring 'im on, that's
what I say. We'll wipe the bleedin' floor with 'im, see if we
don't – oh – are we there?'

'Indeed we are.' Liam, still holding on to her as she
swayed a little beside him, pushed the front door open.
'Wait a sec. Let me put the light on.' She stood obediently
as he clicked the switch. 'My rooms are at the top of the
house.' He grinned a little. 'Can you make it?'

'Course I can!' She was indignant. 'What do you think I
am – drunk or somethin'?'

'Of course not—' he started, soothingly, and then stopped as his eye fell on something that lay on the hall table just inside the door.

It was a postcard. A postcard from New York. Sky-scrapers. The Statue of Liberty.

He picked it up.

*'New York is even taller than you are. What do you think about that? C.'*

'Wassat?' Dol reached for it. He held it away from her.

'It's nothing. Just a postcard.'

'From a f-friend?' She hiccoughed again on the last word.

'Yes. From a friend. A friend I haven't heard from for quite some time.' His voice was thoughtful.

She nodded, gravely. 'Good. Tha'ss good. I like friends. Come on. Up we go.' She turned and started up the stairs.

He looked again at the card, shaking his head a little, before tucking it into his pocket and following her.

'Something rather strange appears to be happening,' Liam said, a couple of weeks later, eyeing Lottie levelly. 'I some-how get the feeling it might have something to do with you.' They were sitting in the lounge bar of a small pub not far from where Lottie worked. The place was decked out for Christmas and a small, cockeyed Christmas tree stood on the bar.

'Oh?' Lottie sipped her drink, eyebrows raised in enquiry.

'My mantelpiece appears to be filling up with post-cards.'

'Ah.' She looked a little wary. 'What kind of postcards?'

'The cryptic kind. From New York. Saying things like "America is *very* American – isn't that odd?" And "New York has lots of weather, mostly terrible."'

Lottie laughed a little, and drew on her cigarette. 'Christine?'

'So it would seem. I just wondered – would you have any idea why the icy silence has suddenly been broken?'

She shrugged. 'I did write to her,' she said. 'Ages ago. After I spoke to you at the wedding. Have you seen the baby by the way? He's the cutest little thing. He's got blond hair and blue eyes, just like Ned.'

'That was, as you say, a long time ago.' Liam was not ready to be sidetracked. 'Did she write back?'

'Not then. But she dropped me a line a couple of weeks ago. Just a scribble – she's a terrible letter-writer.'

'Did she mention me?'

She shook her head. 'No.'

'Then what the devil is she doing? Playing games?'

Lottie put her head on one side, thought for a moment. 'You want my guess? I could be wrong, but I think she's probably come to her senses. She wants to make up. Do you want to write to her? I can give you the address if you want.'

'No.' Liam's face was thoughtful. 'If she'd wanted that she would have sent me the address herself, I guess.'

'Well,' Lottie leaned forward, her face bright, 'you'll be able to ask her yourself quite soon, won't you?' She waited for his question. Liam refused to ask it. 'She's coming home,' she said. 'In a couple of months or so. Apparently they asked her to stay on for the extra few months, because they've had a big exhibition and it was very popular so they extended it. I think she must have been quite a success over there. And speaking of success,' she added, characteristically inconsequential, 'did you ever have any with the horse with one leg?'

'Hmm?' Liam had reached absently for his tobacco pouch.

'The horse you owned a leg of. Any luck with it?'

'Oh – yes. It won a few times and we sold it. I've got a whole one of my own now.'

'Really?' A sharp spark of interest lit the pale eyes. 'A racehorse? All to yourself?'

'Yes. Did she say exactly when she'd be home?'

'No. Just a couple of months or so. She didn't mention a firm date. Does it win?'

'What?'

'The horse. Does it win?'

'Not yet.'

'Oh. Well – let me know when it does, won't you? I'll come along with you and swan around the owners' enclosure or whatever you call it. What fun! I could buy a great big hat.'

Liam rolled the cigarette, sat looking at it pensively. Lottie raised her eyes to the paperchain-decked ceiling. 'Not a chance, Lottie Barker, not a chance,' she answered herself, 'The man's on another planet.' She finished her drink and stood up. 'I must go. No, no—' Liam had scrambled to his feet beside her. She pressed him back into his seat, kissed his cheek lightly. 'You stay and finish your drink.' Then, impulsively, she dropped down beside him again and took his hand. 'Liam – write to her! Sort yourselves out before she comes home.'

He shook his head. 'Like I said, if she'd wanted me to write she'd have sent me the address. Let her do it her way. She knows where I am.'

'Stubborn as ever.'

'I'm not being stubborn.' He leaned forward on his elbows, her hand still in his. 'Lottie, can you not see? There's no future for me and Christine. There never has been. I've had time to think while she's been away. We're chalk and cheese. I've nothing to offer her.'

'You love her. Don't you?'

He ducked his head. 'Yes. Yes, I do. I guess I always will.' 'Then—'

'Lottie, life isn't a Hollywood film! Love doesn't conquer all! I can only be bad for her, you can surely see that? What kind of future could she possibly have with me? Christine is used to money. To a comfortable life. To status. I'm a know-nothing Irish gambler.'

'Then gamble.' Lottie said, surprisingly shortly. 'Life may not be a Hollywood film, Liam McCarthy; oddly enough, even I've got sense enough to know that. But I've known you for as long as I can remember, and I've never heard you spout such tosh before. OK, don't write to her – I

can see your point there – but don't write her off, either.
I think it took a lot of guts for her to send those cards. She's
opening a door. Don't for God's sake slam it in her face or
she will never forgive you! Now,' she stood up again, 'I
really must go.' She hesitated, looking down at him. 'I'm
sorry to lecture,' she added, softly. 'To be honest, I think it's
just that I feel so miserably guilty about causing the row in
the first place.'

He shook his head, smiled faintly.

'Be seeing you.' She stood and watched him for a moment
longer, then turned and vanished into the crowd, turning
heads as she went.

Liam downed his whiskey in one and pushed to the bar
to buy another.

He heard, finally, that Christine was on her way home in a
letter from Ned. To everyone's astonishment – including,
Liam sometimes suspected, his own – the boy, having reluctantly acceded to his father's strongly phrased suggestion
that he should to go to university, had once there taken
to the life like a duck to water. Having spent a year at
a 'crammer' to get there, however, work appeared to be
coming a very long way down Ned's list of priorities. In
his regular and enthusiastic letters the academic side of
university life hardly received a mention; the choir in which
he sang, the Dramatic Society he had joined, the nights spent
drinking with friends, these were the things he wrote about.
Ned, it seemed, had at last broken free of his mother's apron
strings and was enjoying life as a young man should.

The letter from Christine herself arrived a week or so
after Ned's. It was short and to the point. She was home.
She wanted to see Liam; she had something she had to tell
him. She would come to his rooms on Sunday afternoon. If
he wasn't there she would know that he didn't want to see
her. She wouldn't blame him for that. He looked at it for
a long time. Something to tell him. Almost certainly not
something he would want to hear?

Sunday was a day of gales and rain. Liam was standing in the kitchen looking down into the street below when the taxi drew up and Christine got out; he had been standing so for over an hour, waiting. He watched as, one hand to her hat, the skirts of her coat flying in the wind, she ran across the pavement to the street door. She was dressed in red.

He crossed the sitting room and opened the door. She was climbing the stairs slowly. As the door opened she looked up, and for a moment her face lit to a smile at the sight of him; in that second all the self-protective resolutions he had so determinedly and sensibly made were swept away. He held out a hand. She ran up the last few steps and took it. 'Liam.'

He drew her into the room and shut the door. Rain drove against the window; the fire crackled in the hearth. He wanted to kiss her more than he had ever wanted anything in his life before. She stood quite still, her hand in his, the smile gone. Her face was a little thinner, he thought, her hair a little shorter. She looked stylish and sophisticated, yet more fragile than he remembered her. Her eyes were shadowed. 'Liam,' she said again, very softly.

Liam had spent the last months convincing himself there could be no future for him with this woman. He had almost succeeded. Now he suspected she was here to tell him just that. The very thought was unbearable. He took her face between his hands and kissed her.

For a moment her eyes closed and her mouth opened under his. Then she stiffened and pulled quickly away from him. His heart twisted in painful disappointment. 'As bad as that?' he asked, quietly.

She turned and walked away from him, stood for a moment staring into the fire, her back to him.

'Drink?' he asked, his voice more sharply unfriendly than he had intended.

She turned, laced her hands together in front of her. 'Yes, please. I should like a drink. Just a small one.' She watched as he poured whiskey into two glasses. When he handed one to her he noticed, surprised, that her hand was shaking. She saw his look and hastily put the glass down without attempting to drink from it.

'At least take your coat off and sit down. If you've got something to tell me, you might as well do it comfortably.'

She took off her hat and coat, tossed them on the sofa, picked up the glass and walked to the table where she sat, her head bowed, the glass cupped in two small, well-manicured hands. There was an agonisingly long silence.

Liam could bear it no longer, 'Christine—' He stopped. As she lifted her head he saw her tears. 'Let me do it for you,' he said, quietly. 'You've found someone else. Someone more – suitable. It was bound to happen. We've always known there could be no future for us. It was foolish of us to convince ourselves there might be. You don't belong with me, we both know it.'

She wasn't listening to him. Suddenly she had dropped her face into her hands and was sobbing like a desolate child, her shoulders shaking. He so much wanted to hold her, to comfort her, that his self-restraint was a physical, wrenching pain. He spun away from her and stalked to the fireplace, resting his hands on the mantelpiece, leaning over the fire, his shoulders hunched against the sound of her intemperate tears. She was talking now, the words coming disjointedly, almost incoherently, between sobs. 'I was hurt – I was lonely. I was *so* lonely – I didn't mean to. You'll hate me, I know you'll hate me – I don't blame you – after the things I've said to you. Oh, I'm sorry, I shouldn't have come here!' The words were a wail of distress. He was aware of movement behind him. 'I shouldn't have *come*! I'm sorry. I'm sorry! I had no right – I've never done anything but hurt you.' She had jumped from the chair and was struggling back into her coat. With one arm in a sleeve and the coat dragging behind her, she threw open the door.

He flung himself round. 'Christine!'

But she was gone, clattering down the stairs, wrestling with the coat, still sobbing loudly.

He stood for a moment, paralysed. The street door slammed behind her.

'*Christine!*' He could not – he absolutely could not – let her go like this. He went down the stairs two at a time. The wind all but took the door from his hand as he flung it open. Rain gusted into his face. '*Christine!*' He glared up and down the pavement, caught a flash of red. He launched himself after her, caught her by the arm to swing her round to face him. Her curly halo of hair was already dark with rain, her face streaked with tears and mascara. Passers-by, heads down in the wind and rain, eyed them with ill-concealed interest.

'Let me go. Please, let me go. I'm so ashamed of myself.'

He shook her a little, more fiercely than he had intended. 'Will you stop this! It isn't your fault if you've fallen in love with someone else! I knew – we both knew! – it would happen sooner or later.'

She stared at him, shaking her head, rain and tears drenching her cheeks, hair soaked, untidy and dripping. He was suddenly aware that he had run into the street in his shirtsleeves; the cotton shirt clung to his back in cold discomfort. Christine raised her voice against the wind, an edge of the old, familiar impatience in it despite the tears. 'That wasn't what I said! I didn't say I *loved* someone else! I said I'd—' she hiccoughed a little, 'I said I'd *slept* with someone else. And then—'

'What?' His hands tightened on her arms.

'I said I'd slept with someone else. After all the things I've said to you! I didn't mean to, Liam, I truly didn't. I was so angry, and so lonely – and then it all went so terribly wrong and I realised what I'd done.'

As he had done before, he cupped her face between his two hands, holding her so that she had to look at him. 'Say that again.'

'What?'

'About not loving someone else.'

'Well, of course I don't love anyone else! How could I? I love *you*. And – I've let you down – terribly.'

'No. You haven't.'

'Yes, I *have*! Liam, you aren't listening. You don't understand.'

'I understand, darlin',' he said, his accent suddenly lilting, 'that we're both making something of an exhibition of ourselves out here, when there are two perfectly good whiskies waiting upstairs by a perfectly good fire where we could dry ourselves off and talk about this like civilised beings, instead of performing like a couple of drowned rats for my neighbours. Most of whom, I fear, already have a less than favourable regard for me.' He wrapped his long arms about her, pulled her to him.

'Liam,' she tried once more, 'please—'

'Will you shut up, woman,' he said, gently, and kissed her. 'Save your breath. You'll likely need it one of these days.'

'There's going to be a war, isn't there?' Christine was tucked snugly into a corner of the sofa, wrapped – not to say entirely enveloped – in Liam's dressing gown, her hair curling like corkscrews as it dried. The wild evening had darkened. Firelight flickered on her face. Liam could not take his eyes off her.

'Yes,' he said. 'I think there probably is.'

'Poor Czechoslovakia has gone. They're saying Poland will be next. We can't let him get away with it, can we? We'll have to do *something*.'

Liam nodded, sombrely, and sipped his drink. 'Yes.' He was sitting on the floor next to the sofa, his long legs stretched to the fire. Christine stretched out a hand to him; he took it, kissed the palm, rested his cheek on it, looking into the flames.

'If it is going to happen – if the world really is going to go mad – there's something I want to do,' Christine said, softly. 'I thought about it a lot in America. I want to do it more than anything in the entire world.'

He tilted his head to look at her and waited.

'I want to go to Ireland,' she said. 'I want to go back to Ahakista. Not to stay in the big house. I want to stay in the cottage. The one you and Mary lived in when we went before. And – I want to stay there with you. I want us to listen to the sea splashing outside the window. I want us to paddle. And to search for mussels. Will you come?'

He skewed to face her, resting his folded arms on her curled-up legs and his chin on his hands, studying her. 'Will I bring me bucket and spade?' he asked at last, seriously.

She tilted her head haughtily, eyes sparkling. 'Of course. Someone's got to do the digging.'

'So that's it! You just want your very own Irish navvy!'

Her laughter died as she reached a hand to his curly hair. 'You are sure that you still love me? You aren't going to get mad with me when you come to think about—' She stopped as he caught her wrists and pulled her towards him.

'Will you stop it?' He was suddenly fierce. 'I've told you. I won't listen. I don't want to hear. I don't want to know what happened in New York. It's your business, none of mine. And as for loving you – after the past couple of hours, can you doubt it?'

His closeness, the strength of his fingers about her wrists, were exciting her again. 'No,' she whispered. Her eyes were enormous in the shadowed firelight. She leaned forward to kiss him. He pulled her off balance so that she tumbled on to the floor on top of him. She laughed, trying to twist away from him. He held her. She stopped struggling. Kissed the tip of his nose. 'So – will you come to Ahakista with me? Can you manage to afford the time?'

'Jesus, Mary and Joseph, woman!' Liam's hand had found the belt that fastened the dressing gown. 'Why would I need to afford the time?' Her smooth bare shoulders gleamed in the light. 'If a gambling man can't gamble in Ireland, then where the devil can he?'

'Excuse me. It is Ned Clough, isn't it?'

Ned, who had been sitting on a bar stool watching

the river that slid lazily through the pub's pretty garden, jumped and turned. The young man who had addressed him was tall, dark and very slim. His doe-eyed face was narrow and sharp-planed, his hair thick and straight and the blue-black of a raven's wing. The stranger put out a hand. 'Paul DeBar. I do hope you don't mind my introducing myself like this, but – well, I heard you sing at the service the other night. And when I spotted you I just had to come over. It was wonderful stuff! Wonderful! I say, may I buy you a drink?'

'Er – thank you.' Flushing with pleasure Ned indicated his almost-empty glass. 'A pint of bitter, if you don't mind.' The exotically named DeBar, impeccably dressed and with a college scarf, not unlike Ned's own, slung with negligent style about his neck, was equally exotically handsome; his smile was quick and intelligent, his voice musically well-modulated. 'Do you sing?' Ned ventured.

DeBar threw back his head and laughed infectiously. Several people turned to look at him, smiling at the sound. 'Good Lord, no! My only talent for music is in listening to it! In the same way as my only talent for literature is in reading it, and my only talent for work is in watching others do it! I say—' he leaned closer, then winked. 'Do you really want warm beer? I've got a couple of bottles of champers up in my room. Got a few friends coming round. Care to join us?'

Ned glanced dubiously at his watch. 'Isn't it against the rules to—?'

Again the laugh. DeBar laid a hand on his arm. 'My dear thing! What are rules made for if not to be broken? Come on – be a devil!' he slipped a casual arm through Ned's as if they were the oldest of friends. 'In my firm opinion there's absolutely no wrong time to drink champagne. Perish the thought!' Quick glances and smiles followed his laughter to the door; Ned, bemused and flattered, allowed his new acquaintance to draw him through it and out into the sunlit street.

# *Interlude*

## Ireland and England, August 1939

'I do believe,' Christine said, rolling on to her stomach on the towel and squinting out over the glittering jewel that was Dunmanus Bay in the sunlight, 'that this must be just the most beautiful spot in the world.'

Liam smiled down at her. He was perched on a rock beside her, tossing pebbles into the clear, shimmering water. 'There can't be many to beat it,' he conceded. Behind them the little whitewashed cottage stood, windows and doors open to the sunny, salty air. Seabirds wheeled and called. The heron that Christine had christened Harry swooped down and settled on his accustomed rock, a silver fish wriggling in his beak. Christine shaded her eyes to watch it.

Liam stood up. 'Coming in for a dip?'

She shook her head sleepily. 'Nope. I'm altogether too warm and comfortable. You go ahead. I'll get some tea when you're done. I made some cakes this morning while you were out.'

'The devil you did? That's getting a bit domesticated, isn't it?'

She wrinkled her small nose and slanted a grin up at

him. 'Oh, don't worry, I'm sure they're entirely inedible,' she reassured him. 'They're as hard as rock. But at least it will give us something to feed the birds.' She watched as he kicked off his shoes and took off his shirt and trousers. Unlike those many times in the darkness of the summer nights when they had both bathed naked in the cool, lapping waters of the bay, he had, in deference to the nearby lane and its occasional traveller, modestly donned his bathing trunks. She watched as he picked his way through the rocky shingle to the water's edge. Even moving as carefully as this he managed somehow a kind of loose-limbed grace that was totally unconscious. He never, she mused, made an awkward movement. His legs were long, well-shaped and muscular, the wide shoulders and narrow hips almost perfectly proportioned. She smiled. He hesitated, dipping his sun-warmed foot in the water. 'Cold?' she called.

He grinned over his shoulder. 'As a witch's heart.' He waded in, then with a swift and easy push was off, cutting into the water, the sun gleaming on his wet skin and his black, curly head, the drops that were thrown from his moving arms glittering like flying diamonds. He swam strongly and easily for a few strokes before turning on his back and floating, feet paddling lazily. Christine sat up, drew up her knees and rested her suntanned arms upon them, eyes narrowed against the light.

Their time together here at Ahakista had been more idyllic than she had dared hope for; the cottage, on its tiny rocky peninsula, had been a haven of peace, warmth and laughter in a world that by all accounts seemed to be rushing at breakneck speed into chaos and disaster. Her eyes followed Liam as he turned in the water and began to swim with long, leisurely strokes towards the heron's rock. The bird watched him come with a bright eye and a haughty cock of its head. Christine took a slow, deep breath, tasting the sea in the air, feeling the sun on her bare shoulders. She ran her fingers through her tangled, sun-bleached hair. If only, if only. If only she could make time stand still. If only there were no past, and no future. If only life could always be this uncomplicated. If only today could last for ever.

A small, cool breeze ruffled the water suddenly, bringing her skin up in goosebumps. The heron, affronted, rose majestically into the air. Christine stood up, brushed the short flared skirt of her sunsuit free of sand, pushed her feet into her sandals and started back towards the cottage to make the tea.

In the distance, faintly, she heard the sound of a motor-cycle.

She was coming back across the grass towards the rocky shore with a tray in her hands when Liam came out of the water. He leaned against a rock, drying himself lazily, watching her with a smile. The pretty flowered sundress with its short skirt and halter neck suited her marvellously. Her skin was golden in the sun. It was perfectly obvious that the job in America had been a great deal tougher than she had expected, or had admitted; as they had agreed, they had not talked about it, but her physical state had spoken volumes. When she had come home she had been palely subdued, tense and underweight. Now she had filled out again, entirely lost that alarming look of drawn fragility. She had regained her vivacity and the spring was back in her step. She was herself again. He stepped forward to kiss her as she came closer. 'If they aren't the prettiest pair of legs I ever have seen, then my name's Seamus O'Malley.'

She grinned, but her heart was somehow not in it. 'Hi, Seamus.'

Sun-dazzled, he peered at her. 'Christine? Is something the matter?'

She set the tray on the ground and straightened, her movements slow, almost weary, all the blithe happiness gone. Her eyes met his. 'Liam, we – that is I, at least – am going to have to go home. Now.'

'What?' He held out a cool and still-damp hand to her. 'Why? What's happened?'

'A telegram just arrived. From Papa.'

That opened his eyes. 'From your father? He hasn't found out that I'm here with you, has he?'

She shook her head. 'Worse than that.' She reached into her pocket, pulled out the flimsy yellow form. *'Stalin pact with Hitler,'* she read.

*'What?'*

She nodded. 'That's what it says.' She kissed the hand he had offered and let it go, then continued reading. *'War now inevitable. Reserves being called up. Rail and roads chaos. Warning of air raids. Essential you come home at once, while you can.'* She dropped to her knees, started to pour the tea, then stopped, banging the teapot down and closing her eyes. 'Oh, fuck it,' she said, calmly, the first time he had ever heard her use the word. 'Fuck it, fuck it, *fuck it!'*

Liam sat cross-legged beside her. 'In spades,' he said, a little bemusedly.

She lifted her head to look at him. 'What will you do?' she asked, softly, the words almost lost in the wash of the sea.

'What do you mean?'

'You don't have to go back. You're not a British national. You could stay here.'

He stared at her, then threw back his head and defused the moment with a sudden shout of laughter that had the heron, which had a few minutes before returned to his perch, tetchily airborne again. 'Are you right in the head, woman? Stay here? Why would I stay here when the party's over the water? Apart from anything else,' he leaned forward to kiss her sunburned nose, 'you surely don't think I'd let you go to war all on your own? Not even you could take on Herr Hitler single-handed! Not that I've a doubt in the world that you'd try!'

'Damn!' Lottie said, mildly, leaning to the mirror to apply her lipstick as the wireless murmured in the background. 'I suppose that's put paid to *my* chances of dancing the night away on the *Queen Mary*.'

Emma rocked baby Charlie gently in her arms. The soft, blond head lolled on her shoulder. She breathed the warm and milky smell of him. She closed her eyes for a moment. 'Of course I realise you'll have to go,' she said, calmly. 'What choice is there?'

'None,' Alex said, bleakly, gathering them both in his arms and holding them much too tightly.

Ned sighed, rubbed at tense neck muscles and looked into a pair of dark doe eyes. 'I would never have believed,' he said, thoughtfully, 'that I'd be glad that I've got a weak heart.'

'This is it, Jose!' Tom Barker's bright eyes were lit further with excitement. 'This is *it*! The RAF! I'll fly. I'll *fly*!'

'Yes,' Josie said, very quietly.

Siobhan, arms clasped across her breasts, stood at the window of Pamela's small sitting room looking down into the sunny street below. Newspaper boys bellowed their indecipherable messages. A man was standing on a ladder propped up against a lamp post. A young couple strolled past, hand in hand, intent in conversation. They were both carrying gas masks slung across their shoulders. In the clear skies above them a small plane droned, glinting in the sunlight. Siobhan suddenly dropped her face into her hands, covering her eyes. 'Oh, Pamela,' she whispered. 'The children! The *children*!'

# PART THREE

# Chapter *Fifteen*

## France and England, 1940

'Bet y'er glad yer ain't sittin' safely in some pub back in the good old Emerald Isle, eh Sarge? Bet you ain't 'alf glad yer signed on fer this lot, ain't yer?' The speaker, braced wearily against the side of the rattling, bouncing truck, was pale-faced and filthy. Like the other men in the vehicle, he was unshaven and his eyes were bloodshot. 'Bet yer always wanted an unguided tour o' bloody France in June, didn't yer?'

'Think on, Stan,' someone else said, the words sardonic. 'Remember 'oo you're talkin' to there. That's three bets you've laid. Three shirts you've lost, wouldn't be surprised. When did you ever know the Sergeant to lose a bet?'

Liam, driving the vehicle, grinned tiredly and said nothing. He wrenched at the wheel to avoid a young man with a large bundle on his shoulder who, hearing them come up behind him, had turned around and was desperately trying to flag him down. The girl he was with was barefoot, bloody and limping; two small children clung to her hands, too tired, or too frightened, to cry. Grimly Liam accelerated past them. The young soldier sitting beside him leaned forward, his elbows on his knees, shaking his head as he peered out of the dust-clogged windscreen at the endless, shambling column of ragged civilian refugees that stretched as far as the eye could see. 'Where are they all *going*, Sarge?' he asked.

Liam shook his head. Behind them the big guns boomed and growled as the desperate rearguard action to save two routed armies continued. 'God alone knows. Unless they can swim—' He stopped, suddenly alert. '*Shite!* Here comes another one.' He slammed his foot on the brake. 'Out! Everyone *out*! Into the ditch!'

Pandemonium had broken out around them as the civilians, too, heard the sound of the dive-bomber screaming up behind them. Panic-stricken they scattered, scrambling off the road and into the ditches and fields. The plane howled down low and opened fire. Liam crouched in the ditch, clamping his steel hat to his head, curling, wincing, under what small protection it could afford, his skin pricking with sweat beneath the heavy khaki of his uniform. Bullets ripped along the road, churning the dust, their sound all but lost in the shrieks and cries of their victims. Beside Liam the young soldier was swearing, tearfully and steadily, a litany of hate, desperation and helplessness. The plane screamed over them, curled off in a graceful arc into the clear blue sky and was gone. 'Bastard! *Bastard! Fucking bastard!*' Private Reid had jumped to his feet, trembling, and was staring at the bloody mayhem that had erupted about him. His dirty face was tear-streaked. 'Bastard!' he said again, more quietly, his voice choked.

'Back in the truck,' Liam snapped. 'Now! Before – oh, no you don't!' He leaped forward, dragged a man away from the truck door and shoved him, reeling, into the ditch. '*Will you buggers get in here!*' He had launched himself into the driving seat and was revving the engine. The men scrambled aboard as the truck crashed into gear and started to move. The civilians eyed them sullenly. A woman was screaming. Another keened, bent over a dead child.

'Here.' Driving one-handed, Liam reached into his battle-dress pocket and brought out a packet of cigarettes. 'Make yourself useful, lad. Hand them round.' He gave the pack to his companion.

The boy sniffed, surreptitiously rubbed at his face with a filthy hand. 'Thanks, Sarge. Sorry, Sarge. It's just – there's women and little kids out there.'

Jesus, Mary and Joseph, Liam thought tiredly, you're no more than a kid yourself. 'Hand round the fags, will you,' he said gruffly, and the truck ground on, northwards towards the coast.

Dunkirk was on fire; at least that was the first impression that Liam's little band got as they trudged through the blasted and littered sand dunes towards it, the truck having been commandeered five miles back, at Lepanne. Buildings were alight, the docks were on fire, oil tanks were burning. A pall of thick black smoke hung over the stricken town like a curse. The air on the beaches was barely breathable, choked as it was with cordite, sand and dust as the retreating men of the British Expeditionary Force were ceaselessly bombed, strafed and shelled as they waited, helpless, demoralised and exhausted, for rescue. Liam, like his men, was almost too tired to take in the scene before him; over the wide beaches that were scattered with abandoned military equipment, vast queues of weary men, three and four deep, shuffled to the waterline, where lorries and trucks had been driven into the water to form makeshift embarkation platforms, from which a gallant, patchwork fleet of small boats was ferrying them out to where larger vessels waited in the deeper water to receive them. The beach was littered with wreckage and the water too was thick with it. The brutal barrage was taking its toll everywhere. The wounded, the dying and the dead were strewn over the churned and filthy sand. One of the bigger ships – it looked, Liam thought, like a Channel ferry – was pulling away, steaming out to sea, its decks packed.

Anxious and envious eyes followed it. The queues shuffled forward. Liam flinched as a shell landed a short distance away, buried itself in the soft sand and exploded, flinging up a huge pillar of sand and stone. Out at sea the shells were raining down on the rescue boats; even as he watched a small fishing boat disintegrated; so far as he could see, only a handful of men swam away from the wreckage. Flames had begun to blossom on one of the bigger ships. The noise was excruciating.

'What do we do, Sarge?'

Liam shrugged. 'Join a queue, I suppose.'

'Which one?'

Stan grinned, stuck up a thumb. 'The shortest one o'course.'

There was, in fact, more semblance of order than had at first appeared. Moving down the beach, they were accosted by a weary officer who directed them to a queue. Once there they could do nothing but endure the pulverising bombardment and wait, as everyone else was doing.

'Where's the bloody RAF? That's what I want to know,' the man in front of Liam demanded, watching almost dispassionately as a Messerschmitt machine-gunned a mass of men grouped by a stone jetty nearer the town.

'Takin' flyin' lessons,' someone answered, gloomily.

The queue shuffled forward.

Astoundingly, Liam, now that they had stopped moving and despite the conditions, was almost asleep on his feet. He had not slept for – how many? thirty-six? forty-eight? – hours. He and his gunners had been part of a defensive line near the Belgian border until, almost out of ammunition, they had received the order to disable the guns and retreat. Hampered by the fleeing civilians, they had been retreating ever since. They had had one meal in the past two days, courtesy of a field kitchen near Lille. Liam had a splash of carefully conserved water in his water bottle and that was all.

He lost all count of time. Hour by hour, inch by inch, the lapping sea came closer; as did the sound of fighting from beyond the town. The enemy was getting closer every moment.

The sun blazed down from a perfect, cobalt sky. 'Bloody hell could be like this,' someone muttered.

The sleeve of the battledress of the man in front of Liam was ripped from shoulder to elbow. Beneath it was a stained and dirty bandage. The man had his arm about his companion, whose head was swathed in what looked like a bloodstained rag. Flies buzzed.

They moved again.

A shell screamed overhead and landed in the sea not far from them. Water fountained into the air. The little boat that was headed for the makeshift pontoon rocked, then righted itself.

Stan nudged him. 'Wake up, Sarge. Nearly there. Just think of it. Fish an' chips an' a pint.'

Liam blinked and smiled a little. 'Sure, an' don't they say that hope springs eternal?'

He shook himself, forcing himself to sharper awareness. He looked around, wondering if Alex had made it to the beaches. He, too, had been in France when the French army had collapsed and the Germans had overrun the country.

'Come on, mate. Up we go.' Water was lapping at his boots. He scrambled on to the lorry. It wasn't a comfortable place to be. It seemed, somehow, even more exposed than the beach, and if anything even hotter. There was another seemingly interminable wait as the small pleasure boat took on as many as it could carry and set off. A little fishing boat took its place. Minutes later they were chugging through the churning sea towards the mother ship. The fishing boat pulled up alongside. One by one the rescued men set off up the rope ladder that hung down the side. Liam found himself beside young Private Reid. The boy's face was white as a sheet.

'Sarge – I can't!' he said. He was trembling, his eyes on the rope ladder that hung and swayed as the big ship moved on the waves. 'I *can't!*'

'Come on, lad. Move along.' The voice was impatient.

'No.' There was panic in the word. Reid shook his head. 'It's too high. I can't. I'll fall!'

Liam grabbed his arm and pulled him to one side, letting the others go ahead. 'Calm down, lad. Calm down! You have to. 'Tis your only chance. Come on. You go ahead. I'll help you.' He almost physically lifted the boy on to the side of the boat. 'Right. Step across. Grab the rungs. Take your time. Don't listen if they try to hurry you. There – you're on,' he added encouragingly as the distressed boy all but flung himself across the gap between the two ships and, more by luck than judgement, found himself clinging to the ladder. 'Up you go. I'm right behind you.'

Painfully slowly the boy inched up the ladder. Liam swung across the gap and on to the ladder. Above him Reid had frozen. Liam reached up firmly to take hold of his right foot and guide it to the next rung.

The ladder shifted as someone else jumped on to it.

'Come on, Pete. You can do it.' It was Stan, leaning over the rails above, hands held out encouragingly. Reid looked up. And, petrified as he was, he lost his footing on the wet rungs entirely. As he slipped his flailing feet caught Liam, sending him swinging almost off the ladder, hanging by only one hand, smashing his back painfully against the ship's side. Almost at the same moment a shell exploded within yards of the fishing boat, setting it tossing wildly. The man beneath Liam screamed as he dropped. Liam dangled for a moment, then managed, his own legs swinging, to make a successful grab for a lower rung, giving the boy above him a chance to find his feet again. The men above them, seeing what had happened, were hauling up the ladder. All Liam had to do was hold on. When the fishing boat slammed into the side of the bigger ship he was almost free. Almost, but not quite. The boat smashed into him, crushing his right leg agonisingly between the two boats. He screamed once, then gritted his teeth and locked his fingers about the rung, felt himself being hauled on to the deck and heard, just before he passed out face-down on the gritty wet wood of the deck, Stan's voice, oddly distant. 'Che-*rist*, Sarge. Looks like your war's over, at any rate. Lucky sod.'

That day 110,000 French troops and nearly 230,000 British were rescued from the bloody beaches of Dunkirk by, surely, the most unlikely flotilla that had ever set sail.

Alex Barker was not one of them.

'Well, well, well. The lengths some people will go to to get attention!' Startled, Liam looked up from the newspaper he was reading. Christine cocked her head and smiled at him cheerfully. 'No grapes, I'm afraid. Blame the Führer. Like everything else, it's all his fault.' She bent to kiss him gently, and the tenderness with which her fingers brushed his cheek was at odds with the crisp brightness of her voice.

'My!' he said as she straightened, laying the paper aside. 'Don't we look dashing?'

'Like it?' She tossed her cap and driving gloves on the bed and twirled on her heels, showing off her neat khaki uniform. The one-armed sailor in the next bed grinned appreciatively and winked at Liam.

Liam smiled back, then nodded to the chair beside the bed. 'Do sit down, woman. You're making an exhibition of us both.'

She pulled a face. 'Must I?' I thought I might be able to push you around the garden in a wheelchair. You know – like they did in the Great War. I've seen pictures. It all looked very gallant and romantic—' Her voice faltered for a moment. She put out her hand to him.

He took it, squeezed it reassuringly, but shook his head. 'They won't let me move at all at the moment, I'm afraid. So you'll just have to brush up on your bedside manner and tell me all the news.'

Christine eyed the long, cage-like hump in the bedclothes that was Liam's right leg. 'How is it?' She sat down, still holding his hand.

He shrugged. 'They don't know yet. Some pretty important bits and pieces got mangled, I'm afraid. They've oper-
ated a couple of times. Now, as they say, we'll just have to
suck it and see.' He held up his hand as she opened her
mouth to speak. 'My turn. Simple question. What on earth
are you doing here?'

'Visiting you.'

'Twirp. I mean, how did you get here?'

She smiled a little smugly. 'Somebody else's general had
a meeting in Norwich. So I smiled nicely at my general and
asked if I could swop for a day, then I smiled nicely at the
other driver and she agreed, then I smiled nicely at *her*
general, explained the situation and asked if I could come
here while he got on with winning the war, and he said yes.'
She spread her free hand. 'Simple, really. That's one thing
about the war, you know – it does teach you new tricks.'

'Good God,' he said, soberly. 'If you're learning new
tricks, that's another bone I'll have to pick with Hitler.'

She laughed.

Liam settled back on his pillows. 'Right. Bring me up to
date on the news. Any word about Alex?'

Christine shook her head. 'No. Emma's out of her mind
with worry. It's been nearly four weeks. We're hoping that
no news is good news – I mean, I guess it all must be such
a muddle over there that it'll take some time to sort out.
But it's very hard for her.'

Liam nodded. 'I heard from her a week ago. She sent a
picture of Charlie. He looks a grand kid.'

'He's a poppet. And a real monkey.'

'What about everyone else?'

'Papa's in America.'

'*America?* What the hell's he doing there?'

She lifted a shoulder. 'We aren't supposed to know, but
I think it's something to do with this lend-lease business, or
whatever they call it. He knows an awful lot of people over
there from before the war, of course. He's negotiating for
some government department or other, but it's all terribly

hush-hush. Everything is, nowadays,' she added, ruefully. 'Mama—' A shadow crossed her face. 'Well – I told you in my last letter – Mama isn't at all well again. All the talk of an aerial attack on London terrified her, and even though it hasn't happened – well, nothing like they said it would, at any rate – she's a bundle of nerves. She and Mary went down to the cottage for a while but,' she nodded towards the paper that Liam had been reading, 'you can see what's going on down there. They're bombing the Channel ports and raiding the airfields. I told you Lottie's in the WAAF, didn't I? She's at Biggin Hill – that's probably something else we're not supposed to know – and last I heard Tom was stationed at Hornchurch, flying Spitfires.' She looked down at their linked hands for a moment, her face suddenly sombre. 'It hardly seems possible, does it? Little Tom. The baby of the bunch. Up there dodging bullets and trying to kill people. And by all accounts, believe it or not, enjoying it.' She was quiet for a moment, then shook her head and lifted it with a small, quick smile. 'That's something else the war teaches you, isn't it? It doesn't pay to think. Or to remember. Live for the day. Accept it all. And hope for the best. Anyway,' she added, brightly, 'Josie seems to think Tom's got a charmed life. He's already managed to get two wrecked machines back safely, without so much as scratching himself. Now, who's left?'

'Ned and Lottie. Ned's still at university?'

'Yes. Though the war's messed things up there, too, and his course has been cut short. He'll be home soon, I think. He's thinking of applying for the Civil Service. With his heart, of course, there's no question of active service. As for Josie, she's doing something with evacuees.' She grinned suddenly. 'She says it's like trying to keep a genie in a bottle. You get them gone, and then they're back again. You can't blame them, really. I mean, it's been ten months, and nothing's really happened in London. Even the bomb in Birmingham was the IRA and not the Germans. If you ask me, we're all much more likely to break our necks in the damned black-out than to get bombed out of house and home. So,' she sat back in her chair, 'that's about it, I think. London's rather weird at the moment, but quite exciting; full of Free French and Poles and such – Lottie's got a decided pash on the Poles, wouldn't you know it? Rationing's a pain – they've rationed tea now, would you believe! – and the Air Raid Wardens are an even worse pain. A bigger bunch of jumped-up, officious busybodies I don't think I've ever come across.' Quite suddenly she swallowed hard and bowed her head, bringing Liam's hand to her lips. She sat quite still, her soft mouth resting on his fingers. He could feel its trembling against his skin.

He reached his other hand to her short, curly hair. 'Hey,' he said, gently, 'come on, now.'

'I've been so worried.' She spoke in a whisper. 'When your telegram came, I thought—' She swallowed. He tightened his grip on her hand. 'And then, your letters haven't really told me anything. I was afraid—'

'They told you I love you, didn't they?'

She nodded, still hiding her face from him.

He tilted her chin, forced her to look at him. She blinked away the tears.

'Fer Gawd's sake, Paddy.' It was the one-armed sailor. 'Give the girl a kiss! We don't mind. Do we lads?'

'To be sure,' Liam said, cocking an eyebrow, his eyes still on Christine's, 'an' wasn't I just about to do that very thing?'

It was a month later, at the start of a blazingly beautiful August and whilst what had come to be called the Battle of Britain was being fought in the skies above southern England, that Emma Barker finally heard what had happened to her young husband.

'He's alive, Aunt Pamela. He's alive! He's in a prisoner-of-war camp somewhere in Germany. The Red Cross has been in touch. He was wounded, but not badly. He's written me a letter – Aunt Pamela? Are you still there?'

The silence at the other end of the line lasted for a few seconds longer, then Emma heard her mother-in-law clear her throat. 'Yes, darling. I'm still here. You say he was wounded?'

'Yes. A shell splinter in his shoulder. But he says he's all right now. He sends his love. Will you be seeing Mama? Will you tell her for me? Tell her Charlie and I will be round on Thursday afternoon, as we arranged. Oh, Aunt Pamela, isn't it wonderful? He's *alive*! Look – I'll have to go – I think our three minutes must be up. Come to Holland Park on Thursday and you can play with your wicked little grandson.' After putting down the telephone Emma swooped on Charlie, who was sitting in the middle of the floor playing with a set of battered little Dinky toys that Ned had found for him. He giggled as she swept him up into her arms and cuddled him fiercely to her. 'Daddy's alive,' she whispered into his hair. 'One day – one day he'll come back. One day he'll come home to us. You'll see.'

The doorbell jangled. She put the child down and turned. The man who had come into the shop smiled, diffidently. He was of medium height and squarely built. His clothes were shabby and his shoes scuffed. From his swarthy skin and the cast of his features Emma guessed him to be a foreigner. His thick hair was jet black and his dark eyes, even when, as now, he was smiling, were melancholy.

'May I help you?'

'Mrs Barker?'

Emma nodded, puzzled. 'Yes.'

He spread his hands, inclined his head a little. 'I hope I don't inconvenience you. My name is Steinberg. Rudi Steinberg. I am at present doing some research concerning the Labour Movement in England. A friend suggested the works of Charles Booth, and suggested also that you might have copies of some of them.' His voice was soft, his pronunciation a little too meticulous. Emma could not for the life of her place the underlying accent.

'We do have some of them, yes – there are seventeen volumes, you know, but—'

'Would they be very expensive?'

'That's the problem,' Emma said. 'I don't sell books any more. It's the war, you see – the shortage of paper – it's getting harder and harder to replenish stocks. Even second-hand books aren't easily come by any more. So I've turned the shop into a lending library. It costs five shillings to join, I'm afraid, but then you're allowed up to four books at sixpence each, and you can keep them for as long as you like providing another member doesn't request them. Would that be of any help to you?'

'Indeed it would.' Again the expressive and somehow totally un-English spread of the hands. 'As I'm sure you can see, my funds are a little limited.'

Emma scooped Charlie off the floor and on to her hip. The little boy held out his hand to the stranger. 'Car,' he said, solemnly.

Rudi Steinberg touched the child's plump little fist with a long finger. 'Why, so it is,' he said.

Emma smiled at the gentleness of the touch and the words. 'Do you have children?' There was something about this quiet, sad-looking man that she instinctively liked.

'No.'

There was a small, somehow awkward silence. 'Well,' said Emma, briskly, 'if you'll just fill in a form for me.' She went to a filing cabinet, extracted a form, put it on the desk. 'I'll show you where the Booth books are. You can choose which you want. I think most of them are there.'

'Thank you.'

After he had gone she glanced at the form before she filed it. He had given an address in Marylebone, and listed his occupation as 'shop assistant'. Strange. He had not struck her in the least as being a shop assistant. She shrugged, then laughed a little. What was she, if not the same? A shop assistant whose husband was alive after all.

To Charlie's delight she waltzed him around the shop, humming happily.

Alex was safe.

Liam was discharged from hospital at the end of the first week of September; not so much because he was properly mobile again, but because the hospital needed the bed, and he was now considered to be walking wounded. He was, for the moment at least, still in uniform, and he was also still in a considerable amount of pain. There was, the doctor had informed him cheerfully, absolutely no knowing how long that would last, nor how complete a recovery he could expect eventually to make. At least the combination of uniform and walking stick got him a seat on the train and willing hands to help with his kitbag.

The train crawled through the bright and sunny East Anglian morning, stopping and starting, sometimes apparently dying, creeping through stations from which all names and signs had been removed, and through a flat, rich countryside that basked beneath a cloudless sky. It was packed. Every seat was taken. Servicemen sat on their kitbags in the corridors beside civilians perched on their suitcases. A baby in the next carriage cried monotonously. By the time they had been travelling for an hour, as a distraction from pain and boredom Liam had engaged the naval rating sitting next to him in a game of poker, with cigarettes as the stake. The journey seemed unending; it was mid-afternoon before they steamed at last through the crowded slums of the East End towards Liverpool Street station. His new friend, seeing the sweat standing on Liam's forehead as he struggled from the train, cheerfully shouldered Liam's kitbag as well as his own, and slowed his steps to Liam's as they made their way to the taxi rank. Then, having ascertained the direction in which Liam wanted to travel, he disappeared into the seething crowd, to appear a few moments later grinning triumphantly. 'There you are, mate. I've hitched you a lift. Lady over there with the kids is going your way. She says you're more than welcome to join them.' He shook his head at Liam's thanks. 'Think nothing of it, chum. From what I've heard, anyone who was in that shambles deserves a bloody medal, never mind the odd free taxi ride.' He slapped Liam's shoulder and was gone.

London, too, was bright with sunshine. Despite the circumstances the capital seemed to be enjoying its Saturday. Couples strolled amongst the gun emplacements the barrage balloon moorings and neat allotments in the parks, and there were queues outside the cinemas. Children played warlike games in the streets and there were uniforms everywhere, some of which Liam did not recognise.

Liam had decided to go first to Emma's bookshop; apart from anything else, he was not at all certain he could manage the climb to his own rooms. Emma was his best point of contact with Christine; the war had changed many things, but he strongly suspected that it had not changed the fact that a half-crippled Irish gambler was no fit suitor for Christine Clough; so best, he had reasoned, to avoid the Holland Park house.

He bade the little family who had given him the lift goodbye, and the taxi driver helped him with his kit-bag. As they approached the door of the shop it opened, and a man came out into the street. Liam caught only a glimpse of him; shock-headed, swarthy-skinned and with dark and melancholy eyes. The man raised his hat, polite but unsmiling, as he passed.

In the shop Emma was standing, holding a pile of books and leaning against the desk, gazing after the man and frowning. When she saw Liam, however, her face lit in delight and she dropped the books on to the desk. 'Liam! *Liam!* Oh – how splendid to see you! Why didn't you tell me you were coming? Oh, Liam!' She ran towards him, then stopped, as he flinched a little. 'Oh, poor you! Does it hurt very much? Here, sit down.' She pulled a chair forward.

'I'll drop this 'ere then, mate, shall I?' the taxi driver asked, loudly.

'Oh, yes, please.'

The man dumped the kitbag, raised his eyebrows. Liam fished in his pocket for a coin, then handed it to him. 'Thanks, mate.' The driver signalled towards Emma with sly eyes. 'Good luck.'

As the door closed behind him, Emma dropped a kiss on Liam's cheek and gave him a very careful hug. 'Rest for a moment. I'll just put these away, then I'll make a cup of tea and we can catch up on everything.' She picked up the pile of books, stood looking down at them for a moment, shaking her head. 'This blasted war! It's turning everything on its head, isn't it?'

Liam had reached into his pocket and was rolling a cigarette. He looked at her enquiringly.

Emma walked to the bookshelves, talking over her shoulder as she went. 'The man you saw coming out of the shop as you came in? His name is Steinberg. Rudi Steinberg. He was a lecturer at Berlin University until the Nazis came to power. They threw him out, of course, because he's Jewish. He lost his job and his home. He's got no idea what's happened to most of the rest of his family. He escaped and came here in 'thirty-three; he keeps body and soul together by working part time in a shop. And now they're going to intern him as an enemy alien. It's ridiculous! He's so nice – such a gentle man! It's madness – these are the people who *suffered* under the Nazis! What are we doing putting them in prison camps?' She put the books back on the shelf. 'They've closed the Italian restaurant down the road, you know. How on earth could anyone imagine that *Luigi* was an enemy spy – oh, no!' In the distance a siren had begun to wail. 'Oh, blast it! They'll wake the baby—' She stopped. Another siren had joined the first, and another. Gradually all over the city the warnings picked up, one after the other. And now there were other sounds: the rumble of guns, the heavy drone of engines.

Emma looked at Liam with wide, startled eyes, then turned and ran for the stairs. Liam struggled to his feet and went to the door. Others were already in the street, peering skywards. 'God Almighty!' someone said. 'This is it. There's hundreds of them!'

An Air Raid Warden's whistle shrieked piercingly, a man's voice was calling orders. People were beginning to walk quickly, heads still tilted to look at the sky. No-one ran.

'There's a public shelter at the end of the road.' Emma had come up behind him. She was cradling her sleeping son on her arm, his fair head on her shoulder. 'But we're OK here. There's a cellar – I've fixed it up quite comfortably, actually.' The noise of the bombers was coming closer. An anti-aircraft gun opened up nearby. The windows rattled.

'Best you get the little one down—' Liam began and then stopped. The sky had darkened; wave after wave of enemy bombers were droning overhead, shepherded and protected by the little fighting Messerschmitts, which in their turn were being harried by the Spitfires and Hurricanes of the RAF. There were indeed hundreds of them, and they flew steadily in deadly formation over the city that their master had sworn to subjugate. The Luftwaffe had failed in its attempt over the summer to break the spirit and the resolve of the RAF; now it was aiming to break the spirit and the resolve of London and her people. Hitler's long-promised blitzkrieg against the city had begun.

'Where are they going?' Emma whispered.

Liam shook his head.

Charlie stirred, stuck his thumb in his mouth and settled back to sleep.

# Chapter Sixteen

The raiders were heading for the docklands of the East End of London, where the thousands of tons of high explosive and incendiary bombs that they dropped caused raging fires that then guided them back during the night to drop more; a pattern that was to be repeated again and again in the months that followed. After the first wave retreated, leaving an inferno of burning docks, factories and homes behind it, and the all-clear was sounded, Liam and Emma came out of their cellar and went to the top of the house to look out of the window. The vicious glow in the evening sky to the east spoke for itself.

'Jesus, Mary and Joseph. It looks as though the whole bloody world's going up in flames,' Liam said, softly.

Emma clutched Charlie to her, biting her lip. There was a distant explosion and she flinched.

'D'you have a camp bed?' Liam was suddenly brisk, distracting her from the sinister glow in the sky.

Emma turned her back on the window. 'Er – yes. There's a spare one in the cellar.'

'Right. Would you think it a good idea if I stayed for a while? Until we know what's happening? It may be that this is a one-off raid, but – well, it looks as if it might be the start of something nasty. Would you like me to stay? I could sleep in the shop, if you don't mind me joining you in the cellar if there's a raid.'

'Oh, please! Liam – would you?'

'Of course. I may not be a hundred per cent,' he leaned on his stick, shifted his leg a little, 'but at least you'd have someone around. That is, if you're sure you wouldn't rather go back to Holland Park?'

'No.' The word was quick. Emma had regained her equilibrium. 'They've only got an Anderson in the garden. I don't think it's as safe as my cellar, to be honest with you – it certainly isn't as dry! – and anyway, this is my living, and my home. I can't leave it – I won't let them make me leave it.' She jerked her head back, fiercely, towards the fire-reddened sky. The words she spoke were to be echoed all over the city in the days and weeks to come.

'That's settled, then. I'll stay, at least until we know what's going on. And to celebrate the decision,' Liam reached into the pocket of his battledress and pulled out a flask, 'why don't we have a wee nip?'

Emma could not help but laugh. 'Oh, Liam,' she said, 'you may have damaged yourself a bit, but you haven't changed, have you?'

Day after day, night after night, the bombers came to rain death and destruction on the city; and each morning Londoners emerged from their shelters, their cellars and their Underground stations to face fresh devastation. Whole streets disappeared overnight; churches burned, ancient buildings were reduced to rubble. Most raids left hundreds dead and thousands injured; yet, after the first shock of the onslaught, the people of the capital – grumbling, exhausted but grimly determined – adapted to the nerve-racking bombardment and obstinately went about their everyday affairs as best they could. Windowless shops were open for business. Bus drivers created their own imaginative routes when roads were closed. Office staff struggled to work through streets that still burned, past flaming gas mains, broken water pipes and unexploded bombs, feet crunching on broken glass, whilst exhausted rescue workers still dug in the smoking ruins. Many developed a philosophic, almost fatalistic attitude to the bizarre situation; not even the best of shelters would protect you from a direct hit, nor could warning always be given of a rogue, strafing fighter, so if a bomb or a bullet had your name on it, that was that; you were a gonner anyway. Within a very short time cinema audiences stayed in their seats when the 'raiders overhead' sign flashed on, dance bands played on until the sounds of a raid were too close to be ignored, and when, as a warning wailed, a bus stopped next to a public shelter, most of the passengers would simply shrug and stay put.

For some, however, such stoicism was impossible, and predictably Siobhan Clough was one of them. The thought of the bombing had taken her to the verge of breakdown; the reality was too much for her. She was terrified of staying in the house, yet even more terrified of leaving it. She could neither sleep nor eat and she cried almost constantly; before the month was out she was back in the psychiatric clinic, which had been evacuated for safety to a large house near Tunbridge Wells. Since the clinic was very short-staffed, it was agreed that Mary McCarthy should go with her, to help care for her.

'I spoke to your mother on the phone last night,' Christine told Liam. 'It seems Mama is sedated for most of the time. Mary's helping out with the other patients as well. It sounded as if she's quite enjoying it, though she's worried about Mama, of course. And, with Mrs Turner gone off to cook for the army, about Ned and me being here at home on our own.' She grinned, wickedly. 'And with good reason,' she added. They were in her bedroom, Liam lying naked on her bed, his arms behind his head, watching as she dressed to go on duty. His damaged leg was propped on a pillow for comfort. Christine glanced at it. 'When do you go back to the hospital?'

'Day after tomorrow. Do all of you wear such fetching underwear?'

She pulled a face at him. 'Any idea what's going to happen?'

'They're trying to decide if I need another operation. One way or the other the Doc seems to think I'll be on Civvy Street by Christmas. He doesn't think I'm going to be any more use to the army.'

She was passing the bed. She dropped a quick kiss on his forehead. 'Fraud!' she said. 'You were on pretty active duty half an hour ago.'

'Any complaints?'

'None. Are you going back to the shop?'

'Later, yes. I promised to mind it for a bit while Emma takes Charlie to visit Alex's mother.'

She kissed him again, stood back for a moment, looking at him. Liam had never once complained of pain, but the signs of it were etched in the deepened lines of his face, and he was still very thin. 'Rest for a bit. You look tired.'

He smiled, faintly. 'Everyone's tired.'

'That's true. But not everyone's had their leg smashed to smithereens and stuck back together again. I'll have to run. I'm on the long shift tonight, but I'm off tomorrow evening. Any chance of the pictures?'

'Not bloody *Gone with the Wind* again?'

She laughed from the doorway. 'We've only seen it twice. Lottie's seen it three times already.'

'Lottie sees it with a different guy each time.'

She smiled, sweetly. 'Would you like me to try that?'

'You'd better not.'

The nature of her smile changed. 'I do love you,' she said, softly, after a moment, and was gone.

He lay still, listening to her light footsteps, heard the closing of the front door. In these uncertain and perilous times he hated her to be out of his sight, hated to know that she drove, often during air raids, through the blacked-out streets of the battered city at night. Always there was, buried deep, but never quite deeply enough, the all but intolerable fear that each lightly spoken goodbye could be the last. He supposed he was not the only one to find that the threats and dangers of war focused the mind wonderfully on the priorities of life. And Christine – volatile, infuriating, sharp-tongued, wholly enchanting Christine – was increasingly, it might even be said worryingly, becoming a priority in his. Just two days before he had almost asked her to marry him. That was how bad it was. Half-smiling, he rubbed at his eyes tiredly, shifted his aching leg a little. The house was very quiet. A plane droned overhead. In the distance a siren wailed. Sod it! He wasn't moving now. He closed his eyes.

Ned stood in the bedroom doorway, looking at the still figure on the bed. Liam's head was turned away from him a little, the sharp, handsome profile silhouetted against the white cotton pillow. As the younger man watched, Liam twitched a little in his sleep, muttered something. His long body was pale, almost milk-white, and the network of scars on his leg stood out ferociously. The wound and the long stay in hospital had taken their toll; the lean strength that so characterised Liam had, for now, gone. The wide shoulders were bony, he was quite painfully thin. As sleepers do to those who watch them, he looked almost touchingly vulnerable.

Ned leaned against the door jamb, tossed back the heavy lick of fair hair which, as always, immediately flopped back across his forehead, and reached into his pocket for cigarettes. A couple of months off his twenty-first birthday, he was of medium height and was slightly and gracefully built. The forget-me-not eyes with their long, fair lashes still dominated a face that was smooth and tanned after the long hot summer. But there were dark rings under those eyes and he had a nervous habit of blinking fiercely every now and again. The hand that held the lighter to his cigarette was not quite steady. He looked around the room with a practised eye, noting his sister's casually discarded civilian clothes upon the chair, the fact that the hanger on the door of the wardrobe was empty – Christine was in uniform and on duty, then – the dwindling supply of creams and scents upon the dressing table. He must have a word with Piers. He seemed to be able to get almost anything, despite the shortages. It would be no bad thing to keep in with Christine. His eyes came back to the sleeping figure on his sister's bed. After a long, quiet moment Ned lifted his knuckles and rapped sharply upon the open door.

Liam stirred.

Ned rapped again, watching him as he woke.

'Shit!' Only half-awake, Liam had tried to move. He jumped, stiffened, then by an act of will that Ned could almost feel, relaxed, going with the pain. 'Ned. What are you doing here?'

'I live here. Remember?' Ned grinned, louchely, glancing around the room. 'Though not as entertainingly as you do, apparently.'

Liam returned his grin, struggled to sit up. 'Dammit. I didn't mean to go to sleep. What time is it?'

Ned consulted his watch. 'Just gone three.'

Liam was sitting on the side of the bed, reaching for his clothes.

'Do you need any help?' Ned asked quietly.

'No.' The word was a little too quick, a little too emphatic. 'Ned, can I use the phone? I promised Emma I'd get back to mind the shop for her – oh, *blast* the thing!' The sound of the siren had begun to lift and wail. Anti-aircraft gunfire sounded in the distance. 'Haven't those sods got any sense of time at all? They're not due for another hour at least!'

'I'm not sure they set their timetable to our convenience.' Ned's voice was light, but he had stiffened. He strained his ears. Faintly the unmistakable sound of the German bombers was coming closer; a steady, heavy growl that assaulted the eardrums and stretched the nerves to breaking point. Another siren sounded, very near this time. A whistle shrieked in the street outside. 'Come on downstairs. You'll have to stay now anyway. They won't let you through until the all-clear. Come and have a drop of Air Raid Special in the shelter with me.'

Gingerly easing his leg into his trousers, Liam looked up enquiringly.

'Needs must when the devil pushes,' Ned said. 'If my dear Papa is going to spend the war safe and sound in Washington – and it looks as if he is – then I've taken it upon myself to make sure that if a bomb does drop on us his collection of malts will be safe. There won't be a lot left, mind, but it will be safe. He has some very fine whiskies, you know.' He smiled, very brightly, then blinked fiercely as the air vibrated to several explosions. 'I've moved them all into the Anderson. It does help to pass the time, I find. Do you need help getting down the stairs?'

'No.'

Ned took no offence at the brusqueness of the word. 'Please yourself. I'll see you down there.'

'Do we have to go to the shelter? Can't we stay in the kitchen?'

Ned's chin came up. 'The whiskey,' he said, and flinched again as another series of explosions rocked the city, 'is in the shelter.'

Liam shrugged. 'Fair enough.' He reached for his shirt.

By the time he had manoeuvred his way down the stairs there was no sign of Ned. The raid was a heavy one. The noise was thunderous. The house shook every time a nearby anti-aircraft gun opened fire. Liam, privately, had his reservations about the things; understandably no figures were ever given about the amount of damage or the number of casualties caused by stray shells of a friendly nature. Ned had propped open the front and the back doors, to minimise any possible blast damage. Liam saw the sense of this, but questioned the faith in human nature that it implied. He went to the back door.

The Anderson shelter was perhaps twenty yards away, an

earthy hump with an open, sandbag-protected entrance that looked, he thought wryly, a bit like Alice in Wonderland's rabbit hole. His walking stick clicking on the flagstones, he limped across the yard. A squadron of bombers throbbed overhead. He ducked his head into the darkness. Vaguely he could discern candlelight, but after the sunshine of the yard he could see virtually nothing. 'Are there steps?'

'Yes. Hold on.' He felt Ned's hand on his arm. The younger man guided him to the edge. 'Wooden steps. Best to come down backwards.'

Best not to come down at all. Liam did not say it. The atmosphere of the shelter was thick with cigarette smoke. He could smell the whiskey. He sat down, carefully, bumped down the steps on his buttocks with the aid of his cane and his good leg, settled himself on a bottom bunk that had been made up into a fairly comfortable bench.

'It's a good job it hasn't rained recently.' Ned was talking very fast. He stopped at the crump of every explosion before rushing on. 'If we get an inch of rain you can guarantee six inches of water down here.' He handed Liam a glass.

Liam looked round, smiling, trying desperately not to imagine Christine out in this. They had deep shelters at the headquarters where she worked. She'd be safe. She would. 'Nice set-up. All we need is a pack of cards and some willing punters to fleece.' His eyes were getting used to the darkness. The shelter had been made relatively comfortable. There were candles in holders attached to the walls, the two top bunks were made up into beds, the two lower furnished comfortably with bolsters and cushions. The tumbler that Ned had handed him was cut-glass. He sipped it. And for the first time in his life the thought of George Clough brought a slow and appreciative grin.

Ned poured himself another very large glass of his father's whiskey.

It took no kind of expert to divine how terrified the young man was. At first Liam judged it best not to embarrass the boy by letting him see that he knew. They talked in desultory fashion of Ned's appearance before the Civil Service Board, Liam's likely discharge from the army, Alex's fate and Emma's stoical bravery in the face of it. But in this confined, almost intimate space with its sheltering darkness Ned's fear was almost palpable. A bottle was emptied. Another started. There came a time when silence fell between them. The attack was easing. They heard the chatter of machine-gun fire as an RAF fighter took on one of the escorting Messerschmitts; the searing howl as one of them came down.

Ned dropped his face into his cupped hands, shuddering.

Liam reached across the narrow space between the two bunks and laid a quiet hand on Ned's shoulder. He could feel the fragile bones, the deadly tension that tautened the sinews.

'I should be in the same dotty-hospital as my mother, you know that?' Ned said at last, his voice choked.

'Don't be daft.'

'It's true.'

'No.' Liam was patient. 'Don't think it.'

Beyond the fortified doorway an autumn twilight was falling. There was a long moment of silence, which coincided with a lull outside. Faintly, in the far distance, the steady drone of an all-clear sounded, but suddenly, closer, there was the crump of another bomb. Ned leaned his face into Liam's supporting hand. 'I'm so frightened,' he said, simply. 'I hate this war. I *hate* it! What am I doing here? Why is someone trying to kill me? What have I ever done to them?'

Tiredly Liam closed his eyes, cupped his hand behind the boy's neck and drew him closer to him, comforting him. Ned's forehead rested in the crook of his shoulder. Nothing in his privileged life had ever prepared him for this.

'I'm a coward,' Ned said.

'No. You're not.'

'But I'm *afraid*. All the time.'

'So is everyone. You're not alone.'

There was a very long moment of quiet. Ned lifted his head, looked at his companion in the candlelit darkness. The bombers had gone, though every soul in the city knew they would be back when darkness fell. All over the capital now the all-clear was sounding. Liam could not see the boy's eyes; they were tiny caverns of darkness in the candlelight. 'Oh yes, I am,' Ned said. 'That's what you don't understand.'

In the silence that followed the words they both heard the sound of the telephone shrilling from the house. 'You'd best go and answer that,' Liam said.

Ned scrambled up the steps, ran across the yard, taking the bottle with him. With difficulty, Liam hauled himself after him. When he reached the house it was quiet. The half-empty bottle of whiskey stood on the table. He listened for a moment, then went up the steps that led from the kitchen to the hall. Ned was standing looking down at the telephone he had just replaced on its cradle. His face was ashen beneath the summer's tan. His eyes when he lifted them to Liam were huge, and utterly blank.

'Ned?' Liam took a step towards him, alarmed. 'What is it? Bad news?'

Ned tried to speak, swallowed, cleared his throat. 'The clinic,' he whispered. 'A direct hit. Mama – *Jesus Christ!*'

Liam stood as if turned to stone. 'Ma?' he asked, his voice all but expressionless.

'Both of them.' Tears had started to stream down Ned's drawn face. '*Both of them!* They were supposed to be *safe* down there!' He stumbled to Liam, buried his face in his shoulder, sobbing uncontrollably, with wrenching, ugly sobs that shook his body in Liam's arms.

'Nobody's safe. Anywhere,' Liam said quietly, and closed his own eyes against the horror of it. Outside, the last of the all-clear sirens was wailing over the city.

Emma hitched Charlie more comfortably on her hip, slipped

her key into the lock and pushed open the door. She felt drained; oddly detached. Her eyes and her head ached abominably, from tiredness and from grief-stricken tears. Liam had broken the news to her as gently as he could, but there had been no way to cushion the shock. The raids over the last couple of nights had been particularly bad; she had not slept. She felt almost light-headed. Even the weather had changed, seeming to mirror her mood. The afternoon was dismal. A faint drizzle drifted along the drab street. She closed the door behind her.

The house was very quiet. She could hear the ticking of the grandfather clock. 'Ned?' she called. 'Chris?'

There was no reply.

She started up the stairs. 'Stars,' Charlie explained, bright-eyed and solemn, 'ban'sters.'

'Yes, darling. Stairs and bannisters.'

She was rewarded with a huge, pearly-toothed grin.

On the main landing the drawing room door stood open. She walked past it, across the shadowed landing, towards the stairs that led up to the bedrooms.

'Emma?'

She almost jumped from her skin. She stopped, walked slowly back to the drawing room door. 'Papa?' she asked, incredulously.

George Clough was sitting in an armchair beside the empty hearth; he was holding something in his hands. The air of the room was chill. There was a moment of absolute silence. Charlie leaned inquisitively back in her arms, trying to see the figure in the chair. 'Hello, man,' he said.

'I'm sorry, Papa,' Emma said, very quietly, 'I've just come to pick up some clothes. I didn't know you were here.'

'No-one does. I hadn't time to let anyone know. I managed at the last minute to wangle a lift on a government plane.' George's voice was hoarse. He sounded tired. He stood up. Emma took a small step backwards, her arms tightening around Charlie. She saw now what her father was holding; the silver-framed photograph of Siobhan that usually stood on the mantelpiece.

'*Hello*, man!' Charlie, not used to being ignored, said again.

'Hello, little boy.'

'His name's Charlie.'

'I know.'

'Charlie,' Charlie said, proudly, nodding his flaxen head.

Now that he was closer Emma could see the dark rings beneath her father's eyes. If she had not known such a thing to be completely impossible, she would have said there were traces of tears on his face. She opened her mouth to speak. The siren sounded. 'Oh, God,' she said, wearily.

'What are we supposed to do?' George asked.

'We're supposed to go to the shelter, but it's ankle deep in water, so we usually stay in the kitchen. The shelter's only across the yard. We can always nip across to it if they come too close.' She led the way out on to the landing and down the stairs. The kitchen was gloomy. George's hand automatically reached for the light switch. 'No!' Emma said, sharply. 'No lights. The black-out isn't up yet.' She swung Charlie down on to the floor and tucked him under the big pine table, then went to a cupboard and brought out a big box of wooden bricks. 'There you are, Charlie-barley.'

'Will he stay there?' her father asked.

'He's used to it. He's spent more time under tables these past few weeks than he's spent sitting up to them,' Emma said. As she straightened, her eyes lit upon the photograph that her father still carried. She stood very still for a moment. Then, 'We'll leave as soon as the all-clear goes,' she said, quietly. 'I'm sorry to have disturbed you.'

'No need,' he said, brusquely. 'No need at all.'

She sat down, rubbing at her eyes with the heels of her hands.

'You look tired,' he said, awkwardly.

'We're all tired. It's the worst part of it, actually. You

get used to the bombs. It's hard to get used to doing without sleep.'

'I came up from Croydon this morning. I've seen pictures in the Washington papers, of course, but I'd no real idea of the extent of the destruction.'

'You should see the East End,' Emma said, grimly.

Beneath the table Charlie was making little humming noises to himself. There was a small flurry of explosions in the distance. Emma cocked her head and listened.

'How close is too close?' her father asked, his voice just a little too casual.

Emma smiled faintly. 'Closer than that.' She stood up. 'Do you fancy a cup of tea, Papa? I'm sure Chris and Ned won't mind if I borrow a couple of spoonfuls. Ned doesn't like tea anyway.'

'Thank you. That would be nice,' he said, stiffly.

Liam, at Christine's slightly embarrassed request, did not attend Siobhan's funeral, and George Clough, perhaps fortuitously, was on an aeroplane back to Washington on the day Mary McCarthy was buried, so there was no awkward confrontation. A few weeks later, with Christmas approaching, and with the nightly raids having become so much a part of everyday life that only the worst of them was more a topic of conversation than the weather, a large, neatly wrapped parcel turned up at the bookshop. Puzzled, Emma tore it open. '*Chocolate!* And biscuits! Custard creams! And – oh, good heavens! Wherever has all this come from?' She opened the note that was enclosed with the goodies.

Liam was sitting at the desk, a piece of paper in front of him. He was running a finger down what looked like a list, pencilling in ticks here and there. He glanced up.

Emma stared.

'Father Christmas?' Liam supplied, helpfully. 'The Angel Gabriel?'

Emma shook her head. 'Hardly,' she said, faintly. '*Dear Emma, An acquaintance is joining a convoy. I asked him to get this to you if he could. The little boy might like—*' She stopped, blinking suddenly. 'Papa,' she said. 'It's from Papa. He's sent these things for Charlie.'

Liam, manifestly unimpressed, turned his attention back to his list. 'Has he indeed?'

Emma was delving in the box. 'Chiclets. What in the world are Chiclets?'

'Baby chickens.'

'Oh, don't be silly.' Laughing, Emma turned to look at him. Stopped, watching him. 'Liam, what *are* you doing?' she asked.

He scratched his curly head with the pencil. 'House-hunting,' he said, absently.

She stared at him. 'Househunting,' she repeated, blankly. 'Yes.'

'At a time when half of London is being flattened – you're thinking of buying a *house*?'

'More than one, actually.' He was unruffled. 'Can you think of a better time to buy? I went to a couple of agents this morning. There's a whole street in Chelsea where every other house is for sale for a song. A square in Belgravia where thirty-five apartments out of fifty-three are standing empty—'

Emma was still staring at him as if he had taken leave of his senses. 'There is a reason for that, you know,' she said, drily. 'Or hadn't you noticed?'

He grinned, shrugged. 'So – it's a gamble—'

'—and you're a gambler,' she finished for him.

'If ever there was one.'

She deposited the box on the table, sat down opposite him, put her elbows on the surface, resting her chin on her hands. 'You're serious!' she said. And then, grinning suddenly, 'You're mad!'

'Probably. But I can't be sleeping on your floor for ever, can I? And you've enough of your own junk around without putting up with that lot for much longer.' He gestured to several wooden tea chests filled with the possessions he had taken from his rooms when he had given up the lease.

'Thanks,' said Emma.

'And you and Charlie have got yourselves well organised now. You don't need me.'

Impulsively she put a hand across the table to rest it on his arm. 'You've been a really good friend,' she said. 'Charlie loves you to bits.'

'Charlie,' Liam said straightfaced, 'loves everyone to bits. As you well know. Sure, the child has no taste whatsoever.'

'Huh!' Christine said, only half-joking. 'No American food parcels for *us*! Happy Christmas, Daddy dear!'

'He probably knows,' Liam said, helping himself to another generous glassful, 'that you're drinking his whiskey.'

'That's quite beside the point,' Christine said crisply. She was decorating the kitchen of the Holland Park house with prewar Christmas decorations brought down from the attics. 'Oxford Street was absolutely heaving this morning,' she added, 'but I did manage to get some wine. And Ned's found someone in the office with a contact in Suffolk. Chicken for Christmas dinner.'

'Sounds good.' He hesitated. 'Who's cooking it?'

Christine grinned at him around a colourful but fragile paper bell. 'Emma, of course. Who in their right minds would let me loose on a real chicken? And if you don't stop looking so obviously relieved,' she added repressively, 'I might well have to clout you.' She climbed on to a chair, reached to fix the bell to the ceiling. Liam looked on, appreciatively. Christine skipped down from the chair, rummaged in the box. 'How's the househunting going?'

'I've several irons in the fire at the moment. I was waiting to see what they said at the hospital. Now they've told me there's no need to operate again, I'll push on.'

Christine bent to kiss him as she passed. 'That was good

news, wasn't it? So now, here you are – footloose and fancy free.'

He caught her wrist, pulled her closer to him. 'Not the most accurate description I've ever heard,' he said, softly, opening her hand and kissing her palm.

Laughing, she attempted to pull free.

He held on. 'Tell me something.'

'Yes?' She ruffled his hair playfully.

'Do you love me?'

She stilled for a moment, touched a tender finger to his face. 'You know I do.'

'Then marry me.'

Between one breath and another the atmosphere froze. She wrenched her hand from his, turned her back on him. 'No.' Her voice was cold. 'Liam, I've told you before. No. I won't marry you.'

He came to his feet, leaning his hands on the table. 'Why? *Why?* Am I still not good enough for you? Christine – there's a war on – who knows what's going to happen, how much time we have together?'

She turned. Her set face was very pale. 'I hardly think the war can be thought a good reason to get married, do you? I've said no, Liam. I mean no. Why, oh *why*, do you always have to *spoil* things?'

'Is that how you see it?' His temper, inevitably, was rising to match hers. 'I ask you to marry me and you tell me I'm *spoiling* things? For God's own sake, woman, I love you! You know it. You say you love me. Yet you won't marry me and you won't even give me a decent reason!'

'I don't have to give you reasons for what I do or don't do!'

'That's true enough.' The words were bitter. Liam reached for the whiskey bottle. 'Who the hell am I to expect to be given a reason?'

'Oh, don't be so childish!' she snapped.

'And don't you be so bloody arrogant!'

'Bugger off!' She snatched the box from the table and

stormed from the room, slamming the door behind her loudly enough to shake the house to its foundations.

Swearing softly, Liam topped up his glass.

Ned found him a couple of hours later, his head resting on his arm upon the table, his other hand still loosely cupped about the glass. The younger man closed the door softly behind him and crossed the room, a little unsteadily, to stand beside the sleeping figure. Quietly he hitched himself up to sit on the table, then reached in his pocket for his cigarette case. His soft, fair hair was ruffled, his collar open, his tie loosely knotted. He lit the cigarette without taking his eyes off the sleeping man's face; his eyes were heavy-lidded, his face flushed. After a moment Ned put out a hesitant hand and, smiling a little, laid it very gently on the springy black curly hair.

Liam, oblivious, slept on.

# Chapter Seventeen

There followed, for British cities in general and for London in particular, a gruelling winter and spring. As the relentless bombing continued, and in an atmosphere of constant rumour about the possibility – some said the certainty – of invasion, there was hardly a night when the raiders did not attack; and even on those odd occasions people found it all but impossible to sleep. Tempers grew short and nerves were stretched to breaking point; and to make things worse there was little to cheer in the news from the war fronts; in March 1941 Rommel appeared in North Africa and successfully counter-attacked the British lines, though the Australians clung on by the skin of their teeth in Tobruk. In mid-April the raids on London worsened and there were a number of tit-for-tat retaliatory raids on Berlin. Towards the end of the month Athens fell to the Germans. And then, on the night that followed a sunny Cup Final Saturday in May, the capital suffered its most catastrophic raid ever. Terrible damage was inflicted – the Law Courts, the Tower, the Mint were hit, the House of Commons was destroyed by fire – and thousands were killed or injured. For a few days, as Londoners, shocked and weary, struggled once more to clear the wreckage and get their shattered city moving again, chaos reigned. It was perhaps understandable that, as first one night, then another passed quietly, and as the days turned to a week and then two, it took some time for the realisation to sink in; the punishing raids appeared to have stopped. It was as if that last, fearsome, punitive strike had been a final effort to break the city and her people; and it had failed. Whilst endlessly speculating as to the reason why, and despite the odd random raid now and again, people gradually came to acknowledge the fact that the actual Blitz seemed to be over.

'D'you think it's really stopped?' Christine was stacking books on a set of shelves.

'It's been a month.' Liam lifted more books from the packing case and piled them on the table. 'Can you find room for these?'

'Yes, I think so.' Christine reached for them, arranged them, sat back on her heels, pushing her hair back from her forehead and leaving a large smear of dirt on her face. 'Have you met Lottie's Count yet, by the way?'

Liam grinned. 'She brought him round to see me a couple of days ago.'

'I hope you were suitably impressed?'

'To be sure I was. I've never met a Count before. And he plays a good hand of poker. Took ten bob off me.'

Christine surveyed him suspiciously. '*He* took ten bob off *you*?'

'As sure as I stand here.' Liam was straightfaced.

'I don't believe it.'

'Believe it.' His smile was blandly innocent. 'Two things about the Poles. They're all Counts and they all gamble. Stefan was so pleased with his ten bob that he suggested he might bring his friends round for the odd game or two. You've got dirt all over your face.'

'God preserve us from devious Irishmen,' she said, mildly, then she scrambled to her feet and looked around the room. 'Well, I think we're nearly there. What luck the old lady wanted to sell most of the furniture too.'

'She's gone to live with her daughter. There's no room

for it.' Liam too looked around. 'Not exactly what I would have chosen, mind, but there'll be time for that later.' The room was large and square, with a big open fireplace. The furniture was heavy and old-fashioned, but of good quality. The big window, taped against the bombing, looked out on to the Chelsea Embankment. Three doors down two houses had been flattened in the last big raid on the tenth of May. Before the war Liam knew well he could not have afforded the front doorstep, let alone the whole house. At the height of the Blitz it had been, to say the least, a buyer's market. He was well satisfied; the house suited his purposes well.

Christine had wandered to the mirror over the fireplace and was scrubbing at her face with a handkerchief. 'I popped over to Emma's on the way home yesterday.'

'Oh? How are they?'

'They're fine. Charlie is a real sweetheart. Emma's thinking of selling second-hand clothes. Good idea, I'd say, with rationing come in.'

'Any news on Alex?'

'Yes. She's had several letters at once – they must have been held up somewhere. He's well. He's being held in a British prisoners' camp in Germany. He says he's not being treated too badly and he's in good health – bored, though. He's learning German.'

Liam chuckled a little. 'He's in the right place for that.'

Christine turned from the mirror, her face thoughtful. 'There was someone at the shop when I arrived. A German, or perhaps Austrian, from his accent – an internee who'd just been released. Rudi something.'

'I remember. I saw him once. Emma told me about him.'

'They'd been to one of Myra Hess's lunchtime concerts at the National Gallery.'

Liam shrugged. 'Nothing wrong with that.'

'No. Of course not.'

Liam cocked an eyebrow at her tone, but said nothing. He limped to her, kissed her. She leaned against him for a moment, a little tiredly, then pushed away from him, smiling. 'I'll bet you've got not a thing in the kitchen?'

'You'd win.'

'Right.' She was brisk. 'Ned got some real bacon from his Suffolk contact. *And* Mrs Brown – the lady who's looking after the cottage for us – sent us some eggs. Come back to Holland Park. I'll get us some lunch. Ned's out for the day. We'll have the afternoon to ourselves.'

'Done,' Liam said, promptly, and took a last look around the room.

'It looks really nice, doesn't it?' Christine asked.

'Indeed it does.' He kissed her on the nose. 'Thank you.'

'Oh, don't be silly,' she said, looking very pleased indeed. 'Come on, now – I'm starving.'

They were talking about Emma's new venture with the second-hand clothes when they turned into the crescent and walked towards the house. 'Mr Davies is very enthusiastic,' Christine was saying. 'He's really very good to her, you know. He charges her hardly any rent and—' She stopped. 'What on earth?'

Liam followed the direction of her startled gaze. The street door to the house was ajar. 'Bloody Ned!' Christine said in disgust. 'Honestly, that boy's getting more irrespon-sible by the day! You'd think he'd remember to shut the *door* when he goes gallivanting.' She had started forward, hurrying towards the steps.

'Chris!' Liam said, urgently. 'Wait!'

But she was up the stairs and into the house before he could stop her. Limping along behind her, cursing under his breath, he heard her voice. 'Ned? Ned, are you here? Oh, honestly – *Ned?*'

Liam was struggling up the steep steps to the door when he heard her sudden, small yelp of fright. She had run up the curving staircase and had almost reached the top, where she had frozen, one hand on the bannister, the other to her mouth. On the landing above her stood a young man, lean-faced, shabbily dressed, balanced on the balls of his feet like a fighter. If he, too, had been surprised, he had recovered more quickly than Christine. In any case he had the advantage; in his hand, very steadily, he held a nasty-looking service revolver.

The man jerked his head. 'Keep on comin', lady,' he said. 'Nice an' slow.' The accent was unmistakably Australian.

Very slowly Christine walked up the last few stairs to the landing. The man backed away from her, waved the gun a little towards the wall. 'Over there.'

She sidled round, her back to the bannisters, until she stood where he had indicated.

'Hands spread on the wall,' he said.

She spread them, valiantly trying to disguise the fact that they were shaking.

'OK, mate.' The man's dark eyes did not move from Christine as he addressed Liam. 'Now you. Up yer come. Slowly.'

'Sure, an' do I have any choice?' Liam asked, pleasantly. 'Slow's the way I do everythin' lately.'

'Just do as yer told, chum, an' no-one needs get hurt. Leave the stick.'

'I can't manage without it,' Liam lied. He could, in fact, have hauled himself up using the handrail. He could see the man's dilemma. Due to the layout of the house, the only way he could keep an eye on both of them at once was to have them together up on the landing. Liam started, very slowly, up the stairs. Christine was watching the gun with wide, alarmed eyes. 'It's all right, darlin',' Liam said quietly, his own eyes on the young man's face, 'I don't think the – gentleman – wants to harm us.'

'You could have fooled me.' Christine's voice was shaky, but tart. 'Pointing a gun at someone is hardly a gesture of goodwill, is it?'

'Shut up,' the man said, not unpleasantly. 'Come on, Paddy. Up you bloody come.'

Liam was making more of a performance of climbing the

stairs than was necessary; no harm in allowing the intruder to believe he was in worse condition than he actually was. At the top of the stairs he stopped, wincing, and bent over a little. Christine watched him with suddenly sharp eyes.

The other man gave him a moment. 'War wound, mate?'

'Dunkirk,' Liam said. Keep him talking.

'Huh!' It was an expression of profound disgust. 'Bloody shambles, that was.'

'You were there?'

'Yeah. I was there. I was there when we bloody left, but I'll tell you somethin' – I'm not goin' ter be there when we bloody well go back!'

Liam half-smiled. 'Can't say I blame you for that.'

'Over there.' The gun came up quickly as Liam moved. 'Not too close! Turn out yer pockets. You, too, lady – let's see what you've got in yer bag.' Christine opened her bag, pulled out a purse. The man glanced at it. 'Slide it across the floor.'

She slid it across the parquet flooring, but in her apparent nervousness got it tangled in the fringe of the narrow Turkish runner that ran from the top of the stairs to the drawing room door. 'Sorry,' she said, quickly, reaching for it.

'Leave it!' he snapped, her action catching his eye. He half-turned. Liam stepped forward on his good leg and his heavy stick swung, smashing with bone-cracking force on the hand holding the gun. With a yell of anguish, the Australian let go of the weapon and it flew through the air to land by the drawing room door. As Christine scrambled after it, throwing herself forward to prevent him from retrieving it, Liam's stick swung again with all the force of his considerable strength behind it, aimed at the man's head. The deserter ducked, turned to face Liam, nursing his broken hand. He started forward. Liam stepped sideways and brought up the stick again. The Australian stopped, glaring at him. Behind him Christine was scrambling to her feet, the gun in her hand; Antipodean common sense asserted itself; the man quite literally leaped past Liam, raced down the stairs and out of the front door.

Shakily Christine got to her feet, the revolver hanging heavily in her hand.

'And what, exactly,' Liam said, carefully taking it from her, 'do you imagine you were going to do with that?'

'Use it, if necessary,' she said, lifting her chin. Reaction was setting in. Her lips were trembling and her eyes were very bright.

He put an arm about her, drew her to him. 'Do you know how?'

'Not really. But I daresay I could find out.'

He laughed, his own voice not altogether steady. 'We'd best find out what's missing. And I'll have to get something done about the front door lock.'

The drawing room was undisturbed, but in the study the drawers of George Clough's desk stood open. 'There's usually some money,' Christine said, walking round it. 'No.' She shook her head. 'It's gone.'

'Much?'

'No. About twenty quid or so. It's only for emergencies.' She eyed the telephone on the desk. 'I suppose we ought to report—' She stopped. 'Oh, no! I've just thought of something.' She started past Liam.

He watched with puzzled eyes as she flew to the top of the stairs. 'What is it?'

'If that bastard's had my eggs and bacon,' her voice rang fiercely back up the stairwell, 'then, believe me, I *will* go after him with that gun.'

At the end of June Hitler invaded Russia; a rash move if ever he had made one. The people of Britain heaved a sigh of relief. If in some circles the principle of 'standing alone' had been welcomed when France had fallen the year before, the idea had by now worn decidedly thin. Whilst the German armies were pouring into Russia there was little chance they would be trying to cross the Channel. The fact that there were a couple of heavy air raids on London at about the same time was enough to prevent anyone from becoming complacent, however. The raiders came again at the end of July; London's war was far from over. But meanwhile the cinemas and the theatres, the night clubs and the dance halls were booming. As was gambling, even – or perhaps especially – the kind that was not strictly legal.

Ned had his own interests, his own haunts, and most of those were not legal either. He hated the Civil Service, hated the time-serving pernickety rules and regulations, the rigid pecking order, the sheer overwhelming dullness of the work that he was engaged in. Perhaps in consequence, gradually, his social life was becoming rather more flamboyant. University friends flitted through the city, in or out of uniform, and everyone knew a bar, a party, a gathering of like-minded spirits. Teamed with the instability of character and high sensitivity that Ned had inherited from his mother, the atmosphere of wartime London was not exactly conducive to equilibrium or steadiness. It strung his nerves to shrieking point, drove him to intemperate excesses and on occasion stilled any whisper from the voice of good sense. No matter the rationing and the shortages, there was always a good time to be had somewhere, if you had contacts and could afford it; and Ned had both contacts and money.

It was late on a balmy early autumn afternoon that, finding himself at a loose end, he decided, on impulse, to visit Liam. This time, he decided, he'd *make* Liam treat him like a grown man. It infuriated Ned that Liam – as did Christine, from whom, perhaps unconsciously, he took his cue – still tended to treat him with the kind of patronising tolerance he might afford to a slightly backward fifteen-year-old. In all the times he had been to Liam's Chelsea house, Ned had never been further than the shabbily comfortable sitting room. It was a Saturday – there might be a game in progress. If there were, he intended to join it.

The taxi pulled up outside the house. Ned clambered out,

reaching for his wallet, then stopped. A few hundred yards away, walking away from the house, was the unmistakable figure of Liam. Ned opened his mouth to call; shut it again. Liam turned a corner.

'You stayin' or goin', Guv?' the driver asked, irritably.

Ned hesitated a moment longer. Then, 'Staying,' he said, with a sudden, angelic smile. He stood watching the taxi disappear into the traffic, then turned to the house, reaching into his pocket for the set of keys he always carried with him. He smiled again. Serve Liam right. He'd taught Ned how to use them, hadn't he?

The front door clicked open satisfyingly easily. Ned stepped inside. The house was very still. He glanced into the empty sitting room as he passed. It was in a state of comfortable disarray, a newspaper discarded on one of the sofas, a pile of books on the floor by a chair, a used ashtray on the table. He went on, up the stairs. Off a square landing on the first floor there were three large rooms and a bathroom. At the end of the landing a narrow flight of steps led up to the attic rooms above. He pushed open a door. It was an impersonally tidy bedroom, obviously unoccupied. He closed the door quietly and moved on. The next room was just as obviously Liam's. There were books beside the bed, a wireless on the tallboy, an opened bottle of whiskey on the bedside table and a large, well-used ashtray. A freshly-ironed shirt hung from the back of a chair. Ned opened a wardrobe door. The clothes were hung neatly, the smell of rolling tobacco was strong. For a moment Ned saw Liam's capable, long-fingered hands, the deft way he rolled a cigarette, the way he ducked his dark head and narrowed his eyes as he lit it.

He put out a hand to touch a shirt, gently, almost caressingly. Brushed a fleck of dust from the shoulder of a jacket. Liam's dinner suit was there, a long white silky scarf folded carefully on a shelf beside it. Ned reached for the scarf, put it about his own neck, turned to admire the effect in the mirror of the wardrobe door. The bed, reflected behind him, had been carelessly made. He took off the scarf, folded it exactly as he had found it, replaced it on the shelf and shut the door. He went to the bed, lay down on it carefully, his head on the indented pillow. Again that smell. Liam's smell.

He lay very still for a long time, listening to the silence around him, taking in every intimate detail of the room: the used glass beside the whiskey bottle, a tie casually hooked over one of the handles of the tallboy's drawers, a pair of shoes kicked off and left beneath a chair, a collection of cufflinks and collar studs in a glass dish on the bedside table. After a while, careful not to disturb the bedclothes, he got off the bed and went to the tallboy. There was a wallet lying on top of it. He picked it up, rifled through it. There was a good deal of money in it, but nothing else. He replaced it exactly as he had found it, with the speed and care of long practice, then he went through the drawers. Underclothes, socks, belts, braces, all the everyday paraphernalia of Liam's life. There were no letters, no photographs. Ned felt a small twinge of disappointment. He stood for a moment, looking round intently, then, flicking his hair back off his forehead, he left the room and went back out on to the landing, closing the door behind him.

The door opposite Liam's was locked.

Ned fiddled for a moment, and pushed it open. The room was in absolute pitch darkness; the black-outs were up. He switched on the light and looked around. The room was large, and its purpose was obvious. There were several baize-covered tables with chairs set about them. Ashtrays overflowed and the air was stale. Ned wrinkled his nose. A long shelf was stacked with packs of cards. On one wall were several photographs of greyhounds and a couple of a racehorse with a white blaze on its forehead. In one of them Liam, grinning broadly, was holding a silver cup. There were other, smaller cups set upon the mantelpiece. In the corner was a crateful of bottles and a cardboard box full of glasses. So this was where the real business of the house went on. Ned backed out, relocked the door, turned and froze.

A key was turning in the lock of the street door.

Swift and silent as a shadow, Ned sped across the landing, slipped into the spare bedroom, very gently closed the door behind him and stood leaning against it, listening intently over the thumping of his own heart. He heard the door open and close. He heard Liam's uneven step on the stairs. He was muttering to himself, 'Forget my bloody head one of these days.'

He went into the bedroom, and a moment later came out and started back down the stairs.

The wallet. Ned took a long, soft breath.

The front doorbell rang, very loudly.

Ned nearly jumped out of his skin. Liam swore. 'God alive, who's *that* now?' He limped across the hallway to the door and opened it.

Ned eased the bedroom door open a little.

There was an odd and very long silence. Liam broke it. 'What in hell's name do you think you're doing here?' The words were coldly hostile.

'Sure, an' is that any way for a man to greet his father?'

'It's the only way I know.' Liam's voice was terse. 'Go away, Pa. I've nothing to say to you.'

'After all the trouble I've taken to find you?' Dermot pushed past him and stepped into the hallway, looking around. 'Well, well, well!' He whistled, softly. 'It's grand, this is, lad.' Uninvited, he walked into the sitting room.

Liam closed the front door angrily. 'What do you want?'

'I was in London. Passing through, you might say. What more natural than to look up me only son?'

'What are you doing in London?' The question was savage. 'Taking up where Hitler left off? Checking on what he missed, so you and your God-forsaken mates can blow up what's left? Looking for some more innocent kids to murder?' Ned had tiptoed out on to the landing. Liam's voice was uncontrolled and shaking with fury. 'I don't know how the hell you found me, but you've wasted your time. The last time I saw you, you pistol-whipped me, remember?'

'I did it to save your life, boy,' Dermot said softly.

'I – am – not – a – boy!' Liam, emphasising each word fiercely, was literally trembling with rage. 'I want nothing to do with you, you understand? Not with you, nor with your squalid, murderous affairs. Now get out of here before I turn you in.'

'Careful, Liam.' Dermot's voice was suddenly dangerous. 'Think on, boy. Before you threaten me; remember, you're not entirely lily-white yourself. You were well involved too, and there are people who know it. It may have been a while since, but—' He let his voice trail off.

'Bugger off,' Liam said.

'I will. I will. Though 'tis sorry I am you still feel so badly.'

'The understatement of a lifetime,' Liam said, grimly.

Dermot went back out into the hall. Ned drew back. At the door Dermot stopped and turned. Liam was standing at the sitting room door, watching him. 'Your Ma?' Dermot asked, gently. 'You'll at least tell me how things are with her?'

Ned caught his breath.

Liam did not speak for a very long time. Then, 'You don't know,' he almost whispered.

'What?' The word was sharp.

'Ma's dead,' Liam said, coldly brutal. 'One of your mate Hitler's bombs got her.'

Dermot bowed his head for a moment.

'For Christ's sweet sake, Pa!' Ned had never heard such bitterness in a voice. 'What's one more death in the glorious fight for freedom? You'd have blown her up yourself if she'd stood in your way.'

Dermot studied his son's face for a long moment, then, with no other word, he turned and left.

Liam stood like a statue, staring at the closed door.

'Bastard,' he said, a break in his voice. 'You bastard!' He walked back into the sitting room. Ned heard the unsteady chink of glass on glass. He slipped back into the spare bedroom. After a while he heard the tap of the walking stick as Liam came back out into the hall. There was a momentary pause. Liam blew his nose. Then the front door opened and closed and all was silent again.

Ned waited for a moment, then, still treading quietly, he crossed the landing to sit on the top stair, his chin in his hand, his face pensive.

It was just before Christmas that Tom Barker's luck at last ran out. As the Russians' dogged and terrible defence of Leningrad continued to block the German advance in the East, and a week after the Japanese strike on Pearl Harbor had at last brought the United States openly into the war, he was flying escort to a squadron of bombers when his Spitfire was caught in a dog-fight and sent plunging in flames into the Channel. No body was ever found. His death saddened them all; always the baby of the two families, he had been held by them all in great affection. The effect of this fresh, terrible blow on Pamela was predictable; she threw herself with more single-minded determination than ever into her work with the WVS. During the Blitz her sitting room had been turned into a canteen for the rescue services, and now she was running the local Volunteer Car Pool. When, a few months later, the organisation began to set up Incident Enquiry Points – groups of their members who were willing to take on the heartbreaking task of breaking the news of death or injury to close relations after a euphemistically termed 'incident' – she was the first to volunteer.

It was Josie, perhaps, who suffered most. She and Tom had always been closer to each other than to anybody else. The shock was all the greater because Josie had come to accept Tom's own cheerful confidence in his 'charmed life'. She had almost stopped worrying about him. The fact that no body had been found made the grief deeper, too. The sight of an air-force uniform would bring a sudden awful surge of hope; she almost expected to see her brother walking towards her on the crowded pavement, or waiting on the steps of the small flat she had taken just around the corner from the war orphanage where she worked. When she came home late one winter's evening to find a figure huddled in the dark on the step outside her door, for a moment her heart gave that familiar lurch; then the faint light from the torch she was carrying picked out the figure more clearly. It was a girl, with fair hair and a tiny, pointed face. Even in the dim torchlight she looked exhausted, and her eyes were deeply shadowed.

Josie stopped, a couple of stairs down. 'May I help you?'

The fair head lifted. 'Are you Josie Barker?' Her voice was hesitant, and very soft.

'Yes?' Josie put a question into the word, watching the other girl curiously.

The young woman swallowed visibly, ducked her head. 'My name's Lucy Drayton. I'm – that is – I was a – friend – of your brother's.' The words dropped away almost to a whisper. 'He said – he always said—' She stopped, swallowing again, and Josie sensed her sudden tears.

'Yes?' she prompted, gently.

The sad, exhausted face lifted to hers. 'He always said that – if anything should happen to him – and if I should need help – I should come to you.'

Josie came up the steps to stand beside her, held out a hand to draw her to her feet. 'Come in,' she said.

# Chapter Eighteen

And Father Bear said—'

'Someone's been sitting in *my* chair,' Charlie roared delightedly, clapping his hands.

'And Mother Bear said—'

'Someone's been sitting in *my* chair!'

'And then Baby Bear said—'

'Someone's been sitting in my chair and *broked it all to pieces!*'

Rudi lifted his head from the book and looked at the little boy over the top of his glasses. 'And just who is telling this story, young man?'

'We are! We are! Come on! Then they goes upstairs—'

Emma looked up, smiling tiredly. Pale sunshine lit the shabby room. It had been a hard, cold winter and an equally chill spring. The war dragged on. The raids had started again, spasmodic but vicious, and very wearing. Life, it seemed, had become a dreary round of shortages, queues, make do and mend – she was at this moment taping up the spines of several battered books that had literally fallen to pieces – scrimping, saving, worrying and waiting. Waiting for Alex's carefully worded letters. Waiting for news that the war-tide had turned, that somehow, sometime, peace and normality would return to life, and the killing and the destruction would stop. Peace. Normality. She had almost forgotten what normality was. And yet – there was Charlie. Charlie, with his bright, laughing face, his quick intelligence, his utter trust in the world about him, despite the circumstances of his young life. He sat now, watching as Rudi turned a page, wriggling in his seat with anticipation. 'Then they goes upstairs,' he prompted again, impatiently.

Emma put her elbows on the table and rested her chin on her hands, watching and listening.

'The three bears climbed the stairs.' Rudi stopped for effect, glanced at Charlie. Charlie swung his legs excitedly, opened his mouth. Rudi held up a finger. The little boy giggled. 'Into the bedroom they went. And Father Bear said?' Rudi's smile was wide and warm.

'Someone's been sleeping in *my* bed!' Charlie shouted.

'And Mother Bear said?'

'Someone's been sleeping in *my* bed!'

'And Baby Bear said?'

'Someone's sleeping in my bed, and *here she is!*' Charlie gurgled with laughter. 'And she woked up and she runned away.'

Rudi nodded. 'And she woked up and she runned away,' he agreed, solemnly.

'And they all – lived—' Charlie looked from Rudi to his mother, waiting.

'—happily – ever – after,' they chorused, obediently.

Over the top of his half-glasses, Rudi's dark eyes were suddenly intent upon Emma's. She looked away.

'I have an idea,' Rudi said, gently. 'Why don't we visit the zoo?'

Emma rolled her eyes. 'Again?'

'*Yes, please!*' Charlie said.

'Poor London,' Emma said, looking from the window of the bus that trundled towards Regent's Park. 'She looks so *drab!*'

'I think she looks brave,' Rudi said, quietly. 'Look,' he pointed, 'that's not drab.' They were passing a neatly-cleared bombed site. Torn wallpaper flapped in the wind, there were scorch marks on the walls. But in the cleared space where once a house had stood someone had cultivated an allotment. Meticulous lines of vegetables were netted against marauding birds, the earth had been freshly turned and weeded, and set beside the cultivated ground was an ancient garden bench. 'That's London,' Rudi said. 'Carrying on. Feeding herself.'

'Making do and mending,' Emma said with a small smile.

'Exactly. You really ought to be very proud of your city, you know, not feel sorry for her, even battered as she is. I often wonder—' He stopped, shrugging.

Emma looked at him curiously. 'What?'

'I just wonder how Berlin, Vienna, Prague look now – how they are standing up to the war.'

'I've never been to any of them. Tell me – what's your favourite city in the whole world?'

He laughed. He had a rumbling, surprisingly infectious laugh that transformed his usually melancholy face; Emma smiled in response. 'My dear Emma, how do I know? I haven't *been* everywhere in the world.'

She pulled a face. 'Oh, don't be so pedantic. You know what I mean.'

He thought for a moment. 'Vienna, I think,' he said, pensively, his eyes distant. 'Vienna in the winter, crisp with snow. Such spires she has, and wide, tree-lined boulevards. What better to do than to sit in one of her cafés with a sweet, flaky pastry and a cup of hot chocolate listen-ing—' He stopped at Emma's sudden shriek, half-laughter, half-outrage.

'Stop it! Rudi, stop it! You beast! Sweet pastries and hot chocolate indeed! What are you trying to do to me?'

Charlie, who was sitting on the seat in front of them pretending to drive the bus, turned at his mother's laughter and came up on his knees, watching them inquisitively.

Rudi, too, was laughing. 'There is nothing to compare to a Viennese hot chocolate,' he said, mischievously, 'Dark and rich, and as good to smell as to taste.'

Emma groaned and clapped her hands over her ears. Charlie giggled.

Rudi reached and gently took hold of her wrists, pulling her hands away from her ears, and although he was still smiling he was no longer laughing. 'Vienna is truly beautiful,' he said. 'There is nothing I should like so much as to—' They both froze at the same moment.

Very carefully Emma released herself from his grip, ducked her head to avoid the steady, dark eyes. 'When we get to the zoo,' she said to Charlie, quickly, 'what would you like to see first?'

'The sea lions, please,' the little boy said, immediately, and made a loud honking noise. 'Charlie likes the sea lions.'

Over the months that followed the friendship between Emma and Rudi became something of a talking point.

'Do you think they're sleeping together?' Lottie asked Liam, frankly. She was sitting on his kitchen table, her shapely legs swinging. Her red hair curled about her air-force blue cap; Liam had already remarked that in her immaculate uniform and neat collar and tie she looked like an extremely attractive and rather naughty schoolgirl.

Liam, who was beating some dried egg mixture in a bowl, shook his head. 'No. I don't. In fact I'm sure not. Emma wouldn't.'

Lottie raised blue eyes to heaven. 'Saint Emma,' she said, with no rancour, then added, 'You're probably right. And him?'

Liam shook his head again. 'No. I'm not saying they might not want to. But I don't believe they are, that's all.'

'How boring.' Lottie jumped from the table to come and peer into the bowl. 'What's the point of living through this ruddy war if you aren't going to enjoy yourself while you can? We might all be dead tomorrow. You're surely not going to *eat* that mess?'

'I certainly am. With mustard.'

'Cardboard with mustard! How very tempting. Personally I detest the things.'

Liam grinned. 'I gather you won't want any, then?'

'No thanks.' Lottie glanced at her watch. 'I'm meeting someone later. We're eating at the Savoy.'

'Where else?'

Lottie laughed, pulled herself back up on to the table and held out her legs for his inspection. 'What d'you think of them?'

'The legs or the stockings?' Liam asked straightfaced.

'The nylons, daft! A Yankee squadron's moved in. They're a really yummy bunch, and they can get hold of absolutely *anything*.'

'Is it a yummy Yank who's taking you to the Savoy?'

She grinned. 'Yep.'

'What happened to the Poles?'

'The threadbare aristocracy?' she said, airily. 'Several of them became just a little too intense about things.'

'And then the Yanks arrived?'

'Exactly.' She was completely unabashed. 'Now, listen, do shut up for a minute because I haven't finished gossiping yet. What do you think about Josie's lodger? Or rather, I should now say lodgers?'

Liam shrugged.

'Well? Were they married, or weren't they? And is the baby Tom's?'

'As to the first, I haven't the foggiest notion. But Josie is utterly convinced that the boy is Tom's. And I don't somehow feel, seeing how close they were, that she'd be easily deceived about something like that.'

Lottie considered a moment. 'No, I must say I thought

the same. Mother's convinced, too. Mind you, I think she wanted to be.'

'Sure – you can't blame her for that,' Liam said, quietly.

'Oh, I don't,' Lottie said quickly. 'But, honestly, she's quite besotted. Here we are only just into October and she's started saving stuff for Christmas already! Mind you,' just for a moment her bright eyes softened, 'with young Charlie and baby Tom around it could be fun – I hope I'll be able to manage at least a day or so.' She slipped from the table again and wandered to the window. Liam watched her. She stood silently, looking out into the autumnal garden. When she turned she was frowning. 'What do you think, Liam? Are we going to win this rotten war? Or is it just going to go on for ever and ever and ever? I mean, North Africa, Burma, Russia – there's no *sign* of a breakthrough, is there? The bombs are still falling, the boys are still getting shot out of the sky.' Just for one moment she blinked and her voice trembled.

Liam took a step towards her. She warded him off with raised hands. 'I'm OK. I'm a bit browned off, that's all. We've had a nasty few days; the squadron got badly mauled. A couple of boys I was rather fond of caught it. It serves me right. We all know we shouldn't get involved – but it's hard.' She pulled a face, sniffed and then grinned, a little shakily. 'And to cap it all they've cut down the clothing ration *again!*' she added, lightly. 'How's a girl supposed to stay decent, I want to know?'

Liam made a fist and gently grazed her chin with it. Her eyes were still over-bright.

'So,' she said as he went back to his eggs, 'when are you going to make an honest woman of Chris?'

'Huh!' The grunted syllable was singularly expressive.

'You've asked her again?'

'Only about a dozen times. Usually when drunk. I wouldn't dare when I was sober.'

'And?'

'We've had a dozen rows. She flatly refuses and she won't tell me why.'

'She loves you. I'm sure she does.'

'Yes. So am I. It doesn't really help.'

'You mean – you think she won't marry you because it's – beneath her?'

'Yes.'

She shook her head. 'Surely not! I can't believe that.'

'What else could it be?' his voice was grim.

She moved to him, took the bowl from his hands and set it on the table, turned him towards her, looking up into his face. 'If I were Christine, Liam McCarthy,' she said, softly, 'I'd marry you. So there! Don't give up. She'll come round. Now—' She stood on tiptoe and kissed his cheek. 'I must be off.' She winked. 'Enjoy your eggs.'

It was early November 1942 before a war-weary British public at last had real cause for celebration. After ten anxious days following the intense fighting for El Alamein, listeners to the BBC were told one night not to turn off and go to bed, since at midnight news described as the best to be heard for years would be broadcast. And, indeed, it was. The enemy was in full retreat in North Africa, the apparently invincible Rommel had been beaten at last. There was, finally, a real victory to celebrate and Britain had a new hero in General Montgomery, who had won it. It was, as Prime Minister Winston Churchill described it so aptly, 'the end of the beginning', and confidence began to grow that the tide of the conflict was turning. Yet still, as the New Year came and went and another year of war began, despite growing good news on nearly all fronts, it was hard for a population that had endured such hardships and privation for so long to feel entirely optimistic. Few doubted now that the Allies would win – the question most asked now was: when? And what would be left at the end of it all? Early in 1943, usually in retaliation for heavy RAF raids on Berlin or other German cities, the Luftwaffe began a series of raids known as 'scalded cat' raids. A handful of bombers would attack swiftly, often by daylight, and then run for home. They did a fair amount of damage, and civilians again were being killed and injured, but the battle-hardened populations of the cities of Britain that had already survived the worst that the German air force could throw at them simply gritted their teeth and became once more adept at diving into shelters. Here, more and more frequently as the year progressed, the talk, away from official ears at least, was of the likelihood (some thought the certainty) of Hitler at last producing the secret weapon – the vengeance weapon – with which he had vowed to destroy London.

Spring was still spring, however, and couples still walked in the parks and kissed beneath the trees and under the shadow of the barrage balloons. Whenever Emma took Charlie on the tube to see his grandparents, the child was all but overwhelmed by the gifts of sweets and chocolates pressed on him by homesick GIs who would talk to her about their own families and bring out battered photographs to show her. The lilac bloomed at Kew, sheep grazed in Hyde Park, and the bombed sites were cloaked with the rampant pink heads of the rosebay willow herb that thrived upon them. With the threat of invasion past, church bells rang once more, traffic lights were turned back on, however dimly, and villages could be identified again; any small restriction eased, any sign of normality returning, was welcome, an indication that better times must surely be on their way.

On the day El Alamein fell Ned at first thought he had made entirely the wrong decision. Outside, in the streets of London, the population was celebrating the unexpectedly quick and complete rout of Rommel and his forces in Africa. Almost Ned wished he were out there in the jubilant city; the party to which he had decided to come had turned out to be neither as lively nor as friendly as he had hoped. Everyone appeared already to have a partner – everyone except the plump, pink-faced horror who kept trying to draw Ned into simpering conversation – and the host appeared to have no records of any other artist than Noël Coward, to whom, as he kept explaining to anyone who would listen, he had once been introduced. Ned loathed Noël Coward. The only saving grace of the occasion so far was the venue: a large and rather grand house in Cheyne Walk. The drawing room in which he was standing was a delight; a delicately ornate ceiling, panelled walls, a lovely marble fireplace. The cost of the furniture, he reckoned, would keep even a high spender like himself in fair luxury for the best part of ten years. Bored, he sighed, sipped his drink and avoided the eager little eyes of his would-be seducer.

Outside, suddenly, the sirens wailed.

'Oh, shit!' someone said, above the general groan that went up.

The host held up his hands for quiet. 'Anyone who wishes, of course, may go down into the cellars. They are, as you may imagine, comfortable and – er – well equipped.' The emphasis on the words brought laughter. 'However,' he shrugged, then stopped as the door opened and two newcomers entered. 'Bunty,' he called, beaming, 'Bunty, welcome! And who – is this?' His appreciative eyes had settled upon the young man's companion, a tall, dark and slender figure with a narrow face and thick, straight black hair. He was dressed in white tie, tails, a well-cut Crombie draped about his shoulders, a white scarf thrown negligently around his neck with that air of casual, almost insolent stylishness that so many young men attempted to achieve and so few actually did. The slight shabbiness of the prewar clothes actually added, rather than detracted, from his good looks.

Ned stared, his heart suddenly pounding. 'DeBar!' he said, into the sudden hush as everyone turned to stare at the newcomers. 'Paul DeBar!'

DeBar turned and, at the sight of Ned, a sudden, flashing smile lit his handsome face.

The man called Bunty had his hand on his arm. DeBar shook it free and strode towards his host, held out his hand. 'Paul DeBar,' he said in his attractively husky voice. 'I do hope you don't mind the intrusion. I'm afraid I'm gate-crashing – though,' he glanced at Ned again, a gleam of conspiratorial mischief in the doe eyes, 'it does so happen that one of your guests could vouch for me.'

'Perfectly happy to do that for you myself, Paul,' said Bunty, loudly. 'Any friend of mine's a friend of Rollo here. Isn't that right, Rolls?'

'Most certainly.' Rollo's eyes were speculative as he quite openly assessed DeBar's louchely elegant looks. DeBar, used to this, was undisturbed. 'A drink, darling boy,' Rollo said to Bunty, without taking his eyes off the other man, 'get Paul a drink.' He waved a hand dismissively.

Ned watched and waited, moved a little closer, listening.

'So – where on earth did Bunty find you?' Rollo asked, a faint, surprised emphasis on the pronoun.

Paul laughed. 'Where does anyone find anyone, dear thing? In a bar.'

'All alone?' Rollo's voice was quiet, his eyes sharp.

'All alone,' DeBar agreed, in a mock-doleful tone. His eyes, still sparkling with laughter, flickered over his host's shoulder and caught Ned's. The long lashes swept down. Ned's heart turned over in sudden excitement.

'Rollo!' someone shouted from the other end of the room. 'Come and do something about this sodding Heath Robinson contraption of yours! The record's stuck.'

Rollo hesitated for a moment, still smiling into DeBar's eyes. 'Coming,' he called, and, more quietly, 'I look forward to making your acquaintance later,' he said.

DeBar inclined his handsome head a little, watched for a moment as the other man moved through the small crowd. Then, slipping the overcoat from his shoulders, he turned to Ned. 'My dear thing,' he said, softly, 'what luck! What splendid luck! Fancy meeting you here!'

\*   \*   \*

Half an hour later, having managed to evade both the far-from-impressed Bunty and Ned's pink-faced pursuer, they had settled in a small anteroom. DeBar had charmed a half-bottle of brandy from a Rollo who knew a lost cause when he saw one, but perhaps hoped that a favour granted now might be a favour returned at some future date. He poured two large glasses, handed one to Ned, sipped his own, then slouched elegantly back into the feather cushions of the chair, surveying the other man with bright, warm eyes.

Unexpectedly, Ned found himself blushing.

Paul toasted him appreciatively. 'Pretty as ever, dear thing. Pretty as ever. It's been – how long?'

Ned shrugged. 'Two, three years?'

'Something like that. Yes.'

'I've thought of you often.'

'Oh, and I you, dear thing, I you. It was a pity,' DeBar's lashes swept down, hiding his eyes for a moment, and he lifted his shoulders expressively, 'that things ended as they did between us.'

'It couldn't be helped,' Ned said quickly. 'And anyway – it was a long time ago.'

'Good of you to say so. It was my fault, of course. Entirely my fault. Fidelity has never been my strong point, I'm afraid.'

Ned winced a little. 'It's water under the bridge,' he said, shortly, taking a too-large swig of brandy and nearly choking.

DeBar smiled a little. From some distance away there came the crump of a bomb. An anti-aircraft gun crashed twice and fell silent.

'Bloody things,' Ned muttered, almost automatically. 'I hate them.'

DeBar nursed his drink, watching Ned. Their eyes caught, and held. DeBar leaned forward, his elbows on his knees. 'It seems like yesterday,' he said.

'Yes.'

DeBar smiled, his eyes dancing. 'Tell me, dear thing. Have you learned any new tricks since I saw you last?' he asked, very softly.

Ned blushed again, lifted his chin. 'A few.'

Another silence. Then, 'Good,' DeBar said, huskily. 'Tell you what, dear thing – you guard that with your life.' He pointed at the bottle. 'I shan't be long. A small word with our host.'

Ned watched him go, sat quite still, waiting, a sudden, almost painful excitement coursing through him. He was trembling. Of all the lovers he had had in these past two years none had ever come anywhere near Paul DeBar. Perhaps, he had sometimes thought, because he had been the first, though he did not really believe that. Now Ned had no doubt that he would find out.

He picked up the bottle and stood up. DeBar had reappeared in the doorway, holding out a long, slender hand. Ned walked to him and took it. DeBar led him towards a glorious, sweeping staircase that led to a chandeliered landing.

Ned hung back a little. 'Are you sure?'

DeBar smiled. 'I'm sure. Trust me.'

They reached the top of the stairs. DeBar hesitated, counting doors. 'There,' he said.

He led the way to a door, pushed it open, ushered Ned through. The bedroom was as sumptuous as the rest of the house. DeBar closed the door, crossed the room to the huge bed, sat on it and looked back at Ned expectantly.

Ned, still standing by the door, tugged deftly at the knot of his bow tie and undid the top button of his shirt.

DeBar smiled his most exotic smile. 'You do remember, then.'

'Oh, yes,' Ned said.

DeBar lay back on the pillows, his hands behind his head. 'And tell me, dear thing,' he said, 'that soft heart of yours. Have you lost it to a new love?'

There was a very long moment of silence. Ned, who had stilled at the question, pulled the tie free and dropped it on the floor. 'Yes,' he said, 'as a matter of fact I think I have. But then, it never was my heart you were interested in, was it?' He slipped off his jacket, walked towards the bed with it dangling from his fingers, dragging on the floor. Watching him approach, the other man laughed, softly. Ned stood above him, dropped the jacket on the floor, set the bottle he still carried on the bedside table. 'And as for the rest of me – well – you may do as you please.'

DeBar reached a hand to him, palm up, crooked a finger invitingly. 'I always did, dear thing,' he said, gently. 'Why should anything change?'

An early summer dawn was breaking as, achingly tired and a little light-headed, Ned left the house in Cheyne Walk. He hesitated for a moment, tempted to turn left towards Liam's house, just half a mile along the Embankment. But instinct told him that for all sorts of reasons – the least being that Liam would probably only just have got to bed himself – it was best he did not. The skies were clear and there were few people about. To his left the river reflected the fire of dawn in its swirling waters. An ARP Warden lifted a weary hand in greeting, smiling a little at the state of the young man who smiled just as wearily back. Ned's skin felt flushed and hot in the chill, sharp air. He turned up his collar, stuck his hands in his pockets, hunched his shoulders and tried not to think about the night that had just passed. Paul DeBar had not changed in the years since they had last been together. He was still wayward, still amusing, still utterly, gracelessly enchanting. Still brutal.

A cat scavenged in a pig bin. A boy on a bicycle wobbled by. A ship's hooter called from the river. London, exhausted by her celebrations of the night before, was asleep. At least this part was. In the distance behind him, towards the east, a thick column of smoke showed where at least one of last night's bombs had hit. He turned away from the river and set off towards Kensington and Holland Park. The walk, he hoped, would do him good. Christ, he'd be in trouble if he fell asleep at his desk again.

He turned into the crescent and stopped, dismayed. Barriers had been set up, patrolled by two uniformed policemen. One of them held up a hand. 'Sorry, Sir. Can't go in there.'

'But – I live here. That's my house.' Ned pointed.

The officer shook his head tiredly. 'Delayed-action bomb, Sir. Dropped last night, in the garden at the back of number twenty-six. You'll have to stay away until it goes off.'

'But—'

'Sorry, Sir. No "buts". The whole street's closed. You've somewhere to go? If not, they've set up a centre over at—'

'Yes, yes. I've somewhere to go. But – number twenty-six is at the other end of the street. My clothes – my things – I can hardly go to work dressed like this!'

Another tired grin. 'Oh, I don't know, Sir. You look pretty smart to me.'

Ned's brain only just seemed to have started working properly. He stood for a moment, uncertain. 'So – what's the drill?'

The man shrugged. 'Like I say, the street's closed until that little bugger goes off. Keep in touch with the Town Hall. They'll let you know when it's safe.'

'My sister – she lives with me—'

The policeman indicated a small hut that had been set up at the end of the barrier. 'If she's been by, she'll have left a message at the desk. If not, you can leave one for her.'

'I—' Ned shrugged helplessly. 'Thank you.'

There was no message from Christine. Ned's head ached and his mouth was parched. Hastily he scribbled, '*Chris – gone to Liam's. See you there. Ned.*' Then, shoulders hunched and eyes squinting against the sun, he turned on his heel and set off back to Chelsea.

'*My Two Darlings, a line to tell you that I'm well and, all things* considered, in good health. *As I have told you before, boredom is the main problem, but we've got ourselves organised now and there are various activities on offer. I've become a positive whizz at chess, and believe it or not am learning to play the mouth organ! Won't my Charlie be proud of his Dad when he comes home the new Larry Adler?'* Alex's untidy, familiar writing blurred suddenly before Emma's eyes. She blinked. *'But mainly, my darlings, this is to tell you how much I love you, how much I miss you, how often I think of you. In my thoughts in this strange and dreary place I am always with you. The photographs you sent me never leave me. They bring you both so very close. And isn't my little chap growing? It's difficult to believe he's nearly five years old. My greatest regret is that I have missed those precious years. But just wait; when this war's over and the job's done, I'll come home to you and never leave you again. Ever. Chin up, darling Em, it surely can't be too much longer? I can't tell you how much I admire and love you for facing what you have faced alone and for making the wonderful job I know you have made of our boy. Kiss him for me. As I kiss you. I miss you so. Love (what a hopelessly inadequate word that is!), Alex.'*

The flimsy paper trembled in Emma's fingers. She laid it very carefully upon the table, smoothing it flat with her fingers. The room was very quiet. She rubbed with the palm of her hand at the tears that were running silently down her cheeks.

*'I can't tell you how much I admire and love you for facing what you have faced alone—'*

Elbows on the table, she closed her eyes and buried her wet face in her cupped hands.

'I suppose I'd better go and see if I can get through to the Town Hall,' Christine said. 'With any luck that bloody thing might have gone off during the night. Honestly, Liam, how you manage without a phone is beyond me.'

Liam grinned. 'I'll get in touch with Winnie,' he said, amiably, 'see if he'll authorise one specially. I'm sure he won't mind taking a minute or two off from winning the war in order to connect an Irish gambler to the telephone system.'

Christine stuck her tongue out at him. As she passed Ned, who was sitting curled up on the sofa, clad in an old dressing gown of Liam's, she stopped. 'Something up, little brother?' she asked. 'You look a bit peaky.'

Ned shook his head. 'I'm OK.'

'You need a few early nights, if you ask me. Whatever time did you get in last night?'

Ned shrugged. 'Since all I possess at the moment is a dinner suit, I might as well dine in it. Stop being so bossy.'

Liam laughed. 'Well, we can at least do something about that. Come on, let's go and see if we can find something of mine that halfway fits you.' He stood up.

Christine eyed them both doubtfully. 'Something that's shrunk?' she suggested, not altogether joking.

'Bugger off to the phone,' her brother said, mildly.

Liam no longer used a stick unless he was tired or planned to walk a long way – or, as Christine had pointed out tartly, occasionally for effect. He limped to the door and up the stairs. Ned followed him to the bedroom that the Irishman was at the moment sharing with Christine. They heard the front door shut as she left the house.

'Right.' Liam opened the wardrobe door. 'Let's see – what about this? I've had it for a long time and it's always been a bit small for me. I don't think I've worn it since before the war.' He pulled out a dark blue suit. 'Wait – you need a shirt first.' He put the suit back, went to a drawer, tossed a folded shirt to Ned. 'Try that.'

Ned caught the shirt. Liam turned back to the wardrobe. Swift as an eel, Ned dropped the dressing gown from his shoulders and slipped into the shirt. In his reflection in the mirror he caught sight of the livid weals and bruises on his body. Two nights with DeBar had taken their toll. The shirt was all-enveloping. By the time Liam turned back the marks were covered.

Liam chuckled amusedly at the sight of him. 'Oh, Lord. Should I look for a smaller one?' He went towards the drawer.

'No,' Ned said, sharply, turning up the sleeves, 'this will be fine. It'll be covered by the jacket anyway.' He stepped into the trousers.

Liam was rummaging in a drawer. When he turned he had a belt in his hand. He eyed Ned, who was holding up the trousers with his hands. They hung about his hips like a sack and crumpled over his bare feet on the floor. 'The baggy look,' Liam said, straightfaced. 'All the rage this year, I hear. Let's see if we can hitch them up a bit.' He limped to Ned, began to thread the belt through the loops on the waistband of the trousers. Ned stood very still, within the circle of the big man's arms. He closed his eyes for a moment. 'There.' Liam cinched the belt tightly around Ned's slender waist, stood back tilting his head critically. 'Not too bad really. I've needle and cotton. We can turn them up.'

'Shouldn't we wait to see if the bomb's gone off first?' Ned asked, doubtfully.

Liam stopped suddenly, looking at him. Then all at once he began to laugh. For a moment Ned watched him, puzzled, then he too saw the funny side of what he had said. Liam had collapsed on to the bed, his broad shoulders shaking. 'This bloody war!' he said, rocking a little. '*Shouldn't we wait to see if the bomb's gone off first!* We've all gone barking mad!'

In the way of such things his sudden hilarity was infecting Ned. He turned to look in the mirror, held out the baggy trousers like a girl about to curtsey and his giggles redoubled. 'Look at the state of me!' he gasped.

Liam, by now all but helpless with laughter, doubled up again. 'You – look – like – a—'

'—clown!' Ned finished for him, and capered wildly about the room.

Tears were rolling down Liam's face. He mopped at his

eyes. 'Jesus, Mary and Joseph, will you stop that!' The absurd laughter, however, had all but overcome him. He threw himself back on the bed, roaring.

Ned finished his routine with a flying leap on to the bed, landing on his knees and collapsing across the other man, both of them spluttering and gasping for breath. In irrational convulsions of laughter Liam threw his arms about Ned and hugged him, before pushing him off and rolling on to his stomach, still shaking with mirth. Ned lay inert and hiccoughing with giggles on top of him, his hands flat upon Liam's broad shoulders. He could feel the warmth of the other man's skin beneath his shirt, the contraction of muscle as he laughed.

'What on earth—'

Ned jerked upright. Christine stood in the doorway, face startled. 'What's going on? I could hear you out in the street!'

Ned rolled off Liam. Liam sat up, a little sheepishly, his long mouth still twitching. 'Just one of those silly things,' he said. 'I said we'd have to turn up the trousers,' hilarious tears began to run again, 'and Ned said – Ned said—' He could not go on.

Christine's mouth pursed in the manner of one excluded from a private joke. 'Yes?' she prompted, eyebrows raised.

'Ned, quite seriously, said, "Shouldn't we wait to see if the bomb's gone off first."' Liam could not contain himself. He began to laugh again. Ned's shoulders heaved.

Christine looked from one to the other of them. 'So?'

'So – that's it. It just struck us as being funny, that's all.'

'Well, I suppose it's half-funny,' she conceded. 'But not as funny as all that.'

'We know that!' Liam howled, knuckling his eyes again.

'Well,' Christine said, crisply, 'it's as well you didn't ruin a perfectly good pair of trousers because the bomb has gone off and we can go home – oh, for heaven's sake, you two, *now* what's funny?' She surveyed the two laughing men for a moment, her own lips twitching, then she turned and left.

After a moment Liam, still grinning, slapped Ned on the shoulder, hauled himself to his feet and followed her. 'Any damage?' Ned heard him call.

'Not sure,' she replied from the foot of the stairs, where she stood waiting for him. 'They didn't say. But they did say it was safe to go back, so I assume that the house is still there.'

Ned lay back on the bed, curled on to his side, his head on Liam's pillow. He was still laughing quietly; it was difficult actually to pinpoint the moment when laughter became tears.

# Chapter Nineteen

The successful D-Day landings of June 1944, at last opening the long-awaited Second Front in Europe, ended a
lengthy, tense wait during which southern England had
become an uncomfortable and congested cross between a
massive transit camp and a front-line aerodrome. When at
last the invasion fleet sailed there was a general feeling of
relief and exultation; Dunkirk was to be revenged at last.
For Londoners, however, the euphoria was short-lived. At
the beginning of the year the city had suffered yet another
devastating Blitz; for two or three months the raiders had
again attacked, night after night, sometimes twice a night.
The last serious raid, however, had occurred in the middle
of April, and since then an uneasy peace had fallen upon
the capital. It was a peace that was not to last. Exactly a
week after the landings, as the Allies were fighting their
way through France and Belgium, the first of Hitler's long-
anticipated secret weapons was launched against London.
At first there was confusion; many assumed that they
were enemy aircraft shot down by the RAF; then, three
days later, a statement was made in the House of Commons. These were pilotless planes, packed full of high
explosives; literally 'flying bombs'. They came by day,
since there was no need for stealth, and as the everyday

life of the city had to go on they caused much higher
casualties than had the conventional air raids. The capital
was on constant alert, and people got used to the droning
sound of the engines, used to diving for shelter when the
nerve-racking silence fell as the sound died and the thing
plunged to earth. During July and August, as the troops
in Europe advanced and the Russians pushed out of the
East towards Poland, seventy V1s a day were raining on
the city.

All over Europe the destruction was at its height; Warsaw
was in flames, German cities were being bombed and
burned, the Allies were already in Rome, and at the end
of August, with the German armies still fighting a fierce
and bitter rearguard action, Paris was liberated. One by one
the launch sites for the 'doodlebugs' – as the population
had christened them – were overrun. Yet still there was
unease. There had long been rumours of a second and more
fearsome weapon, with speculation ranging from the wild
to the frankly ridiculous. German propaganda had not been
slow to arouse the population's fears; many were ready to
believe the horror stories of a massive rocket with a ten-ton
warhead capable of wiping out fifty acres of London in a
split second. At the end of the first week in September
there was a huge explosion in Chiswick, followed closely
by another in Epping. The official explanation was that two
gas mains had blown up; it did not, however, take long for
a war-experienced – and war-weary – public to work out
what was really happening. The V2, Hitler's final, desperate
attempt to force an end to the war without a dishonourable
surrender, was no figment of the imagination. It was real,
it was quite shockingly destructive and it was aimed at
London's heart.

For Ned the rockets were the last straw. At least there had
been some chance to shelter from the doodlebugs; now
death came silently and with no warning. His nerves were
in shreds, he jumped at the slightest sound. He was tense,

and restless; his characteristic mood swings had become wilder than ever.

'For heaven's sake, dear thing, do leave that nail alone. There'll be nothing left of it.' Paul DeBar's husky voice was mildly reproving. 'If there's one thing I can't abide it's a bitten nail.' He was lying, naked to the waist, on the bed, watching Ned, who had been sitting on the windowsill gazing down into the street below and nibbling his thumbnail fiercely. Ned looked at the chewed nail, picking away at it nervously with his other hand. 'Come and sit down.' DeBar patted the bed beside him. 'And do try to relax, dear thing. You're a bundle of nerves!'

'Yes. I know.' Ned crossed the room to sit on the bed. 'I can't help it. You've no idea, Paul – no idea at all.' He shook his head. 'I'm frightened. All the time. Frightened – and miserable.'

'Miserable?' DeBar's dark eyebrows climbed a little. 'Oh, come on, little Ned. Why miserable?'

'*You know why!*' Ned turned his head sharply away.

DeBar reached a narrow hand to Ned's wrist, his fingers curling about it gently.

Ned shivered.

'I don't like to think of my Neddie miserable,' DeBar said, softly.

'Where were you yesterday?' Ned asked, abruptly. 'And *why* won't you see me tomorrow?'

The fingers about his wrist tightened painfully. DeBar's face changed, the dark eyes suddenly hard. 'I've told you, Ned. It's work.'

'That's what you always say! But you won't even tell me—'

'I can't. I've told you that, too.' The other man had relaxed again. 'You know what they say: *Careless talk costs lives*. I'm not allowed to talk about what I do.'

'I don't believe you!' Ned was suddenly passionate. Tears had sprung to his eyes. 'You're seeing Rollo, aren't you? *Aren't you?* And Christ knows who else as well.' He tried to fling himself away from the other man, but DeBar's strong fingers tightened again, held him, fiercely and deliberately painfully.

'What I do,' DeBar said, very quietly, 'and who I do or don't do it with, has absolutely nothing – nothing! – to do with you. Repeat that, Ned. I want to know you understand me.'

The tears had spilled down Ned's cheeks. He bit his lip.

'Repeat it,' DeBar said, tightening his grip further, bruising the pale skin.

Ned let out a small gasp of pain.

'Repeat it.'

'Wh-what you do, and who y-you do or d-don't do it with, has absolutely n-nothing to do with me,' Ned muttered, dashing away the tears with his free hand.

DeBar smiled, a swift and calculatedly charming smile with not a trace of warmth in it. 'That's better,' he said. 'Now,' he stretched languidly and looked at his wristwatch, 'we have exactly an hour to kill.' He drew Ned, unresisting, towards him. 'You haven't been a good boy, Ned, have you?' His voice was a sorrowful whisper. 'I'm afraid you really should be punished for that. Don't you think?'

The October sky that lowered beyond the window was heavy with cloud, dark and roiling as a witch's cauldron. Wind gusted against the windowpane, rattling it in its frame, and every so often sheets of rain slammed against the glass. Liam, propped up on one elbow, looked down at the quiet figure who lay beside him. Even in sleep, Christine looked tired. Her face was pale and drawn. After the Liberation half of her unit had been sent to Paris; the ones who had remained behind had been working double shifts for weeks. Very gently he drew the sheet down, baring her breasts and belly. Tenderly he ran the palm of his hand over her skin, soft and silkily smooth. She stirred a little, murmuring, half-smiling, but did not wake. Long fair lashes curled against her cheek, and her short, tousled hair was still a little damp with the sweat of their lovemaking.

Rain roared against the window again. Smiling, he traced the line of the straight little nose with his finger. He hated to wake her, but the afternoon was ebbing fast and he knew she was on duty in a few hours' time. He bent to kiss her, long and very tenderly. When he drew back her eyes were open, and she was smiling. 'Sorry,' he said.

She shook her head on the pillow, yawned and stretched sleepily. 'How long have I been asleep?'

Liam looked at his watch. 'About an hour.'

She rolled towards him, entwining her arms about him, burying her face in his chest, snuggling in comfortably. 'Did you sleep?'

'No.' He cupped her head in his hand and held her close. 'No. I didn't. I had better things to do.'

'Oh?' She pulled her head back, looked up at him in surprise. 'What sort of things?'

He smiled. 'Watching you. You're beautiful when you're awake. You're even more beautiful when you're asleep.'

Faint colour rose in her cheeks. 'Don't be silly.' She cuddled back close to him. 'Five minutes. Then I must think about going – golly, listen to that weather!' The wind was howling in the chimney and sending little, skittering draughts through the room. 'Have you got a game tonight?'

Liam shook his head. 'The high-rolling times are over, I'm afraid, at least for a while. The punters are all in Paris, or hoofing it through Belgium.'

She rolled away a little, watching him. He pulled himself into a sitting position and reached for his tobacco pouch. 'Is that bad?' she asked. 'I mean – it's how you earn a living.'

He shook his head. 'No.' He grinned a little, ruefully, as he rolled his cigarette. 'To be honest with you, the fact that Mr Hitler appears to be personally targeting my investments again worries me more.'

She laughed. 'Only you would have gone into the property business just as the whole of London seems to be
blowing up.'

He bent over her, kissed her forehead. 'If you're going to
gamble, my darling, gamble big. If you lose,' he shrugged,
'you lose. But if you win at least you win something worth
having.' He stayed above her, his eyes suddenly intent
and serious. There was a very long silence. Christine was
no longer smiling. As if sensing what was coming she
squirmed a little, trying to sit up.

'Liam, it's getting late – I really must—'

'No.' Liam pinned her where she was, gently but very
firmly. 'Christine – my darling, my lover – whatever happens over the next few months, it's obvious now that the
war will be over soon. We can at least start to make
plans.'

'Liam! I—'

'I love you. I think you love me. Times have changed.
There'll be opportunities – great opportunities – when this
blasted war is over. I intend to be there. I intend to take
them. I want you to take them with me. Christine – please
– marry me? Please?'

This time she threw him off with surprising strength. '*I
can't!*' she said.

He lay back on his pillow, lit his cigarette, watched her
with a set face as in silence she began to pull on her clothes.
Suddenly he was seething with anger, shaking with it.
For a few minutes as she struggled with stockings and
camiknickers and blouse and skirt, and hunted furiously
and still silently for her shoes, he said nothing. Then, 'Why
not?' he asked. '*Why not?*'

Still she said nothing, but straightened, with the shoe in
her hand.

He crushed the cigarette out in the ashtray, leaned forward lifting a hand and stabbing the air with his finger.
'You'll tell me this time,' he said, his voice cold with
controlled anger, 'and what's more, by Christ, if you walk

out of that door you'll never walk back again. I mean it.'

She stood, stubbornly silent for a moment longer. Then she bent to put her shoes on, straightened and walked to the end of the bed, her hands on the frame. 'Why do people get married, Liam?' she asked at last, very quietly.

'Because they *love* each other, you bloody idiot! I keep *telling* you—'

She was shaking her head. 'No. You don't have to get married just because you love each other. Look at us – we're perfectly happy.'

'You might be!'

'People get married to spend the rest of their lives together. People get married to—' She hesitated, swallowed. 'To have children. To establish a family. To watch that family grow.'

'What's wrong with that?'

There were tears suddenly in her eyes. 'I've lied to you, Liam. You remember, we swore – never to lie to each other? Well, I have lied. And once you know that, you won't love me any more, will you? And that will be the end of that.' Despite the tears that were rolling down her face, her voice was perfectly level.

'How have you lied? When?'

'It's more a lie of omission than commission,' she said, 'but it's no better for that. In fact it's worse. When I came back from New York I didn't tell you the whole truth.'

He waited.

'I told you I had—' she struggled for a moment, 'lost my virginity. I was so sure I'd lose you. When I didn't, when I realised—' She stopped again, breathing unevenly. He watched her, puzzled and uneasy. 'I lost my courage. I couldn't, I couldn't tell you the rest of it.' Her mouth twisted. 'Add cowardice to mendacity.'

'The rest of what?'

She let go of the bed, took a step back, lifting her chin. 'I didn't just lose my virginity in New York. I did it in the

most stupid way possible. I got pregnant. I was frantic. I
had an abortion. Don't you see? That's why I was away
so long. It went wrong. Badly wrong. There is absolutely
no chance of my giving you children, Liam. No chance at
all.' She spun and walked towards the door, then turned.
'Haven't you ever wondered – why nothing's happened?'

'I did ask you, if you remember,' he said, tightly. 'You
said – you said you were taking precautions.'

She smiled, bitterly, through her tears. 'I lied about that,
too. Now you see what I am. A liar, a coward and a cheat.
But I can't cheat you for the rest of both our lives, Liam.
I can't.' With no warning she spun round and ran quickly
down the stairs.

Taken by surprise, Liam sat for a moment, stunned and
still. He heard the front door open, scrambled from the bed.
'Christine? *Christine!*' But she was gone, slamming the door
behind her, running out into the wind and rain, struggling
into her coat as she went.

He stood, naked and shivering, in the chill on the landing,
looking at the closed door. 'Shit! Shit! *Shit!*' he exploded.
He walked back into the bedroom, dropped on to the bed,
buried his face in his hands. He sat so for a very long time.
The wind howled and hammered about the house. When
he lifted his head, his bright eyes were wet, the long lashes
sticky, his face grim. He stood up and went into the gaming
room across the landing. There were two bottles left. He
took them both back into the bedroom.

Ned huddled in the wind, coat collar turned up, his hands
tucked into his pockets. He was cold, and wet. The river,
transversed by the dark loom of Battersea Bridge, swirled,
pitted with rain. A ship's hooter toned, mournfully. The fine
houses that still stood on the northern bank of the Thames
did so in defiance of the ugly gaps between them, drowned
and battered by the October storm. Ned pulled out a flask,
tipped the last of the brandy it had contained down his
throat. His hand as he replaced the stopper was unsteady.

He stiffened. The door of the house he was watching had opened. Silhouetted against the dim light – the black-out regulations had been eased considerably; the rockets that were showering on the city needed no lights to guide them – was a tall, slender figure, elegant and unmistakable. Ned drew back. DeBar exchanged a few words with whoever stood beyond the door, then threw back his head and laughed. Even over the wind, Ned could hear it. He bowed his own head, wincing, closing his eyes. When he looked again, DeBar was walking, whistling into the wind, westward, towards the King's Road.

Ned swallowed the tears that recently seemed to threaten so often to overwhelm him. He needed solace. He needed comfort. He needed a strong, protective hand.

He turned east, towards the Embankment, and Liam.

He had no need of skeleton keys now. Since the episode of the time-bomb both he and Christine had had keys to the house. He opened the door quietly. The downstairs rooms were dark and still. The only light came from upstairs, streaming across the landing from Liam's open bedroom door. Ned slipped out of his coat and jacket and hung them on the newel post at the bottom of the stairs.

'Liam?' Ned called softly. 'Liam, it's Ned. Are you there?'

Even over the whistling of the wind he heard a faint, growling snore.

Very quietly he climbed the stairs. Liam was sprawled on the bed, dressed only in a crumpled pair of trousers. An empty whiskey bottle lay on its side on the floor, a newly-started one stood on the bedside cabinet.

'Liam?' Ned touched his shoulder, shook him a little. 'Liam – wake up. It's Ned.'

Liam grunted and rolled on his side. Ned studied him for a moment, then touched an eyelid with a gentle finger. It was hot, damp, a little swollen. 'Liam – wake up, please.'

Liam's lashes fluttered. 'What? What the—?'

'It's me. Ned.' Ned sat down beside him on the bed, his hand on the other man's naked shoulder. 'Is – is something wrong?'

Liam's reddened eyes opened, focused with some difficulty upon Ned's face. Then Liam groaned and flung his arm up to cover his eyes against the light.

'Liam, what is it? What's wrong?'

For the space of several long breaths Liam lay quite still. Then he lifted his arm a little to peer at Ned from beneath it. 'Sure – nothing another drink won't cure,' he said. He pulled himself up to a sitting position, reached for the bottle, splashed a large amount of whiskey into a glass. 'What are you doing here?'

Ned shrugged. 'I was passing. I'd – been to see a friend. I just thought I'd pop in. I hope I'm not intruding?'

Liam gave a small snort of something like laughter. 'Intruding? No, you're not intruding. A man shouldn't drink alone. Even the Irish know that. Have a drink.' He held out the glass to Ned. Ned hesitated. Liam laughed again. 'It's all right,' he said, 'I'll take the big glass.' As Ned took the glass, Liam tilted the bottle to his lips. Ned watched him over the rim of his glass, which shook, very slightly, as he held it. Liam's brilliant blue eyes were bloodshot. He had a day's growth of beard. He leaned his head backwards for a moment, tiredly, resting it on the bedhead, and closed his eyes. Ned studied the face he knew so well. His heart was thumping in his throat. He took a large swallow of whiskey. 'Word of advice for you, lad,' Liam said, without opening his eyes.

Ned waited.

'Stay away from women. They're nothing but bloody trouble. Nothing – but – bloody – trouble,' Liam repeated, slowly.

Ned sucked a lip but said nothing.

Liam put the bottle to his lips again, then slid down until his head was once more on the pillow. His eyes were still closed. Dark curls were plastered untidily on his forehead. His profile was sharp against the white cotton of the pillowslip, his mouth a straight, harsh line. Suddenly Ned ached to touch him, ached to smooth the frown from between the black brows. He put out a hand, snatched it back as Liam opened his eyes. 'Drink up,' he said, blinking, indicating Ned's glass with a wave of the bottle.

Obediently, Ned did. Liam splashed more whiskey into the glass. 'What is it?' Ned asked, hearing his own voice a little slurred. 'Christine?'

'Who else?' Liam leaned on an elbow, took a swig from the bottle. 'Who bloody else?' He sat up unsteadily, swung his feet to the floor, shook his head. 'Told her if she walked out I'd never let her back. And she went – she went.' Suddenly and shockingly his shoulders began to shake. He bowed his tousled head, rested his forehead on the back of his hand as the sobs racked him. 'She went,' he repeated, desolately.

'Liam, don't! Please don't!' Ned set his glass down and put an arm about the other man, pulling him close. For a moment Liam relaxed against him, accepting his comfort. Ned closed his eyes. Liam's weight was warm and heavy against him, his hair, crisp and thick, was against his cheek. It was too much for Ned. He turned his own face and brushed his lips against the curly hair, gently kissing it. His arm tightened around the broad shoulders. 'Liam, listen to me.' His voice was very low, the words tumbling over each other as he spoke. 'Let me help you. Please let me help you. I wouldn't hurt you like that. I never would. I love you. I've always loved you.' His fingers were caressing the other man's face, light and fluttering about his wet eyes and cheeks, soft upon his lips. 'Let me show you how much I love you.'

Liam's body had stiffened in Ned's arms. The dark head came up sharply.

'Liam, please,' Ned clung to him, terrified of what he had done, unable to stop now, 'please, listen to me.'

With a wordless sound Liam flung the smaller man from

him. Ned, unprepared, reeled away from him and sprawled
to the floor. Their eyes held. There was a moment of utter,
horrified silence. Then, 'Get out,' Liam said, his voice low
and shaking, *'Get out*. Get away from me! Christ alive, has
the whole world run mad?'

Ned shook his head, opened his mouth to protest.

In one movement Liam stood up, stepped to him and
cracked the back of his hand across Ned's mouth, his full
weight behind the blow. 'Get out,' he spat again, revulsion
in his face.

Ned scrambled to his feet. Blood seeped from his split
lip, spattered the front of his shirt. He backed away from
Liam, breathing heavily, eyes wide and wild on the other
man's face. 'It isn't my fault,' he said, 'it isn't my fault I'm
– different. It's yours. All of you. Your fault! I've thought
about it. I've thought about it a lot. You're all against me.
You always were. You always ganged up on me. Always
shut me out. None of you wanted me – none of you ever
cared. Only Mama ever cared. And she left me.'

Liam turned from him, tiredly. 'Just get out, Ned. Be
thankful I don't turn you over to the law. Just keep your
dirty little pansy-tricks away from me.'

Ned's eyes flared, viciously. 'The law?' he said. 'Oh, I
think not.'

Liam dropped tiredly back on to the bed and buried his
face in his hands. 'Bugger off, Ned. For Christ's sweet sake,
just bugger off.' And then, realising what he had said, he
made a small, savage sound that hung somewhere between
laughter and tears.

'Oh, I will,' Ned hissed. He had pushed himself from the
wall, stood swaying for a moment. 'I will. And you'll be
sorry for this, Liam. Believe me, you'll be sorry.' He was
sidling towards the door. Liam did not – could not – look
at him.

'You think I'm a coward,' Ned said. 'You think I won't
do it.'

'Won't do what?'

Ned shook his head. 'You wait. You wait and see. Just remember – I told you – you'll be sorry, Liam.' He turned and fled, clattering down the stairs, flinging himself out through the front door. '*Believe me. You'll be sorry, Liam.*' Upon a gust of buffeting wind his high, wild voice echoed up the stairwell, then the door slammed and all was quiet.

Liam dropped belly down on to the bed, his face buried in his crossed arms, and lay very still for a long time. At last, sighing, he rolled over, pushed himself upright, limped slowly into the bathroom and, without giving himself time to think about it, stuck his head under the cold tap.

Christine awoke with a start. She was stiff, uncomfortable and totally disorientated. Her head hurt, and her aching eyes would not open properly. Where was she? What had awakened her? She sat up, rubbing at her face with her hands. Slowly her surroundings came into focus. She had been curled into one of the sofas in the drawing room. The door was open. Bars of light from the landing fell across the carpet. Piece by piece memory reasserted itself. That must have been what had woken her. She had not switched the lights on. She had fallen, weary and miserable, on to the sofa in the wind-buffeted twilight. Now it was fully dark. What was the time – God Almighty, what was the time? She peered at her watch, cursed under her breath. She should have been on duty half an hour since – she stilled, as a sound caught her attention. Someone had begun to sob, loudly and uncontrollably, words mingled with the wild sound. 'I'll sh-show – them – sh-show them all.'

'Ned?' Startled, she came to her feet, alarm shaking the last of the sleep from her. 'Ned, is that you?'

She ran out on to the landing. The study door stood open, a light showing.

'Ned?'

She sped to the door. Stopped, shocked to stillness.

Ned was sitting at the desk, rummaging frantically through the drawers. In the moment that Christine reached the door he found what he was looking for and straightened, the service revolver that Liam had taken from the deserter in his hand.

'*Ned!* What are you doing?'

Ned looked at her, his eyes unfocused. He was in his shirtsleeves, shivering, drenched with rain. His lower lip was split and swollen and still oozed blood, the front of his shirt was pink with it, rain-diluted. His fair hair, darkened, was plastered to his skull. His breath hiccoughed in his throat.

'Ned—' Christine took a step towards him.

'No!' He lifted the handgun, pointed it at her too steadily for comfort, despite his shaking. She heard the click as he cocked it. 'No,' he said again, suddenly and terrifyingly calm. 'Stay away from me.' Eyes still on Christine, he reached towards the telephone, which sat on the other side of the huge mahogany desk. It was just too far for him to reach.

As his eyes flickered towards it, distracting him, Christine took a step forwards. 'Ned—'

The gun swung back to her. 'I mean it, Chris.' A sob caught at his throat. 'Stay away. I'll shoot. I mean it. It makes no difference, you see. I'm going to kill myself anyway.'

'*Ned!*'

'But not before I've shopped that Irish bastard. Not before I know he'll swing after I'm gone. I told him he'd be sorry. And he will.'

'What are you talking about?'

Ned smiled, a ghastly, bloodstained, sly smile. 'You don't know, do you? He's IRA. Your gallant, romantic, gambling Irish swain is IRA. And I'm going to shop him.' He reached again for the telephone, which was still just out of his reach.

'What makes you say that?' Christine asked, quickly. Anything to keep Ned talking. His instability shrieked at her. Somewhere in the back of her mind she realised that it always had. 'How can you know such a thing?'

'His father came. To Liam's house. I was hiding. They didn't know I was there. I heard them talking.'

'You always were a little sneak,' Christine said, quietly, and took another step.

'Yes. Wasn't I? But believe me, it's true. They'll investigate, and they'll find that it's true. With any luck they'll hang him. Will you cry, Chris? I hope so.'

'Ned, you're unhinged. For goodness' sake, put that damned thing down. You need help.'

'Too late for help.' Ned hefted the gun again and, shockingly, began softly to sing, *'Oh, God, our help in ages past, Our hope for years to come – Our shelter from the stormy blast, And our eternal home.'* His voice was still clear and true and lovely. Christine swallowed. The hymn died away. 'Too late for help,' Ned repeated very softly. 'What do you think, Chris – is there a God? Is there anyone?' Once again his hand crept across the desk towards the telephone. This time he rose a little from the chair and managed to catch hold of the flex of the instrument, pulling it towards him.

'Ned—' Christine took another careful step forward. 'Ned, listen to me.'

'No. You listen to me. Listen while I turn Liam in.'

Another small step. 'What good will it do? You'll be sorry later.'

'No. I told you. I won't be here. It's you who'll be sorry. All of you.' Eyes still steady upon Christine, he closed his hand about the receiver. As he did so the gun wavered a little. Christine dived, throwing herself not at Ned and the gun, but full length on the floor under the desk, wrenching at the telephone wire. The suddenness of her movement startled her brother: and he totally mistook her intention. As the wire snapped away from the wall the sound of a shot crashed above her.

*'Ned! Ned – no!'* She pulled herself to her feet.

Ned lay sprawled across the desk, lax fingers still curled around the gun, eyes staring, a pool of blood spreading from beneath his head.

Christine put her hand to her mouth, stepping backwards, away from the body. The blood ran across the desk to drip to the floor. The ticking of the clock was loud in the sudden, awful silence. Retching, she clamped herself against sickness, as she backed towards the door. 'Ned!' she whispered, once; then she whirled and ran down the stairs as if pursued by demons.

Liam was in the kitchen drinking the last of the coffee that Lottie had got for him from one of her obliging GIs when he heard the frantic hammering on the front door.

'God Almighty, what now?' He ran his hand distractedly through his already untidy hair and stood up. 'Coming. I'm coming.' He opened the door. Stared. 'Christine! What the devil?'

Christine was drenched, breathless and hysterical. He drew her to him, shut the door, rocked her for a moment.

'Christine, Christine, what is it? What's happened?'

For a moment she sobbed helplessly on his shoulder. He ushered her into the warmth of the kitchen, sat her down at the table. She was crying with such abandon that for the moment she could not speak. He poured coffee, splashed whiskey into it. She shook her head.

'Try,' he said.

Ten minutes later, calmer, her story told between wild bouts of tears, she took a long, wavering breath. 'I couldn't think. I didn't know what to do. I could only think of you.' Her face was scarlet and blotched with tears, her breath caught in her throat at every word.

'You are sure he's dead?'

She nodded, still sobbing. 'Oh, yes. I'm sure. Liam – we're going to have to go to the police, aren't we? We'll have to report it.'

'Yes. Yes, we will. But—' Liam's face was grim. Ned's last cry echoed in his ears. *'Believe me. You'll be sorry, Liam!'*

Christine had begun to cry again. 'But, Liam, why? *Why* did he do it? And why did he want to harm you? He's never been exactly stable – we all knew that, I suppose – but what *happened*? What sent him over the top like that? He's always been so fond of you.'

Liam got to his feet, pacing the floor. 'He came here earlier. After you—' he hesitated, 'left. I'd been drinking – we both had, I think. We quarrelled.'

Christine was watching him. 'It was you who hit him?' she asked suddenly and very quietly, remembering Ned's split lip.

'Yes.'

The silence was a long one. Then, 'I don't want to know why,' Christine said, quickly, as Liam opened his mouth to speak. Her pale face had coloured uncomfortably. She lifted a hand defensively as if to ward off the words. '*I don't want to know why!*' she repeated. She dropped her aching head into her hands for a moment. 'We all failed him. Didn't we?'

'Yes,' Liam said.

In the distance, to the west, a loud explosion reverberated.

'Bloody things,' Christine said, miserably, 'are they never going to stop?' She stood up, wearily. 'Will you come to the police with me?'

'Yes. But not just yet.' Liam was reaching for his coat. 'Here, put this round you. You're shivering.'

Christine was staring at him. 'What do you mean, "not just yet"?'

He put an arm about her. 'Think, Chris,' he said gently. 'You pulled the telephone wire from the wall.'

'Yes?'

'Don't you think that might look a tad suspicious? Why would Ned to that?'

'I—' She shook her head, helplessly; then suddenly and sharply lifted her head, staring at him. 'Was it true?' she whispered. 'What Ned said about you?'

He took both her hands in his. 'Not exactly. But yes, there is something that I was involved in, when I was very young, that I'd rather wasn't – investigated. I swear to you, *swear*

to you, that's all it is. I was sixteen years old. I learned my
lesson, and a hard one it was. I promise you – I *promise* you
– that I've never had any contact with them since. Do you
believe me?'

She looked at him for a long time, biting her lip. 'Yes,'
she said.

Liam was rummaging in a drawer. When he turned he
had a small screwdriver in his hand.

'What are you going to do?'

'I'm going to see if I can mend that wire. Then we'll go
to the police. There's no need to say that you spoke to Ned.
You can simply say you found him when you got home
from here.'

'No! Don't leave me alone! Liam, please, I couldn't stand
to be on my own.'

'Come with me, then. You won't have to go upstairs. You
can wait by the door. If I can do it, it won't take long. Then
we can go to the police together.'

The rain, at least, had stopped at last. As they hurried
through the dark streets it quickly became clear that they
were moving towards the site of the latest rocket blast.
Police cars, ambulances and fire engines howled through
the streets. As they neared Holland Park and saw the
position of the fiery glow in the sky, without a word
and hand in hand they quickened their footsteps, Liam's
damaged leg swinging awkwardly. Once again, the crescent
was barricaded; this time with very good cause. Christine
stared. Where the house and its neighbours had stood was a
raging inferno, fanned to worse by the wind. Hardly a wall
stood. Even as they watched there was another explosion
as the gas main cracked. 'Ned!' she whispered. *'Ned!'*

Liam, his face set with shock, put an arm about her
and pulled her to him. Firelight flickered ruddily upon
the figures of the firefighters; it was truly, he thought, a
scene from hell. As they watched, one of the remaining,
gutted houses collapsed into a slithering heap of smoking
rubble. Christine was crying, helplessly.

'Best you take the lady home, Sir,' said a quiet voice beside them. 'You wouldn't want to hamper the rescue services, now, would you?' A policeman had come up behind them.

'No. No, of course not.' Liam's arm tightened about Christine. 'Come on, my darling. The man's right. There's nothing we can do here. Come away. Come home.'

# *Epilogue*

## VE Day, May 1945

'I wonder how soon he'll be able to come home?' Pamela and David Barker were standing at the window of their bedroom, looking down into the street. A party had been organised for local children and was in full swing. Long tables had been set up in the road; Union flags and red, white and blue bunting were everywhere. 'And I wonder how much he will have changed?'

Her husband rested an arm across her shoulders. 'He's bound to have changed a bit, my love,' he said, gently. 'He's five years older, five important years.'

Pamela nodded. 'I wonder if he's serious about standing for Parliament?'

'It isn't the kind of thing Alex says lightly. So, yes, I imagine he is.'

'Would you mind?'

'Of course not. Ah! Here they come, look – the girls and Tommy.' David pointed. Two young women, one tall and dark, the other small and fair, had turned the corner and were negotiating their way through the excited children below. Josie was carrying a small, dark, laughing child pickaback. She looked up, saw her parents at the window and waved, smiling. Pamela's heart lurched, as it always did, when she saw in her daughter's face the likeness of her son's. For her, as for many other people, today could not be a day of unbridled celebration; the war was over at last, Alex would come home. Tom would not.

She blinked. 'I wonder,' she said, brightly, as she turned, 'where Lottie is? Do you think we'll see anything of her today?'

Lottie's father laughed, quietly. 'I think it highly unlikely,' he said. 'London is one big party at the moment. You can count on it; that's where our Lottie will be.'

Lottie was, in fact, sitting on the roof of a taxi, flanked by two broad-shouldered, gum-chewing GIs in smart khaki, their caps tipped to the back of their heads. In friendly manner they had each taken possession of one of her hands. The vehicle was inching its way through the celebrating crowds towards Trafalgar Square. When at last it stopped, the way entirely blocked, one of the Americans thumped on the roof. 'OK, buddy. This'll do us.' He jumped down, lifted Lottie as if she were a feather and set her upon her feet before pushing a bank note into the hand of the driver. 'Keep the change.' He straightened with a grin. 'Right. Now what?'

'A drink,' his compatriot said. 'Where's the nearest bar?'

Still holding Lottie's hands, they shouldered their way through the friendly crowds, into a hotel foyer and through to a busy bar.

'Well, little lady? What're you drinking?'

Lottie smiled a little, shrugged. 'Whatever you're having. Whatever there is. The war may be over, but I doubt the champagne is exactly flowing yet.' To her own surprise she felt a disconcerting sense of anticlimax; try as she might, she could not enter wholeheartedly into the spirit of the occasion. She perched on a table, swinging her leg, and watched absently as her two companions pushed their way to the bar, a series of images flickering in her mind. Young men – boys in another era – alive and laughing in the Mess one moment and shot from the skies in flames the next. The scramble to get off the ground, the anxious wait, the mental counting as the squadron returned, the weary quiet after the last of the planes had limped home. There had been camaraderie and laughter, tragedy and tears. There had been fear and courage, and the gallant support of trust and friendship. What now?

Someone had put a record on. A young couple had pushed back some tables and were jitterbugging expertly. In the street the happy crowds were conga-ing past the door.

'Hey!' The Americans were back. The one called Gus was looking at her quizzically. 'Why so serious? Come and dance with me.' He took her hand in his and spun her on to the dance floor. He was good, and so was she. The crowd watched, clapping appreciatively. He spun her to him, grinning, lifted her from her feet.

Lottie, laughing suddenly, kicked off her shoes and danced.

Charlie loved the swings and slides. Especially the swings. He was too grown up to need anyone to push him now, he could work his own way up to the level of the bar, his feet high in the air as he leaned back, head dangling, letting the wind blow through his hair. Usually his mother would watch him anxiously, calling to him if she thought he was going too high; but today she and Uncle Rudi were apparently too busy talking to each other to notice his energetic efforts. They sat on their usual bench by the side of the little playground, not watching him at all. Even when they had stopped talking, he noticed, they still sat looking at each other, rather than at him. Feeling just a little peeved at this unusual lack of attention, he let the swing slow a little, its arcs becoming shorter and shorter. Before it had come to a stop, however, Uncle Rudi had stood up abruptly and walked away. Charlie looked after him in astonishment. Uncle Rudi never left without kissing him goodbye.

He jumped from the swing and ran to his mother. 'Where's Uncle Rudi gone?'

Emma took out a handkerchief and blew her nose. 'He's – had to go – to meet someone. Someone important. He said to say goodbye.'

'Is he coming back to tea?'

Emma shook her head. 'No.'

'Well, will we see him tomorrow?'

His mother took a long, shaky breath. He looked at her curiously. 'No, Charlie,' she said, quietly, 'we won't be seeing him tomorrow. He's had to – go away.'

The little boy sucked his lip, frowning. 'How far away?'

'Very far. So far that – I don't think he'll be able to come and see us again.'

'But—'

'Charlie, please!' Emma's voice was sharp. 'I'll explain later. Would you like to go to Grandma and Grandpa's? Little Tommy will be there.'

'Oh, good. Yes, please.' He swung on her hand as she stood up. 'Is Uncle Rudi going home?'

Emma hesitated for a moment, then nodded. 'Yes. He's going home.'

'Daddy's coming home, isn't he?'

'Yes.'

Charlie was a logical child. His face brightened. 'Is that what it is? Now that the war's over, is everyone going home?'

Emma stopped in mid-stride and turned suddenly to hug him, burying her face in his dark hair, but she did not reply.

Christine and Liam were strolling hand in hand by the river. Night had fallen, but the celebrations had if anything intensified. The dome of St Paul's Cathedral, valiant symbol of the city's survival, shone triumphantly against the dark sky, lit by the searchlights that for so long had scanned the skies for raiders. They stopped, leaning with their backs to the water, looking at it. Christine put her head on Liam's shoulder. 'It doesn't seem possible it's still there, does it?'

Liam shook his head. 'No. It doesn't.'

A small boat full of singing, flag-waving revellers passed them, lit up like a Christmas tree. They turned to wave back, stood for a moment in silence, their elbows resting on the parapet. A family was walking towards them, the father in army uniform, a small boy waving a Union Jack riding high on his shoulders, a little girl holding her mother's hand.

Christine glanced at them, returned their cheerful smiles, then turned abruptly back to study the dark waters of the river.

Liam took her hand, turned it palm up and studied it in the light of a street lamp.

She turned her head to watch him, smiling a little. 'What do you see?'

'I see a tall, dark gambling man.'

'What's he doing?'

He held her eyes for a long moment. 'He's asking you to marry him. Again,' he said, quietly.

She took a breath and opened her mouth to speak.

He lifted a hand. 'Don't answer. Not yet. But promise me you'll think about it? Today somehow seems like a good day for new beginnings, don't you think?'

Her eyes flickered to the little family group, and back to his.

He shook his head, gently.

She leaned against him, sliding her arm about his waist. There was a small silence. Then, 'Yes,' she said softly, 'you're right. So it does.'